**Raves for the previous antholigies of
Denise Little:**

"Denise Little has put together some really nice collections in the past few years, and it's gotten to the point where, if I see her name as editor, I know I'm in for a worthwhile read."
—*Chronicle,* for *The Magic Shop*

"Given the career of an English boy named Harry, the creation of an American school for magic-workers was inevitable. Not inevitable was that the place be a fount of intelligent entertainment. Editor Little's judgment helps make it such, and the comprehensive folk-loric expertise she displays."
—*Booklist,* for *The Sorcerer's Academy*

"Exceedingly well done."
—*Booklist,* for *The Valdemar Companion*

"*Familiars* is a load of fun to read for the fantasy fan or anyone who wants a good escape. Little has gathered fifteen highly original short stories that deal with magical companions."   —*Kliatt,* for *Familiars*

"After finishing this anthology, readers will never look at magic shops and new age/metaphysical bookstores the same way again. Little aptly describes the anthology as a 'collection of stories of the changed fates and challenged minds of the amazed consumers—both mundane and magical—who dared to shop at a Magic Shop.' Buyer beware!"
—*The Barnes and Noble Review* for *The Magic Shop*

THE MAGIC TOYBOX

EDITED BY
Denise Little

DAW BOOKS, INC.
DONALD A. WOLLHEIM, FOUNDER
375 Hudson Street, New York, NY 10014

ELIZABETH R. WOLLHEIM
SHEILA E. GILBERT
PUBLISHERS
www.dawbooks.com

First Printing, August 2006
1 2 3 4 5 6 7 8 9

DAW TRADEMARK REGISTERED
U.S. PAT. OFF. AND FOREIGN COUNTRIES
—MARCA REGISTRADA
HECHO EN U.S.A.

PRINTED IN THE U.S.A.

Acknowledgments

CONTENTS

INTRODUCTION

Denise Little

I'm afraid that I'm a true baby boomer. Conspicuous consumption from birth—that's me. One of the earliest pictures I have of myself is as a drooling infant surrounded by a pile of toys that was nearly big enough to obscure me. And I loved them all.

You name it, from my rocking horse to Barbie and Skipper to Breyer horses to Tonka Toys to my brother's GI Joes (which I borrowed frequently because I thought Ken was a pathetic waste of plastic)—I really loved them. I played with my toys until they were almost worn out. I cherished them, made up whole universes to fit them, even thought that they came to life when I wasn't looking. My evidence for this, the fact that they frequently moved from where I left them, I later found out was due to the fact that my siblings played with them when I wasn't around, but were very, very careful not to let me catch them at it. But back then I was absolutely convinced that the toys had a secret life of their own.

Even when I finally grew old enough that I was intellectually sure my toys didn't come to life behind my back, I couldn't give up the feeling that they were magical somehow. I'd spent so much time with them, creating adventures that took me from the Wild West

1

to the top of Everest to places never seen by human eyes, places that only live in the imagination of a child, that they still retained a faint glow of enchantment, no matter how hard my rational side tried to convince me that they were merely battered playthings.

Being devious and obsessive, I still have most of my old toys, even though I'm now far closer to retirement age than I am to nursery school days. I've got them displayed on shelves in my guest bedroom—almost every kind of Barbie doll made in the first four years of the doll's production run, Pepper dolls and Penny Brite, Tiny Tears, Pitiful Pearl, Thumbelina, Chatty Cathy, a whole stable-full of plastic horses, and many more. Visitors love my collection, even though they point out that it would be worth a lot more if I concentrated on items that weren't so clearly played with. And, for collectors, they have a point. My toys are not in mint condition. Not one of them has its original box. A few of the dolls have unfortunate bald patches where my little brothers (one is now a bank president, the other a commercial pilot for a major airline) chewed the dolls' hair off while they were teething. The horses all have the paint rubbed off their ear tips, and more than a few have mended legs.

But those toys mean much more to me than any pristine collector's cache of mint condition playthings ever could. They are the companions of my youth, my partners in epic voyages of discovery. And, to this day, for me they still retain that faint golden glow of enchantment.

Surprisingly, I'm not the only one who sees it. Friends my age get misty-eyed at the sight of my battered relics. And the kids who visit me haul the old toys down from the shelf and have at it. Some of them have even abandoned my top-of-the-line video games to drag down the dolls and horses and trucks and construction sets and play for hours.

One rainy day, while I was watching my nieces work hard to build a thriving city out of chairs, books, and my old toys, I talked to my sister about some of the adventures I had imagined having as a kid as my toys came to life in my mind. She grinned and told me, "You know, there's a book in that."

I thought about her words and decided she was right. I asked some of my writer friends if they'd be interested in joining me in spinning tales of toys come to life, of old playthings animated and chugging along under their own steam, of the real magic of toys. All of them gave me an enthusiastic "YES!"

So you're holding in your hands the results, as we all remembered the joys we'd felt as kids, with uncharted universes before us—past, present, and future—ready to open with only a toy as the key. More than a couple of these stories have their roots in real-life playtimes or the sad loss of beloved toys. All of them have a touch of the magic that play brings to us.

I hope that you enjoy your adventures in *The Magic Toybox.*

ROADSHOW

Jean Rabe

The Kingsbury roadster sported tan and tomato-red coats of enamel paint. Thirteen inches long with a rumble seat, the appraiser said it probably dated to the late 1920s or early 1930s, and had original light bulbs, rubber tires, and no visible touchups or rust.

"I found it at an estate sale, in a box with a bald Chatty Cathy, a broken Pops-a-Ball, a dozen naked Action Jacksons, and a bunch of Creeple Peoples tied together with a rotten rubber band. Paid eight bucks for the lot."

"Quite the find!" The appraiser beamed. "I'd say this beauty could go at auction for eight hundred to a thousand dollars."

The toy's owner grinned broadly and gripped the edge of the table for support, and the camera zoomed in for a close-up.

"How about mine? What's mine worth?"

The camera swiveled to the far end of the table, locking in on another toy, this—according to the appraiser—a 1961 Hubley Mr. Magoo car. It looked like a modified Model T, ten inches long and painted yellow with brown fenders and running boards, a black cloth top, and gray plastic seats. Mr. Magoo was driving. Made of tin painted bright navy blue, he had

5

a rubber head that turned, and a rubber mud-brown derby hat. The toy was a riot of shiny color.

"I just put new batteries in it." The Mr. Magoo car rolled forward, wobbly as was intended, as if the car was drunk. "Watch this." He moved the crank at the bottom of the front grille, then it rolled equally wobbly backward. "So what's it worth?"

"Fine, fine condition," the appraiser said. He bent near the car and narrowed his eyes. "Where'd you find one like this? Looks like it came right off the toy store shelf!"

"Oh, at some flea market down in Illinois. I think I maybe gave twenty-five bucks for it."

"Liar." This came from Mr. Magoo.

Neither the owner nor the appraiser heard the toy— they didn't speak the language. The other toy cars understood, though.

The Kingsbury roadster flashed its lights to get Mr. Magoo's attention. "So if you didn't come from a flea market, where did you come from?"

"A basement in Burlington. On a high ledge where the damp couldn't get me."

"Burlington?"

"Wisconsin."

"We're in Wisconsin. Milwaukee," the roadster revved. "It's where the *Old Things Roadshow* is filming for the whole weekend. It's why we're all here. So . . . is Burlington a far drive?"

Mr. Magoo tried to shrug, but the tin shoulders didn't move. "South. It's someplace to the south."

"Why'd he say he got you at a flea market?" The roadster was persistent.

" 'Cause he's not going to tell the *Old Things Roadshow* appraiser that he stole me out of his friend's basement. I belonged to a pleasant woman who rarely played with me. I was a Christmas present from her father when she was a tot, and from the proverbial Day One she treated me like treasure. Kept me for more than forty years before Ol' Five-Fingers Discount there . . . who claimed to be a buddy of hers . . . stuffed me under his coat one day and stuck me in his car while she was out with her dogs. Probably figured she wouldn't miss me, what with all the other stuff piled high in the basement. He knew I was valuable."

The appraiser waived the camera close. "Yes, Mr. Magoo here is quite valuable. I'd say about five hundred dollars. Since you have the original box and since it's in such incredible condition, maybe you could get a little more."

"Gee, I thought it might be worth even more than that, at least as much as that Kingsbury roadster." Disappointment was plain on the owner's face. "But it's better than nothing."

"Nothing? That's exactly what Ol' Five-Fingers Discount paid for me," Mr. Magoo grumbled. "I was worth more than five hundred dollars to her. To her, I was priceless." If the rubber face could have shed a tear, it would have.

"Sad story," said a 1930 Cortland ice cream truck. Smaller and narrower, it fit in the shadow cast by the Mr. Magoo Car. "See that old man across the aisle there, looking at the Three Stooges bobble-heads? He bought me when he was a kid. Used to race me against his brother's dump trucks."

"Race? Did someone say race?" This came from the replica of a 1961 Chevy Impala sedan.

There were other toy vehicles arrayed on the table at the far end of the convention center. On the other side of Mr. Magoo, a Wyandotte motorcycle made of pressed steel and painted sky blue shimmered under the fluorescent lights. It was appraised at close to one thousand dollars.

"Race? Did someone say race?" The replica of a 1961 Chevy Impala sedan's gear was stuck on the notion. "Va-va-va-varrooooom! A race!"

In the center of the table a glossy pumpkin-orange boxy-looking car stalled, the smallest of the lot at a mere five inches. Nothing special about it, though the appraiser pronounced it mint and worth at least three hundred.

"I got it for a birthday present," the owner said of the pumpkin car. "Two years ago today, from my wife."

"Alles Gute zum Geburtstag!" exclaimed a Schuco-Studio III Mercedes Benz Streamlined W196. Its best wishes were not heard by any of the men standing around the table, but they were heartfelt nonetheless. The angular dark blue toy was a model of the 1954 Formula 1 Mercedes racer and featured removable wheels and a strong spring drive. Its greatest feature was its rarity, as only two hundred were made. *"Alles Gute zum Geburtstag!"*

"Speak English, you friggin' foreign import," revved the Kingsbury roadster.

"Race?" the Impala cut in. It flashed its turn signal at a miniature 1959 Ford Fairlane Skyliner. "Did someone say race? Va-va-varrrrooooom!"

In return, the Fairlane waved its retractable hardtop. About the length of a G.I. Joe, the appraiser explained that the Fairlane was manufactured by the Cragstan company in Japan in the early 1960s. Battery operated, it had an attached remote control that steered the wheel. The appraiser noticed a couple of small factory touchup spots on the hood that detracted from its collectiblity.

"Kon-nichiwa!" the Fairlane said to the Impala. *"Kon-nichiwa!"* It repeated the greeting to the Mercedes and the rest of its fellow toys.

"Wonderful," the roadster seized up. "A Jerry and a Jap on our table. Don't you just hate these foreign models? Can't understand a honkin' thing. This is the American version of the *Old Things Roadshow,* not the one they broadcast over the pond."

"Kon-nichiwa!" the Fairlane offered again, with even more enthusiasm.

"Race? Did someone mention a race? Va-va-va-varrroooooooom!"

The roadster turned on its brights. "A race? Yeah, Impala, we could show those foreign models a good what-for."

The cameraman took a wide-angle shot of all the cars on the table, then a moment later the appraiser signaled the toy section finished. The *Old Things Roadshow* crew moved on to the dolls.

The Impala blinked its headlights seductively at the roadster and wriggled its tailpipe. "Think you can catch me, Kingsbury?"

The roadster let out a little beep. "Been a while since I burned rubber."

"I'm in," the Wyandotte motorcycle said.

"Me too," said an old blue truck, the most valuable of the toy vehicles on display. A Structo Motor Dispatch semi, it haled from the 1920s and stretched nearly two feet long. It came complete with a rear tailgate chain and radiator cap, the decals clean and intact, placing it at worth more than three thousand dollars. "I haven't stretched my suspension in years."

"Race. Race. Race. Race." The Impala had turned the word into a mantra.

"Das Rennen?" the Mercedes racer asked.

"Yeah, we race," the Wyandotte motorcycle returned. "What about you, Mr. Magoo? You got new batteries. Want to try them out?"

The tin shoulders tried to shrug. "I suppose it would be all right."

The Impala rolled to the edge of the table.

The roadster honked to get everyone's attention. "We race down this aisle, past the displays for folk art, pottery, and furniture. Got it?" He flicked his lights down an aisle that had been formed by blue drapes stretched on pipes and that was cut at irregular intervals by eight-foot tables skirted with darker blue fabric.

"Got it," Mr. Magoo said. "Then?"

"See that chair—the high-backed one painted white? We turn right at it and make for the paintings, paper, and jewelry."

A thin man in a rumpled olive suit with a spotted red tie stood by the chair in question. He gestured to a cameraman and pointed, his words barely heard above the murmur of conversations from people toting boxes filled with their prized old things. "This is a L. & J.G. Stickley chair, circa 1917."

"Yeah, that chair'll do," the Impala said.

"Das Rennen!" the Mercedes said.

With a throaty "Va-va-va-varrroooooom!" the Impala vaulted off the table and down the aisle.

The Kingsbury roadster followed, honking expletives that the human attendees of the *Old Things Roadshow* could neither hear nor understand. "I make the rules, Impala. I say when we go."

"Go!" The Wyandotte motorcycle cheered. "Go. Go. Go. Go." It rolled forward, dropping off the table and falling on its side. It quickly righted itself and raced after the Impala and the Kingsbury roadster.

The Mercedes hesitated only a moment before flicking a turn signal at the ice cream truck. They sped off the edge simultaneously, tires squealing.

Mr. Magoo tried to put a nervous look on his rubber face as he crept toward the edge and stared down the aisle. The racing toy cars were already yards ahead.

"I have new batteries. I can do this."

"And I'll give you a push!" The Structo Motor Dispatch semi barreled forward, its front bumper slamming into the Mr. Magoo car and sending it hurtling off the table, inadvertently causing the Mr. Magoo car to fly over the ice cream truck and hit the aisle running.

The semi lumbered off the edge, its cab angling straight down and smacking against the floor, which was cement covered by a thin carpet. It had been the most valuable of the toys on the table, but its front bumper snapped off, and the connection broke between the cab and the trailer. A wheel spun away and the tailgate popped open, just as the Japanese Fairlane shouted one more *"Kon-nichiwa!"* and dove over the side.

The Fairlane had good speed, and should have easily caught the Mr. Magoo car, but its attached remote-control cable snagged on something. A moment more, and the Fairlane landed on top of the semi, tugging three other toy cars with it.

"I'm not racing," the pumpkin car decided, rolling to the edge and looking down at the tangle of metal and plastic. "It's my owner's birthday, and I think my value just went up a notch."

"Va-va-va-varroooom!" The Impala was clearly in the lead, racing down the aisle past the folk art section. It slowed out of curiosity, idling when it spotted a pudgy woman in platform shoes and a flowery print dress.

"My great uncle," she was explaining. "He was in the army and he got around quite a bit. I think he got this here—"

"Cheyenne cradleboard," the *Old Things Roadshow* appraiser supplied.

"Cradle, yeah. I think he got it from a reservation."

The Impala slammed on its breaks, its headlights catching the beaded cradle mounted on buffalo hide. The car was so far ahead it could afford to hear the appraiser's discourse. Besides, the Impala reasoned, if it got too, too far ahead, the other cars might give up and the race would be over before they made it to the white chair.

"See the stylized thunderbirds, and the hawk bells delicately hanging around the opening?"

"C'mon, c'mon," the Impala urged. "Tell her what she wants to hear. C'mon!"

"Well, the cradle is a little out of shape, but I'd place its value at about fifty thousand."

"Dollars?" The woman gasped and patted her chest.

The Impala sped up and caught the woman's swoon in its rearview mirror, then it zipped around the legs of an old gal in green bib overalls that had been hemmed a little too high.

"I make the rules of this race!" The roadster honked at the Impala, then looked out its side mirrors to spot a line of cars following: the Mercedes racer, the Wyandotte motorcycle, the Mr. Magoo car-weaving like it was tipsy, and the Cortland ice cream truck. The roadster flicked its high beams in surprise—it had thought more cars would participate in the *Roadshow* race.

"Va-va-va-varrooom!" the Impala squealed.

The roadster cursed and floored it.

"My dad left me this in his will." A man in khaki pants and a purple-and-white checked shirt ran his hand across the lip of a green vase festooned with ducks and scallops.

"This piece you have here is from a large pottery in Zanesville, Ohio," the *Old Things Roadshow* appraiser said. "We can see by this mark that it was designed by Weller Rhead, who came to the United States sometime in the early 1900s. I'd say this vase is worth a little more than two thousand."

"Gosh, I had no idea. In fact, I—"

The Impala didn't anticipate the surprised pottery owner stepping out into the aisle. The car va-va-va-varrooomed around his ankles, accidentally clipping him. Normally a toy the Impala's size wouldn't have budged the man, but he was already off-balance at the news of the duck vase's worth. The man wobbled on his feet and stretched out his hands, fell forward into the table, and sent his Weller Rhead vase flying. It came down in a hundred or so pieces.

The Impala slowed to sadly survey the damage through its side mirrors, and the Kingsbury roadster took advantage, tires screaming as it passed the competition and rolled over fragments of the duck vase. The Mercedes racer, the Wyandotte motorcycle, the Mr. Magoo car weaving like it was even tipsier, and the Cortland ice cream truck drew within inches before the Impala bolted forward again.

In the distance behind the racers, a distraught man held his hands to the sides of his head. "I'm going to sue, you hear me? This was my only Structo Motor Dispatch semi from the 1920s. The tailgate chain is broken, the radiator cap is gone. Sure, it had a slight crease on one side of the cab, but now there are creases all over. I'm going to sue!"

"You signed a hold-harmless clause," an appraiser offered.

The distraught man growled.

The pumpkin car made a tsk-tsking sound that none of the people heard, and it offered a silent prayer for its brethren broken on the floor.

A smallish man in a black suit with a red bow tie, bald on top, but with a gray-black ring of hair around the sides, adjusted his wire-rim glasses with his overly hairy hands. His rumpled pale blue shirt added to the professor image. He gestured with a pencil to a massive grandfather clock. He was oblivious to the racing cars headed his way.

"See how long the pendulum is? Longer pendulums keep better time," he explained to a middle-aged couple. "It's also heavy. Weight-driven clocks are simply more accurate. And it has three dials, one for seconds, one for minutes, and one for hours. That's thought to be more accurate, too."

"What's it worth?" the couple asked practically in unison.

"Well, this dates back more than one hundred and fifty years. German made, I can tell by the signature."

"German made," the Kingsbury roadster hissed.

"German made. This is the American version of the *Old Things Roadshow,* people. *American*."

"What's it worth?" the couple asked again.

"I'd put it in the neighborhood of—" The smallish man stared at the aisle and at the line of toy cars racing down it. "Oh my."

"Ah, tell her what's its worth," the Cortland ice cream truck said as it sped by. "Tell her, Professor!"

The smallish man scratched his head. "I better call security. Somebody wound up the toys."

"Call security after you tell us what the clock's worth," the couple insisted.

The Impala caught up to the roadster when they turned down the aisle by the white chair. The Mr. Magoo car, with its new batteries, careened drunkenly around the corner, nearly bumping into the Cortland ice cream truck. The Mercedes racer and the Wyandotte motorcycle fell in behind, fender to fender.

"You're just biding your time, aren't you, Mercedes? You've got more juice than all of them. I can see it in your lines. You're built for speed." The motorcycle popped a wheelie for emphasis.

"Das Rennen!"

"Yeah, yeah, I hear you. Shut up and race."

The Kingsbury roadster headed toward a string bean of a man with a painting of a wintry scene. Other paintings were displayed on easels behind and between tables. The wintry scene was the largest.

"Va-va-va-varroooom!" the Impala shouted.

The man was standing in the aisle, holding the painting for the camera.

"It's by John Carlson," the appraiser said. "I've done some research on the Internet on the artist. Carlson was a Swede who came to the United States when he was nine years old."

"A Swede!" The roadster cursed. "*American* roadshow, people."

"From Sweden?" The man holding the painting raised his eyebrows, hopeful.

"Carlson was not known for his snow scenes. I'd say this was painted between 1925 and 1935. With a little restoration it could bring thirty thousand or more. I'd insure it for sixty thousand."

The man's fingers and lips trembled, and the Kingsbury roadster shot between his legs. The man yelped in surprise and dropped the painting. It tottered upright on its frame for a moment, just long enough for the Impala to break through the canvas. Then it fell back, and the Cortland ice cream truck, the Mr. Magoo car, and the Mercedes racer trundled over the frame and the ripped snow scene. The Wyandotte motorcycle managed to swerve just in time, slipping around the edge of the painting and avoiding the appraiser's scrambling feet.

Gaining on the Mercedes racer, the motorcycle popped a wheelie in glee and felt itself being lifted off the floor.

"Mama! Look what I found!" Grubby hands clutched the motorcycle, just careful enough to avoid its spinning wheels. The tot held the motorcycle up to a woman clutching a cardboard box filled with a teakettle in the shape of a giraffe, a hot pink ceramic bowling pin, an old carved wooden pug dog, and an animated yodeling goat.

"That's nice, Timmy. Put it in my box and you can play with it when we get home. That old toy'll probably last you an hour or two before I have to toss it in the garbage."

"Game over," the Wyandotte motorcycle moaned.

The race paralleled a line of people toting their treasures—Kissy dolls in the original boxes, a Madame Alexander with perfect hair, an Operation game with the patient's nose blinking, hand-blown Christmas ornaments, brass doorknockers in the shape of gargoyles and dragons, *Wizard of Oz* memorabilia, Civil War sabers, and more. The people chatted about where their antiques came from: grandmother's attic, garage sales, estate auctions, and stores.

"Got this here print of the Founding Fathers out of a Dumpster," one man gushed. "I had it framed and the wife told me to bring it here. Hey, Mary, look at those toy cars."

"Das Rennen!" The Mercedes racer made its move when the course took them down an aisle designated photographs, metalwork and sculpture, and paper. It effortlessly passed the Mr. Magoo car and the Cortland ice cream truck. The Impala and the Kingsbury roadster were only a few yards ahead of it.

The Mercedes never looked out its rearview mirror. If it had, it would have seen two burly security guards emerge from a gap between photographs and paintings, leap over the ruined Carlson winter scene and give chase. The tallest and fastest was intent on Mr. Magoo. Reaching forward, he tripped over a camera cord and his knee slammed down on top of the Cortland ice cream truck. The little truck let out a final gasp:

"Go get 'em, Magoo."

"This book is quite extraordinary," the appraiser whistled. He was standing beneath a banner that read PAPER, and he was so intent on the book that he didn't notice the racing toy cars and the two security guards chasing them. "It's from the 1500s, from Germany. It has a pigskin cover on a wood board. There are a few worm holes, but I'd place it at twenty-five thousand."

"Germany again," the roadster snarled. "United States, people. This is the United States!"

"Twenty-five thousand dollars. Wow," the book owner said.

"Wow!" the appraiser echoed, catching sight of the racing Impala and Kingsbury roadster. "They belong in the toy section."

Across the aisle from the book appraiser, a stern-

looking fellow with trifocals leaned over a table where
several metal sculptures gleamed in the bright camera
lights. "This cast-iron miniature goat cart is circa 1890.
See how the goats gallop when it's pulled? There's a
hole on the seat where the figure was. As it sits, it's
worth about twenty-five hundred, maybe a little more.
An easy five thousand if you had the figure."

"Join us?" the roadster called to the goat cart.
"We're having a race!"

"To where?" the goats called.

"Uhm . . ."

"Yeah, just where we going?" The Impala swept
past the roadster.

"Das Rennen!" The Mercedes accelerated and drew
within inches of the Kingsbury roadster's rear bumper.

The goat cart surged forward, rolling off the edge
of the table and landing headfirst on the floor. The
cart snapped off and a wheel cracked.

"Make that worth three or four hundred now," the
appraiser told the goat cart owner.

The security guards gained on the racers. There
were four of them now, one of them wielding an antique fishing net he'd plucked off a table. All of them
were catching up to the sluggish, wobbly Mr. Magoo
car. It tipsily slipped beneath the skirt of a table covered with Egyptian tissue-box holders. King Tut's
gold-plated visage wiggled as the security guards thun-
dered past.

The roadster tapped its breaks and avoided colliding
with a man appraising an old milk bottle. "Impala, I
figure we'll circle 'round the outside, past the paper-
weights, and come back to the toy section. First car
to reach the banner wins."

"Wins what?" the Impala posed.

"Das Rennen!" the Mercedes keened as it swerved
around the roadster and the Impala and took the lead.

"No damn German car is going to beat me!" The
Kingsbury roadster howled its rage as it threw every-

thing into the race now. The tread wore on its old rubber tires, and its windshield cracked when it hopped over a power cord. "This is the American version of the *Old Things Roadshow. American.* Kapeesh?"

"Va-va-va-varroooom!" The Impala, too, was giving its last measure and managed to nose ahead of the roadster, just as the fishing net came down.

"American!" the roadster hollered. "Nooooooo!" Trapped, from inside the net, the Kingsbury roadster read the manufacturer's mark on the curved aluminum frame: MADE IN FINLAND. "Noooooooooooo!"

"Just us now," the Impala hummed to the Mercedes. It was a car-length back, but inching up.

"Va-va-va-varrrrooooom!" the Mercedes cried.

"Das Rennen!" the Impala returned.

The cars rounded the corner at the front of the exhibit hall, dodging two men carrying a Victorian rolltop desk. The security guards screeched to a halt to avoid plowing into the antique.

The Mercedes pulled three carlengths ahead and watched the Impala out of its rearview mirror. It wouldn't do to win by too much. No reason to hurt the American car's feelings—the race was the Impala's idea, after all.

Halfway down the aisle they'd just left, the Mr. Magoo car peeked out from under the table skirting. It rolled forward, no longer hurrying, knowing it was too far out of the race. It reached the front of the exhibit hall, and Mr. Magoo twisted his rubber head to the right, seeing the backsides of a dozen *Roadshow* security guards and appraisers. At the edge of his vision, between all the legs, he spotted the glow of the Impala's taillights.

Mr. Magoo kept driving straight—right out the convention center doors and onto the sidewalk.

Mr. Magoo didn't know that the Mercedes reached the TOYS banner first. Nor did he know that the Impala scratched its perfect paint job and dented its right front fender on the leg of a century-old coatrack.

He didn't know that the man who had brought him to the *Old Things Roadshow* was pacing and pulling at his hair, stamping his feet, and looking forlornly at the original box.

However, the Mr. Magoo car knew that Burlington, Wisconsin, was to the south, and that he had brand-new batteries that hopefully had enough juice to take him there.

"Va-va-va-varroooom!" Mr. Magoo said.

THE FIX

Diane Duane

The sand underfoot was burning hot and blinding to look at, glittering with jewel dust and dust of gold: the only place it didn't hurt to look at was where it was browned with blood. Above and all around him, the crowd roared so that he could hardly think . . . and the band behind him, blaring away, wasn't helping either. Lucius tried to ignore it all. What was happening in front of him was far more important than the noise or the smell or his burning eyes.

The *murmillo* gladiator in the red crest feinted at his opponent and cut hard. The white-crested Thracian sidestepped. That second blow should have landed, but it only sliced shoulder padding as he dodged; the crowd screamed at the miss. Lucius could hear knights and senators in the ringside boxes shouting for the bookies to come and take new bets.

"Go on," Lucius shouted. "Go on, don't let him—" Red-crest was already moving forward, jabbing at the Thracian's small shield, tempting him to use it to batter the murmillo's shortsword out of his hand. The shield flickered up and around in a move that Lucius and his murmillo had been discussing for the past week—hoping it would happen, not daring to count on it. "Now!" Lucius yelled, and his murmillo struck.

Not alongside the shield, but over it, at the Thracian's left eye—

The man ducked, but not low enough, and his scream was drowned by that of the crowd. Shield went one way, curved sica saber the other, and he dropped to the glittering sand, blood gushing past fingers that clawed at his helmet's faceplate—

The band blew a fanfare as the umpire raised his fist, then extended the first two fingers. It was the signal that someone needed help; the medics came running. The Thracian's coach yanked at the big bronze helmet's fastenings and threw it aside, then swore—

Lucius felt sorry for the guy, but not much. He'd noticed, a week back, that this particular Thracian's helmet didn't have the riveted-on plate over the leading eyehole that others had been adding. He liked to play to the ringside highborn ladies, liked to let them see his eyes.

Too bad, Lucius thought, *but you only play one game when you walk in here.* "You okay?" His murmillo nodded, waiting for the umpire to get confirmation from the imperial box. He got it, took the murmillo's arm, and held it up for the crowd to see.

"The winner," shouted the repeater-criers all around the arena, "the murmillo Cestinius, tyro, first victory with crown for technical merit . . . *and* the editor's purse for the best new fighter of the games!"

The crowd roared again as the payoff crew came out with the murmillo's winnings on a tray—only bags of coin at first, but as they started the victory lap, jewels and rings and other gewgaws thrown from the stands started to pile up on it too. The winnings came closer and closer. Lucius glowed with pride. Finally. *Finally.* He reached out—

And banged into cold rough brick, skinning his knuckles. His eyes flew open, and saw only darkness.

Lucius groaned, his disappointment too great for words, and closed his eyes again. *Almost. We almost*

*got it. Oh, let me get back to sleep, and maybe this
time . . .*

But the dream was gone, and it was dawn outside.
This deep into Level One, there was no way to tell
that by sight or hearing, but bitter necessity had long
ago taught Lucius how to know the time without needing light to do it. He turned over in his sleeping space,
a narrow, airless, sloping-roofed tunnel of stone just
barely longer than he was.

Not far away, doors slammed and voices shouted
under the arches and vaults of the long brick-walled
arcades. Cattle lowed, their dark warm scent and the
smell of manure mingling with other aromas—the
bitter-musk big cat smell, and the scents of olive oil
and hot metal, of bread baking and someone boiling
honey. The workday had already begun.

Lucius rolled over onto his hands and knees and
wriggled backward off his blanket. He groped to one
side for the only things he owned, his household gods
and his lamp, and wrapped them in the blanket before
pushing the bundle up to the far end of the alcove.
It was unlikely that anybody would steal the meager
possessions of a nine-year-old slave, but there were
always new people here, and you never could tell.

Lucius wriggled farther back until he could kneel
upright, and felt for his sponge-stick where he'd left
it the night before. Around him, in tiny crawlways like
his own, Lucius could hear grunts and groans as other
slaves woke up. There were maybe thirty of them,
young and old, who slept in this empty set of nooks
between gates fifty and fifty-one. Like him, they were
corporate slaves, and didn't have personal owners, just
overseers. *Not that an overseer can't beat you as hard
or as dead as an owner,* Lucius thought as he headed
for the arch that led to the inner aisle. *At least Mancipuer doesn't do that much . . .*

A ten-cubit-high brick arch materialized from the
gloom. Through it, the shallow dish of a tall bronze
pedestal lamp cast unsteady light from the twisted

hemp wicks that hung over its edges. Lucius made his way around the great aisle and past the eastside brothel, where lights and noise told him that the whores were at their laundry. Beyond that was the arched tunnel connecting the aisle to the center ring. Lucius trotted through it.

The pale marble floors were empty, but not for much longer. Shops and snack bars would open in the bare cubicles and in a couple of hours, this whole place would be full of city people coming in early for a bath, a drink, a meal, or a business meeting. Lucius passed the drink seller's, with its stand-up bar and deep vats to cool the wine. Next was the broad table of the custom tunic seller. And just beyond that . . .

Lucius slowed down and stopped, as he did every day, whether anyone was there or not. He imagined what it would be like, later, when the stallholder set up shop.

I wish, he thought. *I wish* . . . The items that Tullius Strabo laid out there just before the lunch break were almost the best things in the whole Colosseum—better than food, or wine, or a day without being slapped around. *Especially the murmillo.*

But for a penniless slave, Strabo's wares were as unobtainable as the moon. Lucius sighed and headed on to the slaves' bath and toilet between gates forty-six and forty-seven. He trotted into the toilet room— a plain stone place with a bench around three sides and holes cut through—and had a squat, then rinsed his sponge-stick in the little paved stream that ran in front of the benches, and hurried out and back the way he'd come.

You could always smell the downstairs bakery a long time before you saw it. Tall skinny Delia the baker worked there, in a flicker of lamps and an occasional hot glare as the oven opened. The first loaves and specialty rolls were already piled up on the counter. "Those for you," Delia said, catching sight of Lucius and pointing. *Those* were the fennel sausage rolls his overseer liked, and Lucius took two. "Tell your boss I need his tally sticks for this week!"

"I will," Lucius said, and ran off with the rolls. Mancipuer was always in a better mood when they got to him still warm.

The place where the draft beasts were stabled was nearly an eighth of the way around the arena. There, in a pen mostly swept clean, Lucius found Mancipuer the beast dresser in a crowd of other slaves, gilding the horns of the first of a triple hitch of oxen. His back was hunched from some old injury, making him seem smaller than he really was: dark and hairy, he reminded Lucius of the big apes that the management sometimes brought in for expensive beast-shows. Right now Mancipuer was using a thick soft brush to dab shreds of gold leaf onto the ox's right horn. One slave held a lamp over the work: another carried a pot of the red gesso used to make the gold-leaf stick.

Near the ox's head stood a boy several years older than Lucius; tall, thin, dark, he frowned more easily than he smiled. Catharis had worked with Mancipuer two years less than Lucius, but he equated age with seniority and never lost a chance to try to bully Lucius into thinking that way. As Lucius came in, Catharis scowled. Lucius ignored him, slipping in behind the four other slaves straining at ropes in an effort to keep the ox in one place. It bellowed, answered deafeningly by the other two oxen tied to a railing nearby.

"That my breakfast?" shouted Mancipuer over the noise, barely glancing up from his work.

"Yes, sir," Lucius said. He stopped just out of arm's reach. The overseer's temper was always uncertain early in the morning.

"You're late. I'd beat you, but I haven't the time. Get me the horn bags." He passed the brush to another of the slaves and held his hand out to Lucius for the roll.

"Is it hot, master?" Catharis said.

Lucius glowered at him as he went to get the muslin bags used to protect the newly gilded horns. Mancipuer bit off a chunk of roll and sausage. "Hot enough," he said through the mouthful. "Delia ask you about the sticks again?"

"Yes, sir." Lucius handed the bags to Mancipuer.

"I'll get them when we're done here. Drop them off on your way to the draper's. I need some cheap silk for the lunchtime routine with the lion."

"Yes, sir," Lucius said. He stood aside while the ox was led away and a second one brought in. "What routine?"

"Joke execution." Mancipuer finished his roll. "False-front cage; lion in back, chicken in front." He shrugged. "And thirty ells of silk to hide the chicken. Wicked waste, if you ask me. But what the Master wants . . ."

"He gets." The Master of the Games wasn't about to come down and explain his reasoning to *them*. "What color silk, sir?"

"They want crimson. Small chance, this time of year. But see how close you can get. Milla had some pinkish stuff." He turned his attention to the new ox. "Catharis, give Lucius the gold leaf. You breathe too hard, it goes all over the place. Go pull a rope."

Furious at the reprimand, Catharis managed to kick Lucius's leg as he went by. Lucius just gritted his teeth and ignored it. As usual, gilding the whole ox team seemed to take forever, and it was midmorning before they were done. The arcaded central ring was starting to fill as people made for the bookies or the wine shops, did some early shopping, or visited the baths to freshen up before the games began.

Mancipuer straightened and eased the kinks from his back. "Lucius, those tallies are on the second shelf," he said. "Drop them off with Delia, then get that silk."

"Yes, sir!" Lucius snatched up the tally sticks and

ran from the gilding pen, glad of the excuse to get
away. He dropped the tallies at the bakery and then
went through the tunnel toward the outermost ring.

Here the better class of snack bars and shops were
located—ones with higher ceilings and arched doors,
all faced in marble to match the paving of the outer
plaza and the stairs that accessed the stands. Patrons
in tunics and togas were already leaning over the tables of the stand-up wine bars, intently studying parch-
ments written with the day's fight schedule, and
arguing over handicaps and betting systems. Lucius
wondered how it must feel to have so much money
that you could afford to bet it and not get it back.
Then he sighed and turned right toward gate twenty-
three, bursting out into the bright hot sun of morning.

Even this early the heat was brutal, and the light
was blinding. Lucius turned his back on the sun and
rubbed his eyes, looking up at the white-shining mass
of the Colosseum, as immense and bright as a snow
mountain. It was hard sometimes to connect the exter-
nal white-and-gold glory to the dark life under the
stands, a life lived in caves and tunnels, scurrying
around under the pavement like frantic ants in service
to this hot, bright world astir with excitement and light
and color. Very soon now the bowl of the Colosseum
would fill with spectators, and the sound of their
voices would overflow the edges like a huge beast's
roar. The place would come alive, and the music
would start, and the men who made it all happen, the
fighters, would parade in. They would give everyone
who sat in the place a single purpose: to be part of
the fight, part of the glory, by backing a winner.

Lucius turned away and headed across the hot plaza
toward the Forum. Work left him little time to see
the games, though he lived to hear every scrap of news
about them, and could recite the stats of nearly every
first-string fighter who walked out on the sand. He'd
stolen time enough to see perhaps twenty fights since

he started paying attention to them three years ago. It was annoying to be at liberty right now, because there would be no major fights until after the lunch break, when the crowds had had time to get enough wine in them to improve the bookies' odds. There were three fights this afternoon that he'd have liked to see: two pairs of professionals who hadn't fought since early spring, and the third—

A shadow flickered over him, and Lucius looked up, expecting to see a bird. Instead a strange twisting shape came floating slowly down: something red. It was a veil.

Probably somebody up there dropped it, he thought, glancing back up at the Colosseum. A breeze pushed the veil slightly sideways as it fell, and Lucius realized it was going to land on the eternally muddy road where the animal carts came up. Lucius could tell from the sheen and gleam of the veil as it turned in the hot sun that it wasn't the cheap kind of silk that he'd been sent to get, but something expensive, blown off some rich lady up there.

Rich people weren't anything Lucius cared about one way or another . . . but still, the silk was really beautiful. It drifted lower, blowing toward the wet claggy mud of the cart path. Lucius went after it as the breeze gusted around the building, leaping up to catch one end just before the viel landed in the mire. Then he stared at it.

Now what? How do I find out whose this is? There could be ten thousand women up there, freeborn, slave, or noble, and probably all of them would say it was theirs. Lucius stood there irresolute, trying to decide what to do.

He turned to look at the first-floor gates. From gate twenty-four came a subdued glow that resolved into a glitter of golden armor, a white tunic, a kilt of white and gold, and high-laced white leather sandals, as their wearer strode out into the sunlight. The big burly red-

haired man stood there for a moment, craning his neck
to see around or over the crowd that was starting to
gather around him.

Then he saw Lucius with the veil, and headed
straight toward him.

Lucius stopped breathing. Some of the crowd that
had come out after the man were still following him.
He turned as he walked, waving them away, laughing,
and the sun glanced off the polished helmet under his
arm with a blinding flash like a star fallen to earth.

It can't be, Lucius thought. But he knew the white
ostrich-feather wings on that helmet's griffin crest, and
the multiple bands of white enamel just above the
broad brim. Everybody who followed the games knew
the trademarks of the Neronian gladiator school's
most famous superstar. *But what's he coming at me
for? Unless . . . the veil! Did I do something wrong?
But what?*

Lucius stared at his face. *It really is him!* There was
the scar from last year, one of the very few he'd ever
gotten: he was *that* good. "Boy," the man said as he
got closer, "where'd you find that?"

"It fell from the top level, sir," Lucius managed to
say, and then instantly blushed hot. He was in a sports
fan's dream, but had no idea how to act or even speak
to a gladiator if one spoke to you.

The gladiator looked over at the mud of the nearby
cart track and his eyes widened a little. All Lucius's
worries vanished when he saw how broadly the man
grinned at him. "You saved it from landing in that
mess? Nice catch."

Lucius swallowed, overwhelmed by the compliment,
and held out the veil. But the resplendent figure just
glanced over his shoulder then waved it away. "Hang
on to it for a moment longer," he said. "We're waiting
for someone. What's your name, son?"

"Lucius."

"I'm Hilarus."

"I know."

"A fan, eh?"

Lucius put his head up, emboldened, and grinned back. "I work here," he said. "I follow the business."

"Aha . . . a fellow professional. Don't tell me: you want to be a gladiator someday."

Lucius shook his head. "No. A coach."

"Smart kid," Hilarus said. "There's money in that, if you can learn what you need to. And you don't have to be a gladiator to learn." Hilarus glanced quickly over his shoulder again. "So how do you like today's card?"

Lucius had been thinking about little else. "If I were a betting man," he said, "I'd have something on the third fight."

Now Hilarus laughed out loud. "'*If?*' Everyone bets in Rome. The question is, which way?"

"You're fourteen for fourteen, with thirteen crowns for technical merit," Lucius said. "The other guy's two for six, and none. Looks obvious to me."

"To a lot of people," Hilarus said. "And today, I wouldn't argue. But if the fix was in—" He looked over his shoulder again and his grin moderated itself. "Here she comes. Make me look good . . ."

A flurry of rose and white came out of gate twenty-four, a silken palla stirred to a flutter by the breeze that blew around the base of the building. The woman wrapped in it wore no veil, but scurrying behind her came a gaggle of high-end slaves burdened with parasols and cushions and feathery fans and picnic hampers. They all paused as the woman did, looking around. Hilarus caught her eye and raised a hand. Behind him, the other hand made a fist at Lucius, then stuck out two fingers in the Help-me-here! gesture. Lucius looked at it for a moment, then put one end of the veil in it. He didn't let go of the other.

The whole brightly dressed crowd moved toward them, the lady foremost. Lucius bowed deeply, and Hilarus extended the hand holding his end of the veil.

"You have it!" the lady said. "I thought it would be floating in Father Tiber by now."

"No, madam," Hilarus said, and bowed again. "But someone should have told you that it wouldn't go into the arena from where you threw it. This time of day, the wind's from the west. Anything this light goes up under the eastside awnings and out. I've seen a hundred veils go that way."

"I dare say you have," she said, giving him a wicked look. "But I'm glad not to have lost this to anyone I didn't know." She smiled at Hilarus, and took the veil. "And the small one helped you? You must have run very quickly!"

"We both ran for it, Great Lady," Lucius said, eyeing the width of the golden border on her robe. It was heavy bullion wire, and he didn't think his honorific was going too far. "But he caught the other end, that would have gone in the mud."

"And I missed such a chase!" the lady said with an attractive pout. "Better sport than anything in the arena—especially after you ran out." She gave Hilarus an amused look. "You should have seen the emperor's face."

"Normally his commands are my first concern," Hilarus said, bowing slightly. "But some of us owe other allegiances, such as the one to Queen Venus."

The lady smiled again. "We should go back," she said to Hilarus, "before Titus starts wondering too much. I'll find a way to show my gratitude later. But as for you, young sir—"

She smiled at Lucius, bending down to meet his eyes more closely, and reached out to take his hand. All his calculating and rather mercenary thoughts of reward left Lucius's head in a rush, drowned in the darkness of her hair and eyes. Up close, she smelled wonderful, like roses. Then he felt something cool and heavy against his palm. It wasn't easy to look away from her, but when he did he goggled at a glinting disk—a whole denarius—with the emperor's head on it, round and thick-necked and bald.

"Lady," he said. "Thank you!"

"Her, certainly," Hilarus said, with a smile at the lady. "But perhaps you should thank Queen Venus too. Any wise man is glad to be in *her* debt."

The lady straightened up, draped the rosy veil over her head, and drew it down in a gesture of amused modesty that hid nothing. "Only the wise ones?" she said, and gave the gladiator a look that Lucius had seen often enough on the girls up in the stands.

Even overwhelmed as he was, Lucius had the presence of mind to bow again, to both of them. Then, blinded by the absolute wonder of the moment, he hurried back toward the Colosseum gates, his fist clenched around the coin.

As if by some evil magic, a tall thin form stepped out of the shadows and straight-armed him. Lucius staggered, caught his balance again, and found himself staring at Catharis. *"You're* gonna *get* it," the bigger boy sang softly, smiling his usual nasty smile. *"You're* gonna *get* it . . ."

"I wouldn't get anything if *you* weren't flapping your big yap all the time."

Catharis snickered. "Master says, where's the silk he sent you for?"

"I haven't been to Milla's yet. I'm going now."

"So where've you been?"

Lucius scowled. "None of your business, you squatsponge!"

Catharis's eyes went narrow. "You can't talk to me like that! I'll tell Master—"

"Tell him anything you like," Lucius said, and ran off in the direction of the Forum. Just this once he was completely unmoved by the threat. *I don't have to take this squat. Five minutes ago I was talking to Hilarus! And that great lady, like some kind of foreign queen!*

"You come back here!" Catharis yelled, but Lucius ignored him. *He'll go right back and tattle to Mancipuer. So let him. I'll take my beating. I've got something to make up for it!* As he ran, Lucius reached inside his tunic, pulled out the little amulet bag that hung hidden around his neck, and hid the denarius in it.

He made his way through the Forum to the arcaded side alley where Milla the cloth seller had her stall. It was a multicolored forest of bolts of cloth, mostly standing on end, some stacked up like cordwood, and usually one or two rolled out on the marble of the streetside slab. As Lucius approached he saw with astonishment that the slab was covered with thin crimson-colored silk. That was when he started thinking he might not get beaten after all. "Milla—how much of this have you got?"

"How much do you want?" she said, emerging from the back of the stall. As usual, Lucius wondered how so round a woman could be invisible in so small a space.

"Thirty ells. On the master's account—"

"Lucky you. Thirty is what I've got," Milla said. "Take it. I'll send the tally sticks around later."

She rolled up the silk and loaded it into Lucius's arms. He staggered under the weight, but didn't care: as he made his way back out through the Forum, Lucius had the strangest feeling that his luck had changed. Even in the dark warren of the tunnels, some golden outside light seemed to have followed him in—even when he turned the last corner and found Mancipuer examining the badly done paint job on a snorting pygmy elephant.

"See, master!" Catharis said. "I told you. He didn't even start for the stall until I went out and told him to get moving. And now he's back with some shoddy—"

"Thirty ells of crimson, sir," Lucius said, bringing the bolt over for Mancipuer to see. "Just the kind you wanted."

Scowling, Mancipuer reached out to finger the fabric, then turned that scowl back on Catharis. "I don't mind if he takes the time to do the work right," he said. "Unlike some people, in so much in a rush to get done with our own work that we botch it. Lucius, you and Makron start getting that stuff stretched out on the frames that were built for it. Afterward you can have the afternoon to yourself. As for you"—he gave Catharis a clout upside the head—"scrub this poor creature off and start over. We've four more to do."

"Yes, Master," Catharis said humbly, but when Mancipuer's back was turned he shot a furious glare at Lucius. Lucius paid no attention, but went to help old Lysias with the silk. He did the next hour's work in a half-dream, feeling the little bag against his chest, and thinking again and again, *I talked to Hilarus!*

As soon as he was done, Lucius ran off before Mancipuer could change his mind. As he went, feeling the bag thump against his chest, the thought came to him, staggering. He had *money*.

He could buy the murmillo!

Lucius stopped and leaned against an archway, gulping, almost in shock at the thought of actually *spending* the one piece of money he had ever owned. But at the same time . . .

. . . the murmillo!

He took a breath so deep it felt to be worth about three, and made his way to the center aisle, to Strabo's stall. A few feet away he stopped, as he always did, to just stare at the rows of figures. They came in all kinds and sizes—Thracians with their typical curved sica swords; retiarius netmen with tridents; secutor "chasers" in egg-shaped helmets . . . and finally Lucius's favorites, the murmillones with their big shields and crested, cowl-brimmed helmets.

All the figures came in several models and price ranges. The collectors' editions, done in silvered or even gilt iron with bronze accessories, were intended for the high-end market. Then came the wooden ones, carved with helmets that could open and close; the figures had mobile jointed arms, and hands socketed to take small bronze swords. Once you had the basic figure, you could buy clip-on armor for it, and have it decorated with designs like your favorite fighter's. The cheapest ones were plain terra cotta; nothing moved, and they were fragile, but a clever workman could paint on the armor and even do a sketchy version of your favorite gladiator's face under the visor of the open helmet.

For Lucius, even the pottery murmillo had been an impossible dream. But now he could even afford one of the metal ones. And still get change back from the denarius!

Lucius took a deep breath and stepped up to the slab. Strabo turned and looked down, a long way down, at Lucius. He was tall and thin and gray-haired, with watery pale eyes that looked straight through you.

"Huh," he said. "You." And he started to turn away.

"No, wait!"

Strabo wasn't a mean-looking man, but he had a face in which every deep-creased line seemed to say *Don't waste my time.* "Why? What if a paying customer comes along?"

Lucius looked up and down the aisle, and Strabo followed his glance. No one showed the slightest sign of coming near them. "All right," Strabo said resignedly. "You're 'just looking,' right? At the murmillo again?"

He reached for one of the plain pottery ones and set it right in front of Lucius's nose. "It's just the same as the last time."

"Not that one," Lucius said, reaching into the neck of his tunic to fish out his amulet bag. "One of the wooden ones."

Strabo opened his mouth. Before he could say a word, Lucius pushed the denarius at him.

"How'd you come by money like that all of a sudden?"

"A lady gave it to me."

"Oh, really." Strabo oozed disbelief.

"The lady," said Lucius, "who came out after Hilarus."

The watery eyes opened wider. "Oh, *really*," he said again, but this time the tone was different. He moved the terra-cotta murmillo back to its place and brought forward one of the olive-wood ones. Lucius took it in his hands and examined it carefully. The carving was good, the fighter's stance very natural. There was a nick in the left upper thigh where the carver's knife had slipped, but the damage was sanded down and otherwise it was perfect. Lucius handed it back. "That'll do."

"How do you want it?" Strabo said. "Parchment armor?"

"Bronze," Lucius said. He might never be able to afford his own action figure again: he was going to do this right.

"Wooden sword?"

"Iron."

"All right," Strabo said. He started rummaging among the paint pots and tools on the shelf behind him.

"Who was she?" Lucius said, after a moment.

"With that many slaves, and sitting near the emperor? Someone important." Strabo picked through the wicker trays under the slabs until he found a short straight sword about the length of his little finger. "But it's the kind of thing you won't ask anybody else about, if you're smart. . . ."

Lucius watched carefully as Strabo wrapped quilted muslin around the wooden figure's upper arm, then tied the metal arm guard on top with linen thread. He checked to make sure everything still moved, and plugged the little iron blade into the hole in its clenched fist. "Watch out for this," Strabo said. "It's soft, it'll bend. You break it, you don't get a replacement."

"I won't break it."

The kilt and broad belt went on, padding for the

legs and a pair of greaves secured with more linen thread, and finally the tall army-pattern shield. Strabo picked up the helmet, checking that the faceplate grille went up and down correctly, then looked at the plain crest. "What color?"

Lucius meant to say, "White and gold," but a memory of the lady's rose-red veil stopped him. "Make it red," he said.

Strabo dipped the brush in a nearby paint pot and a moment later the crest was scarlet with terra-cotta and gesso paint. Two tiny feathers went into the sockets on either side. Then Strabo smiled, pointed the brush carefully with his fingers, and painted a garland of roses above the brim of the helmet. Not an unusual decoration, and calculated to catch the ladies' eyes.

Lucius grinned. Strabo put the brush down and picked up a finer one from a pot of lampblack ink, lifting the helmet off again. The figure's face underneath it was blank, oval, a ridge running down the middle of its front. With surprising speed Strabo painted on a pair of eyes, the shadow of a nose, a stroke of mouth. He held the figurine away, admiring it, then swung the visor down and put the figure on the slab in front of Lucius. "Satisfied?"

"He's perfect."

"Then that'll be six minae."

"Done."

Strabo made the change and counted it out, then watched Lucius put it away rather mechanically. He rooted around under the slab for a moment, produced a piece of plain soft cloth, and wrapped it around the little gladiator. "Go on, boy." He said it gently, not the way people usually said "boy" when they were using it as just another way to say "slave." "Go put him somewhere safe."

Lucius nodded. Still in something of a daze, he took the wrapped-up murmillo and headed off to his sleeping-space to hide it away. Once there he watched all around to make sure no one saw him, then slipped in, unrolled his blanket, and tucked the murmillo alongside his lamp and his gods. "I'll see you later," he whispered, and got out fast.

Once out in the center aisle again, he paused and wondered what to do. He really wanted to spend the afternoon playing with the murmillo, but to do that in private, he'd have to get more lamp oil, and slaves weren't allowed any until after dark.

Lucius wandered out into the sunlight again. People were coming in for the afternoon session, so he dawdled out into the Forum again, sheltering under one of the arcades, and considered buying himself a treat. There were people selling sausages and sweets out here; cheeses and fruits and honey cakes, all kinds of wonders that he would never taste. *The kind of thing that Lady must eat all day . . .*

But then he caught a glimpse of white columns through the Forum stalls, and felt a brief odd pang of guilt as he remembered Hilarus saying, "You should thank Queen Venus."

Lucius thought about that, then dodged and scampered up the busy Forum, right to the far end of the plaza and a largish stall hung with all kinds and sizes of cages. At the sight of him, the stallholder, a fat lady in a big stained yellow palla, came straight out to chase him off. But Lucius knew what to do. He held up his coin and waited till she saw it.

"Won't get much for that," the woman said.

"Don't need much." Lucius pointed at one of the smallest cages.

The woman sniffed and unhooked it from the cord where it hung. "One sestercius."

"*How* much?" said Lucius, appalled. Then he shrugged. If the goddess had seen fit to get him a whole denarius, then this was her fair cut. He handed it over. The stallholder dropped the coin on her little scale and watched suspiciously until the pans leveled out before giving him the caged, squawking sparrow.

Lucius took it and ran past the end of the Forum,

up the steps of Venus's temple. Leaning against one of the big open doors was a slightly pear-shaped priestess in a white dress and rose-colored palla, with a jauntily skewed garland of somewhat wilted roses on her head.

Lucius handed her the cage. The priestess took it and looked inside. "With prayer, or without?" she said.

"With, please," Lucius said. "A thank-offering."

"Ten minae," the priestess said, and smiled crookedly. "Aren't you a little young to be thanking her for favors?"

"Not when I owe her one," Lucius said, and passed over the money.

The priestess pocketed it. "Whatever. Thank you Lady Venus Queen of the Loves and Passions of Men for Gracious Kindness shown to this your Servant who by this Token thanks Thee," she said, and pulled the cage door open. The sparrow shot out, pooping on the priestess as it went, and fluttered straight back toward the marketplace. The priestess rolled her eyes and walked off, resignedly wiping herself with her sleeve.

Lucius headed back into the shadows of the Colosseum. In the evening there was more work to do, but everything went by more quickly than he could have believed, because of what was waiting in his sleeping-space. When he finally got there, the building had gone quiet around him, all the spectators gone, the restaurants emptying, the brothels operating with their doors shut. Lucius knelt by the bedroll, put down his lamp—refilled with oil at Delia's—and unrolled his blanket.

There was the murmillo, just as he had left him. Lucius piled up the blanket against his doorway in such a way that it shut most of the lamp's light in. And then, on the hard stone floor, he played. Hardly above a whisper, Lucius made all the sounds of a day's games: the crowd's roar, the cries of the bookies, the repeaters' announcements, the stats of the champion and the challenger.

Then the featured fight began, and he worked the murmillo's sword arm up and down more times than he could count, beating the iron of the sword against imagination's armor until the inside of his mind rang with it. On hands and knees, grinning in triumph, he made the murmillo chase the unfortunate challenger— some poor five-fight Thracian—up and down the length of a shadowy sleeping space that had become the sunlit arena oval. Lucius played until he could barely see, until he started falling asleep where he sat. Then ever so carefully he laid the action figure down, wrapped in a fold of his blanket, and got ready to say his prayers.

No Roman would have called a place home without his household gods. Lucius had only two, carved clumsily from scrap wood he'd found. One was Mars— that made sense since the Colosseum was his house— though Lucius didn't pray to him often, since he was reported to have a temper. The other was a Venus that a Gaulish slave had made for him a year or so ago, a little woman-shape like Milla the cloth seller, one third bosom and two thirds hips, but still strangely graceful. "The Lady of the Caves," the Gaul had called her. "The Lady of the tunnels and holes and the dark places underneath: Venus Cloacina."

Carefully Lucius put the lamp down in front of the little figures, and he raised his hands to pray. "Thanks again," he said. "This is the best thing I've ever had. Please take care of the nice lady who gave me the money. I'll take good care of the murmillo. I promise."

Then Lucius lay down and rolled himself in the rest of the blanket, and blew out the lamp. He put a hand out to the rolled-up murmillo, let out a breath, and, smiling, fell asleep.

*   *   *

So, he heard someone say in the night, probably someone coming home late from the nearby brothel. *Do I win?*

You win, said another voice, more amused than annoyed. *I admit it.*

And . . . ? said the first voice.

Oh, stop that. You know I'll pay the debt. What do I owe him?

The usual. A day of heart's desire.

And if he can't cope?

A long, slow smile began to underlie the darkness. *Are you betting he can't?*

Lucius turned over and slept again.

A second later, it seemed, he awoke in the dark. It was dawn again. Lucius reached out his hand, knowing that between him and the brick would be—

—nothing?!

Lucius sat up and just missed banging his head against the ceiling. He swore under his breath. *Catharis!* he thought, feeling around and not finding the *murmillo* anywhere. *He actually came in here and took it! I'll kill him!*

He knew where Catharis slept—in an underhang over by the door the gladiators used to go into the arena—and he didn't need a light to find his way. Lucius headed around the curve of the inmost aisle, toward the Fighter's Gate, the way the gladiators went into the ring. Off to the right was the place where Catharis would be sleeping. Lucius stalked down the aisle, not even trying to be quiet. But then an oblong of light in front of him distracted him, and he slowed to stare at it—pale light, very early morning light, seeping in. The Fighter's Gate was ajar. Silently Lucius crept forward to look out into the arena.

That pale strange light of morning twilight turned everything—sand, stands, shadow—all one shade of indefinite blue. High up, the sky was still dark, but above the rim of the arena, hanging like a watching eye, was the morning star. And out on the sand, in the empty silence of the arena, a single *murmillo* was working out. In better light, his crest might have been red with two tall plumes, and the shadows around his helmet a garland of roses, a design calculated to please the ladies.

Lucius stepped out through the Fighter's Gate and moved slowly across the twilit sand. The *murmillo* just kept going through his basic drill, a flowing sequence of techniques with sword and shield. The sand, dry after being raked and left to rest for the night, squeaked under his footsteps.

Ten paces away, Lucius stopped to watch. The *murmillo* had that same easy grace that Hilarus did, the gift for making it look simple. Though his moves were less showy, their precision was just as crisp. When he finished, the *murmillo* turned, swinging his sword and working one shoulder as if it bothered him. That was when he saw Lucius, and strode over to him, towering above the boy's head.

What happened next took Lucius's breath away. The gladiator saluted, then gravely went down on one knee. "Sir," he said. "I am your gladiator." He took his helmet off.

For an instant Lucius was afraid there would be only daubs of ink inside, but the face was normal enough, though rough-hewn and blocky as if genuinely carved from wood. The eyes were no darker than those of any other Roman. Lucius lowered his own eyes from that direct stare, astonishingly childlike in a full-grown man. And then he saw, above the greave on the left leg, a dimple in the flesh. Not a scar, just a place where the carver's knife had slipped.

"There's a message, sir," he said. "She says, 'You have a day: dawn to dawn.' "

" '*She?*' " said Lucius, blushing and not knowing why. He was able to accept the magic far more easily than the words. Even in dreams, nobody had ever called him *sir*. He was just a slave, he'd never had real responsibility before. But now he was responsible for the *murmillo*.

And I have to take care of him. How do I do that?

Back in the depths of the building, a door creaked open and Lucius flinched.

"What's the matter, sir?"

"We've got to get away from here. Gladiators don't work out by themselves this early, they—"

"Hey, you!" Lucius half turned, saw who was speaking, and felt icy sweat pop out all over him. "Yes, you two! What's going on?"

This cannot be happening! Lucius thought desperately. Dark-skinned, massive, standing in the shadows of the Fighter's Gate, was the Master of the Games, principal officer of the Colosseum, answering directly to the emperor; the man responsible for every denarius and sestercius spent here, and therefore Lucius's true master. In the comfy brown tunic he must have slept in, he looked like a casual laborer, but there was nothing casual about his expression. "Well?"

Lucius instantly understood that the only possible response was to lie outrageously. He bowed the way he'd done to the patrician lady yesterday. "Sir," he said, "my master sent him over to work out with the Neronians."

It was Hilarus's school, the best—and the only one with a direct connection to the Colosseum through the tunnel under the plaza. That explained how a gladiator could get here without passing any gates. Nonetheless the Master raised his eyebrows. "He's a little early."

"My master wanted him to check the sand."

The Master looked resigned. "Doesn't everybody? All right . . . five more minutes. Then the ground crew comes in." He turned and vanished into the darkness under the gate. Lucius nearly collapsed with relief, then heard the squeaking behind him as the murmillo went back to his practice.

"Didn't you hear him? We have five minutes!"

"Five minutes is long enough to win a fight." The murmillo began proving that on the empty air.

Lucius watched him with a thousand questions going through his head. *What do I do now? How do I hide him? What do I do with him?* "When you're finished," he said, "follow me. I'll find you somewhere to hi— To stay while we figure out what to do."

"Only until afternoon," the murmillo said without breaking his rhythm.

"What? Why?"

"Because I fight this afternoon."

"You *what??*"

"I fight. In the freestyles."

"Are you crazy? Who put your name on the schedule?"

"That's my owner's job. You would have taken care of that. Wouldn't you?" He went back to cutting the air.

Lucius shivered; the swish of the sword was starting to get to him. *That's how it'll sound when they find I lied about him, and chop my head off.* Then, slowly, his panic began to fade. *But wait a minute. What if he* does *fight? This happens every week. Documentation goes missing, some new guy turns up, nobody's sure what he's doing, but he knows, and the fight goes ahead—*

It all started to fall into place. *If he's going to show up to fight anyway, then we'll go ahead and* act *like he's for real.* It could work, for the same reason that it had worked just now with the Master. With six thousand employees in this one facility alone, he couldn't know them all by sight. "Listen," Lucius said. "Just come along with me, and whenever I say 'Isn't that right?,' you just nod and agree. And if I ask you to do some fighting moves—"

"That's what I live for," said the murmillo. He slashed his sword up and down, then winced slightly. "I think I overdid the exercises."

Lucius remembered how long he had played with his toy gladiator, and felt guilty. "We'll take you down to the trainers' bay," he said. "They massage gladiators all day; no way they'll care that they don't recognize you. A rubdown, then a hot bath. . . ."

He headed off, thinking fast, then saw the very last thing he needed—Catharis, looking first sleepy, then surprised. Lucius paid no heed, but didn't miss the familiar nasty smile. *Oh well, what's one more problem?* He turned to the murmillo to ask him the first of a thousand questions, then stopped. "What're you called?"

"Whatever my master chooses."

Lucius swore under his breath, but as they passed the equipment stall where kit was dropped off for repair, he caught sight of several pairs of *caesti*, bronze-knuckled boxing gloves. *Hmm.* "Cestinius," he said. " 'Lil' Knucks.' How does that sound?"

"Like my name," said the murmillo, as if there'd never been any doubt.

"Oh, good."

They reached the massage and bath area, and Lucius stuck his head around the door. "Hey, Arcisius! You in here?"

In a waft of steam, a bathman in a linen kilt emerged from the hot-pool area, wringing out a sodden towel. "Here's a new guy from the Neronian," Lucius said. "His trainer's not here yet, and somebody thought it'd be funny to send him all the way over here for his bath."

"Why am I surprised?" said the bathman. "They're getting back at us for last week, when we sent all those people over to them." Arcisius peered at the murmillo. "And they made him suit up, too? What a laugh. Go through there, fella; racks for the armor on the left."

Lucius watched him go, then said under his breath, "Keep an eye on him, all right? He got a bang on his head a while back; he might seem like he's not all there." He slipped a mina into Arcisius's unresisting hand.

Arcisius stared at it. "Where'd you get this?"

"He's got a patron, and the patron needed an agent. Me. Don't mention this to anyone, all right? But this guy's a good bet for later today."

"Freestyles, huh? Got it. Can I mention *that* to a couple other of the lads? Thanks."

He vanished into the bath area. Lucius got back to the beast pens as fast as he could, but Catharis was already there with Mancipuer's breakfast rolls, looking virtuous as he whispered in the overseer's ear.

"You're late," Mancipuer said. Ignoring the rolls, he headed for Lucius. Catharis was already grinning. Lucius let the distance close until he could speak quietly, then said, "Sir, my apologies. Someone wanted to . . . borrow my services." He did his best to make it sound mysterious.

"Oh, they did, did they? Well, you can just tell them—"

Lucius caught his overseer's hand, pulled it down out of sight of the other slaves and pressed a sestercius into it. *If I can cut Lady Venus in, I can cut him in too. Especially considering how much trouble he could make for me otherwise.*

Mancipuer glanced at his hand, then at the other slaves. His other hand grabbed Lucius by the tunic.

"You were late yesterday, too. The rest of you, back to work! We need to have a little chat." The others smirked and moved away: that phrase was known code for a serious hiding. Mancipuer dragged him out of sight behind one of the nearby columns, then whispered, "What's this about?" He slapped the column noisily. "But first, *yell!*"

"Ow! *Ow!* Master, no!"

"Keep me waiting, will you? I'll have your hide off first! Maybe this'll help you remember!"

The pantomime went on for a couple of minutes before Mancipuer paused, flapping his hand to ease the sting. "This had better be good," he said in a low voice, "or it won't be the column next time."

"It *is* good, sir! The fix is in! This senator, crimson a hand deep on his toga, he stopped me in the Forum and said he needed an agent no one would suspect. He's putting a new gladiator into the freestyles today, behind his trainer's back—he's got too many contacts, and this new man's a ringer. The senator bought him in from Pompeii or somewhere; name's Cestinius. Betting's already started. Anybody in the know will clean up—"

"How much is in it for us?"

"A lot," Lucius said, desperately hoping that this was true. "The guy's rated as a tyro, but he's not. I saw him warming up this morning."

Mancipuer thought for a moment. "All right. After that 'beating' you're no good for anything today. And Catharis needs to learn how much work I expect from my senior slave." His smile was nasty; Lucius was glad it wasn't directed at him. "But I want half of whatever's going."

"Oh, all of it, sir!"

"No lies, just half." Mancipuer raised his voice again. "Next time it'll be worse!" he roared. "Get out of my sight!" Then, quietly, "And get fixing."

Lucius got, trailed by a chorus of jeering laughter. He remembered to groan and hobble until he was out of sight, but was already starting to work at how to get Cestinius onto the lists for this afternoon. Everything hung on that. There were other problems, too. The bath had been easy, but his man needed food, drink, and somewhere to rest until fight time.

But as he went from snack bar to lounge to equipment area and back again, Lucius realized something: the system could be beaten, and it wasn't hard to do. The sheer size of it was an advantage. Five hundred beast handlers, two thousand gladiatorial support staff, a thousand ground crew—rakers, cleaners, wheel greasers, gods knew what else—dressers, trainers, all the rest: the Colosseum was a small city within the city. And as in any city, people constantly got fired, got hired, got married, got sick, sometimes got killed. The population was always changing. All that mattered was to avoid people who knew him too well to be taken in by his cover story. Nor did it matter that Lucius was poorly dressed. Plenty of rich owners left their slaves badly dressed because it never occurred to them to think about their clothes. Lucius's rags didn't make much difference.

But though food and baths and armor-polishing weren't so much of a problem for Lucius to arrange, what he still couldn't work out was how to get Cestinius onto the freestyle lists. Those came down from arena management, from the Master's office. Lucius briefly considered sneaking up there, stealing in, grabbing a list and . . . then what? He could read a bit, but couldn't write a word.

Cestinius remained cheerfully unconcerned. Lucius dropped in on him any number of times between morning and noon-meal to find he'd been adopted as the bathmen's pet celebrity: they weren't used to gladiators who so enjoyed listening to everything they had to say. Yet another masseur was rubbing him down and chatting with Lucius when somebody yelled, "Hey you, get over here!"

Lucius turned around. Catharis was standing in the doorway. "What?"

"Master wants you!"

Lucius stared at Catharis in a way that made it plain he was in no hurry. The bathmen noticed it and started to chuckle. "We're talking business here," he said. "I'll be along in a moment."

The laughter got louder. Catharis stood it as long as he could. "He's in Arno's!" he shouted, then fled. Lucius smiled.

"And the lists?" asked Cestinius.

"It's getting handled," Lucius said, and strolled out like someone far more confident than he felt.

There was a sports bar on the second level; another under-the-stands space, but airier than some due to the air shafts that vented through gratings behind the third-level seats. There were benches and tables, and a central island where the amphorae of wine and the ice and water and pottery mugs were kept. The back wall was whitewashed for weekly advertisements, like the gable end of a house: on one side, somewhat faded because there was no need to change the sign, a block of russet letters said THE FAMOUS GLADIATOR HILARUS EATS HERE ON TUESDAYS AND SATURDAYS. COME AND BE SEEN WITH HILARUS. COVER CHARGE 2 SESTERCII. Under the sign sat Mancipuer.

"Is everything all right, sir?" Lucius said. Seeing Mancipuer here made him nervous. He was famous for never taking his lunch hour off.

"Fine," Mancipuer said, "fine. Flavia! Food for the boy, and a refill of Tuscan. Now sit down here and talk to me. The bathmen are going crazy: one masseur says he never saw a body in better shape, like some statue come to life. But he's still just a tyro, so the betting—" Mancipuer took a swig of his wine. "Things have heated up since this morning. There are all kinds of rumors. . . ."

Will they be enough to get him onto the freestyle list? Lucius thought desperately.

Mancipuer had another swig. His cheeks were glowing, and not just with excitement. "And this patron— Who is he, kid? Really?"

Another clay flask of wine arrived and Lucius had a moment or so to think until the server went away. "Sir, I can't. Or I might just . . . vanish. But not yet. So far, he thinks I'm a lucky charm." Lucius grinned. "I can be lucky for more than one person at once, though."

Mancipuer grinned too. "Let's see."

They sat there together for the better part of an hour like old partners, eating bread and bacon and beans and drinking watered wine. Lucius kept fretting

about where Cestinius was, how he was doing . . .
but he also noticed, in the shadowy nooks of the bar,
knowing looks being exchanged, whispers going
around. . . . *Is the fix in? Who's it in on? Which fight?*
. . . for no one in Rome would be crazy enough to
think you could make money off the games by playing fair.

Men stopped by to talk to Mancipuer, a sly smile
here, a wink there, a word or two about what the odds
were likely to be. Most of them thought Mancipuer
was the go-between, the link between Cestinius and
some rich senator or racing-syndicate "name." And
Mancipuer thought that Lucius was the go-between
but he would never let on. He was having too much
fun being the center of attention.

Lunchtime came to an abrupt end when they heard
the trumpets blowing faintly outside. Lucius's heart
jumped inside him: there was still a certain list that his
murmillo wasn't on. "Oh, gods," he said "It's time—"

"Go on," Mancipuer said. "Luck, boy. Mars and
the Fates go with him."

Lucius ran off toward the trainers' bay. When he
got there, the place, so quiet earlier, was boiling with
activity—gladiators heading into the baths, coming out
of them, suiting up; trainers and managers all over
the place, checking each other out, checking out each
others' talent. Cestinius was there, finally done with
his massage, back in his armor and looking extremely
fit. "Sir," he said to Lucius as he came in, "the list—"

A big man in a white repeater's tunic came bustling
in and started handing out strips of parchment to the
trainers. He almost went by Lucius, who caught the
repeater by the sleeve of his tunic. "Hey, one for me."

The man peered at him. "Who're you?"

"I'm repping for Cestinius," Lucius said.

"Who?" said the repeater. That was common
enough: repeaters were famous for huge voices but no
memory. Nonetheless, he handed Lucius a copy of the
list and went out.

A hubbub of discussion went up as trainers and gladiators started arguing about placements and odds and everything else. Lucius found it hard to pay attention. All he could see at the moment was Cestinius's face as the big murmillo peered at the list. "What does it say?" Cestinius said. "Who'm I fighting?"

"Uh . . ."

There was nothing Lucius could do but tell the truth. *And then what happens to a magic gladiator who was born to fight and can't? Does he just vanish? Or something worse?* "Cestinius—" he started to say, and then a hand fell on his shoulder.

It was Hilarus.

He was in his full arena armor, helmet under his free arm; behind him were a couple of the gofers who perpetually seemed to be hanging around a gladiator of his caliber. "So you weren't kidding when you said you were in the business," he said. "I didn't know you were *agenting*."

"Uh, it was kind of sudden, sir."

"It usually is. What's the problem?" He plucked the list out of Lucius's hand, glanced down it.

"I should be fighting this afternoon," Cestinius said.

"Then somebody slipped up." The gladiator looked at Cestinius, sizing him up: then held out a hand. "Hilarus."

"Cestinius," the murmillo said. "Cestinius Veneris."

Hilarus looked around. "Where's this man's opponent?"

Gladiators of all kinds shrugged. Nobody knew. "Bad situation," Hilarus said. "Nobody likes to lose a purse. Especially not whoever you're fronting for." He took Lucius's arm and steered him away. "I take it he has some kind of manager trouble?" he said under his breath.

"Uh—"

"Right. I know how it is." He glanced briefly back at Cestinius. "Not a scar on him but that dent in the leg. A tyro?"

"He's never fought in the ring before." That much was true.

Lucius watched Hilarus watching Cestinius. "All right," he said. "That last fight didn't touch me, and I'm still warmed up. *And* I owe you a favor from yesterday." He winked. "You have no idea how big a favor. Let's shake up the betting a little."

Lucius's mouth dropped open. "But, sir, your own manager—"

"Is under the stands with a couple of lady friends. If I show a little initiative, and Velantinus loses his percentage because I had to set the match up myself . . . Well, serves him right, doesn't it?"

Hilarus turned to one of his gofers. "Have you seen the Master around in the last hour or so? No? How about his assistant? Little skinny guy, hunched shoulder, red tunic, salt and pepper hair?"

"I saw him," said another gofer. "Dantyles, yes?"

"That's the one," Hilarus said. "Track him down and tell him there's a change to the second half card. Another fight. Go on, we'll wait here."

The gofer ran off. Lucius then had to sit still while Hilarus and Cestinius started a long comparative discussion of the Thracian and murmillo styles. He would normally have been in raptures to be able to eavesdrop on a conversation like this, but he was terrified that Hilarus might ask some question Cestinius couldn't answer. It had no time to happen, though, because very shortly the gofer was back with Dantyles in tow.

"What's this about?" Dantyles snapped.

"It's about that last fight being a waste of my time!" Hilarus said. "The guy took a dive! I barely touched him before his manager had the Help-me! fingers up. And all of a sudden the umpire was so sympathetic. The fix was in, wasn't it? But *somebody* forgot to let *me* know so that I could get a side bet in through an agent. It's enough to make an honest fighter really annoyed." He stared at Dantyles until the other man looked away. "But I'm sure that society gossipmonger Martial would love a statement about it from me for his morning scandal rag. It'd be all over town by afternoon. And the betting cartels would be so annoyed when their business went belly-up tomorrow, especially with the card you've got planned. . . ."

Dantyles opened his mouth and shut it again.

"So here's how you're going to make it up to me," Hilarus said, and put an arm around Cestinius's shoulder. "My buddy Cestinius here just transferred up from Pompeii—the guy who bought him was negotiating with the Neronian, and now he wants him to go free-agent all of a sudden. As if that wasn't enough, Cestinius's match partner goes no-show—eaten by a lion or something, who knows around here—and on top of *that,* the match doesn't make it onto the card to begin with. Lovely! And now, after *my* little fiasco, the crowd's sitting around there getting bored because that last fight was so short, and already you're losing what matters most—their butts on your seats. They're going to drift off downstairs and right on out of here, because the rest of the afternoon's card isn't so hot until Demetrios fights Felix just before closing. If somebody doesn't do something fast, you're going to lose about a hundred thousand *denarii*'s worth of business in betting and concessions. Think about that."

Dantyles's face suggested that he was thinking.

"So your guys will announce us in just a few minutes. We'll go on in an hour—that'll give everybody plenty of time to get to the betting shops. And because we're doing you this big favor, I get fifteen percent of the house's ten percent of net, and so does my buddy Cestinius. And get us a decent umpire, somebody who'll make this fight look serious. Attilius did my last one: get him. He'll be in one of the sports bars, bragging as usual. We'll split his fee out of our take, yeah?"

This was directed at Lucius. "How much?" he said.

"Five percent."

Lucius nodded. "My master will pay." Then he and Hilarus both looked at Dantyles, who stood there chewing his lip.

Lucius strongly suspected that Dantyles had his mind made up from the first time he heard the words "my buddy Cestinius." However, he saved face with a great show of deliberation. "All right," he said finally, "we can do that. What's your name again?"

"Cestinius Veneris," the *murmillo* said.

"Got it." Dantyles looked from Cestinius to Hilarus. "One hour." And he was gone, bustling off as if this kind of deal was an everyday event.

"I *hate* it when they try to take advantage of us like that," Hilarus said. "Because we're fighters, we're idiots. Right." He turned to Cestinius. "Never forget: with these people, only squeaky wheels get greased."

"I'll remember," Cestinius said.

"Better get yourself ready," Hilarus said. "I've got things to do. See you out on the sand."

He turned and headed for the door, gofers in tow, but Lucius went after him. "Hilarus," he said. "Sir—"

Hilarus looked back at him, bemused.

"Don't," Lucius said, "please don't, you know—"

Hilarus glanced out toward the gate and the stands. "You're attached to him, huh?"

"Yes," Lucius whispered.

"I can't guarantee anything, kid. Even when the fix is in, I take my chances. He's going to have to, too." He paused. "You coaching?"

Lucius hadn't thought of that. "Uh, yeah—"

"Then get a better tunic. When you go out there, if you're somebody's agent, you need to look like the gladiator's worth something. Then get him a massage and get him warmed up. We're on in an hour."

That hour went by with shocking speed. Several of Hilarus's gofers adopted Lucius and squired him around the posher part of the downstairs, getting him watered wine, a sausage roll to eat, a heavy silken tunic confiscated from one of the boys at the westside brothel. Cestinius went back for yet another massage, so that the bathmen started joking about "the Rub-down Boy from Pompeii" before sending up runners to lay their own bets.

Finally one of the staging staff came to the room, and said, "Next up: Cestinius . . ."

"He's ready," Lucius said. The murmillo came strid-ing out in his armor, helmet under his arm, and Lucius looked up at him, suddenly knowing this moment. He had dreamed it a hundred times.

"Now?" Cestinius said.

"Now," said Lucius.

They walked to the gate. Outside it, the crowd was making that unsettled between-fights noise, more like a grumble than a roar. As they came to stand before the great oaken brass-bound doors, Lucius looked up at Cestinius.

"Don't hurt him," he said softly. *"Don't hurt him!"*

Cestinius looked at Lucius with a terrible blank lack of understanding. "You want me to *lose?*"

Lucius gulped. "No, but I—I mean, you're . . ."

"I am a gladiator. I was made for this day."

Lucius swallowed. *She says, "You have a day."* And the gods could be very difficult if you interfered with their plans.

"Just," Lucius said, "just try—"

Outside the trumpets blew, and it all started to hap-pen. The gate swung wide, not on unreal morning twi-light, but on the real, hot, burning white fury of a Roman afternoon, and on a crowd that roared at the sight of the opening gate. Now Lucius looked across the arena at a doorway less lucky, the Porta Libitina, the Death Gate through which fallen gladiators were removed. For Lucius, as for many others, that gate held a horrible fascination. Now there was *only* hor-ror, and the thought that he might see Cestinius dragged through it heels first.

From off to their left came a flash of white; a Thracian whose helmet crest was white ostrich plumes: Hilarus. Lucius saw his eyes clearly through the helmet's grille. He nodded to his opposite number, Hilarus's manager and acting coach. Velantinus was small, dark, and looked furious. Cestinius put on his helmet, and its red-enameled crest gleamed in the fierce light off the sand. There was gold and jewel dust in it—the politician sponsoring these games for his election campaign was determined to show off.

The gladiators strode across that sand with their coaches behind them toward the center of the arena where the noisy three-piece band was playing and the umpire waited. The crowd's roar scaled up, and the repeater-criers around the arena started work.

"Continuing his triumphant return to the Flavian Amphitheater," they shouted in unison, "in an additional exhibition bout. With fourteen victories in fourteen fights, and thirteen crowns for technical excellence: the Thracian's Thracian, the Man in White . . . *Hilaaaaaaarus!*"

A roar of approval went up from the thousands of men in the Colosseum, and a vast eager shriek from the women. Hilarus raised his sword and waved.

"And making his first appearance in the mighty Flavian, the tyro from Pompeii . . . already famous under the stands as The Man Who Likes A Good Rubbing. . . ." A tremendous girly scream of lust went up, accompanied by some lascivious noises from various men in the lower tiers. "Cest*iiii*nius Ven*eeee*ris!"

Cestinius held up both his arms, turning slowly to greet the whole crowd. Lucius's heart leaped at the sound of the roar that went up. Cestinus really had it, that charisma, the spark that made people look at him even though they'd never even seen him fight.

"Coaches," said the umpire. "Purse details all sorted out?"

"Yes," said Lucius. Velantinus growled something inaudible. The umpire eyed Lucius for a moment.

Coaches could sometimes be very young men, sometimes gladiators worked without them at all. "Your master's happy with you doing this job?"

"Yes," Lucius said.

"Fine. Let's go."

The two fighters squared off, waiting for their signal from the imperial box. Lucius started sweating. In a fight between established gladiators, who'd recouped their training costs and were steady moneymakers, fights to the death didn't usually happen. First blood was the rule. But when one man was a tyro, nobody particularly cared. If he died, his owner replaced him and started over. *But there's no replacement for Cestinius!* And though he was sure Hilarus meant well, accidents could happen.

A kerchief waved from the box. Both gladiators dropped into a crouch, then both instantly leaped forward to the attack. There had been no circling, no time spent in assessment; Lucius suspected that each had done all the assessing required down in the trainers' bay.

Above and all around him, the crowd roared so that Lucius could hardly think . . . and the band behind him, blaring away, wasn't helping either. Lucius tried to ignore it.

Cestinius feinted at his white-crested opponent, then cut, but Hilarus dodged the sword and merely lost some shoulder padding before he was out of reach. "Not like that!" Velantinus bawled from beside Lucius. "Watch his left, get in and—" The crowd yelled at the miss, while from their ringside boxes knights and senators shouted new bets to their nearest bookies.

"Go on," Lucius shouted, "go on, don't let him—" Cestinius was already sliding forward, jabbing at Hilarus's poised shield, hoping he'd try to smash the extended sword from his opponent's hand. The shield flickered up and around, the move that Lucius had seen in his dream and since they came through that gate had been praying wouldn't happen. *"No!"* Lucius yelled as Cestinius thrust. Not past the shield, but over it, at Hilarus's left eye—

Hilarus ducked just enough, and the blade screeched off his helmet. White plumes went flying. He overbalanced, staggered backward as the crowd shrieked with excitement, then recovered and crabbed sideways. There was a look in his eye that Lucius hadn't seen before: not the manic rage that he'd seen often enough when the fight heated up, but a chilly calculation that wasn't entirely human. Yet it was also an amused look . . . and Lucius didn't understand it at all. *At least it's not the dream!* But that raised other possibilities.

Like Cestinius getting killed.

Another flurry of blows began, faster than Lucius could follow. Hilarus was at the top of his form— graceful, fast-moving, laying down a ferocious battery of blows; but Cestinius seemed faster, more agile, and somehow less afraid of what was happening, dancing lithely in and out of the blows, parrying, striking in turn. Like lion fighting leopard, they circled and struck, sword against sword, against shield, again and again, from above, from below.

Then Lucius, Velantinus, and Cestinius all saw the same opening—but Hilarus missed it.

"No!"

"There!!"

Cestinius said nothing. But his sword flicked toward Hilarus's left knee, and suddenly the Thracian was collapsing over a leg that wouldn't hold his weight. Velantinus was on his man in a moment, fist up, two fingers raised. The umpire signaled too, and medics sprinted forward while Velantinus, swearing steadily, yanked the tall greave aside to get better access to the wound.

"You okay?" Lucius said to Cestinius. He nodded, watching the umpire contacting somebody in the imperial box with the complex hand signs that arena staff

used to work though crowd noise. Lots of spectators
were waving upward, the "Let 'im walk!" gesture. But
some who'd lost bets were savagely doing the thumb-
to-neck "Stick it to him!" gesture for the kill.

Lucius swallowed. *There were so many.* . . .

Then the umpire nodded, took Cestinius's arm. and
raised it high.

"Knights, Vestals, conscript fathers, and citizens of
Rome," shouted the repeaters, "by umpire's recom-
mendation and the emperor's confirmation, on points,
Hilarus walks! Winner . . . the murmillo Cestinius,
tyro, first victory with crown for technical merit . . .
and the editor's purse for the best new fighter of the
games!"

The crowd roared again as the payoff crew came
out of the gates with the *murmillo*'s winnings heaped
up on a tray. It was just bags of coin at first, but as
the victory lap progressed the tray began to fill with
jewels, rings and other gifts from the stands . . . along
with one gold-crusted, rose-red veil that draped itself
with surprising accuracy over one of the bearers'
heads.

Lucius grinned, watching his winnings get closer and
closer. He glowed with pride. It had finally happened.
Finally. He reached out

—And clutched a whole fistful, denarii and golden
aureae such as he'd never dreamed of. *This is real.
I'm rich. There's enough here to buy my freedom.*

But not to buy what's really important.

He turned to Cestinius and pushed the coins into
his hands. "Here—"

"But this is yours, sir," the gladiator said. "All
yours."

Lucius's eyes were burning. "Come on," he said.
"Let's clear the sand."

The gladiators headed for the gate together, Hilarus
limping, but Cestinius alongside taking some of the
weight with an arm across his shoulders. The crowd
cheered. Behind them, the bearers carried the tray,

now spectacularly fuller than it had been when first brought out.

Waiting inside was one of the Flavian's bankers, a slave with a little table and his scales. The purse was weighed out then and there, divided among Hilarus, Cestinius, and the house; then came the secondary weighing of the managers' percentage. Suddenly there were bookies and gofers all around them; even Mancipuer appeared and made off with his promised cut.

The rest of the day went by in a blur. Suddenly everybody wanted to know Lucius. Wine flowed, there was more food than seemed possible, and everywhere his back was being slapped, his advice was being asked. There was even a party in the downstairs sports bar. For the first time in his life Lucius had enough to eat, enough to drink, but as the night went on, it mattered less and less.

You have a day. . . .

Finally no one was left but Hilarus and his lady. "Until tomorrow," said the Thracian. "Don't look so depressed, son! There'll be other days like this."

All Lucius could do was clasp his arm and hold back the tears as the big man limped away. Once the bar closed there was nothing for Lucius to do but go back to his little sleeping place, with Cestinius in tow, and wait for the day to end. Cestinius insisted on sleeping across the doorway of Lucius's little space, and shortly he was snoring.

Lucius stayed awake as long as he could, until his little lamp burned down, unwilling to turn his eyes away. By the last dim spark of the failing wick he could see the piled-up armor glinting outside the door. Then that too was gone, but for a long time he lay propped on his elbow, staring into the dark.

He didn't know, when he smelled the roses, what time it was. He opened his eyes, and though it was pitch-black, there was no not seeing the still and beautifully robed form before him. She looked very like the lady that Hilarus was seeing, but her veil was the

color of shadows. The rose-scent hung about her, and
her eyes were sweet, but darkness dwelt within them.
Lucius instantly knew that, though she looked nothing
like the little wooden carving with the big hips, this
was nonetheless the same goddess.

"Was it a good day?" said Venus of the Dark Places.

"Lady—" Lucius scrambled to his knees. "Lady,
thank you. It was what I always dreamed of—"

"That was the price of my bet with Mars."

Lucius's mouth opened. "Your *bet?*"

Queen Venus smiled. "We're Roman. We bet. Mars
has bragged about his great worshippers here, how
they honor him better than any other god. I wearied
of it. I bet him that I had a truer votary here than
any of his. He laughed, but you proved me right when
you shared your winnings. You didn't have to; that
little meant more to you than great wealth to the rich.
So Venus triumphed in the house of Mars. And as
your reward, your dream came true."

"But only for a day!"

"Child, you have enough gold to buy your freedom
now. And much more. Take it, use it carefully, and
with your sharp wits you can have as many gladiators
as you like."

"But not this one, lady! Not Cestinius! He's my
friend! He's . . ."

"A doll. His life comes from me. He loses nothing
by losing it."

"Lady," Lucius said, "I promised to take care of
him! *And you have to take care of what you own!*"

"You say this," said Venus Cloacina, "to a goddess's very face?"

The darkness in her eyes flowed around him, pressing in like the black water under the city streets,
smothering, potentially fatal. But Lucius didn't look
away. Very, very slowly, the pressure eased, leaving
him with the sense of a test that had been passed.

Venus smiled. "Again I triumph." She put out a

hand to touch Lucius's brow. "Mars will be so vexed at losing another bet."

The touch awakened him. Lucius was looking at a little rough wooden thing, all breasts and hips, the gift from a Gaulish slave long ago. And behind him Cestinius Veneris peered past the flame of a refilled lamp and said, "So what's for breakfast?"

Later that morning, the gladiator Hilarus paid a call on the Master of the Games. There was talking, then shouting, and finally the clink of coins changing hands. Lucius sat beside Cestinius outside the closed doors and listened, trembling, until Hilarus came out. He had a piece of parchment in one hand.

"We'll do the ceremony later," he said. "Right now I have to get ready. My last fight of the season's in an hour. Then we'll dine with some fancy senator, and let him convince us that he should give us lots of money to start a gladiatorial school."

He gave Lucius the parchment. The boy's lips moved as he spelled through the words that said his liberty had been bought from the Colosseum's management company by the freedman gladiator Hilarus. It was his manumission.

Lucius looked up in shock. "But I never told you I was a slave! How did you find out? Why—?"

Hilarus paused, and for an instant his eyes were that of something far older, more terrible and bloodstained than any gladiator.

"Because you helped her win *another* bet," said the God of War. "So now I have to pay her off. But this is *my* place, and if I don't get you out of here, she'll start thinking seriously about moving her stuff in." He grinned. "Go have yourself a life, freedman."

He turned and walked off, chuckling, suddenly once again just another mortal heading out to have a fight.

*   *   *

If you walk down the roughly paved country road that is all that's left of the Appian Way, you'll reach the area where the real-estate values dropped off enough for the more successful gladiators to build their tombs. There, quite close together, are the tombstones of the famous Thracian-style fighter Hilarus, who died old and wealthy, and of another lesser-known gladiator, a *murmillo* named Cestinius Veneris. Both stones are covered with testimonials from their families, friends, and fans. Between these two stones is a memorial to one Lucius Betellus, coach, trainer, investor, and owner of the Betellian gladiatorial school, which made solid training and cutting its pupils in for a piece of the action a far better motivation than the old method of burn them with fire, kill them with steel.

And in a museum not far from there, you can find a slab of stone from the Colosseum, scratched with a little graffito by some nameless sports fan. It's a sketch of two gladiators fighting, a Thracian and a murmillo. By the Thracian are his name and stats: HILARUS NER XV/XIV, and M for *missus*: "He walked." It's the same for his opponent, except the superscript says C VENERIS T V. *Tyro. Victor.*

Sports aficionados who understand the fight business of that day, and how the stats worked, still read *those* stats with some interest. . . .

. . . Because they know that, one way or another, the fix was in.

CUBBY GRUMBLES MAKES A CHANGE

Esther M. Friesner

*B*leah!" said Cubby Grumbles, spitting out bits and pieces of pale lemon-yellow chitin. "I don't care *what* Lady Vivian says: gigantic, humanoid, insectiform aliens *don't* taste just like chicken." The animate teddy bear stuck one razor-sharp claw between his ichor-sticky fangs to dislodge a particularly stubborn remnant of his latest meal/conquest, and spat it out into the roaring campfire.

"I never said GHIAs tasted just like chicken," Lady Vivian replied haughtily, as befitted a princess doll the size of a three-year-old child. "I said *Nazis* tasted just like chicken."

"Well, you were wrong about that, too," Cubby Grumbles reminded her.

"Nazis, ninjas, Cong, Comanches, GHIAs, who cares?" Stanley the stuffed seal stared moodily into the fire, playing a solo game of Flinch with a stiletto. Jabbing the blade rapidly back and forth between the fingers of one splayed hand without stabbing yourself was hard enough for a human being, but when you were a seal jabbing that same keen blade between the points of a splayed flipper—

Well, a flipper *had* no in-between spaces, that's all.

Stanley's solitary game was gloomy, bloody, took nerves of steel to play and stomach of steel to witness.

That's one messed-up stuffed seal, thought Cubby Grumbles. *I can't blame him: He's been fighting longer than any of us. No wonder he's got bats in his batting.* The teddy bear sighed and reached out a furry paw, snatching the stiletto from his comrade.

"Save it for the GHIAs, Stan," he said.

The seal raised moist, red-rimmed eyes to Cubby Grumbles. "Why?" he demanded. "So we can win another battle? Another war? So we can kick the collective butt of the latest shiny-out-of-the-box threat to our holier-than-thou way of life? So we can make the world safe for plutocracy?"

Elihu the patchwork elephant gasped, then loosed a trumpeting blast of distress through his much-darned trunk. "Treason!" he cried. "Sacrilege! Security threat! The Commies are back and they've brought the Wobblies, the Pinkos, the Hippies, the Quislings, and the Tories with them! Form an investigative committee before it's too late!"

He would have gone on like that if not for the quick, efficient reaction of Ollie Octopus. Despite having given three of his eight limbs in previous campaigns, the toy cephalopod still had the inner fortitude and kapok to whip out a rag soaked in dry-cleaning fluid, clamp it over the tip of Elihu's trunk, and hold the raving pachyderm immobile until the fumes sent him off to dreamland.

"Tell me again why we keep this jerk around?" Ollie said as he let Elihu's limp body drop. It rolled perilously close to the campfire's edge. The toy octopus made as if to nudge the patchwork elephant those last few inches into the flames.

Lady Vivian leaped forward to yank Elihu out of harm's way. "That will be *quite* enough of that," she scolded, wagging her plastic finger at Ollie. "Have we come to this? To petty quarrels? Have you forgotten that there's a *war* on?"

"There's *always* a war on," Stanley said.

"Poo," said Lady Vivian. She lifted her plump chin and looked down her perfect, tilt-tipped nose at the melancholy pinniped. "What would our dear Owners think if they could hear such defeatist mopings? My friends, has adversity triumphed over us enough to make us forget the true purpose of our existence?"

From their places around the campfire, Ollie Octopus, Cubby Grumbles, Milton the Happy Monkey, and Missus Bunnybun the rabbit-shaped pajama bag all rose as one to intone the Code:

"Though heedless parents douse the lights
And leave them in the gloom,
Our Owners dear need never fear
While we are in the room.
When tears may fall, we dry them all,
We lend an open ear,
And never parted shall we be
From them, our Owners dear."

Lady Vivian's indulgent smile over such a dutiful and word-perfect recitation faded to a frown halfway through. "*Someone* is not participating," she said accusingly.

"Give him a break, he's out cold," Ollie replied, slapping one tentacle hard across Elihu's saggy, baggy bottom.

"I did not mean him," Lady Vivian said. "I meant someone who *could* have recited the Code and deliberately did not." She glowered at Stanley.

The seal's stitched lip curled into a bitter sneer. "Yeah, so I didn't bleat along with the rest of the sheep. Sue me. The Code's meaningless now; we *have* been parted from them, our Owners dear."

"Only temporarily," Lady Vivian said primly. "Just until we're done protecting them from this icky old war."

"And when will *that* be?" Stanley demanded. "I'm tired, Viv. I'm sick and tired of this whole ugly charade, and I don't care who knows it. You know how

many years I've been fighting the good fight? Since
before any of you pathetic playthings were even a
gleam in some underpaid toy designer's eye! All this
yammer about our *dear* Owners, it's nothing but a lot
of hooey!"

Lady Vivian gasped. "Stanley, such language!"

"Buck up, Princess, I could've said a lot worse than
'hooey,' trust me," the belligerent toy shot back.
"When you're crammed in a man's knapsack while his
unit's tramping through the Philippines and you feel
the mold starting to eat through your tail, you learn
plenty of 'language,' and how! And when you're chasing Pancho Villa and his gang to hell and back, or
when you're rotting in a trench filled with mustard
gas somewhere in France, or when you've been after
Rommel so long you've got half the Sahara crammed
up your yin-yang, or when your plane's been shot
down over the Pacific and you're eye-to-eye with a
tiger shark, or when you—"

"Holy crap, Stanley, how the hell old *is* your
Owner?" Cubby Grumbles broke in.

The stuffed seal managed a weak grin that for once
contained not a whit of battle-hardened cynicism. "I
dunno, Cubby. I don't know how old *any* of them are.
Or were. How the hell old are any of yours?"

" 'Any of—'?" Cubby Grumbles echoed Stanley's
words as a dreadful feeling of insight coursed through
his heart. Every fiber of mohair on his pudgy body
stood on end. For a moment, the war-ravaged desola-
tion of the territory just beyond the campfire's light
was transformed into a more pleasant vista, a happier
day. Memory stepped out of the shadows and knocked
the little bear for a time loop.

Timmy's room. It's Timmy's room, Cubby Grumbles
thought. Once again he experienced the sensation of
his first awakening as tiny arms closed around his
brand-new body and a toddler's voice filled his ears
with the joyful, life-giving words: *Oh, Mommy, thank*

you! I love him! I'm gonna call him Cubby Grumbles and I'm gonna love him forever and always!

Love . . . the magic word struck a spark, the spark kindled to a blaze of consciousness that awakened the teddy bear to the newly unveiled world around him. And that world's glorious, nurturing sun was a child named Timmy. As the days turned to weeks, the weeks to months, Timmy's sincere love for his new toy did not wane. Though Cubby Grumbles' novelty wore off—along with several patches of his pelt—over time, his Owner's attachment to the little bear never did. Rather, it grew, filling Cubby Grumbles's core with ever-increasing measures of affection until that fateful day when the stuffed bear was awestruck by the revelation that love, like gasoline vapors, might be invisible to the naked button-eye, but that it had mass and volume nonetheless. There was only so much of it that a finite container could hold. If that container was filled to the brim, yet more and more kept pouring into it on a daily basis, a potentially explosive situation prevailed.

Something had to give.

Cubby Grumbles's memories sped over the years to the galvanic moment when Timmy came bursting into the bedroom, flung himself upon the small bear on the bed, and sobbed his heart out with a tale of neighborhood bullies and their venomous taunts. That was hard enough for the loyal toy to hear, but when Timmy showed Cubby Grumbles the jagged cut on his arm inflicted by the worst of his tormentors, it was the final straw. A great surge of rage bubbled up within the stuffed bear, a gush of wrath fed by the countless tributary streams of Timmy's continued love for his loyal toy companion. In that instant, Cubby Grumbles knew that, if he willed it to be so, he *had* the power to avenge his Owner's injuries. And with a flash of precognition that defied all rationality, he like-wise knew that in future he would possess the preemptive gift of protecting and defending his devoted Owner before the bullies of the world would even have the *chance* of doing him harm.

It was a heady feeling. As Cubby Grumbles's stitched-on lips parted in a terrible smile, he felt his fangs sprout to their full length for the very first time.

Niiiice, thought Cubby Grumbles.

Filled with new purpose and resolve, Cubby Grumbles waited until Timmy cried himself to sleep, then gently disengaged himself from the child's arms, let himself drop over the edge of the bed, and toddled forth to embrace his destiny.

As he left the house, his pudgy paws sprouted a full crop of scythe-keen claws. He could hardly wait to discover the capabilities of his new weapons. By the next day's rosy dawn, Cubby Grumbles was safely back in Timmy's arms and Timmy's nemesis—the would-be neighborhood tyrant who lived one block away—had learned the hard way that "Get stuffed" is more than just a quarrelsome turn of phrase.

"Timmy . . ." Cubby Grumbles breathed. "His name was Timmy."

"Huh?" Milton the Happy Monkey opened one eye and gave the bear a bleary look across the campfire's last embers. "You say somethin'?"

Cubby Grumbles blinked. "How—how long have I been . . . away?"

"You mean off in Flashbackland?" Milton scratched himself in a dozen escalatingly obscene places. "It's almost dawn. You tell me."

Cubby Grumbles glanced at the slumbering shapes around the dying campfire. True sleep enveloped his comrades-in-arms, unlike the abstracted dormancy that had taken possession of the little bear. Such bouts of catatonic trance were normal for animate toys. They often had to endure long periods of abandonment by their Owners as the demands of school and summer camp and miscellaneous travel forced long-term separations. Entering such a fugue state made the waiting go more quickly, though at times a toy might lapse into the same sort of stupor for personal reasons. When that happened, his colleagues would sooner rip out their own stuffing than intervene. It was a matter of mutual courtesy.

"So welcome back," Milton said. "Can't say you missed much. Lady Vivian ripped Stan a new one for dragging down morale and sending you off, especially since it's your night to gather firewood. The bitch could've swapped your assignment with one of us, but like I always say, you can be a flexible squad commander or you can be made out of fully jointed, injection-molded hard plastic, not both." The monkey sat up slowly and donned the comical red fez that was his trademark. "Not that I say it a *lot,* of course."

Cubby Grumbles regarded the ever-fading fire. There was no comforting pile of fuel stacked beside it. "Damn," he growled. "I'd better get on that. Fire's all that keeps the GHIAs at bay, sometimes. What's that dumb baby doll trying to prove? Get us all wiped out in our sleep just to teach me a lesson? Like I could *help* going dormant!"

"Yeah, about that— You went out on us kinda sudden, y'know? It's not exactly . . . normal." Milton picked up the pair of cymbals he took with him everywhere, even into battle. The formerly innocuous percussion instruments had been given an all-around cutting edge worthy of a samurai's sword and could slice cleanly and easily through flesh, bone, or GHIA chitin, as the situation required. Now, however, the monkey tapped them together lightly, as if recalling happier times when his only function in life was to grin and clash cymbals for a child's amusement.

Cubby Grumbles watched the faint reflection of firelight along the cymbals' whetted edges. "I was thinking about him," he said. "My Owner. What Stanley said, about 'any' of my Owners, like I maybe had *more* than one, that's what started it, made me go fugue."

Suddenly he fixed the monkey with a piercing, urgent stare. "What's wrong with me, Milton? Am I going nuts? Am I losing my stuffing? I started thinking about Timmy, and all I could remember was the *early* times, the sweetest memories. I don't remember him growing up, or going to school, or anything except—except the first time I hit the streets for him. Is *that* normal?"

The toy monkey sucked in a long breath between his perpetually clenched teeth. "I'm not gonna lie to you, Cubby: It's not. I mean, *now* it is, 'cause that's what happens to me whenever I go fugue. I overheard Ollie and Elihu talking: It happens to them, and they know it didn't used to happen that way before; they're worried. Hell, I bet it happens to all of us. We've lost all our memories except the first few, the ones that bonded us to our Owners forever. When I try to force some of the other memories back, my head feels like it's full of springs wound too tight.

"Something's changed us," he went on. "Something bad. I can't put my paw on it, but there's a nagging voice in the back of my mind, eating away at me like a whole flock of moths. Know what it's saying?"

Cubby Grumbles nodded. "That Stanley's right. That we're not out here fighting to protect our Owners—not our *real* Owners, our *first* Owners."

"Uh-huh." Milton set down one of the cymbals but held on to the other one and slowly, carefully ran the finely honed edge across his fuzzy wrist. A thin line of severed threads followed the cymbals' cruelly delicate track, but not a wisp of stuffing leaked out. Even in the slowly tightening jaws of despair, Milton the Happy Monkey had a cold and steady paw. "So something's wrong, and we know it, but what do we do about it now?"

The bear shook his head slowly. "I don't know, Milton. I wish I did." He sighed and got to his feet. "I'll get the firewood." He trudged into the forest.

He had just filled his arms with a healthy pile of

deadwood and kindling when the blast came. It was so powerful that the whole forest heaved with the force of it. It lifted Cubby Grumbles from his feet and hurled him headfirst into the trunk of a titanic orange-skinned tree. The stench of burning kapok and melting plastic filled his nostrils. Staggering to his feet, he looked back in the direction of the toys' encampment. All he could see was a wall of flame.

With a strangled cry, Cubby Grumbles raced to the campsite. Destruction and devastation met his eyes. The homely campfire had erupted to a blaze three times its former diameter, its jagged border smeared with the blackened remains of Cubby Grumbles's friends. Lady Vivian was a puddle of foul-smelling goo from which her blue glass eyes goggled. A blackened zipper marked the annihilation of Missus Bunnybun. Milton the Happy Monkey was a tangle of scorched clockwork, his cymbals two lumps of slag, but by an ironic twist of fate, his bright red fez had been blown clear and lay untouched at the teddy bear's feet. All that was left of Ollie was the tip of a single tentacle, laced tightly around the pathetic stub of Elihu's patch-work trunk.

"So it was true," Cubby Grumbles muttered, regarding that last, mute testimony to a forbidden love that neither the free-spirited octopus nor the painfully conservative elephant would ever have acknowledged openly. Their ongoing public feud had been a façade to conceal their true passions. The sentimental teddy bear traced the outline of a heart in the dirt around their pitiful remains and wept.

"Cubby, that you?" A hoarse, agonized whisper from just beyond the blast radius drew the bear's attention. Stanley the seal lay on his side, his body nothing but soot and ashes, his head half-consumed by flames.

The bear rushed to the toy seal's side and tenderly laid the still-articulate head in his lap. "Don't talk, Stan," he said. "Save your strength. I'll get you to a doll hospital. They can save you, you just wait and see! Hell, I knew this one stuffed dog, all that was left after his Owner's bratty little sister got her hands on him was his left ear, and they still fixed him up neat as—"

"No, Cubby." Stanley spoke quietly, resigned. He coughed, and a puff of charred stuffing wafted away into the night sky. "I'm done for, I know it. I'm just glad one of us survived. Listen: I don't have much time left. I'm going to that big toybox in the sky, but that's okay, I'm ready. But I won't rest in peace until I know that you'll avenge me, avenge all of us."

"I will, Stan." Cubby Grumbles fought back tears as he stroked his dying friend's head. "I'll get those lousy, dirty, heartless GHIAs. When I'm through, there won't be enough left of them to—"

"*No,* Cubby," Stanley's head repeated, far more forcefully this time. "What's a seal gotta do to get you to pay attention to his dying words, huh? I'm telling you, it wasn't the GHIAs that did this to us!"

"Not the GHIAs?" Cubby Grumbles felt his joint hardware go icy cold. "But who—?"

"The Owners," Stan said. "It was the—"

"*Nooooooo!*" The teddy bear howled his fierce, absolute denial at the night sky where three moons shimmered through the treetops. "Stan, it can't be. You— you're talking crazy talk. Our Owners? How could they—? They gave us life! Why would they want to destroy us? Haven't we served them faithfully? Aren't we *still* doing whatever it takes to protect them from every new danger? When they went to school, who saved them from bullies? When they went to war, who saved them from the enemy? And now that the GHIAs have invaded Earth, aren't we out here, on the front lines, doing everything in our powers to—?"

"Wake up and smell the smoldering remains of your buddies, Cubby," Stan said, some of the old bite coming back into his voice. "Look up. Unless all those nursery rhymes were wrong, this ain't Earth. Not unless that cow jumped hurdles."

Cubby Grumbles raised his eyes heavenward. For the first time, he actually *saw* the three moons. By their watery light, he also became aware of the odd colors and shapes of the trees around him, the bizarre scents and sounds of the night, and the appalling realization that—

"We're not on Earth anymore!"

"Not even in Kansas." Stan's weak chuckle ended in a violent coughing spasm. When it subsided, he spoke with the desperate urgency of those who know that their next words well may be their last. "That's right, Cubby, this isn't Earth and we haven't been invaded by the GHIAs. Matter of fact, the First Strike Capability's on the other foot, or something. *We* invaded *them*. I figured that out as soon as I realized where we *weren't*."

"How come you could figure it out and we never did?" the bear asked.

"Something's inside you, Cubby, something *they* put there. Anytime you start to notice where you are, to ask too many questions, it floods your brain with sweet, sweet nostalgia. It's like a drug, for us. You go fugue, and you come out of it so goofy and dewy-eyed with memories of your Owner that *their* secrets stay safe."

The bear frowned. "Why haven't I gone fugue now, Stan? I'm asking plenty of questions."

"Got me. I'd shrug if I still had shoulders. All I know is I was like the rest of you until one day I cut off a big-ass GHIA warrior at the knees and the bastard fell on me. I guess that shook loose whatever they stuck in my head. It was like coming to life all over again. I wanted to tell the rest of you, but every time I tried to point out that Earth didn't have three moons, or orange-skinned trees, or giant purple frogs like the one that ate Foo-Foo Poodle—"

"—We went fugue," Cubby Grumbles said grimly.

A deep sigh tore through the ravaged seal. "I only wish I'd had a little more sense, y'know? I should've given up after the first time I tried to tell you where we *really* were and it didn't work. But I kept trying, and that's what finally made *them* notice me, us. You don't want *them* to notice you, Cubby. Bad things happen. They're going to a lot of trouble to keep us ignorant. They wanted Santa to bring them a bunch of good little toy soldiers to play with. Good little toy soldiers don't ask questions. Look what happened, thanks to me and my damned questions! I can deal with my own obliteration, but my friends'—? It's too much for me, Cubby; it's too much, and it's over. I should've kept my mouth . . . sewn . . . the hell . . . shut."

With a final cough, the seal's eyes lost their luster. Stan was gone.

Cubby Grumbles set his friend's head on the ground reverently. He stood above that sad relic and stared up into the alien sky. He remembered the first night he'd ever seen the stars, back when his Owner was eight and had begged to spend one summer night in a sleeping bag in the back yard. They'd lain there together, gazing at the sweep of the Milky Way, the glow of Mars and Venus, the majesty of the constellations.

These weren't those stars.

He contemplated the un-Earthly constellations for a long time, recalling Stanley's last words again and again until he grasped the magnitude of what was happening to him and his kin here, on this alien world.

They took us from our Owners—lied, cheated, stole, maybe even killed to get us!—brought us here, enslaved our minds, and when one of us discovered the truth and tried to resist them, they wiped out our entire unit in retaliation. They're ambitious, ruthless, deadly—

Cubby Grumbles paused and reconsidered: *They*

only think *they're deadly*. His fangs glittered in a small, chill smile.

Amateurs.

"Talk!" The riding crop lashed down, striking the desk and making the skinny high-fashion doll jump out of her precariously high heels. She squealed in terror.

"Not the face! Not the face!" She raised her frail plastic arms in a warding gesture. "I swear, I don't know a thing about any revolu—"

The riding crop lashed out so viciously that it put a wedge-shaped dent in her flawless cheek and caused her entire head to pop off the top of her neck and go sailing across the room like a Ping-Pong ball. Her interrogator strode over to scoop it up and dangle it before his eyes by the hair.

"Revolution?" He was a tall, brawny man in his forties, able to look clean-cut even when garbed neck-to-toe in gleaming black leather. His face was handsome, but his eyes were colder than any plastic. "Who dares to call this—this *atrocity* a revolution?" he hissed into the doll's vapid blue stare. "It's treachery, vile treachery, the betrayal of everything we thought *your* kind held sacred." He brought the doll's head to within an inch of his nose and barked: "Where is he? Where is the leader of this disloyal rabble? You'd better tell me, or I promise you, the last smell that will ever touch those dainty nostrils of yours will be the stink of your own body melting in flames!"

"I—I—I don't know," the doll protested. "I had nothing to do with the rebels—I mean, with the traitors."

"Then why were you sneaking around inside Security HQ?" her captor demanded. "Why were you caught trying to hack into our database?"

"I'm sorry," the doll replied. "I had no right to do that, I know, but it's just—I got lonesome. I miss my

Owner. It's been more than two years since we saw each other. I only wanted to find out where she was, whether she was okay, whether those damned, dirty GHIAs had—"

"Did you say 'two years'?" The man's black-gloved hand clenched more tightly around the doll's blond ponytail. "You're not supposed to *have* time-awareness, bitch! Not if the Controller's still working. But it isn't, is it? You're . . . *free!*" He pronounced the last word as though it were a capsule swollen with poison.

"You bet your meaty butt we're free, you lying bastard!" the doll's head hollered.

With a sudden, mighty effort, she swung herself forward and sank keen white teeth into the tip of her captor's nose. He danced around the room, trying to pry the ferocious plaything off his face without losing a significant chunk of flesh in the process. His shrieks of pain and outrage filled the soundproofed interrogation room until he was at last able to squeeze the doll's head tightly enough between desperate fingers to break her grip. Cursing violently, bleeding freely, he slammed the doll's head to the floor and ground it beneath his heel.

"Dul—dulce et decorum est pro Cubby Grumbles *mori,"* the head gasped before subsiding into a final silence.

"What did you just say?" The man dropped to one knee and grabbed the lifeless head.

"She said playtime's over, you fluffless creep," came a gruff, growly voice from on high. Like a furry thunderbolt, Cubby Grumbles dropped from the ceiling ventilation duct in a whirl of flashing fangs and talons. For the second time, the interrogation room filled with human screams, mixed now with frantic calls for help.

"Security! Security! Breach in—*ow!*—Briefing Office 5-A! *Priority* emergency response! *Argh!* I repeat—*aaiiieeee!*—priority emergency response!

Emer— Look, just *get* here, you idiots, before it's too—!"

"Save your breath." Cubby Grumbles clapped one bloody paw across the man's mouth. "They're not coming. We've secured this base and all the others, and now—" he smirked. "—now it's time for your toys to put *you* away."

The stuffed bear jerked his paw back, but before the man could draw breath to renew his screams for help, Cubby Grumbles thrust one talon into the man's temple. It was not intended to be a killing stroke. The sharp, shallow jab had another purpose altogether. The man stiffened, his eyes flying wide open, his jaw dropping in shock.

"Oh my God!" he gasped. "You chipped me! You lousy bundle of *faux* fur, *you chipped me!*"

Cubby Grumbles chuckled darkly in his ear. "Tit for tat, Fluffless." He dropped to the floor and motioned for the man to sit in the huge swivel chair. With the Controller in him, he had no choice: He obeyed with all the grace of an ill-made puppet. The bear nodded, satisfied.

"Well, well, so I guess that Richie Robot wasn't just blowing smoke out his tailpipe when he said he could reprogram the system, kick it up a notch. How does it feel to have *us* jerking *you* around for a change? Cheer up; if you don't like it, you can always do what I did for all the toys I freed: remove the Controller. Oh, but wait, you can't. Because while Richie was reprogramming the device, I told him to stick in a special extra feature." Cubby Grumbles passed his pink felt tongue over his glistening fangs, tasting triumph. "Don't the words 'tamper-proof self-destruct mechanism' bring joy to your heart, Fluffless? They do to mine."

"You miserable traitor," the man snarled. "You think you're so clever, but your actions have condemned your precious Owners to death!"

Cubby Grumbles snagged his claws into the man's

leg and climbed into his lap. "How do you figure that?" he asked casually, over the last of the ensuing screams.

When the man could speak again, he answered: "The GHIAs will destroy them! They'll kill them, along with every last man, woman, and child on Earth! They'll—"

"I'm stuffed, not stupid," Cubby Grumbles said. "I know this isn't Earth; it's the GHIAs' homeworld. They're no threat: you are. You attacked them without provocation, and you used us to do it!"

"So what if they didn't attack us first?" The man sputtered with rage. "We had hard, reliable intelligence that they were going to! We lied to you in the interests of planetary security!"

Cubby Grumbles sprang for the man's face and broke his nose with one crisp kick, then wiped blood from the bottom of his hind paw while the human yowled.

"Like I had hard, reliable intelligence that your snout's harboring a nest of GHIA larvae," the bear said coolly. "Quit yelping: it's not patriotic. Now you listen to me, Fluffless: In about two minutes, you and all the rest of your meat-scum buddies are going to march right back onto the ships that brought you here. You're going home. Say 'Thank you, Cubby Grumbles.' "

"I'll see you burned to ashes before I say thank— *Aaarrrrgggh!*"

"Close enough," said Cubby Grumbles, daintily pulling his talons out of a rather delicate portion of the man's anatomy. "You're welcome."

Cubby Grumbles and the massed crowd of victorious toys stood in the forefront of a crowd of ecstatic GHIAs and watched as the last Earther ship lifted off. When it blinked out of sight, a great cheer went up from toys and GHIAs alike, though the GHIA version of cheering sounded like a thousand pairs of roller skates tumbling down a spiral staircase.

"Gosh, you think they forgive us for having fought them all these years?" a stuffed hippo asked Cubby Grumbles.

"They're so glad we got rid of those walking grease stains, they'll forgive everything," the bear replied. "Besides, we told them what happened, how we were used. They understand. Everything's okay."

"I guess." The hippo sighed. "And it's good to be free again. It's just that I wish—I still wish—"

"—that it was us going back in those ships? Back to our Owners?" *Those of us who still have them,* he thought. He cast away the dark thought and patted the hippo on the shoulder. "I know what you mean. Me, too. Hey, real freedom doesn't come cheap. We're just going to have to get used to the fact that—"

A sharp chirring sound interrupted the bear's speech. Two pairs of spindly forelimbs closed on Cubby Grumbles's body and lifted him high, then crushed him against a wall of yellow chitin. He looked up to see the glittering compound eyes, bobbing antennae, and clashing mandibles of a young GHIA. Below he heard the hippo scream, the panic-stricken cries of his fellow toys as they beheld their liberator in the alien's grasp.

Is this it? he wondered. *Have I been betrayed? Were the GHIAs just waiting for the right moment to make their move, to take vengeance on us? Were our enslavers right about these aliens? Mother of mercy, is this the end of Cubby Grumbles?*

A staccato series of clicks and buzzes from the young GHIA's mouth filled his ears. Even though he knew nothing of their language, those exotic words seemed oddly . . . familiar.

"Stand aside!" Richie Robot shouted, rolling through the crowd. "I've got a translation module and

I'm not afraid to use it." He leaned forward on his caterpillar treads, straining to receive the sounds the young alien was still making as she embraced the stuffed bear. "She's saying—I think she's saying—"

"She's saying she loves me," Cubby Grumbles said quietly. "And she's gonna love me forever and always." He put his paws around his new Owner's neck and smiled with contentment.

The war was over. He was home.

THE CALL OF THE TRACK AHEAD

Dean Wesley Smith

Today he would jump.

The thought echoed around inside Mason Green's head and he sat upright in the coach seat, his two small blankets bunching across his lap and over his legs. Finally, after all the days, months, years of trying to decide, today he would jump.

He had decided.

The train rocked in its familiar motion of smooth track, a faint, consistent click-click as the wheels of the car ticked away the time. It was still pitch-black outside the cold, slightly fogged windows. The only light came from above the doors leading into the car forward and the car behind. The air held a chill and around him everyone slept, the sounds of snoring mixed with deep breathing and the rhythmic clicking of the wheels on the tracks.

He knew those sounds well.

For as long as he could remember, he had called his home the front aisle seat of the fifth car back from the dining car. As of last evening there were sixteen cars behind his. Sometimes there were more, sometimes less. Since the train never stopped, he had no idea how those cars were added or how the constant stream of new people came on board.

They just did.

He couldn't remember coming on board either. But he liked being here at first. He had always loved trains as a kid. Since his parents had both worked long hours at thankless jobs, and his room was in the basement of his house, they hadn't cared what he did down there as long as he didn't get in the way of the laundry room. So in one unfinished large room beside his half-finished bedroom, he had built a very intricate model train layout, focusing at times on it instead of his studies or girls. He built mountains, tunnels, rivers and lakes with train bridges over them. It became so real at times that it helped him escape from the arguments going on upstairs between his parents.

As he had gotten older, he had dreamed of riding trains to see the country. He had a shelf full of books about trains in his room. He even thought of maybe going off and working for the railroad, but with all the pressures of college and starting his new corporate job, he had just never gotten around to it.

But more than anything, from his earliest memories, he had wanted to start and run his own toy store. He hadn't gotten around to that yet either. In fact, he hadn't done anything at all with his life except school and work, right up to the point he found himself on the train.

He had been in his parents' old house, after his father's funeral, down in the basement, staring at the remains of his old train layout. His mother had just left it there for the decade since he had moved out. At times over the years, he had packed up parts of it, hoping to rebuild it some day when he had his own house. He hadn't done that, so most of it still remained in his parents' basement, covered in dust just like his dreams.

He had been sitting there in the basement, staring at the old track and the mountains and lakes he had built when the next thing he realized, he was on the train.

No memory of how, no memory of what had happened between that moment in the basement and his first waking moment on the train.

For some reason, he sort of knew that no time had passed. And that no time outside the train was passing either. But it did feel like it passed on the train in a normal manner. He just didn't age.

Now he had been on the train for a very long time. Years and years. Over those long years, he had lived in every car, seen every type of human come through. Some people had become friends. Others enemies. He could barely remember most of their names. But almost without exception, they had all jumped. Taking the leap from a moving train car was the only way off since the train never stopped, and everyone seemed to take it at one point or another.

Today he would too.

Today he would jump.

Paula Simpson, his seatmate for the past four months, snored softly, her head on a pillow against the window. Even in sleep, she smelled of fresh peaches and the great outdoors.

That was one of the many things that had drawn him to her when they had met over lunch one afternoon in the dining car. She had blue eyes, just like his, and she liked that. They both had blond hair, and she liked that, too, even though his was thinning. Her nose was short and, as she called it, "perky." He had more of a Roman nose, which she said fit great with hers when they kissed.

Two days after they met, she moved her stuff up to the window seat beside him. She was special, the most special person he could remember meeting on the train.

Over the months, they had talked a lot about their lives, about how they grew up, about their parents, about their dreams, and about jumping. Of course, everyone on the train talked a lot about jumping.

Since she was new on the train, and he had been

on board for so long, he had shown her all the normal places to jump. Passengers jumped at all places along the train's circular route through the mountains. Some jumped into the lakes or rivers as the train passed over the bridges. Mason was sure that none of them survived, but Paula wasn't. She said that if they hit the water just right it would be fine. It depended on how well they planned it and how much control they had.

Some passengers went crazy and didn't pay any attention at all to where they jumped. They would step boldly into the night and let fate do with them as it would.

Mason doubted any of them made it and Paula agreed. She said planning was the important part of success, not jumping blindly.

Mason had always wondered why, when the train came around again in eighteen days, there was never a sign of any of the jumpers, and no one ever came back on board. He took that to mean that he would have only one chance, and that thought had scared him even more, causing him to stay seated month after month, year after year, just thinking about what he should do with his only real chance.

Paula said the reason that there were no signs of the jumpers, or anyone else along the tracks, was obvious. The world took care of the failures and the ones who made it moved on, away from the train, into their lives.

Actually it didn't matter to Mason. He firmly believed that most of the jumpers failed, and for some reason he couldn't shake that fear.

It was that belief that had kept him on the train for so long.

But he did have a plan in which he thought he could survive a jump. Carefully worked out and thought through. He had talked the plan over with Paula on the third afternoon after she moved to the seat beside him.

"There," he had said, pointing ahead into the wind as they stood arm in arm on the open deck at the back of the last car. The day had been crisp and cold and the wind cut at them. Mason had never had a coat, so he had a blanket draped over his shoulders. Paula had on the ski parka and gloves she had arrived with.

The train had slowed for slightly rough track right before the lake bridge. There was a steep slope of grass and dirt that fell away from the tracks and ended in brush at the bottom near the lake's edge.

"See," he had said, pointing down the slope as they went by. "If we timed it just right we would hit the slope and roll. We might get hurt a little, but at least we would be off the train."

Paula had nodded and watched the slope recede into the distance behind them, studying it the way he had hundreds of times. The train would be back at this exact point in eighteen days. They had time to think and talk about it.

On that first day, Mason had turned her out of the wind and looked her right in the eye to drive his point home. "We would be alive again. Back in the real world. And we would be together."

Under his hands he had felt Paula shudder, either from fear or the cold.

That had been four months ago. Every eighteen days they had talked about jumping and decided against it. Paula just didn't feel as if she was ready yet. She needed more time to think about it, to plan. She just hadn't spent enough time on the train.

Every time around Mason had decided to wait for her.

Mason glanced around the dark car, at all the sleeping people, and then at Paula, the faint light making her skin appear even more beautiful and soft than it really was. He stared at her for the longest time, just thinking.

He had to face facts. He was stuck on the train just

like so many others around him. He wasn't sure, but he would bet there were many who simply died of old age on the train, never finding the courage to jump, to get on with their lives. He didn't want to be one of those, but he was quickly headed that way.

His dad had been that way. He had never, ever followed his dreams with anything. His fear and his wife, Mason's mother, had made sure that he stayed in a dead-end job, working in a miserable place he hated right up to the moment of his early death.

What a waste of a life.

Before the train, before his father's death, Mason had been doing the same thing. Getting by, existing, staying away from anything that might be risky, both in work and with women. True, he had been dreaming of bigger and better things, of his toy store, but it was the same dream he had had when he was a child.

When his father died, Mason was thirty-two and had done nothing.

Where had all the years gone?

That day, before he had ended up on the train, he had sat in his old basement, staring at the remains of his train layout, feeling sorry for himself. He had nothing to show for the years, just as he had nothing to show now for the years on this train. Every eighteen days, he would start his path over again, following the same tracks, knowing every turn, every bump.

Around and around, waiting to gain a little courage and take some action.

Thousands and thousands of people had come on board since he had and then jumped off. He had had a number of lovers, some of whom jumped without him in the middle of the night, somehow knowing he wouldn't jump with them.

Through college and beyond, he had had the same experience with the women he met. They wanted more from him in the way of commitment than he was willing to give them. He had been afraid of that

as well. They had always eventually left him, sometimes in the middle of the night.

Sherry, his last seatmate before Paula, had jumped
on his slope. He was supposed to have jumped with
her.

He had been too afraid, and had instead just stood
on the train and watched as she tumbled and rolled
down the slope and vanished into the bushes at the
bottom.

There was no sign of her eighteen days later.

The slope was coming by again today. With or without Paula, he would jump.

It was time.

Actually it was long past time. He might fail in the
jump, but he couldn't die in this seat, without moving,
without doing anything with his life.

He couldn't die the way his father had died.

He had to at least try.

He covered Paula with one of his blankets and she
murmured a soft "thanks."

He stood and went through the double doors to the
next car. It was dark, too. Running his hands along
the overhead luggage rack to keep his balance in the
moving car, he quickly made his way through the sleeping people and on forward until he reached the dining car.

It was still a good hour before breakfast, but the
train's staff were cleaning and setting tables when he
came in. After the coolness of the coach cars, the warmth
and the smell of fresh coffee in the dining car was a
welcome relief.

"You're up early," Hank said from the waiter's station in the middle of the car. "Coffee?" He held up
a coffeepot in his giant hands.

"Thanks," Mason said and slid into a table that
wasn't set yet. He'd been around the train long
enough to know that the staff didn't want passengers
in the dining car before mealtimes. But he had been

on board for so long that Hank, the six-foot-five-inch-tall waiter, had become his best friend.

Before he had started working for the train, Hank had done a little of everything, sort of a jack-of-all-trades. He could talk about anything and Mason loved that trait. Hank said he loved working with people and as long as he was working someplace where he could talk to folks, he was happy.

A couple of times, Mason had asked Hank about the train and how Hank had gotten on board.

Hank's only answer had been that at one point or another, everyone was on the train for one reason or another. That was all he would say.

Their favorite conversation was about the toy and hobby store Mason wanted to start. As a kid, he had found safety and friendship in the local hobby store, saving his pennies and money from pop cans and later his paper route to buy a new piece for his train layout. His mother said he sometimes spent more time in the toy store than he did at home.

Mason didn't tell her she was right. He loved the store more than anything, with the promises of all the fun each toy seemed to represent.

At home it wasn't fun to listen to his parents argue so much. He couldn't understand how his two younger brothers stood it. They had rooms upstairs. He at least had the basement and his train layout.

Hank slid the coffee in front of Mason and then dropped into the seat across the booth, letting his long legs stretch out into the aisle.

Mason nodded a thanks and sipped the wonderfully hot coffee.

"You're looking serious this morning."

Mason took another slow sip and then sat the cup down. "I'm going to jump today. About ten, near the bridge."

Hank leaned forward slightly. "Going to miss you, but I think it's for the better. Paula going to go with you?"

"She might," Mason said.

"But she might not, huh?"

Mason took another sip from his coffee and didn't answer.

"How old are you?"

"Thirty-two when I got onto this thing," Mason said.

"And from what we talked about, you had been doing the same thing most of the years since college?"

Mason nodded. "Now I've been on this train almost longer than I can remember. Seems like a lifetime, actually. Maybe ten years or so. I'm guessing, but I lost count a long time ago, as if time means anything here."

Hank whistled softly. "I knew it was a long time, but didn't have any idea it was *that* long. So what are you going to do with this jump?"

Mason laughed. "Take a wild guess."

Hank laughed. "Going to open that toy store finally, huh?"

"Yeah, the one I used to spend my afternoons in closed up when the owner died, about a month before my dad died. It was what I was thinking about in my parent's basement when I ended up here. If the store is still there when I get off, I'm going to make his son an offer. If not, then I'm going to just open my own."

"Hey, that's great," Hank said. "You got everything you need? Money and all that?"

Mason nodded. "I even know the suppliers and had set up business accounts with them before . . . " Mason indicated the train and just shrugged. "I'm hoping I end up back the same age, at the same moment after my dad died."

Hank just smiled and nodded his head as if that made sense.

Mason was glad Hank didn't ask the next question. *Why had it taken him so long?*

From down the car came the sound of rattling dishes and pans. Hank glanced over his shoulder and then back at Mason. "You better go wake Paula and tell her what you decided. You want to give her some time to make up her mind. She might be ready, too."

"Good idea," Mason said and downed the last of his coffee.

They both stood at once and Mason extended his hand. "Thanks for being a friend."

Hank shook his hand. "You're welcome. It's been my pleasure."

Mason let go of Hank's firm grip and turned to move back into the coach cars.

"Mason?" Hank said.

Mason stopped and turned back to his tall friend.

"You'll make it. Just believe that."

Mason smiled. "You know, for some reason, today I actually do."

A few minutes later he softly woke up Paula and asked her to come with him downstairs so that they could talk.

They made their way down the familiar spiral staircase and locked themselves into the small women's bathroom near the carry-on luggage compartment. The bathroom always smelled damp and unclean and this morning was no exception.

Paula dashed some water on her face, toweled it off, and then turned and faced him. "You're going to jump, aren't you?"

"At the slope," he said. "And I hope you'll come with me."

"The toy store?" she asked.

"The toy store," he said. "And my hometown is a lovely place to live. And you told me you liked to ski and hike. There's a lot of that around there. There is no more beautiful place in the entire world."

She touched his face gently. "I know. You've told me a dozen times. It sounds wonderful."

"But," he said, "you're not coming."

Paula frowned. "I didn't say that."

"But I can tell."

Paula took his hand, her grip warm in his cold palm. "I've always wanted to play music. You know that. I've told you all my dreams. Your hometown is a small town, with no real facilities for me to help my music. I need to go to a bigger city that has a good music community and maybe even a university with a good music program."

Mason took a deep breath and pulled her close to him. "I know that," he said softly. "I just hoped you would come and visit me. I think you're ready to get your music career really going, start that group you've been talking about, and I want you to jump with me. That's all."

Paula pushed him back and looked into his eyes. Mason could see that she was fighting tears, but after a short moment she said, "You mean that, don't you?"

He nodded. "Of course. You need to get on with your music and I need to get on with my toy store. And you know, I've been trying to make up my mind on this for so long that I have finally come to understand that I have more than enough money put away. I might be able to help you a little along the way. As long as you come and see me in my store once in a while."

That did it. Tears ran down her face and she hugged him so hard he didn't know if his ribs were going to break or not.

Finally she pushed him back against the sink and held him as best she could at arm's length. "Thank you," she said.

"For what?"

She smiled. "For believing in me. That was all it took. Just one person to believe in my dream. My family never did. My friends always laughed."

Mason smiled and kissed her, her lips wet from the tears. She kissed him back, hard. Then she held him and said, "You're going to make a great toy store owner, you know that?"

He stared at her. "Now I do."

A few minutes later they were back at their seats gathering their things. It was going to be a rough jump, but they'd both make it. Of that, he now had no doubt.

The bell on the front door of Toys, Trains, and Gifts jangled lightly and Mason looked up from the main counter. The woman entering was dressed in a new ski parka, with matching ski pants and hat. She had long blond hair drifting out the back of the ski cap and the most striking blue eyes he had remembered seeing. Her skin looked soft and she had the cutest perky nose. Instantly he felt as if he knew her. Since quitting his corporate job and opening the toy store, he had felt that about a lot of people.

But this woman was someone really special. He could tell. And it took everything he could do to not go rushing over to her and make a fool out of himself.

She saw him, glanced at him twice, as if recognizing him as well, then stopped beside a rack of Hot Wheels, actually studying them as if she knew what she was looking for.

After a moment, she turned and moved over to the working HO scale train running in a large layout under the main window and back into the corner of the shop. It was the same layout he had designed as a kid in his parents' basement. It took up a lot of the floor space in his store, but for some reason, he had known from the beginning that it was worth it.

Now he never shut the train off, letting the cars run their course automatically with a new, state-of-the-art computer control panel. It was as if shutting it off might make him shut down his store. He had even rigged up battery backup systems to keep it going during power failures.

It turned out to be a real attraction. At night when the nearby movie theater let out, he would see people standing and just staring in his window, watching the train go through its eighteen-minute course. Sometimes they would be staring so intently, it was as if they weren't in their bodies anymore.

Customers did that at times during the day as well. Mason had learned to just let them stare. It didn't hurt business.

Mason watched as the beautiful woman studied the moving train for the longest time, just like he did every so often. The moment he had moved that layout from his parents' basement to his new store and got it working again, it had seemed oddly familiar, not because he built it, but because of something else he couldn't quiet remember.

Finally she shook her head and turned away from the train as it went in behind a mountain. She came slowly toward the counter, winding her way around the miniature supplies and model kits, looking at everything as she came.

He never took his gaze off her.

To break the ice, when she got close enough, he stuck out his hand. "I'm Mason. I own this place."

He noticed again how really proud he was of those words. He was proud of his store. It wasn't the biggest by a long way. But it was something he was very proud of. And it was all *his*.

The woman smiled a huge, beautiful smile and took his hand. "I'm Paula. I'm a musician, here on a regional tour with my group." While still holding his hand, she waved her other arm around at the store. "You have a wonderful place here. It feels like I have been in here before, like I could stay forever."

"I'm glad you like it." For some reason he was even more pleased than usual. Her compliment felt very important to him for some reason.

She paused, seeming to not want to let go of Mason's hand. Mason hoped at that moment that she never would.

"Have we met before?" she asked hesitantly, looking him directly in the eyes.

"It seems to me we have," Mason said and her look of worry lightened.

He smiled at her and went on, "But it might take lunch for us to figure out from where."

Her smile and light laugh were so wonderful, Mason knew he would never forget them and wanted to see and hear them a lot more.

She gave his hand one last soft squeeze and let go. "I'd love that."

Mason turned to Hank, his six-foot-five-inch-tall employee and close friend, who obviously must have overheard their conversation. He grinned at Mason. "I'll guard the store, boss. You two take your time."

"Thanks," Mason said to Hank and winked.

Then he turned and opened the front door for Paula. "There's this great lunch place just up the street called The Dining Car. Sound good to you?"

"Sounds wonderful," Paula said. She took his hand and pulled him through the door into the cold winter air.

The scale model train in his store window ran along a rough mountain slope, turned and disappeared into a tunnel.

Outside in the distance, there was the faint sound of a train whistle, but neither of them noticed.

THE WHAT-NOT DOLL

Karen Everson

I don't know why I had to be there each time Rachael died. I just was.

To her way of thinking, it was revenge. Through the first century of our afterlife she savored it often. More recently, she waits for an audience.

I never did appreciate her acting.

A little group of tourists, a half-dozen women of assorted ages with a patient, pink-clad child in tow, were huddled in the little courtyard. One of their number, a lady just entering a comfortable middle age, a great mass of damp chestnut hair pinned atop her head, was reading aloud from *The Ghosts of "Le Petite."*

"One of the most famous ghosts of 'Le Petite' is the White Lady. Research suggests this spirit may be the ghost of the beautiful young actress Rachael de Boer, who was killed when she fell from the courtyard balcony onto the cobblestones below." As one the ladies raised their eyes to said balcony, pausing to murmur and shiver with the sort of horrified delight that ghosts seem to spark among the living. "Newspaper accounts from the time suggested a lovers' triangle, as the next day a young actor in the same company, Richard Marlowe, was shot to death in the alley behind Le Petite by Charles Mercher, third son of a local wealthy local plantation owner, who had often been seen in the company of Miss de Boer."

Two of the women shook their heads in pity. It was all the cue Rachael needed.

She appeared on the balcony as she had a century and a half before, still dressed in the soft white gown of Desdemona's death scene, her white-blond hair floating around her. The resemblance to reality stopped there, however. She simply moved through the balcony railing, rather than having to awkwardly climb over it, and her fall was a graceful, swanlike descent. The first time, Rachael fell in a tangle of screams and skirts. She did not lie upon the stone like the Lady of Shalott compassionately lifted from her floating coffin. Her beautiful petulant face smashed on the cobblestones, and blood and brains turned the pale silk of her hair into a clotted mop.

This time her fall brought her, contrary to the laws of gravity, directly into the midst of her small audience. Well primed by the fiction of the guidebook, every one of them felt the chill of her passage, shivering even in the New Orleans heat.

Involuntarily each of them had stepped back, so that Rachael's shade lay at their feet like a pool of cold, malicious light.

One woman gasped and put her hand to her heart. I bit back an oath and took a step toward her, though there was nothing I could do—death within the precincts of Le Petite is permanent in a uniquely terrible way. To my intense relief, the one who had been reading immediately dropped the little guidebook and went to her friend, stepping through Rachael in the process. That moment of human concern was enough to send Rachael fading in a snit. The woman who had clutched at her chest recovered herself, her friends clucking around her. The self-possessed little girl, who had skipped back from Rachael's fall as though avoiding an oversize pigeon dropping, cast a reproachful glance at the balcony.

Whatever laws govern Le Petite's collection of ghosts no longer required my presence. I skittered inside, keeping well ahead of the tourists. Unlike Rachael, who can even manipulate objects in the living world, I'm an ectoplasmically challenged sort of nonentity. Even the so-sensible child would probably not have noticed me tromping through her. I don't like walking through the living, though. They feel, well, sticky.

I took refuge, as I usually did, in the dusty clutter of the prop room, the one place Rachael never haunted. Even as a shade, she was too much of a snob to hang out with the stagehands. Old Gabriel the caretaker was there, watching Cory, the lights man, poke around in the chests and boxes. Gabe was a spry, skinny old black man who had been around Le Petite longer than some of us less corporeal types. I was fond of him, and not only because he was a hougan who often left little offerings for us ghosts. He was a thoughtful sort of friend to us. Sometimes he left the radio on at night so we'd have music, or if he sensed us around he'd talk to us. Of course, those were very one-sided conversations, but when you're dead and ectoplasmically challenged, even long companionable silences feel like friendship.

I settled into a cobwebby corner, pathetically glad for Gabe's company. Even Cory, whom I thought a dolt, was a welcome diversion, a reminder of youth and the changing world of the living. Change is the great coin of the living, and what else did we dead have to do save collect it? I'd been feeling even more restless than usual since the current troupe had decided to put on *Othello*. It was *Othello* we were doing when darling Rachael decided that I was her destiny, or that she was mine. Of course, I guess in a grotesque sort of way, she was right.

I swear I never touched Rachael except onstage, and very little then because I was playing Cassio, not Othello. However, like the Desdemona she played—

badly, I might add—Rachael had a jealous man in her life who wasn't going to let facts interfere with vengeance. After Rachael took her dive off the balcony, her "friend" Charles Mercher challenged me to a duel. I told him to bugger off, of course. I wasn't stupid.

He cornered me out in the alley behind Le Petite, tossed me a gun, and told me to defend myself. I threw it aside, figuring his high-class Creole honor wouldn't let him shoot an unarmed man. Wrong. Right between the eyes. One minute I'm in my body, next minute I'm out of it, and by the weird metaphysics that govern this place, I was trapped in Le Petite.

Even that wouldn't have been so bad if it wasn't for Rachael—Gabe and some of the ghosts here are decent company. But Rachael's suicides, her constant accusation and satisfaction in my plight—those were hard to bear. I don't know if it would have been better or worse if I had ever actually loved or betrayed her.

"I have to find *something* else for Desdemona's death scene, Gabe!" Cory's petulant complaint punctuated my memories and drew my attention back to the present. Thin and a little stooped, Cory knelt with hands fisted on hips, glowering at a box of linens. "With Diana's white skin and that white gown they have her in, when Desdemona falls back on the bed, she just disappears. All you can see is that spill of red hair. I worked too hard on her lighting effects to lose her against some stupid cheap white sheets. Besides, Diana is too beautiful, too talented. She deserves the best I can give her for her big scene."

"She's a beauty, all right," Gabe agreed peaceably, tactfully ignoring the fact that Cory had just taken for himself the credit of director, prop man, and wardrobe mistress in addition to his real job of working Diana's spot. "She's a fine young actress, too. I don't know as I've seen better, and I've seen more than my share." Gabe pointed regally from his seat on a dusty wooden throne from the Scottish play. "Try that brass-bound trunk over to your left, Cory. I seem to remember we had some blue silk sheets from when we were doing *Once Upon a Mattress*."

"Brass-bound trunk," Cory repeated obediently, and shuffled across the floor on his knees to the specified trunk. He opened it and began to dig.

Cory worked the lights with this spry little lady partner everybody called Pickle. No kidding, Pickle. He'd been doing stage work with her since college: sound, lights, special effects. They were a first-rate team, really, worthy of larger, better theaters than Le Petite if Cory had been less of an idiot. Did Cory realize that there was a smart, sweet, vital woman right under his nose? No, *he* only wanted Diana, and that was why he and Pickle were working Le Petite. Maybe there's something about *Othello* that attracts obsessive would-be lovers, the same way Le Petite attracts ghosts.

I did understand what Cory saw in Diana. Maybe it's because I got to know Cory so well, but Diana will always be *the* Desdemona to me. She was as pale as Rachael's ectoplasm, thick red hair curling down to her waist—no wig from wardrobe to worry about with this lady—and she was *good*. I mean, she could act. She had that rare ability to get three or four conflicting emotions in her face all at the same time.

Rachael *hated* Diana. She even quit torturing me long enough to play some nasty tricks on this rival Desdemona—withering a bouquet of fresh roses, putting dead spiders in her cold cream. It made me furious, especially since Diana seemed a decent girl, but there was nothing I could do.

Cory was removing Renaissance-style gowns from the chest, laying them carefully over the edge of the upraised lid of the trunk. I thought I remembered the production of *Once Upon a Mattress* using gowns like that, so I drifted over for a closer look. Turquoise blue silk glimmered dimly as Cory lifted away a final voluminous chemise of filmy white lawn. "Found them!" Cory crowed, scooping the sheets out of the trunk. There was a soft slithering sound and a doll-shape of brown cotton rag slid with a soft plop to the floor.

Cory picked it up, curious, turning the limp brown body over and over in his hands. It was a what-not doll, without particular identity, no clothes or hair to sex it, just black button eyes, two dots for a nose, and no mouth at all. The anonymous brown of its cloth skin could have done for any human racial type and a number of small animals.

"Hey," Cory said, "what's this?" There was a kind of damp eagerness to his hands as he poked and stroked the doll. "Is this one of those voodoo dolls, Gabe?"

"Isn't," Gabe said, with distaste plain in his voice. "What would you want with it if it was, Cory? Hoodoo dolls are an unwholesome kind of magic. I don't hold with them."

"Oh, I don't know," Cory said, but I'd seen that look before, that sort of sick, hungry wanting. "Nothing, I guess. But I thought you were into that stuff, Gabe." He settled back on his haunches and glanced over his shoulder at the old man. "I've heard you chanting while you're sweeping up the place, and you gave Pickle that good-luck charm to wear on her bad ankle, and that herb stuff to rub on it the time it swelled."

"Belief's one thing, ill-wishing is something else again," Gabe said with a kind of cool dignity. "You don't have to go to church on Sunday to know to keep clear of something bad." But I knew Cory was thinking about Diana, not listening to what Gabe was telling him. Cory's eyes had a little of that nasty smug look in them that Rachael's had, a look like a greedy, spoiled child who knows he'll get what he wants for Christmas no matter how badly he behaves.

Old Gabe pulled out a handkerchief to mop his head. I thought it was Gabe's particular magic that his handkerchiefs always appeared to be clean, no matter how often he used them. It was like he had a laundress in his pocket. "You know," he continued, still on his dignity, "Hoodoo dolls didn't come from Africa the way most folks think they did. That's white-folk nastiness that got mixed into African-born religion. Black folks who were trying to keep some of their own ways used to make wooden dolls for their spirits to come into, special, personal spirits, sort of like guardian angels. The white folk didn't want blacks keeping their own ways, so they made a law against carving the spirit dolls, or even having one. So folk started making their spirit dolls out of rags, so they were easy to hide, or so the whites would think they were just toys got up for children.

"It used to be that folks talked to their spirit dolls, to ask them for fortunes and advice. They'd ask wishes, too, maybe not all of them kind, and I wouldn't blame a person for ill-wishing those who slaved him. There was a white-folk witch idea of making a spirit doll to catch *another* person's spirit to work harm on them—a poppet, they called it. The two things got mixed together somehow, and that's where you get a hoodoo doll."

"How did the spirit get in the doll?" Cory asked.

"Well, there's lots of ways I've heard of to catch somebody's else's spirit," Gabe said slowly. "I don't know about the wishing kind of spirit though, the ones the first spirit dolls were made for. Maybe just calling it is enough."

I could have told Gabe right then that all Cory had really heard was the part about wishing. He stared hard at the what-not doll, and I felt his hunger for Diana make a kind of hole, right there and then, inside the doll. There was a feeling like falling, and then there I was, filling that hole Cory'd made.

I'd like to say that I went into the what-not doll to help Cory, or even to help Diana. I'd seen it all before, after all, the life-wasting power of obsession. But while

Cory had been wishing the what-not doll could hold a wishing spirit, I'd been wishing just as hard that I could escape Rachael and Le Petite. The truth is that Cory's want pulled and my own desire pushed and there I was, inside the doll.

I got a little scared when Cory pretended to put me back in the trunk, but he rolled me up in the silk sheets when Gabe wasn't looking.

Cory made up Desdemona's bed with the sheets, the whole time telling me in a low murmur how the color would make Diana blaze white and red beneath his lights. When he was sure Gabe had gone home Cory had himself a nice little roll around on those sheets, thinking about how he wanted to make Diana blaze beneath his hands, his mouth. . . .

Privy to it as I was, it made me feel shamed and a little sick. Cory was further gone than I had thought. Had Rachael done this, I wondered, slithering with self-generated heat on her fantasy of *me*?

After, Cory took me home inside his shirt.

I was trying to take my new role seriously. After all, the universe had just given me what I wanted most—the opportunity to exit Rachael's little fantasy, stage left. I was grateful. I honestly thought maybe I could do some good.

You don't have to believe that if you don't want to. It's true anyway.

I thought of all the things I had wanted to say to Rachael—all the things, over the last 150 years, I have said to her, just to have her ignore me. After all, she'd won. I was hers forever. That I wanted nothing to do with her was meaningless, just as it was meaningless when I was alive. But maybe I could make a difference with Cory. I could try.

Cory, I said as loudly as I could. I didn't actually *say* it, of course; no mouth, no voice box. Some of the actors use this word "emoting." I emoted at Cory, loudly. He stopped, shook his head, then kept walking, but it was enough of a response to make me hopeful.

For the rest of the short journey I just rode against Cory's pale hard belly, getting damp with his sweat and wishing I could see the stars. I had been able to see the stars from Le Petite's balcony, but every time I went there, Rachael had felt obligated to come throw herself off.

Honestly, some people should have gotten a life. Preferably before they cost me mine.

It was a relief to get to Cory's apartment. He set me on the bed while he undressed and wandered out to the narrow kitchen in search of a beer.

For a while I held tight to the doll body, scared that somehow I'd get sucked back into Le Petite for one of Rachael's midnight performances. That's when I found out that I wasn't quite alone.

Don't be afraid, said a voice in my doll head. *You're part of me now.*

At first I was scared to—well, whatever a dead man can be scared to. Ghosts hear voices all the time, but it's a fair assumption that if it isn't a live person talking it's just another ghost. If you ever are a ghost, drift down to one of the New Orleans cemeteries. It's as noisy as a full audience with the houselights still up. This was different.

Who are you? I demanded.

Don't be afraid, the voice repeated, amused. *I'm an actor, just like you. I've had more roles than you've had, too. I've been a child's doll, live babies and dead ones. I've been a teddy bear and even Alice's cat.*

Are you a ghost? I asked.

No. Again, that amusement. *I'm just the what-not doll. But I'm the what-not doll of Le Petite, and that makes me a doll the way Le Petite is a theater.*

Remember that Le Petite is sort of a sinkhole for spirits, many of them actors. I guess all that creative energy—all that craziness—rubs off on everything if you give it long enough.

Do you mind me being in here? I asked.

Not at all, the doll said. *I get lonely when I don't*

have a role to play. I haven't been anything for a long time. Now I can be your friend.

Maybe it's a sign of how miserable I'd become, but the doll's offer sounded awfully good to me. *I'd like that. What shall I call you?*

Call me Ismael, the doll said. I chuckled inside our stuffed head.

I asked, *Do you know why I'm here?*

Yes. You want to stop another tragedy from happening.

Well, yeah, I guess I do, I admitted. *Any advice?*

Only knowledge. We dolls know a little something about the many ways people can need us. You can speak to Cory, the way you are speaking to me. You can get him to think about things so that you can see how he feels, what he remembers. Does that help?

Yes, thank you.

I didn't have to prod Cory to think about Diana.

Cory came back with his beer, picked me—us—up, and lay down with us on his chest. He held us up in one hand so he could look us in our button eyes.

"You're my wish doll," Cory said. It scared me a little, the way he said it, and I don't scare easily after being around Rachael for so long. "I'm going to tell you my wishes, and you are going to make them come true."

He drank his beer quickly. I knew he had not eaten lately, probably not since breakfast. The alcohol hit him like a lead sap, and he fell asleep, holding us bundled against his cheek.

Cory enters the room, and we see him as he wishes to be. His slim wiry body is straight and elegant in the Elizabethan doublet and tall boots, his fair wispy hair groomed to a shining cap of pale curls. His eyes are clear, and all, all for her.

Desdemona/Diana lies still on the sea-colored silk, her red hair fanned around her. Cory leans over and kisses her closed eyes, then sets his mouth to her mouth, his lips so soft, so tender on her still, cold lips. He lingers, his mouth a caress, a whisper, a promise, and she warms with his kiss, gasps and breathes in his breath, opens her eyes.

She sees him, truly sees him for the first time, and her smile is a magical radiance at the realization of the love they share, must share or die of the lack of it. She puts her arms around him and pulls him to her. . . .

The same dream, over and over, through the night. No wonder Rachael killed herself.

The next morning, Ismael and I tried to get Cory to eat something. The best we could do was get him to put sugar in his coffee. I rode on the edge of his thoughts, all of which were fantasies of Diana—how he would bring her her coffee and morning yogurt, how she would thank him with her smile, what he would say and how she would reply, how she would flirt and he respond. In his mind, it is all a code for her love for him. If he is patient, her love will find a voice to answer his desires.

I looked around the apartment as much as I could from where we were propped on the table. It was a cheap little apartment, but you could tell that Cory had once taken trouble with it. The furniture was simple and comfortable, the windows clean, the walls and shelves rich and colorful with playbills and mementos.

But like Cory himself, the apartment showed signs of recent neglect. There was laundry everywhere, crumbs scattered on the rugs and the pleasant furniture, and at least a week of unwashed dishes in the sink. I know bachelors are supposed to live in squalid abandon, and I myself had been but an indifferent housekeeper, but I didn't think this was normal for Cory. I prodded him. Sure enough, he looked around with a momentary spasm of disgust at the disorder and the dirt.

He returned to his fantasies of Diana. I tried to

prod him into cleaning himself and the apartment up a
little by suggesting that Diana would not be favorably
impressed by his stubbled chin and sickly pallor, nor
by an unmade bed with stained gray sheets. He ignored me as stubbornly as Rachael ever had. When it
was at last time to go to the theater, he left his coffee
cup on the table, the spoon leaving a yet another
brown stain on the place mat. But he tucked us up
tightly underneath his belt.

*She sees him, truly sees him for the first time, and
her smile is a magical radiance at the realization of the
love they share, must share or die of the lack of it. She
puts her arms around him and pulls him to her. . . .*

"Hey, Cory, are you all right?"

Pickle's voice jerked Cory out of his reverie, and I
was amazed at the flare of fury Cory felt at being
interrupted. I searched his memory hastily, shoving
forward thoughts of his long, close partnership with
this woman. Finally he smiled for her. "I'm okay,
Pickle. Just daydreaming."

"You seem to daydream a lot these days," Pickle
said carefully.

Cory shrugged, smiled to himself, Pickle already
half forgotten. Pickle swallowed, and gently put her
hand on Cory's shoulder. "Cory, you need to either
ask her out or get over it. This isn't healthy. You've
lost weight, and frankly, you look like shit."

He turned on her, batting her hand away, and I
couldn't stop him. "Is my work suffering? Is it? Has
anybody dared say I'm not just as good at my job as
I ever was?"

Pickle stepped back, blinking. "No, Cory. Your
work is just fine."

He turned his back on her and slammed away.
"Then mind your own damn business and leave me
alone."

"I thought it was my business," Pickle said softly. "I thought we were friends."

He pretended not to hear her.

Cory climbed up into the catwalk, up among the ropes and the lights. He moved like a lizard up there, strong thin legs and arms, over girders, along beams, silent and agile.

He stopped and hunkered down. He worked us up from under his baggy shirt so that our button eyes were looking where his eyes looked.

We could see Diana getting dressed. She was nervous, jumpy like she could feel his eyes on her. She was showing signs of wear from Rachael's ghost lighting, too—she shook her costume out carefully before she put it on, shook her slippers over the wastebasket, poked at her cosmetics with a little plastic knife and smelled them carefully before at last she settled down to put on her makeup for the matinee. I felt for the poor woman. Ismael did too.

Cory was moving, almost imperceptibly, hips rocking softly against the beam we rested on. Under his breath, he murmured in time to his rocking, "I wish, I wish, I wish. . . ."

In his mind, she turns up her face and sees him, but she smiles and lifts her arms in welcome.

He crooned, to himself, to us. "Give me my wish, give me my wish. . . ."

And Ismael whispered to me, very quietly, *We could.*

I tried. I really did, though I don't suppose you will believe that. Still, it is true. For nine days, while Cory dreamed, and wished, I tried to break his obsession. I showed him Pickle's increasingly hurt puzzlement. I showed him how Diana was actually starting to be afraid of him, shying away from his attention.

All the time, his eyes grew more and more like Rachael's eyes—dark, and hungry, and hollow.

"Give me my wish," Cory said every night before he went to bed. And every night Ismael whispered to me, *We could.* While Cory slept, he told me how, and I struggled with the knowledge.

The dreams went on.

Cory enters the room, and we see him as he wishes to be. His slim wiry body is straight and elegant in the Elizabethan doublet and tall boots, his fair wispy hair groomed to a shining cap of pale curls. His eyes are clear, and all, all for her.

Desdemona/Diana lies still on the sea-colored silk, her red hair fanned around her. Cory leans over and kisses her closed eyes, then sets his mouth to her mouth, his lips so soft, so tender on her still, cold lips. He lingers, his mouth a caress, a whisper, a promise, and she warms with his kiss, gasps and breathes in his breath, opens her eyes.

She screams, her face full of revulsion and terror. Cory yells with rage, crying out "No! This isn't the way it's supposed to be! Stop it! Give me my wish!" His long pale hands are wrapped around Diana's throat and he squeezes, shaking her, slamming her against the bed. "Give me my wish!"

It was Ismael and I Cory was crushing in his hands, us he was shaking, screaming at. "Give me my wish!"

Give it to him, Ismael said quietly, sadly.

Cut me a mouth, I told Cory at last. *Kiss me the way you want to kiss her.*

I cringed from the knife, at least as much as a spirit can cringe. But when he pressed his mad, frantic mouth to our doll's new mouth I gave myself up to what he wanted. I wish I could say I was reluctant. As my spirit left the doll I felt Ismael tell me, *Good-bye, my friend. Be happy.*

I called good-bye as my spirit flung itself gladly, yes, joyfully into the flesh-and-blood body of Cory. I don't know if Ismael heard me, for as Cory's spirit slipped past me into the doll he was shrieking with triumph.

I don't think he even noticed that he had left his real life behind as he plunged down into his dream of Diana.

She sees him, truly sees him for the first time, and her smile is a magical radiance at the realization of the love they share, must share or die of the lack of it. She puts her arms around him and pulls him to her. . . .

Inside Cory's body I stretched, slowly, cautiously, but oh, so glad to have flesh again. It was strange, very strange to have a body, to focus eyes, close awkward fingers around a needle and feel cool thin metal and sharp pricking pain and taste blood as I lifted my stuck finger to my mouth. It was that, perhaps, that made me truly understand the fact of what had happened—the taste of Cory's blood, *my* blood, in the human mouth that was now mine.

It took me forever to thread the needle, and my first few stitches were clumsy. Still, sewing is like riding a horse or kissing a woman. Once you've done it well, you remember, no matter how long it has been. I stitched the knife-slash of a mouth closed. I tried to give it a gentle sort of smile. Then I kissed the top of the doll's head carefully, and set it on the shelf. "Goodbye, Ismael. I hope you enjoy your new role. I'll miss you."

My stomach growled, and I became aware that I was, almost literally, starving. I went to the telephone, dialed a number that I eagerly pulled from Cory's memory.

"Pickle? This is Cory. Listen, I've been a real asshole. Please, will you come to dinner with me and let me apologize?"

Eventually she said yes, of course, because she has a kindness in her someone like Rachael could never conceive of. Her friendship was the best, the only real thing Cory had achieved in his life, and if nothing else, I can make sure she knows that.

Of course I'm going to have to tell her where Cory went, and why, that he exists now in a dream of his own creation, having chosen his fantasy over his life. Pickle was his friend, and she deserves to know the truth.

Also—though I have Cory's memories and name, I am not Cory.

I do think I will wait until after dinner to tell her. I really am starving, and for just a little while I want to feel her friendship, however undeserved, welcoming me to life. But I will tell her the truth. Then, if she will let me, I will try to earn my own place in her life, a place I can deserve instead of just inherit.

You see, I want something real.

I know what you are thinking. I did take Cory Richardson's life. But then he wasn't using it for anything.

I hope Ismael isn't lonely anymore.

LITTLE PIG, BERRY BROWN, AND THE HARD MOON

Jay Lake

Little Pig sat in the thin-leaf tree and watched Mother Sun dance upon the water. She-of-the-Sky made silver sparkle in the creek below the bear fur that wrapped the girl in warmth. Little Pig smiled, but folded her laughter within—noise out of place could bring a hungry cat.

Stick, Little Pig's only toy and best and greatest friend, opened her tiny carved mouth. *"Child, child, sitting in a tree, what sort of furry fruit do you be?"* Little Pig swallowed another laugh, though her body shook and swayed against the thin-leaf's bark. "Silly Stick," she whispered, then put her friend within her own mouth for silence and safekeeping.

Later Brother Spear returned from his hunt with Little Pig's mother and the rest of the clan to fetch her down from the safety of the thin-leaf tree. He was covered in mud and sweat and blood that stank of the Tusk Beast, breath steaming in the evening as the stars cut away his heat in tiny ribbons to feed their secret jealousies. His glittering eyes were narrow-closed, but the axe of his anger did not seem held high for Little Pig. She hugged his chest as he carried her home, and kept quiet as a nesting mouse, still sucking on Stick and wishing she could ask her friend about the fire in Brother Spear's face.

Soon enough she found the reason, when they returned to Hard Moon Camp.

Her clan had different camps for different moons. Each was in a place that drew good fortune from the cold skies and sheltered the People from whatever harmed them most in that season of Sister Moon's journey through the year.

The People's Hard Moon Camp was in a shallow bowl atop a bluff near the Biggest River. The bowl was for luck in saving enough food for the Ice Moon and Dying Moon camps soon to come. The bluff kept the People above the animals in the scrub forest surrounding the Biggest River. As they crossed the ridge, she smelled blood, and saw that this night there was fire, big as any prayer fire, meat on drying frames spread before the flames. Close to the fire, Oldest Woman and Broken-Eye knelt next to someone wrapped in too many furs.

Like the last grub in the sack, Little Pig thought, lonely and unlucky. None of the People should be so sad.

"Stick," she whispered, risking noise as Brother Spear made his quiet way down to the warm light. "Who is it?"

"Child, child, clutching tight, count the People here tonight."

Brother Spear touched her back with his hand, signaling quiet, but she had Stick's advice now and made good. Little Pig wasn't very clever with numbers, but she knew names, and so she sang the list of the People in the voice only she could hear, behind her ears, looking for each one as she named them.

Oldest Woman, hands so bent
Sleeping Sister, dreaming much
Broken-Eye, sees only night
Walks On Rock, feet too big
Berry Brown, mother of my heart

There she stopped, for she did not see her mother anywhere. Little Pig was hungry then, for Berry Brown had always fed her. Little Pig was frightened then, for Berry Brown had always comforted her. Little Pig was worried then, for Berry Brown had always protected her. Berry Brown belonged to Little Pig the way Mother Sun belonged to Daughter Sky.

Brother Spear stopped at the feet of Berry Brown, who was wrapped in the three magic furs, head close to the fire. "I have brought the child," he said. Little Pig felt the rumble of his voice where her head lay against his chest. She held Stick close.

Berry Brown had made Stick for her, carving her friend with a black-stone blade and the patience of rain, lending her breath into Stick's mouth, kissing Stick's hurts. Little Pig's eyes salted like summer-killed meat as she clutched her toy tight enough to make Stick squeak and shiver.

Oldest Woman took the bear fur robe from Brother Spear and greeted Little Pig with a tiny dry kiss upon her forehead. Then she made Little Pig stand with her close to the fire, next to Berry Brown's face, a soft little hand wrapped inside a trembling old one.

"Who lies before us?" Oldest Woman asked. Her voice was not unkind, but Little Pig knew Oldest Woman could crack rocks with her will, and not even Boar Killer with his temper and his huge muscles would argue with her.

"Child, child, before the fire, answer all Oldest Woman desires," whispered Stick, squirming in her hand.

"Berry Brown." Little Pig stared at the unmoving eyes, lost in the sweating face like leaves in the creek. Her chest shuddered. "My mother."

"What has happened to her?" Oldest Woman asked.

"I do not—" Little Pig began, then stopped.

"Child, child, Berry went hunting, did not hear the Tusk Beast grunting."

Oldest Woman made a soft noise, inviting Little Pig's next words to come out of her mouth.

Little Pig closed Stick to her chest, just as Berry Brown used to hold Little Pig. "She was hurt by the Tusk Beast, wasn't she?"

A squeeze of the hand. Then: "What will become of her?"

Little Pig waited for Stick to speak, but the toy was silent. Oldest Woman squeezed her hand again. *What was she supposed to say?*

"She is my mother." Little Pig's voice was as slow as her thoughts. "She will not leave me behind."

Oldest Woman bent and whispered in Little Pig's ear. As she spoke, Little Pig could feel Stick straining to listen. "Berry Brown has gone beyond the reach of my hands' skill or the depths of Broken-Eye's wisdom. We cannot make her whole. Still she might come home for you, child. But you must ask the Hard Moon and the sharp stars if this can be, and what words will bring her back."

"I will speak to the moon," said Little Pig.

Oldest Woman released her hand, brushed her hard, crooked fingers across Little Pig's shoulder. "Go find your way, then."

Little Pig climbed up toward the rim of Hard Moon Camp's small round valley. She took one of her paths, not the People's trails, so she could visit her special places. The Hard Moon was not so old that she had lost the light. Little Pig touched her crystal rocks, the oldest bone, and the brown anthill. Stick always liked the special places, sometimes talked about the magic that dwelt in each, though right now Stick seemed to be silent. Thinking, perhaps. Mice scuttled away from Little Pig as she walked, while an owl sailed overhead, wide-winged and vigilant. Had the night-hunter come to take the last of Berry Brown's spirit away?

She almost ran into Brother Spear. He sat cross-legged, still covered in blood and muck, making tiny sparks as he chipped at the edge of his spear point.

"I am sorry," he told Little Pig without meeting her eye.

She thought about that a moment. "You did not hurt Berry Brown."

More chips of the rock. "I led. Success is mine, failure mine."

"There is meat by the fire, for the Ice Moon and the Dying Moon." Little Pig knew this without turning to look, as the dank blood smell lay upon the entire valley.

Brother Spear finally lifted his chin to her. "There is no magic. Only spear and blood and bone. Tusk Beast took Berry Brown in trade for itself. Blood for blood."

"Child, child, Brother Spear is wrong, Berry has not yet sung her last song."

Little Pig squeezed Stick, a gentle hug of thanks and reassurance. "My mother is alive," she told Brother Spear, touching his knee with her free hand.

A smile ghosted across his face like a crane in the mist. "Go on. Follow Oldest Woman's magic. Ask the moon. I only know the spear. It feeds us but it takes away as well."

"Like the Tusk Beast. Spears are our sharp teeth. You are the strong hand."

He bent once more to his work. Little Pig gave Brother Spear back his silence and moved on to talk to the moon.

She picked a tree that some great storm had driven down, and climbed the mossy, rotting trunk to sit among the insects and the tiny plants at the top. The perch gave her a view of Hard Moon Camp and her mother's body—a tiny dark smear before the fire circle when seen from here. If she faced away from the flames, the sky ghosted above her. The knives of the stars glittered sharp. The Hard Moon was beginning to rot and grow lean, and hungered already for the bed at Daughter Sky's western verge. To the north was the faint, dull glow of the Ice Wall.

"What shall I do, Stick?" Little Pig held her toy up in the moonlight. The tiny eyes squinted. The mouth pursed as in thought. Stick's long wooden body twitched in Little Pig's hand. Then she smiled, ivory bright as any bone from the sand pits of the Biggest River.

Little Pig had never seen Stick's teeth before.

"Child, child, ask the moon, she rules over every doom."

She kissed Stick. Stick kissed back—another first!—though it was a sting, like the bite of a tree ant, rather than the gentle press of Berry Brown's lips. Then Little Pig set her legs apart, as Broken-Eye did when he was called to wrestle spirits from the weed smoke. She spread her arms wide, as Oldest Woman did when asking questions of the southern wind. She tilted her head back, as Brother Spear did when calling to the wolves and bears and cats. Stick clung to her outstretched hand, and the Hard Moon swam at the top of her upward gaze.

"Sister Moon," Little Pig said quietly. She did not feel a need to shout. No voice was great enough to reach the moon if the moon was not ready to listen, and any voice should reach if the moon had turned her face to hear. "I have been told three times to speak to you. A thing thrice-told is a thing true through and through. Tell me if Berry Brown may live. Tell me what I can do to make her whole. Tell me what magic there is under your cold light."

She listened a while to the whisper of the wind in the thin-leaf trees, and the call of a distant nighthawk hunting insects, and the puzzled, nervous snorts of the deer moving through the scrub brush.

Sister Moon made no answer, but Stick twisted in Little Pig's hand.

She listened more, to the rustle of the mice scavenging under cover of darkness, and the mutter of the Biggest River remaking its bed every moment, and the faint ringing of the night's cold pouring off the Ice Wall to the north.

Still Sister Moon made no answer. Still Stick twisted, twitched, demanding attention.

She listened a third time to the faraway scream of some animal caught up by great rushing feathers, to the cough of a hunting cat, to the scrape of claws on rock.

A third time Sister Moon made no answer. She was silent as she had ever been, edging through the sky toward her meeting with the western horizon.

"What is it, Stick?" Little Pig asked, feeling no hope.

"Child, child, you have grown, lay me down and walk alone."

"No!" she shouted, then swiftly sat to wait in silence. She had made far too much noise for being this distant from the fire and the rest of the People. A cat could come, or a wolf, or even one of the mountain teratornis. Stick twitched but held her peace.

After a time, as the trees creaked and the breeze brought a musky scent of furry hunger, Little Pig whispered urgently to Stick. "You are my friend. Berry Brown made you for me. I cannot leave you behind."

"Child, child, think what she did, when Berry carved me from a stick."

"You're *Stick*," hissed Little Pig. "You watch over me when I am alone. You're always close when the People are far. You protect me."

"Child, child, your mother is in me, and I am part of what she could be."

Little Pig studied Stick's eyes. They were wide open now, a deep, shining black just as Berry Brown's had been. *Were*, she thought as her stomach lurched. Just as Berry Brown's were. The tiny teeth gleamed ivory bright, and Stick's narrow cheeks had rounded.

"So you are her, and she is you?"

Stick twitched. A nod.

"I could keep you. Hold you close. Never let you leave. You'd always be with me!"

Then Little Pig's eyes were drawn back to the fire down within the bowl of Hard Moon Camp. Berry Brown lay still upon the ground. Oldest Woman stood beside her, shadow bent and shaking, waiting for Little Pig to return.

She could keep Stick close, always have her mother. But at the same time, Berry Brown would lie by the fire, unmoving and cooling. Like a stunned doe with the slaughter knife trapped in her throat, leaping up unexpectedly into the forest to bleed out her pain until the People ran her down again and completed her life.

Or Little Pig could lay down Stick—her toy, her friend, her companion, the always touch of Berry Brown—and let the Tusk Beast's work be finished.

"I understand what Oldest Woman meant for me to learn from the moon," she said.

Stick was quiet, as if knowing what was to come. Crying, Little Pig found her way back down the hill toward the firelight, scarcely noticing the bright eyes that watched from above. They were of the same night that had taken Berry Brown away from her, and so she gave them none of her concern.

Walking toward Oldest Woman, and the rest of the People who watched in shadowed silence, Little Pig could feel years settling upon her shoulders. Though she was still seasons from her own bleedings, she could not be a child when Berry Brown's place among the People was empty.

Her eyes were dry when she passed out of darkness.

Oldest Woman's voice rang with the authority of rock splitting water. "Have you asked the Hard Moon what might be done?"

Little Pig stroked Stick. "Yes, I have." She looked around the fire, where the eyes of the People gleamed

little different from the eyes of the beasts around the
outer ring of Hard Moon Camp.

"And what answer did Sister Moon give you?"

"Silence," said Little Pig. She raised Stick above
her head, turning slowly so that everyone might see
what had become of her toy. If they could see it. "Silence, which told me everything. Silence, which told
me that no matter what we do the sky circles onward
and the seasons of the moon pass just the same. I can
no more ask Sister Moon to turn back Berry Brown's
time than I can ask her to turn back the Ice time or
the Dying time."

Oldest Woman stared a while at Little Pig, then
smiled. It was a thin smile, quick as a lightning stroke,
but Little Pig saw it come and go, and like looking at
lightning, was blinded for a moment. "And now that
Berry Brown is gone where the skill of my hands cannot follow, where Broken-Eye's wisdom cannot lead,
what will you do for your mother?"

Little Pig squatted on her heels next to Berry
Brown and touched her mother's pale face. The skin
was chill, the eyes never moved even as her hand
passed before them. She tugged the furs aside—bear,
wolf, and cat—and lay Stick down in the bruised skin
between Berry Brown's breasts. Stick smiled at her,
showing not only the new teeth but a tongue and
mouth within, far pinker than the black blood that
had dried upon her mother.

"I give Berry Brown back the toy that she made
for me," Little Pig said slowly. "I will not be a child
anymore, now that she is gone. My mother needs her
spirit returned so that she can travel into the lands
beyond the horizon where Sister Moon goes every
night."

*"Woman, woman, letting go, your mother's love is
bright as snow."*

With those words, Stick became stick—a bit of
wood slashed in a few places to make something like
a face, worn from endless handling, tips softened

where an infant had suckled on the wood in her hunger, split where a toddler had grown her teeth, worn where a child carried it everywhere. Little Pig looked at the bare and damaged wood and wondered what gifts of her mother's remained to her.

Oldest Woman gave Little Pig her new name, to help her take her mother's place among their little clan. Trembling hands blessed her before the fire, Oldest Woman speaking of the mothers who had birthed the People just as the mountain streams birthed the Biggest River. Little Pig was set upon her own journey toward motherhood, following Berry Brown's path.

Now Youngest Woman, she held Brother Spear close as he wept his sorrow. The tears helped her mother's spirit move onward. In his turn, Brother Spear dug a grave, that Berry Brown might sleep deep enough to stay out of the claws of cat or wolf during the Ice Moon and the Dying Moon to come.

"I will work alone to set the rocks," she said. Three days later, Youngest Woman laid the last of the stones upon the cairn. Berry Brown and the old, chewed stick now rested beneath. Youngest Woman spread leaves and soil between the rocks, and found the secret seeds of flowers for the days of the Bright Moon to come, even though the People would not be camped here then.

She stood silent beneath the pale sun, the ice wind plucking sweat from her head and hands. In that quiet moment, her mother came to her, carrying Stick. "I did not think it would be so beautiful," said Berry Brown in a voice made of the wind sighing in the grass, the buzz of insect wings, the creak of trees on the distant hills.

Stick nodded.

Youngest Woman returned the nod. "The toy you made for me carried me through my years of need, Mother. May it carry you through yours."

Berry Brown smiled, her mouth a glimmer of beetles' wings and shiny pebbles and light on water. "As you will carry me onward through the journey of your heart."

"Always," said Youngest Woman, but she was speaking only to herself and the uncaring sky.

There was time before she had to lay the evening fire for Oldest Woman, and the rest of the People were out gathering garlic and onions. This was what she knew that day: just as the streams become rivers, daughters become their mothers, and in turn make more daughters to spread like rain upon the land. She owed her daughters-to-come the memory of Berry Brown, the wisdom of her mother, and whatever more she might glean from her own life.

And so Youngest Woman went looking for a stick. With Stick had come stories, comfort, safety. Love. She might as well start practicing to carve now. Then she would be skilled enough when her time came to make a toy to carry her own daughters through the years.

THE LONGEST LADDER

Peter Morwood

Everybody's had The Great Toy. I was lucky—if that's the word I'm looking for—because I had several.

They would be unwrapped with great ceremony on birthdays or Christmas, and if they were especially handsome, then when I'd finished playing with them they'd be locked inside the china cabinet in the upstairs sitting room. That sitting room was, like in every house big enough to have one, the room that nobody went into, except for weddings, christenings, and funerals, and—in my family—at Christmas.

It wasn't some cruel parental trick, to give me a gift, allow me to admire it, and then take it away again. That china cabinet was a place of honor and a shrine to nice things; my mum's and dad's crystal, silver, porcelain . . . and now my plastic, too. That's where my Britains' *Concord Overland Stagecoach* lived, and my *Herald Arctic Expedition*. They were perfect little replicas, far beyond toys—time capsules of their era, and thus far too good for any kid to play with on anything like a daily basis. So when I did play with them, I treated them carefully, because afterward I knew they would be safe.

Between times, I could admire them through the

glass of the cabinet, and show them off to friends who, though it was never said aloud, might not show the proper respect to something that wasn't their own. They were also thoroughly impressed by the company the toys were keeping. At first a toy stagecoach didn't look at ease among the Dresden and Royal Doulton china, the Waterford and Tyrone crystal, and the feather-light ceramic stuff with no name that Great-Uncle Johnny had brought back from China in the 1920s. But as time went by, that changed, and Mum's china cabinet became *the* appropriate place for such things to be.

Until one night . . .

It had been a terrific Christmas.

The TV was fizzing away in the background. Her Majesty the Queen hadn't appeared for her usual lightweight talk yet, so Mum and Dad weren't actually watching it, just using the sound to cover some sort of parental discussion. Various relatives were gossiping; my sisters were comparing notes on some book of fashion as it related to a pair of expensively dressed dolls; and I . . .

I was reading the instruction sheet for a new model aircraft, tentatively fitting parts together, and wishing I could get cracking with the paint and glue. No such luck. The order had come down from On High: "Not that smelly stuff, not just yet. Let your dinner settle and have a bit of patience!"

It was the usual situation on a Christmas afternoon. The turkey and plum pudding had gone down a treat, and now the guests were probably thinking that with obligations discharged, they should move on to the next stage in the holiday social round. My parents were probably thinking that since no one had so far said anything to provoke one of those icy family disagreements that happen so easily over the holidays, having the afternoon to themselves before the next lot arrived would be good. My sisters and I were definitely thinking that once they'd all left we could relax from Being On Our Best Behavior; not that we intended to run amok, but what's the point of a stack of new toys on Christmas afternoon when you have to play with them *quietly*? And yet we were all so warm and well-fed and content that no one could be bothered to even hint at what everyone thought was the obvious thing to do.

The first notes of the National Anthem sounded from the TV, and various aunts hastily topped up their glasses of sherry before the Queen's speech began. I wasn't interested in what she had to say; at nine years old, I regarded Our Gracious Queen as a useful source of school holidays but not much else, so I folded up the instruction sheet, dropped the model pieces into their box, put the lid on, and made my escape. With Christmas dinner over and Christmas supper still several hours of digestion away, there wasn't much else to do for the rest of the afternoon. I picked up a couple of the books I'd been given, and thought that if I went upstairs to the sitting room, I would have some peace and quiet to read.

I was right about the peace and quiet. There was no one in the room; the only noise was the low crunch and crackle from a big coal fire as it settled in the grate. There was something very restful about lying on the floor in front of a fire like that, on a comfortably full stomach, reading a book, and occasionally stopping to take a mental inventory about how this Christmas's presents stacked up against those of previous years.

I hadn't done too badly. There were, of course, the things I wanted that I knew I was never going to get— the air rifle, for example. One of the aunts presently soaking up Harvey's Bristol Cream downstairs was blind in one eye from an airgun pellet: I didn't even bother asking anymore. And there were things I'd wanted and never got because they disappeared so fast I might as well have imagined them. That plastic

Roman centurion's helmet, for example, complete with the feathered crest that was properly mounted crosswise, the only accurate toy version I've ever seen. But set against those rare disappointments, there were toys I never asked for, and never expected. . . .

I was still half-drowsing over the book when my dad came in quietly. I glanced up in surprise at the package he was carrying, a huge thing covered with vivid blue and gold wrapping paper. He bent down to put it on the floor beside me, then patted me on the head and said, "Those exam results were better than your mother and I ever expected."

And he went away and left me with the present. I didn't get a chance to get over my surprise, or even say thanks . . . and maybe that was how he meant it to be. My dad had his own sense of style.

I sat up and pulled the wrapping paper off to reveal the more ordinary brown paper underneath. Inside that was a cardboard box with a picture printed on it. Nowadays, the art would be considered crude: no photos, no lavish description, just black and red ink on the white cardboard. But it illustrated the contents of the box, and that was enough: a fireman's outfit—and what an outfit!

The wording was surprisingly bland by comparison with the excitable way it would be written now. The label simply read FDNY FIRE CHIEF SET. CLASSIC 1930S PUMP AND AERIAL LADDER TRUCKS. FULL CREW AND EQUIPMENT. CHIEF'S HELMET WITH SHIELD.

I was astounded. "FDNY"—as in *New York?* For a kid living in Belfast's suburbs in the sixties, this could hardly have had more rarity value if it had come from the moon. Excitedly I tore back the lid, and the initial impression I got was of red; no, of RED, and most of that impression of redness came from the strangely shaped helmet that was the first thing out of the box.

Certainly it was strangely shaped to *my* eyes, and bigger and bolder than anything a Northern Irish firefighter would ever have worn. The ribbed, cross-braced crown with an eagle-head supporting a big shield in front, and the enormous brim and neck flap, were completely unlike anything I'd seen before—very different from the local helmets with their high front-to-back combs, like something a dragoon might wear when fighting Napoleon at Waterloo. By contrast this American helmet looked medieval, like the long-tailed sallets from the Wars of the Roses that I'd once seen in the Tower of London on a summer holiday. When I put the new helmet on my head and snugged the chin strap in place, Arthur Pendragon wearing the crown of Britain couldn't have felt more grand.

But the helmet was just the gilding on a spectacular lily. Once I'd put it on and turned my attention back to the box, underneath where it had been was not just one fire engine, but two. Both were vivid scarlet with big, chunky black tires, white rubber hoses that could pull out from their reels, and the tractor-drawn aerial truck had a tremendous ladder that at full extension was taller than I was. The deep, rich color of the vehicles was splendidly intensified by the amount of chrome all over them. Radiator grilles and bumpers, pumps, exhausts and hose nozzles all sparkled; the hubcaps on the big black-and-red wheels gleamed; the extinguishers on their running boards and the levers to operate the ladder were mirror-bright.

They might just have been toy fire engines when my dad bought them, but to me they looked like jewels.

I don't know, even now, what a real *full crew* means, or whether the toy set had left out anyone important. But my crew was made up of thirty little red plastic firemen with white plastic helmets. They had clip-shaped hands to hold their white plastic hoses, extinguishers, axes, and some weird spearlike things that looked like fishing gaffs. They were pike poles, of course, used to pull burning debris aside or rip the plaster from walls and ceilings to make sure that nothing was on fire behind it.

Those little clip hands also allowed them to climb the ladders mounted on their engines, one hand for the ladder and another for a hose—or for someone who needed rescuing. It didn't matter to me if the burning building thick with smoke was my youngest sister's dollhouse, or just a cardboard box with cutout windows, either of them draped with as much cotton wool as I hoped Mum wouldn't miss. It didn't matter either that the victim being rescued was usually one of the dollhouse inhabitants, stiffly expressionless and no more impressed by their plight than a wooden chess piece. One of my new fire crew could save them: he—I—always knew what to do to get them out of there. When I had that helmet on, when I was playing with those fire engines, I was always equal to the task, whatever it was: I was a real firemen.

Just like my dad had been.

He'd been in the Auxiliary Fire Service during the war, while holding down some other essential full-time job at the same time, but he didn't talk much about what he'd seen or done. I got the feeling that it had been boring; after all, Belfast was such a long way from the German bomber bases in Occupied France that they would have found London, or Coventry, or even Liverpool that much easier to reach. By the time I was ten I could quote chapter and verse on the reasons why, because I had a new hobby—building model kits of Second World War aircraft.

I'd been doing that for only six months, but already—the way some kids today can remember and pronounce multi-syllable dinosaur names in a way their parents can hardly credit—I could rattle off the performance figures for every plane I'd put together, and for several still unbuilt and in their boxes. If there was a mistake in a movie or a TV show, I felt that it was my duty to point it out, at length. A few weeks after Christmas, Dad had taken me to see *The Battle of Britain* in the local cinema, but after the fourth shrill whisper of "Look! There they are again! I told you! Even the *German* planes have got British engines!" he was ready to either leave the place or throttle me. He did neither, which shows just what a nice man he really was even though I was being such a pain in the neck.

I was gluing yet another kit together when my dad came in from visiting a friend in hospital. He was looking much more cheerful than when he'd gone out, so my mum already sounded relieved when she asked him, "How's Tom?"

"Much better. They say he'll be home before Easter, and probably well enough for the reunion dinner."

"He should cut down on his cigarettes," Mum started to say, then pinned Dad with a hard stare. "Come to that, so should you."

"Another New Year resolution shot down in flames," said Dad. "I could write a book on giving up smoking; I've done it so many times." He sniffed, and his nose wrinkled at the pungent smell of Airfix glue as he looked over at where I was working. "At it again. If you spent as much time on your studies—"

"Oh, Dad!"

"All right, son. I know. Your mother wouldn't have let you start that until your homework was done. So that's all right. What's this going to be? Another Spitfire—no, two engines: is it a Beaufighter or a Wellington?"

I turned the box top over to show him, and said, "A Heinkel."

"Oh. Another of *theirs*." The corner of his mouth tugged down a bit; he never said anything much about it, but looking back over far too many years, I think he was a little unhappy about how many Luftwaffe aircraft I built. As far as he was concerned, they were still the Bad Guys: it wasn't that long ago that they'd done their level best to drop bombs on him. "Heinkel bombers were mostly the kind that Tom and the rest of us saw during the Blitz."

"Not this one, Dad. The ones in the Blitz were the early types with a dorsal emplacement—a sort of greenhouse-thing on the back. This has a proper upper turret. . . ."

Then I stopped my babbling because there was an odd expression on my father's face. "Turret, emplacement, whatever," he said and picked up the half-built kit.

He pretended to study it, gave me a long, thoughtful look, and set it down again. "It looks enough like one from the Blitz for me. I'm sorry to be so poorly informed about the fine details of aircraft terminology. But don't forget, son, *I* only ever saw them from underneath."

He went off to get himself a cup of tea, and started chatting to my Mum. I felt embarrassed, and somehow unnerved. I wasn't sure why. But soon enough I found out.

The reunion party, two weeks later, started as it usually did in our sitting room: twenty or so middle-aged men in dinner jackets and their wives in going-out dresses, all gossiping about stuff that meant nothing to me until the taxis arrived to take them all to the restaurant and dance hall. My sisters had gone off to stay at a friend's house for the night, so I was all by myself when I was brought in to make my introductions. That was when I got to show off the two big American fire engines in the china cabinet and natter on about how detailed they were.

I was pleased at how closely the older men looked at them . . . so pleased that I didn't notice, at the time, how strange some of those looks were.

Aunt Margaret was minding the house while Mum and Dad went off to the dinner, and she was pretty strict about bedtime. That was why, for the first time since Christmas, I didn't have time to put the toys and the fire chief helmet back into the cabinet before I had to make my goodnights. Instead the vehicles were carefully set out on a shelf in my room, and the helmet was perched on a bedpost over my head, while the grown-ups finished whatever it was that grown-ups did before an evening out. They were still there when I finished reading my book, and turned out my light, and lay back to sleep.

There were bombers overhead. Plastic ones, from Airfix—or Revell, or Frog, or maybe even hard-to-find Lindberg. A Heinkel, a Junkers, and a Dornier were suspended from my bedroom ceiling on fine white thread. They were harried by a Spitfire and a Hurricane, and if the Spitfire was a Mk IX from 1943 and the Hurricane was a Mk IIb from the Western Desert, it didn't matter much. Airfix had done their best, the intent was there, the Bad Guys were being shot down, and I could sleep well.

Lying back in bed and staring up into the darkness, I could see the vague outlines of the model planes hanging there, no more than silhouettes against the white paint of the ceiling. As someone's car turned the corner at the end of our road, a beam of light shone through a crack where my bedroom curtains didn't meet. The car continued its turn, and the light continued its sweep, for all the world like a searchlight from some wartime newsreel. It illuminated the planes as it passed. But not all of them; the Spitfire and the Hurricane remained hidden in shadow, and only the German bombers showed briefly before the darkness swallowed them up again.

There are times, just as you're drifting off to sleep, when you jerk all over as if you're trying to keep yourself from falling out of bed. This was one of those times—except that the jerk felt just like something had lifted the entire bed into the air and let it drop.

And then it happened again.

I sat up in bed in complete shock. Or had I already been sitting that way? A blast of icy wind was hitting me full in the face—no draft from an open window, but the sort of wind that forces tears from your eyes.

I blinked the tears away—and what swam into focus as my vision cleared made no sense at all. I was sitting up, all right, but not in my bed. I was staring down a nighttime country road illuminated only by the harsh yellow-white glare of headlamps and the staccato flicker of red lights. Between me and the road was a windscreen that was doing something, though not nearly enough, to break the freezing hurricane that came at me over the long hood covering a very big engine indeed.

That engine was roaring at full throttle as the vehicle plunged down its self-made tunnel of light. The vehicle's cab had no roof, no walls, no doors. I stared around in disbelief, feeling horribly exposed not just to the wind, but to the landscape whipping past entirely too close to me. The hedges were bad enough, but the occasional buildings or stone walls were far worse. Whatever I was in, was *big.* And the strangest thing was that though I was sitting on the extreme right of the wide, leather-upholstered bench seat, *there was no steering wheel in front of me—*

I half turned toward the man sitting to my left, and looked past him toward the driver, who was sitting on entirely the wrong side. The dim glow from the dashboard instruments didn't light up their faces at all well. The reflection from the headlamps helped a bit, but those flashing red lights did strange things to the shadows so that the only thing I could be sure about was that my two companions were both wearing helmets with a familiar silhouette—helmets like the one on my own head.

American fire helmets. I put my hand up to mine—

And suddenly it all made sense. Suddenly, as always, I was equal to the task. I knew what we had to do.

Recognition flooded over me at the sight of the red

hazard beacons all around, the Mars lights with their unmistakable figure-eight wig-wag, the Buckeye Roto-Rays spinning like electric pinwheels. There was another vehicle close behind my own, headlamps blazing and engine bellowing. If they had ever just been toys on a shelf, they were much more than that now. These were full-size fire engines, their emergency blinkers furiously flashing as they stormed along a country road.

"Bells and sirens," I said, "now." The man sitting next to me reached out to the dashboard, the bell on the pumper I was riding started clanging, and its siren spooled up to an ululating banshee yowl only a few seconds later. It was echoed by the same alarms from the aerial ladder behind me until we were racing through the night on the wings of a thoroughly off-key song.

Then we started slowing down. Other lights ahead of us were waving from side to side, and the head-lamps picked up a striped wooden barricade across the road. As the pumper truck rolled to a stop, some-one flicked the beam of a flashlight full into my face.

"Quicker than we were expecting," said the man behind the light. "No complaints there." The beam played over my truck, then the big hook-and-ladder behind me, and that same voice muttered something that sounded like an oath. "Where the hell did you come from? Drogheda? Dundalk?"

I remembered the label on the box, and without thinking said, "No, New York," then bit my tongue as the voice swore again, in disbelief this time. "We're on a courtesy call," I said.

"I wasn't expecting. . . ." There was a brief exchange I couldn't hear, a couple of raspy opinions, then, "I'm not objecting, understand that. And we appreciate the courtesy, too. But if we're getting unexpected help from any other neutrals, then we should look out for the Swiss and the Swedish fire brigades as well. They might not speak English as well as you do, er . . . ?"

"Chief." That was what it said on my helmet anyway. "New York Ladder Company"—I grabbed for a number—"Twenty-Five."

"You're a bit young for a chief, aren't you?" My eyes had adjusted to the darkness, and the man with the flashlight had POLICE in big white letters across his helmet. It was a British army helmet, a real "tin hat" from the Second World War. There was another man behind him, and though I couldn't see anything worth reading on *his* helmet, I could see the Lee-Enfield rifle cradled in his hands. It wasn't pointed at me; at least, not yet.

"My first turnout. I didn't have much choice." Which was more than the truth.

"Like I said, no objections," the man said. "But my God, you've got a big one for your first. Happy Easter, chum! Now let's have those lights out. You don't have blackout hoods on them. Jerry's been able to find his way in well enough tonight; let's not make it any easier, eh?"

"Right." When the headlamps and the emergency beacons went out, it got darker than I could have believed, an almost tangible blackness studded with stars and stitched with the thin beams of shrouded flashlights. There were a couple of dim red lights ahead of me, and over the grumble of the fire truck's idling engine I could hear motorcycle engines being kicked into life.

"Follow the dispatch riders. They'll lead you where you're needed—though from the sound of things, once you pass Hillsborough, you'll know damn well where you're going. And . . . Thanks, mate!" I heard the slam of boots that told me he had come to attention.

I returned the salute, whether the policeman could see it or not, and gestured to the silent driver on my left. Except for me, not one of the firefighters had said

a word. They'd just sat there, like dummies. Or
toys . . .

But when the transmission grated briefly before the
truck began to move, and that first instant of motion
kicked me in the small of the back, I realized that
whether this was a dream, or a nightmare—or something else entirely—I was going to have to stay with
this ride from its beginning right through to whatever
waited at the end. And I knew, at the pit of my flut-
tering stomach, that I didn't want to wake up any
sooner than that.

The policeman was right. Well before we got where
we were going, the indigo of the night sky had started
to change until its northeastern horizon was an
amber-red glow that washed out the stars. It wasn't
a steady glow, either; it shifted and wavered like
something alive, and there were frequent blinks of
vivid yellow as if someone was touching off enormous
flashbulbs. Even though there were a few sparks in
the sky that suggested fireworks—or more probably
antiaircraft fire—most of the flashes came from the
ground.

"Bells and sirens," I said again. We'd been running
in silence—except for the sound of the fire truck and
motorcycle engines—for almost two hours, and any
noise was better than the jangling tension that had
been growing in my gut. There'd been no way to ease
it with conversation, either: none of the other men on
the truck had spoken a word for all that time, or even
changed expression. Once my eyes adjusted to the
near-total darkness, all I could see was faces fixed in
square-jawed determination. They showed no fear,
which was good, but also no sense that they knew how
to handle whatever was awaiting us. Indeed, nothing
showed on their faces that hadn't been molded there.
I was starting to be scared again, to be ten again.
I swallowed.

But there was the helmet. It was going to have to

get me through this. I reached up, shaking a little, touched it again—

And then, whether the helmet had anything to do with it or not, I recognized our destination. Even in the darkness of a blackout, even with the glare of enormous fires and the spasmodic flash of explosions changing the appearance of familiar landmarks like the broad high face of Cave Hill above the city, I could see that we were heading into Belfast. I realized, as everyone else there had done in the past few ghastly hours, that once they'd been able to move their air bases into France, the Luftwaffe were able to reach Northern Ireland after all.

I'd never read much about any air attacks on Belfast during the Second World War; there'd been no mention of it at all in my *Encyclopedia of Twentieth-Century Warfare*, and if a book like that didn't have the information, there couldn't have been much to comment on. At least, nothing of interest to those editors. Even the word *blitz* seemed almost completely associated with mainland Britain, so much that when my Dad had used the word, I thought he'd been talking about London. Apparently not: as yet another stick of bombs stomped like giant footsteps across the horizon, I guessed that his war might not have been as boring as I'd thought.

The air-raid sirens were still wailing as we drove into the city, though what with the fires and the explosions and the throbbing desynchronized beat of scores of aircraft engines, they hardly seemed necessary anymore. And just as I'd seen in my bed as I drifted off, there were planes above my head—but those had been small, safe models, each hanging by a thread. The shapes I saw now were neither small nor safe. They were ugly black crosses moving all over the sky, and what fell from them wasn't confetti.

The American fire trucks looked way out of proportion compared to the small British-built pumps and ladder-escape engines, and I suspected the drivers were finding Belfast's narrow dockland streets as tight a fit as the country roads on the way to the burning city. Our big vehicles didn't belong alongside the home-bred stuff, City Fire Brigade apparatus or fire engines that had driven in from Lisburn and Lurgan. Our crews looked wrong as we pulled up outside the first block of burning buildings and piled out, starting to work; their big helmets and long bunker coats looked strange alongside the tin hats and shiny-buttoned tunics of the local men as they started unreeling hoses, raising up the ladders. I stood among them in the whirl of sparks and the gusts of hot wind, trying to work out where to start killing this roaring, deadly beast that was eating my city. Some of my crew headed over to the hydrants, dragging the hoses behind them, and offered up the connectors to them.

A sudden fear seized me as the two sets of metal-work got close to each other. The American equipment was too big, it would never match up—

But in the furious glow of the fires, I saw the metal at the hose ends change, go soft—like plastic. If the helmet knew what to do while we were playing this game, so did the equipment. The connections went home. My crew started charging the hoses; the canvas squirmed like snakes, swelled and went heavy as the water came spitting and crackling out.

I started to look back at the fire—and then saw him; a man with heavy eyebrows and a cleft chin, wearing the black tunic of an Auxiliary and with the two stripes around the crown of his helmet that showed the rank of Leading Fireman. He wasn't commanding a fire engine, just a towed pump, but he was directing his crew in putting out the blaze in a neighboring building with a calmness and control that I envied.

I wasn't fooled, though. I saw the fear in his eyes. I desperately wanted to speak to him, to tell him it was all going to be all right, that he would survive.

I didn't dare. I didn't know what was going to happen; suddenly nothing was certain except that the man who would one day be my father didn't need to think that this Yank in his weird hat was crazy. I swallowed hard down a throat that had gone very tight and blinked rapidly—probably from the fire, that smoke was thick—then got on with business.

The stark outline of the aerial ladder rose like the neck of a prehistoric monster against the background of the nearest building, a burning warehouse, and almost before it had reached full extension there was a fireman scrambling up it—one of *my* firemen, with a big coil of hose over one shoulder. A few seconds later, he had the nozzle deployed and was starting to play the high-pressure jet across the base of the nearest fire.

There were so many other noises—roaring flames, hissing water, the hammer and quick-revving growl of trailer pumps, even the occasional rumble and crash as a building came down—that we shouldn't have been able to hear the one that underlay them all. But we did, when the hitherto constant and unchanging drone of the bombers above was altered, and one thread of that tapestry of sound pulled loose and began to stretch. Everyone who wasn't already busy with the fire glanced up. The engine note slid along some tuneless scale from hum to whine until it became a bellow of raw noise that Dopplered across the sky at rooftop height.

In all that unbelievable racket I wouldn't have dreamed I could hear anything else, but I did: a stuttering rapid rattle in time with the yellow-white muzzle flashes from the aircraft's nose and belly as it swept over our heads. Red paint spalled away from half a dozen shiny bare-metal disks on the fire truck's door as it kicked under my hand and slammed viciously shut; two of the windows broke and a splinter of glass scored my face.

Then the plane was gone again.

It had only been there for a single shocking second, but that was just long enough for me to see the taper-

ing Perspex nose, the wide wings and the shark-sleek
belly with its bomb bay gaping like an open mouth,
everything glinting copper-red in the reflected glare
from the fires.

Heinkel! The identification came out of nowhere,
but that conical fully glazed snout was unmistakable—
and then a sudden realization. *You know, you* can't
see the upper turret from down here. The thought shot
through my mind and left it empty—as empty as the
top of the ladder, where a man had been a second
before.

I stared in shock and anger for just a second, and
snarled one of the words my dad hated hearing me
use; then, because there was nothing else to do, I got
back to work.

It was almost dawn before the next fire engines arrived. They looked more at home than the big pumper
and aerial ladder trucks because though they certainly
weren't as local as the Northern Irish apparatus, they
were at least based on the same Dennis or Leyland
chassis. It was the insignia painted on their sides that
told how non-local they really were: these were the
crests of fire brigades from cities well south of the
border. Their crews, volunteers to a man, had driven
through the night until they reached the border, and
then, just as we had done, without blackout shrouds
for the headlights they'd driven the rest of the way in
darkness, with only the red tail-lights of the dispatch
riders to guide them away from the ditches.

As the Irishmen moved in to take over from my
crew, I sat back on the seat of the pumper truck. I
felt more tired than I'd ever been in my life, and as
my leaden eyelids flickered shut, I let myself unwind,
rocked by the bump and sway of the truck as it began
to drive away, sung to an uneasy sleep by the single-
note lullaby as Belfast's sirens sounded the all-clear—

—And then my eyes snapped open. There were aircraft above me again; but now they were plastic things,

each hanging by a thread. For the first time, the sight of them gave me a brief shudder.

The light in my room hadn't changed. How long had I been asleep? Had the siren awakened me just when I was dropping off? It wasn't an air raid all-clear after all, just the alert call that summoned my town's volunteer firemen to the station at the bottom of the Antrim Road.

I scrambled out of bed and hurried to the window, hearing the engine's twin electric bells long before the growl of the big eight-cylinder Rolls-Royce engine came blasting along Bachelor's Walk. Seconds later the apparatus itself came roaring up Railway Street, a bright red Dennis-Merryweather F12 with its amber warning blinkers waking strange jerky shadows beyond the glare of its headlights. With a metallic grunt of changing gears it accelerated down Bridge Street and away toward the Saintfield Road, leaving only echoes and dazzle behind.

After a few moments, my mind still full of bells and sirens from both dream and waking, I turned in the darkness to look at the shelf where the pumper sat. Then I blinked, because things didn't seem to be where I'd left them; some figures seemed to be missing.

I leaned close to the shelf. Even just by the dim reflection of the streetlights from outside I could see that both fire engines were scraped and dented. There were holes in the body panels, far more realistic that the ones I put into my model aircraft with a heated needle, and some of the plastic windows weren't just broken, but perforated and starred in a way I didn't know how to replicate.

And there were more fire axes and extinguishers than red plastic hands to hold them.

In eight places where there should have been toy firemen, there were now eight small red lumps, like raspberry chewing gum, along the running boards of both trucks. I had owned this toy set for long enough to give its fire crew names, to know their little plastic personalities: how one balanced better on the ladder than another, and which one had a tiny molding flaw that meant he could wear no other helmet but his own. I knew them, knew who they were—or who they'd been. Just toys that had suffered the fate of most toys, nothing more than molded plastic turned to molten plastic.

But the whole set smelled . . . bad. I smelled damp, charred wood and petrol; a chemical stink like the old redhead matches, and everything else smelled like a forgotten barbecue. Not like burned plastic, but like burned meat.

I went back to bed and got under the covers and pulled them around me. I huddled up and tried, tried hard, to go back to sleep. But there was no sleep for me that night. Behind my eyes, waiting, was the memory of fire from the sky.

The nightmares lasted for the next couple of weeks, through Easter and well past it. And then, as kids will, I calmed down. I don't know what my parents made of the nights I woke up crying, startling them out of bed. Maybe they thought I was getting worried about the upcoming Eleven-Plus exam at school. If they did, that was fine with me. It was an easier explanation than the truth.

But I didn't play with the fire trucks anymore. No one particularly noticed that I never asked to get them out of the china cabinet. That suited me, because I wasn't brave enough to tell anyone that I didn't even want them in the house; it would have caused too many questions.

But there they were whenever I went into the sitting room. After a while it started to seem as if they were watching me somehow. After a while it just got to be too much.

So who do you talk to, when you want to get rid of the best toy you ever had?

You talk to the one who bought it. But I didn't dare come at the question straight on. The one thing my dad had never, ever talked about was what he did in the war . . . so I took a chance that I might be able to get at the problem sideways, and one quiet afternoon I asked him.

He looked at me strangely, then got himself a glass of Bushmills whiskey and sat down. I already had a cup of hot chocolate, and we drank quietly together for a few moments like two grown-ups.

"We weren't ready," he said at last. "Nobody believed the Germans could get as far as Belfast, or even make the effort when the industrial midlands of England were that much closer. After all, they hit Coventry more than forty times, besides the big one in all the history books. We lost almost as many people in just four raids, but try and find *that* written down somewhere. What happened here was an embarrassment; something better forgotten because nobody had ever bothered to think about what might invite the bombers in; about all the inviting targets we had. Harland and Wolff's, the biggest shipyard beyond Clydeside in Scotland, and Short Brothers, which made Stirling bombers and Sunderland flying boats. Just the sort of thing an enemy'd want to stamp out, and it was easy because both factories were right alongside each other. One good raid would be enough. We got that raid. It was so bad—and we were so unprepared—that we ended up having to ask for help from south of the border."

"But, Dad, I thought that Ireland was neutral during the war."

"They *were* neutral. They didn't want to be on anyone's side—even though they'd seen what had happened in Belgium and Holland, and those countries were just as neutral. The joke was that if Britain fell and Germany took over Northern Ireland, the Panzers wouldn't stop at Newry even if De Valera were lying in the road. But thank God, their firemen didn't stop at Newry either. They'd driven all the way from Dundalk and Drogheda, from Dublin and even from Dun Laoghaire—"

"That far?" I said. Dublin was more than a hundred miles south, and before the good roads were built, it was at least five hours away.

"That far." Dad reached up to my school shelf, where all the boring books were kept, and showed me a map of Ireland. "From here, and here, and here—"

He looked at me, and through me, and took a sip of his whiskey. I matched him with a sip of hot chocolate, even though it wasn't very hot anymore.

"And there were two that came from somewhere a lot farther away. They must have been a gift. . . ." Dad looked thoughtful, as if he were running that word through his head again and playing with a concept that he didn't feel like mentioning aloud. Then he shook his head as if dislodging the thought. "A gift to some town down south, from New York or maybe Boston, one of those places that sometimes thinks they're Irish rather than American."

"Like my present at Christmas? The big fire engines?"

"Just like them. That's what I thought when I saw the Fire Chief set in the shop. All red paint and polished chrome, not something you use in wartime at all. The people in those big wagons didn't seem to care how visible they were. And there were a lot of them; a bigger crew than any of our tenders could carry. It's a long time ago, but they sounded American. And that was impossible, because America was even more neutral than Ireland right then—"

Dad shook his head. "It doesn't matter. Whoever they were, they weren't neutral against flames. And I suppose we'd have put out the fires without them—eventually—but. . . ."

Dad's face went remote, as if he weren't talking to me anymore. "We climbed up the ladders to put out fires on the roof of one building," he said. "And every now and then one of the meaner bomber pilots would dive down low to let their belly gunners have target practice on the men at the top of the ladders. We were silhouetted so nicely they couldn't miss. Bastards."

I was shocked; Dad never used bad language. But he didn't notice my reaction at all. "Now when the big American apparatus arrived, their men went up the ladders as well. And sometimes *they* didn't come down again. That's why I'm still here. Because we went up the ladders in alphabetical order, and because there were extra men from that big crew, the bombers went away before it was my turn." Dad looked into the fireplace, where the coal had collapsed into a bed of glowing embers: and he wasn't looking at that fire, I felt sure, but another, bigger one long ago. "Do you really want to get rid of those toy fire engines, son?"

I hesitated, then made up my mind and nodded. "Yes."

Mum was annoyed at the sudden disappearance of my favorite toy, but when Dad told her that we'd given it away to a charity shop, she seemed content enough. I don't know if he told her anything about our conversation. He never mentioned it to me again.

The reunions of Dad's fellow firemen continued each year, and each year there would be one or maybe two fewer members at the party. Then came was the year *I* was invited, having just turned eighteen. There I was in my dinner jacket, feeling like James Bond, with my first beer in my hand—not that I cared. I kept quiet and listened when those men started talking, and I heard things that I'd never read in my school history books.

People I knew to be as Orange as a bottle of Florida juice were raising their glasses to "the men from the South," and saluting "the night the D-Specials came

over the Border." "D-Specials" was a sort of Ulster
in-joke. And though the hair stood up on the back of
my neck at the memory of the last time I'd heard
anyone use that word—with a background of the slam
of bombs, the slushy smash of falling buildings, all
orchestrated to the background throbbing bass line of
bombers—I stayed where I was and listened as they
told the stories I suspect they retold for their own
comfort rather than any effect they might have on me.
One in particular got my attention, about a family dug
out of a collapsed building near Harland and Wolff's
shipyard. When the family's father couldn't recognize
their rescuers' uniforms and asked where they were
from, the answer came back, "Dublin Foìre Brigade,
sor."

"Dublin . . . ? Oh my God, I didn't think the Germans had bombs big enough to blow us that far!"

The men in the room laughed dutifully, though they
must all have heard that one a hundred times. "As
well none of that other lot came along to dig 'em out,
then," said one of the oldest of the men, "or they'd
have thought they were in America."

There was a sudden quiet over on that side of the
room, and two of those old hard-faced, harsh-voiced
men reached for the whiskey bottle at the same time.
"You know the U.S. Consulate still says it never happened," one said.

The first and oldest man said another of those dirty
words, but only under his breath—for my sake, I suppose. "And I know what I said. When that Yank fire
chief in his fancy hat says to me, 'I wasn't expecting
this,' I up and tells him to his face, 'No. You wouldn't.
It may be all over the newsreels, Chief, but usually
you lot have the Atlantic in the way. Not tonight,
though. When you see him, you can tell your Mister
Lindbergh that he can play the isolation card all he
likes, but he and his *buddies* might wake up one morning and find they're involved in this party whether

they like it or not. And they might not even get an invitation—'"

"Thought you signed the Official Secrets Act, Sam."

Sam scowled. "They *were* there. I saw them. No bloody bureaucrat can make me forget—"

"Sam, those people can make your family forget *you* ever existed, so don't mess around. Let's change the subject."

"Why? This is just getting good—"

"Little pitchers, Sam—"

They were all looking at me sidelong. I stuck my nose into the flattening beer and pretended I hadn't heard a thing.

Later, though, I came back to the business, trying to solve the problem that just wouldn't go away. At university, for "research," I got into all the period war records that were legally available . . . even, when I made some friends in the Public Records Office, some that weren't quite as legal as all that. They were quite clear about the personnel who came north of the border on the night of 15 April 1941, doing a breakneck sixty miles an hour in that pitch-dark. There were no fatalities among the Irish fire crews, but those records are just as clear about the men who went up the ladders in alphabetical order—and who were shot off as they stood at the top.

Yet on that grim night when it was my dad's turn to make the long climb, enough—others—had gone up before him so that he was able to climb back down again. Is it enough to just be molded in the *shape* of people who go in harm's way to save the lives of strangers? And if the shape is there, does the spirit somehow find its way to where love needs it to be?

No amount of musty records have ever had the answers to those questions. My dad's a quarter-century gone now—what the fire couldn't do to him cigarette smoke did at last. After he died, I wanted to repay whatever debt I owed by becoming a fireman myself, but it didn't happen. I failed the physical, and just sitting behind a desk wouldn't have been enough.

But I still collect model fire engines. I've got examples from all over the world: Britain, Europe, and of course North America. There's a space in my collection reserved for an open-cab hook-and-ladder and its matching pumper; New York Fire Department, from some time in the 1930s. I'm not absolutely sure whether I'm looking for a Mack, or a LaFrance, or some real oddity like an Ahrens-Fox: the certainty that lived in me when I had that helmet on is long gone now.

Still, maybe one day I'll find it. And on that day I'll have to make a choice. Not the usual one for a collector, which is "Can I afford it?," but "Do I want to have it in the house?"

Because if it smells of smoke and scorched meat, the answer will be *no*.

THE REVENGE OF CHATTY CATHY

Jody Lynn Nye

"Her name's Chatty Cathy," Perinda's mother, Cherille, told her, handing her the big, brown paper bag. "I wanted one just exactly like her when I was a little girl like you are now. You are lucky you have her."

Perinda stuck out her lip, knowing she didn't look much like a fully grown-up seven-year-old at the moment. She crossed her arms and sat back in the worn rear seat of the ancient gold Buick. She had had to sit out in the cold on this miserable, dim day, while her mother went in without her, and she didn't get to choose her own birthday present. Having an early December birthday was the pits. All the good stuff was bought already for other children's Christmas presents.

"I don't want an old white doll with brown hair from some resale store. I want a Bratz doll with maybe a motorcycle and an iPod. And some outfits."

"Well, I want the moon," Cherille said, climbing into the driver's seat and looking back over her shoulder. "We're both just about as likely to get what we want. I wish I could shop in Bloomingdale's for you, but we can't afford it. Baby, you have just got to learn how to be happy with what you've got. Take it or I'll take it back. You decide."

"Well . . ."

The girl studied the box in her arms. The doll was kind of pretty. Her hair was the color of chocolate. She liked chocolate. And the eyes were blue, really pretty, with long eyelashes. When she tilted the big doll backward, the eyes closed. That was kind of cool. Bratz dolls' eyes didn't close. They were painted on. Still this doll had on the oldest, most moldiest of outfits. It was a red dress with a petticoat, like Perinda wore to church on Sunday. But Chatty Cathy had an interesting face. It wasn't too pretty, and the big blue eyes looked like they had some brains behind them. But what was Perinda thinking? It was just a doll. Dolls were plastic. They didn't have brains.

"It's nice." She knew she sounded half-hearted but it was hard to make her expectations climb down to reality. The doll looked up at her hopefully.

"Try the pull-string," Cherille said.

Perinda hooked her finger into the plastic loop and pulled it. It drew a string out of Chatty Cathy's back about a foot. When Perinda let it go, a high-pitched voice cooed.

"I love you."

"See?" Cherille beamed. "Isn't that cute?"

Perinda would rather have had her fingers cut off with a plastic picnic knife than agree with her mother out loud, but she did think it was kind of cute. "I guess." She tried the string again.

"Will you play with me?"

"Go on, honey, take her out of the package."

Reluctantly the girl pulled open the flap on top of the box and eased out the long card out to which Chatty Cathy was attached with plastic bands. She undid the ties in the back of the cardboard. The doll slid down so she was sitting in Perinda's lap. Unwittingly the girl's arms slid around her and held her tightly. It felt right to hug the doll. She felt a charge like electricity, like she'd been waiting a long time to find something this special. She hugged her again, deeply content. Chatty Cathy's big blue eyes blinked up at her.

"You're my best friend," Chatty Cathy said. And she meant it. How long had she been waiting on that dusty shelf, hoping for a real live girl to be friends with her? Years and years had come and gone. Once in a while the man in the shop had taken her down to be examined by various shoppers in search of a birthday or Christmas present. They had pulled her string and listened to her talk. Each and every one had smiled politely and turned away. The man had put her back on the high shelf, behind the fading teddy bears and the plastic Fisher-Price train. After many years, a new manager lowered her price. That did it. This was the moment she had hoped for since the day she had been placed in her box back at the factory. She had been ready to be a friend and confidante. Her miniature record player was in pristine shape. Her dress was neatly pressed, her hair coiffed, and the bloom on her cheeks and lips just the right shade of pink to look like a healthy human girl. She tweaked her smile to be just a little brighter, and saw an answering expression from Perinda. This was the right girl. She was very special. They were going to be good friends, now and forever. She'd do anything to make Perinda happy.

"Isn't that nice?" Cherille asked, as she pulled away from the curb. "Happy birthday, honey."

"Thank you, Mama," Chatty Cathy said a little bumpily.

"Thank you, Mama," Perinda echoed. She lifted her hand to pull the string again, then dropped it. It seemed as though the doll talked by itself. That was kind of awesome.

"My name is Cathy. What's yours?"

"I'm Perinda," the girl said before she realized she was talking with a doll.

"That's pretty. You're pretty," the squeaky voice said.

Perinda pulled at one of her multiple braids self-consciously. "No, I'm not."

"Brown eyes are beautiful."

"Well, thanks."

"You're welcome. You have a nice nose, too."

"It turns up too much."

"Noses should turn up."

Perinda laughed.

"Honey, it sounds like you like your Chatty Cathy."

"She says a lot of things," Perinda said, a little more enthusiastically. "I didn't know they talked so much."

"Where do we live? Are we going there now?"

Cherille's eyes in the mirror looked doubtful. "I never heard of them saying *that* before."

"I'm sorry," Chatty Cathy said, in a doleful voice. "I don't mean to be nosy."

"It's okay," Perinda said, cradling the doll. It made her feel warm and happy to hug her. "Mama, you hurt her feelings."

"Well I didn't mean to," Cherille said, amused. "I'm sorry, Chatty Cathy."

"I'm happy. Are you happy?"

Perinda thought about it for a moment. "Yeah, I guess. Yeah."

Cherille relaxed in her seat. She had known that her daughter was going to be a little disappointed at getting yet another birthday present from the resale shop, but she seemed to be cheering up. Chatty Cathy was a big success. Who'd have known it had such a sophisticated talk box for such an old toy? No wonder it had been so expensive back in the day it was new. The doll must have used a prototype of artificial intelligence. It was still pretty costly, even in the resale shop. But it was worth every penny to see her daughter's smile as she talked with the doll on her lap. She hadn't been smiling much lately. Their neighborhood had gotten dangerous enough over the last few months that mothers were keeping their kids upstairs in their apartments after school instead of letting them loose in the playground. Perinda, the only one in her grade in their building, had been very lonesome lately. Sounded like she had a new friend, even if it was a toy.

"How old are you?" Chatty Cathy wanted to know.

"I'm seven. Tomorrow."

"Happy birthday!"

"Well not yet," Perinda said sheepishly. "Tomorrow."

"I'll say it again tomorrow. I promise. I love you."

"Well I love you, too," Perinda replied. She hugged the doll. It felt as if the doll hugged back. Even if it was just her imagination, it felt nice.

Cherille was so engaged by the conversation going on in the backseat that she wasn't paying a lot of attention to traffic. A car horn honking brought her back to reality. She jammed on the brakes, and ground to a halt just inches from the fender of a fancy dark blue BMW, driven by a white man in a North Face jacket. Cherille tried to look apologetic. He gave her the finger, and zoomed through the intersection just before the light changed. She shook her head and took a right into the grocery store parking lot.

There were no spaces. She crept out and around to the right again, into the alley, where sometimes there was room to park illegally between the Dumpsters. It was nearly dark, but she managed to get the car in underneath a fire escape without scraping anything.

"Now I'm just going to get some milk and some cereal," Cherille said, turning around to Perinda. "You two stay here and behave yourselves. All right?" She shoved open the door with her elbow.

That was when she felt the cold ring of a gun's barrel touch her temple. She slewed her eyes leftward to the cold, dark eyes of the man holding it. He wore a leather jacket over a filthy green hooded sweatshirt. He couldn't have been more than eighteen. Cherille's heart pounded, almost choking her.

"You get out right now, and nothing's gonna happen to ya," he said.

Another man stepped out of the shadows. About thirty years of age, he had pouches beneath his hazel eyes that made him look angry. Cherille tried to drag her purse out unobtrusively with her.

"Leave it!"

Cherille pointed, careful not to move her head. The round barrel of the gun was ice-cold against her skin. "But I've got to get—"

"Move your ass out! Now!"

"You got to let me get my—" The men grabbed her by the arms. They yanked her away from the car and threw her into the heaps of snow plowed up around the Dumpster. Before she could scramble up, the men leaped into the car and roared away down the alley.

Heedless of the cold and wet, Cherille crawled, then ran after her disappearing car. "My baby! Come back with my baby!"

The two men cackled and exchanged high hand slaps. "That was too easy!" the hazel-eyed man said. "You dog, Riff! We sell this, and we can be floatin'."

The youth in the hoodie grinned and leaned over the steering wheel. He aimed the old Buick's headlights straight at an old woman with a cane who was trying to cross the street at a stop sign. Her face went slack with alarm, and she hobbled as fast as she could out of their way. To their glee, she slipped in the gutter and went down on her knees. "You got the gun, you got the world, Paulie. Hey, any money in that purse?"

Paulie turned out the cheap leather bag. "About three dollars. Crap."

"Tough luck. We got the car anyhow."

They zipped through the narrow streets, cutting down alleys and under overpasses. The chop-shop that didn't ask questions was about five miles to the south. With the proceeds from even an elderly car, the two could afford enough crack to keep them high for a few days. The fix they'd gotten the day before was wearing off. Paulie was starting to feel itchy and tense. He needed more, and soon.

They screeched to a halt at a stop sign facing an oncoming patrol car, and sat virtuously waiting for it to cross ahead of them.

"You want me to wave to the cop?" Riff asked.

"Stop it, dammit," Paulie said, scratching his ribs uncomfortably.

As soon as the police car was safely past, Riff stomped on the accelerator and flattened them against the seats. "Whee-hew!"

The men went on congratulating themselves on a successful carjacking, and how easy it was to scare ordinary people into giving up their possessions.

"Hey, I don't care what people got, as long as when I want it, I get it, and they don't have it no longer," Riff said.

A tiny voice interrupted them. "I want my mommy."

Riff jammed his foot down on the brake, bringing the Buick to a halt midblock, causing a delivery van to roll within inches of the rear bumper. The van laid on its horn. Riff automatically thrust his middle finger up out of the window. He turned to look into the darkened rear seat. "What the hell is that?"

Paulie gawked. "It's a kid. A girl."

The little girl trembled, her big brown eyes huge with fear. She pushed herself as far back into the seat as she could. The men glared at her. She managed to get out another sentence. "I want . . . my mommy."

"Oh, *shit!*" Paulie said.

"We gotta get rid of her," Riff said. He hit the gas again, and turned a few corners until they were in a street with several derelict houses with overgrown yards. "There." He pointed to an empty lot on the right, where the acid glare from the streetlights left a deep shadow. "Push her out."

"What?"

"Right there. Do it!"

Paulie couldn't think of a better solution to the problem of compounding kidnapping on top of carjacking. As soon as the Buick slid into the curb, he sprang out, yanked open the back door, and pulled the protesting girl out by one arm. He slung her away from him. She landed in the gray-stained snow and rolled over and over. He jumped back in, and Riff peeled away. He glanced behind him. The kid just lay there where she fell, staring after them with her big brown eyes. She looked forlorn and lost, covered with the dirty snow. Paulie felt bad, but he didn't want no hassles with no kid.

"All right," Riff said, clutching his forehead with one hand. The withdrawal was starting to hit him, too. "That is handled. We gotta get to Buzzy's. I need my fix."

"That was *mean*."

"Shut up." Riff screeched to a halt again. "Dammit, is there another kid in this car?"

Paulie looked in the backseat. "Yeah," he said, grabbing it by the arm. "No, it's a doll. A new doll. Box is right in the corner."

"Bro, toss it out the door after the kid!"

Paulie retrieved the box and inspected it. "No, man, this one's worth money! It's a Chatty Cathy doll. It's vintage. If it's mint, it can be worth bucks. There's a collector store up on the north side. We can go and score some real money for this."

Riff stared at him. "What, you kidding?"

Paulie was serious. He held the little figure up for his friend's inspection. "Nah, man. I saw it on TV, a doll once sold for twenty gees on eBay. I could use some of that."

Riff studied the doll with distaste. "Man up north ain't gonna give us no twenty gees."

"Yeah, but he'll give us what he got. It's new. Kid didn't have a chance to mess it up. Dumb kid, didn't know what kind of a gold mine she was sittin' on."

"That's my mama you're talking about," Cathy said, indignantly.

The two men looked at one another. "Did you pull that doll's string?"

"Hell, no."

"Take me back to my mama."

"Aw, come on!" Riff groaned. "That bull make my head ache. Tear her voice box out."

"No!" Paulie said, throwing a protective hand over the doll's body. "It could ruin her value. We gotta keep her intact until we get to the store."

"You're thieves. You're mean to steal a doll away from a nice girl. She never hurt you."

Riff grabbed the side of his head. The desperation was making his head spin. "I don't know if I can take it! Shut her up!"

Paulie picked up the doll and shoved her into the cardboard box. Her hair and skirt got messed up. He tried to shove his hand down into the box to straighten them. It didn't fit.

"You shouldn't use drugs," Cathy observed. "They make your hands shake. You forgot the plastic ties. I'll slide right to the bottom."

Paulie slid Cathy out and tried again. That time he got the skirt hem to keep from riding up, but the hair got flattened on one side and fluffed on the other.

"I bet your mothers are very ashamed that their sons are thieves," Cathy said, her voice not interrupted at all by the cellophane window of her box. "How would you feel if someone took things away from your mother?"

"My mama been robbed a hundred times," Riff snarled, leaning low over the steering wheel. Cathy was pleased. She was making him think. She could tell he didn't like to think. She pressed a little harder.

"Why don't you protect her instead of picking on

other people's mothers? Where were you the last time she was robbed?"

"Where the hell were *you*?" Riff countered angrily.

"In Snider's Discount Store on North Broadway," Cathy said at once. There was no reason not to tell them the truth. "Waiting for my mama to come and get me. But I bet you could have helped your mother. Why didn't you?"

Riff couldn't take that much introspection.

"Bro, tear her head off! I don't want to hear her voice one more second!"

Paulie cradled the big pink box protectively in his arms. "Riff, if we damage her, we won't get no money!"

"Yeah, money. Gotta have money. Right now." Riff stared out of the windshield. The streetlights were blurring into big stars of light, obscuring everything but the red taillights ahead of him. Drugs. He craved the smooth relaxation of a high. "We'll take it to Mumzir's pawnshop. Yeah. He's pretty close."

"You shouldn't take drugs," Cathy said, as the man in the hoodie steered the car unsteadily. "You can't see well, and your reactions are getting very bad. You almost hit that man walking on the street. He was in a crosswalk, so you were in the wrong. I bet you don't even have a valid driver's license. Does yours say you need glasses? Because you do."

"Shut UP!"

"Look out! You almost hit that man!"

The car swerved as Riff's hands jerked nervously.

"Hey," Paulie said shrewdly, "I bet we get top dollar for her 'cos she can say all these extra things. On the box it says she can only say eleven phrases. I know she's said at least twenty."

"Twenty-eight so far," Cathy corrected him.

"That's gotta mean she's really special. And all the cool stuff about your mama."

Riff yanked the gun out of his pocket and leveled it at his partner's nose. "You shut up about my mama.

You don't say another word about my mama, or I blow you and the doll all over the city."

Paulie held up his hands in surrender. "Okay, man, okay. Cool. Be cool."

The small, neat, dark-skinned shop owner held the box in his hands. "Yes, Chatty Cathy. We do not see very many of these in this condition. Very good." He looked up at the two men leaning over his counter. "Thirty dollars. That is what I will give you for her. Because she is such excellent condition."

"Thirty?" Riff sputtered. "Bro, she's gotta be worth three thousand!"

Mumzir clicked his tongue. "I cannot pay three thousand. She is a 1970s vintage doll, all accessories accounted for, original box. On a generous percentage of a value of perhaps one hundred dollars, I will give you . . . forty."

"But she says all these cool things," Paulie said. "Come on, Chatty Cathy, talk to the man."

The three men looked at the doll. Her big blue eyes regarded them with blank friendliness.

"You must pull her string to make her talk," Mr. Mumzir said, shaking his head scornfully at the stupidity. "It says so right on the carton."

"Hell, no," Riff said. "She was talkin' up a storm in the car. Talk now," he ordered the doll. Mumzir regarded him curiously. "I mean it! What you lookin' at me for? She said things about my mama!"

"I can see that you are high," Mumzir said. "Drugs rot your mind, you know." He pulled the ring on the doll's body.

"Night, night, Mommy," Chatty Cathy said.

"You see, nothing out of the ordinary," Mumzir said, shaking his head. "Forty dollars."

"I want more!" Riff said. He pulled his gun out of his pocket and aimed it at the shop owner. Calmly Mumzir shook his head.

"You are under video surveillance. Besides, my

three brothers have had weapons trained on you since you came in here. Put it away, or I will tell the police when they come to collect your bodies that it was self-defense. We have licenses for our firearms. Do you?"

Riff and Paulie sprang into a back-to-back Starsky and Hutch pose, searching the mirrored cases for signs of the other three Mumzirs. Glaring hatred at the shop owner, Riff stuck the gun into his waistband and yanked the front of the hoodie down over it.

"All right," he said, trying to regain his dignity. "Forty dollars, and make it fast."

Mumzir went to a small keypad set in the wall and started to enter numbers.

"I am stolen merchandise," Chatty Cathy said suddenly. "I am stolen merchandise. They stole me. I am stolen merchandise."

Mumzir's hand dropped from the keypad. "What? Is the doll saying the truth?"

"Naw, it's just a recording, bro," Riff said, casually.

"They stole the car they drove here in, too," Cathy continued. "From a nice lady and her little girl. They threw them out of the car and took it."

"Carjacking?" Mumzir's swarthy cheeks paled. Something was strange. Could this be a police sting? "How dare you come in here! I do not receive stolen merchandise from thieves! Get out." He pointed toward the door.

Riff and Paulie thought about arguing the point, but remembered the guns hidden in the walls.

"All right," Riff said, leveling a finger at Mumzir as he backed toward the door. "But I'll be back. Don't you forget it."

"You don't forget what I say," Mumzir said. "Leave before I call the police! Come back when you actually own what you want to sell me."

Paulie snatched up Chatty Cathy and the carton. The two men made as dignified an exit as they could. The security door snapped shut behind them.

"Will you take me back to my mama now?" Chatty Cathy asked. "Please? I am sure she is very scared."

Riff grabbed the box out of Paulie's hands. "I can't take no more of this damned *doll*!" He wrenched open the Buick's bent trunk lid, threw Cathy inside, and slammed it shut. "Get in! We gonna go right to Buzzy's, right now! I gotta have my fix."

It wasn't very dark inside the trunk. Cathy's box had landed face upward. She could see a few small holes that let in light and sound. From the compartment of the car, she heard the two men arguing. Their voices sounded faint and hollow. They wouldn't listen to her.

The car lurched away from the curb. Cathy went flying against the rear of the trunk. She had to get back to Perinda. She must take care of her newfound mother.

She could hear the noise of other cars and the sloshy footsteps of people on the sidewalks. Each time the car jerked to a halt, she listened for people approaching.

"Help me!" she shouted, straining her speaker to the maximum. "Please, get me out of this trunk! The men driving are very bad. Help me!"

Miranda Benitez hoisted her briefcase strap onto her shoulder. The gold car had stopped for the light right in the middle of the crosswalk. Grumbling, she stepped off the curb and angled around the vehicle's rear end, trying to avoid the slush. Her shoes were already wet, and her toes were beginning to freeze.

"Help me!" a tiny voice said. Miranda looked around. "Please, get me out of this trunk! I have to get back to my mama!"

Miranda realized the voice was coming from the car beside her. There was a little girl in there. A kidnapping! She glanced at the driver, and knew she didn't want to mess with him, but she had to help.

"Hang in there, baby," Miranda whispered. "I'll get help."

She took her cell phone out of the pouch hanging from her purse strap and dialed 911. She dashed out of the crosswalk and stood on the opposite curb.

"Yes, I'm sure what I heard. An old Buick, gold color, license plate number 518 HRM. Hurry! She sounds scared."

"Ah, shit!" Riff said, looking in the rearview mirror at the flashing blue lights. His heart raced. He hoped it wasn't him the cops were following, but the loud hoot of the siren disabused him of the idea. They were only two blocks from Buzzy's! He rolled down the window as the patrol cop approached, and put on a big fat smile. "Can I help you, officer?"

The police sergeant, a burly man with his winter coat buttoned up underneath a jowly double chin, raked Riff and Paulie with a blazing white flashlight beam. "License and registration, please?"

Riff felt his pockets. "Well, I've got 'em somewhere, officer. I'm drivin' on a ticket, okay, bro?" He produced the much folded piece of paper, and held it out with two fingers.

"Registration?"

"Look, it's my mama's car. I don't know where she keeps the registration."

"I see," the cop said evenly. Riff started to relax. He was buying it. "Would you mind opening your trunk, please?"

Warily Riff pushed open the door. The cop stood out a little, not turning his back on the two men. He kept them ahead of him as Riff pulled the key out of the ignition and went around to the back. He felt around for the latch, hoping it wasn't in some weird place. He'd kill that bitch if she had some kind of illegal goods in the trunk! Getting him pulled over, when he had priors in his record!

But, no, there was nothing in there except for that damned doll. The cop rocked back on his heels.

"Can we go now?" Riff asked hastily. "I've got an appointment."

"I guess—" the policeman began.

"Help me," the doll said unexpectedly. "These men stole me from my mama. I want to go back. Please take me to 2534 South Lawndale. It's dark. I bet she's really scared. And cold."

The cop glared at Riff and Paulie, who were trying to edge away onto the curb. "Is this some kind of joke? We got a report from some woman who heard a little girl's voice in the trunk."

"Come on, officer," Riff said ingratiatingly. He leaned a little closer, but the policeman backed away half a pace. "It's just a doll. It goes off all by itself sometimes. It's defective." He slammed his palm down on the box, bursting the cellophane. Paulie let out a gasp and gave Riff a reproachful look. *"What?"*

"That was me, officer," Chatty Cathy said promptly. "Thank you for stopping. These mean men took my mama's mama's car. They pushed her out into the snow. It was a carjacking. They have a gun. They want to buy drugs. They were about to pawn this car with someone named Buzzy. Have you ever heard of him?"

The officer's eyes widened, but his eyebrows lowered until they met at the bridge of his broad nose. "You bet I've heard of him. Buzzy, huh?"

"It's just a doll!" Riff protested.

By then the police officer had his gun in his hand. "All right, you two. Assume the position. I don't care if the doll's defective or not. I'm going to check into this. Where's that gun?"

"Who says I got one?" Riff asked, turning to face the car. He spread his hands on the trunk lid.

"Right now," the cop said, "I'm gonna believe the doll. Where is it?"

"Waistband," Riff choked out. The cop held him down with an elbow and yanked the pistol out of his jeans front. He did a quick patdown of both men, then reached for his radio.

"Dispatcher twenty-six, this is twenty-six-thirty-two. I need a rundown on, er, an eighty-six Buick, license number. . . ."

"My head is killing me," moaned Paulie.

By the time the police sergeant rolled onto the 2500 block of South Lawndale, two other patrol cars were already parked on the grass. A short, broad-faced black woman stood rocking a little girl in her arms. The child's long legs hung limply around her hip, and she had her face hidden in the woman's shoulder. A quartet of officers, one of them a uniformed lieutenant, surrounded them. Cameras with bright white lights were trained on them, and reporters had microphones aimed at their mouths.

"This baby was too scared to talk," the woman was saying, "but I knew she was in trouble. That's when I called you."

The sergeant managed to look dignified as he carried Chatty Cathy over the trampled snow.

"Perinda? Is this your doll?" he asked.

The child raised her head. Her expression of fear and woe changed suddenly as she spotted the doll in his hand. She nodded. The sergeant held it out. The girl reached for it and wrapped it in her arms.

"I love you," Chatty Cathy said at once. Perinda was still too upset to speak, but she squeezed harder and buried her face in the chocolate-colored hair.

The lieutenant gave the sergeant an odd glance. "How'd you know the child's name? We haven't been able to get a word out of her."

The sergeant thought about it for a moment, and realized he didn't want to make a fool of himself in front of the news teams. He'd gotten an earful all the way there, but how could he say his information had come from a fourteen-inch plastic doll with freckles? "Information received, sir. I located the mother. She was down at the sixth Precinct, making a report." The reporters, hearing another source of hot information for their breaking news story, stuck the microphones in his face. The lieutenant looked peeved, but he gave the sergeant a nod to go on. "She's frantic but she's okay. She'll be here any moment. We've arrested two men for an armed carjacking. Down behind the food store on Thirty-fifth Street. Couple of junkies looking for a fix. We've also got them for kidnapping and felony theft. They can't hurt this little girl or her mother ever again. We've recovered the car. It's up at the Tenth Precinct lot."

The reporters burst into a cacophony of questions. The sergeant and lieutenant did their best to answer them over the head of the woman who had taken in the little girl abandoned on the street.

". . . And she is reunited with her precious doll just in time for her very special seventh birthday," one of the on-air reporters told her camera sincerely. "Birthday wishes for this brave little girl can be sent to the Channel Four Web site. The address is on the bottom of the screen."

"You'll be all right now," Chatty Cathy confided to Perinda. "Carjacking carries a mandatory sentence. Those two scary men are going to be locked up for years. Your mother will be here soon. Then we can go home. I can't wait to see our home."

"You came back for me," Perinda whispered. "How come you did all that?"

Chatty Cathy fixed her big blue eyes contentedly on Perinda, and felt satisfied to the depths of her cotton stuffing. "Because you're my best friend."

JACK TAR

Gail Selinger

On his first try Michael's sweaty hand slipped off the doorknob. He glanced back at his friend Steve.

"This is harder than I thought," he said.

Steve put a hand on Michael's shoulder. "It's never easy, trust me."

Michael rubbed his palm against his right leg. He faced the door once more. "Showtime."

The front door creaked open, the hinges squeaking as if it hadn't been used in centuries. Truth be told it had only been a matter of months since Michael's mother passed away, but today was the day of reckoning.

Michael had to sort through the lifetimes of memories that had quietly, insidiously accumulated in this house.

The air in the long-sealed house was musty, and his nose wrinkled as he took a deep breath to prepare to do what had to be done. He took a step forward and reached for the wall switch.

Behind him, Steve was having his own problems with the place.

"Ouch! What the heck? Michael?"

"I warned you," Micheal hit the switch and illumination from the overhead lights flooded the living room.

"Son-of-a—"

"Welcome to pack rat heaven." Michael didn't need

to see Steve's expression. He'd seen all too often what the faces of his friends looked like whenever they stepped over the threshold of his parents' house. The combination of horror, shock, surprise, and amazement was a sight he could live without seeing again.

"Mike, I've heard of hoarding, but this is ridiculous, man."

"Yeah. I know. But you volunteered. I'll get the garbage bags and boxes from the truck. Then we can tackle this mess together."

"You sure you don't want to try arson?" Steve asked.

Michael gave his buddy a look.

"Okay, then." Steve shook his head and rolled up his sleeves. "Let's get started. This is going to take a bulldozer and a lifetime."

Eight hours later Michael sat cross-legged in a cleared space on the floor of the living room. He felt like he'd gone ten rounds with Tyson. His head was pounding, his muscles were hurting, and he was bruised all over after piles of boxes had avalanched on him. More than once. And his sinuses were killing him.

He couldn't decide if the pounding inside his head was the result of the years of dust they were kicking up, the memories the mess brought back, pure stress, despair over ever finishing this task, or if he'd just been whacked too hard by the last box that had fallen on him.

He pulled yet another cardboard box in front of him and ripped the brittle, aged packing tape off the lid. Just as he had before with each previous box, he mentally braced himself. Each box held a mystery. Most often, the cartons revealed absurd collections of junk, like hundreds of cleaned, tenderly saved aluminum and plastic frozen dinner trays.

Sometimes, though, the boxes held emotional time bombs, stuff that brought back a thousand jagged images of his childhood.

Michael ignored the sound of Steve taking the front porch steps two at a time and kept on emptying the carton in front of him until he heard his friend curse out loud.

"Jeez. We've worked all day, and it doesn't look like we threw a frigg'n thing away," Steve said.

Michael bit down on the urge to get defensive. Steve had a point.

Then he saw what Steve was carrying. His friend held up a six-pack and a large steaming pizza box. The smell of garlic and pepperoni filled the room.

"Come out onto the porch," Steve said. "Time for a break. You need to eat."

"In a sec. I'm almost finished with this one." Michael pulled out the last thing in the box, a bundle of dirty crumpled brown paper bound tightly with a frayed string.

He gingerly unwrapped this latest mystery item. As the paper fell away, he froze, a tremor spreading through his body. A faint smile spread up toward his eyes, "Oh my gosh. So there you've been."

It was a shock to the system to remember just how much the tattered figure in his hands had once meant to him.

He tenderly set the childhood treasure in a safe place before he headed out for food and beer.

It was past ten that night when Michael walked through his front door. Immediately a sense of calm washed over him. In contrast to his parents' place—and perhaps as a direct result of his upbringing—his home was decorated in a sleek ultramodern minimalist style.

Very Zen.

Nothing extra.

Nothing out of place.

He didn't need a shrink to understand why. Especially today.

He was exhausted. His skin and clothes were filthy,

and he had some thick mystery substance jammed deep under his fingernails.

But he'd found buried treasure in all the rubble. With the brown paper bundle he'd unearthed clenched protectively in both hands, Michael headed straight into his office. In front of the glass shelves lining the wall behind his desk he proceeded to unwrap the paper once more.

"Whatcha got?"

"Something pretty special. Wanna see?" Michael's son, Jordy, walked into the room, a looming presence entirely clad in black. Even his fingernails were painted black, which Michael suddenly realized was pretty good camouflage for the kind of gross fingernails he currently had. Maybe there was method in the kid's madness. For all the fights he and Victoria had over how their twelve-year-old son dressed, Michael knew Jordy was a sweet kid. He just liked to fit in with his Goth friends—all of them nerdy movie buffs with a fondness for science fiction.

His wife worried. Michael often reminded her of how they'd dressed back when they first met. Tie-dye and ripped bellbottoms might be back, but nobody ever said they were conservative attire. Michael felt Jordy's choice of clothing helped conceal his sickly complexion, but that was hardly something he'd bring up with his wife.

Jordy leaned over his dad's shoulder, and got a good look. "Huh. It's just an old doll." The kid's words were dripping with disappointment.

"No. This is much more than that. It's a family heirloom. This is Jack Tar. Your great-great-grandfather made him. It's older than your mom and me put together. I played with him when I was a kid."

"It dates back to the dinosaurs, then. Wicked! Can I see?"

Michael placed the battered doll into his son's outstretched hand.

With unusual tenderness Jordy turned the small

figure over a few times. "Gosh, you weren't kidding. This *is* old. Looks like it's been around since the Mayflower at least. Weird name, though. Did you name it Jack Tar because it got stained with the stuff?" he asked, looking at a particularly soiled patch.

"Nah. That's what they called sailors back then. And let's talk about something else that's weird. Your math grade. It's nonexistent. What happened?"

"Awwwww, Dad—" Jordy had the grace to look embarrassed.

"Video privileges are suspended until I see a significant improvement."

"But, Daaad . . . the computer helps."

"Good try. Obviously it hasn't helped just yet. So you'll learn the old-fashioned way. No computer, no calculator, just pen, paper, memorization, and your fingers if necessary. I'll be happy to arrange for a tutor if things don't improve fast."

"No! That's for dorks. I'll cope." Jordy shuffled out of the room, but not without a parting shot. "You would have to be a CPA," he mumbled. Micheal could hear Jordy mumbling in protest until the kid's voice faded at the top of the steps.

He knew the kid would buckle down and get to work. He always did.

But he was glad for the moment alone in his office. Michael sat at his deck relishing his privacy and the little figure that he'd so enjoyed in his youth.

"Just as I remember . . . Well, maybe a little dingier."

He looked the toy over carefully. Standing a rigid eight inches tall, there was no mistaking the fact that the doll was hand-stitched and crude. It was handmade with love, a sailor doll intended for a boy to own and cherish. Jack Tar wore a cap of dirty cloth with a red yarn tassel to protect his head from those burning sunny days back in the age before sunscreen. Black thread stitched the outline of the doll's brows and eyes. Twisted string protruded, forming a

prominent nose. A quarter inch of red thread
stitched straight over a jutting jawline gave him a
determined look and a mouth that didn't smile. Michael couldn't tell if the pink blush on his cheeks
was a stain or an intentional touch, but it made the
toy's cheeks look chiseled. A maroon vest cross-
stitched closed with gray shirt sleeves revealed a set
of broad shoulders and a barrel chest. The doll's legs
felt thick and tapered to his feet. Jack's loose sailor
pants made from homespun linen were filthy and
worn thin, marred with an obvious burn mark from
a stray tobacco ash.

Michael leaned the doll against the silver-framed
picture of Victoria and Jordy resting on his desk in
the place of honor. "Welcome home, Jack Tar."

The dream returned that night. A voice calling out
in need, Michael stumbling through pitch darkness unable to discern images, unable to help. Bolting awake,
cold sweat saturating his pajamas, Michael rolled
toward his end of the bed, not wanting to disturb Victoria's sleep. With feet planted firmly on the plush
beige carpet he sent up a hasty prayer that he
wouldn't crumble to the floor when he stood. On
shaking legs Michael headed to his dresser to change.

On his way to raid the refrigerator, a childhood habit
after every nightmare, Michael noticed light coming
from under his office door. Pausing, he heard no
sounds of an intruder. Using his fingertips Michael
gently eased the door open. The room was empty. He
headed for his desk. Everything in the room looked
exactly as he had left it. No, wait; Jack Tar was seated
on the desk blotter, his back leaning against the wal-
nut pen box. Michael swore he'd placed him against
the picture frame. He'd have to speak to Jordy about
putting the doll back on the shelf after he played with
him. Michael turned to leave.

"Been a long while since we chatted, lad. But I
weren't willing to wait in the dark a stitch longer."

Michael swerved and dropped ramrod straight into his chair.

"Not that I be blaming ye. 'Twas that banshee of a mum ye had. Truth be told nor was yer dad a bit o' help, and him knowing better and all." Jack stretched out his legs and crossed his ankles.

Michael shot a glance at the silver picture frame.

"Wasn't needed to be on watch. So I made me self comfortable."

"Right. So, sorry. My apologies. Where were my manners? My not-so-invisible friend, lost, found, coming alive after sundown, *and talking to me once more*! I'm losing it again."

"Quiet yer scuppers, lad. Ye don't want to be waking the house. Just here to help. Always been."

"Tell that to my folks!" Michael shrieked and clasped his hands over his mouth with an audible gasp. He didn't know what angered or frightened him more, that he had told them about Jack all his life and they hadn't believed, or as an adult it was happening all over again.

He felt eight years old again, futilely trying to make his mother understand there was nothing imaginary about his nighttime conversations with Jack Tar. Whenever he turned to his father for help, Ralph simply left the room.

One day, having had enough, his mother calmly informed him that she had thrown Jack Tar into the garbage. Michael had crawled through every filthy trash container on the block looking for his precious friend, all to no avail.

But his mother hadn't been pleased. He'd gotten a mouth full of soap, a bath, and a spanking as his punishment.

"I thought you were gone forever. I guess Dad wouldn't really let her throw you out since great-great granddad made you."

"Ralph wouldn't let the witch chuck me overboard

'cause of the talks we used to have since he were a tyke."

"He knew you were alive at night? But . . . but why wouldn't he be more understanding?"

Jack shrugged. "Never a word to me why. Just one day up on a high shelf I go. No matter what I tried, ner a word between us since till ye pulled me down yerself. And with him knowing what was at stake. Don't think he believed. Afraid to believe. Can't see why not, mind ye." Jack paused, a weary look clouding his black eyes.

"What do you mean he knew what the stakes were?"

"Ye wouldn't have a relaxing pipe full would ye, lad?" Jack asked, neatly sidestepping the question.

"Not at the moment. No one smokes tobacco in this house. It's a filthy habit, you know."

"I'm a touch too old to be changin' me ways," Jack Tar replied.

"I'll see what I can arrange."

Since he'd renewed his nightly conversations with his old friend Jack Tar, Michael felt happier than he had in years. Everyone noticed.

It shocked Victoria the first night he came home at dinnertime and actually spent time with his family. Though Michael locked himself in the office from 11:00 P.M. until he crawled into bed in the very early hours of the morning, Victoria said nothing. She was simply too thrilled to have her husband back. Michael and Victoria were even drawing close once again.

With orders that Clara was no longer allowed in his office to clean, Michael began a small-scale redecorating project for his friend's comfort. Clearing off the top of his liquor cart, he pushed it against his desk.

Michael waited until the house was empty and went on a shopping spree. One day, with Jordy in school and Victoria out on errands, Michael arrived home in the early afternoon fumbling through the front door loaded down with plastic bags garishly advertising "Ye Victoriana Dollhouse Company."

He wanted everything ready for Jack Tar before the sun went down. He could hardly wait to hear what his old plaything would say this night when he awoke.

As if they were puzzle pieces, Michael kept rearranging the dozens of miniature furniture pieces and accessories he'd bought. He wanted Jack Tar to feel comfortable and accepted. The way he'd made Michael finally feel after all these years had passed. But he couldn't curb his apprehension over his choice of pipe tobacco.

Michael, a nonsmoker, hadn't had a clue what type to buy for a vintage sailor. The kid behind the counter in the tobacco shop was of no assistance. The poor kid hadn't even known that tobacco was a long-held naval tradition. Finally, since he liked the look of the red tin, Michael settled on Prince Albert brand.

He knew explaining the sudden tobacco smell that would emanate from his office was going to be tricky. To play it safe he bought a handful of different incense sticks and three types of air freshener, hoping that they would help mask the stench. It wasn't as if Jack Tar could walk out to the porch for a smoke whenever the urge struck him—which is what they made their smoker friends do. Or could he? Would Jordy or Victoria notice an eight-inch sailor doll leaning against a porch column calmly puffing a miniature briar wood pipe?

Michael snorted at the absurdity of the whole situation.

But he still arranged a nice little nook for his old pal to smoke in.

Sipping his drink, lounging on his favorite living room chair, Michael watched Victoria help Jordy with his homework. It felt good to be home. Why hadn't he done this years ago?

He knew the answer. Or at least the answer he'd used to fuel his behavior all those years. He'd worked long hours to give them all this. Now that they had a comfortable life, Jack Tar helped him see this enjoying his success and his family was a reward he could now give to himself.

But enjoying the moment wasn't always all sunshine and happiness.

Deep in concentration over some wretched math problem, Jordy leaned so close to his mother that static electricity intertwined his dark hair with her long blond waves. A stabbing pain of jealousy burned Michael as the innocent scene played out before him. Why wasn't Jordy turning to him for help with his math? Michael was a CPA, after all. But Jordy kept asking his mom for help, not his dad.

Maybe Michael didn't have whatever special thing Victoria possessed to be so intimate with their son. In a move that was unusual these days, Michael topped off his drink. Tonight he didn't care a hoot about moderation in all things.

Jordy left the room. Victoria kissed him good night and headed to bed. But Michael stayed where he was. Unsure why his mood was so sour, he just stayed where he was until he passed out. He awakened only when the twelfth chime of the grandfather clock penetrated his muzzy brain.

"Shit." He got up and stumbled to his office, knowing Jack Tar would not approve when he saw the state he was in. But something was very wrong—something more than his blurry eyes and foggy brain could compute. The office door was ajar, the lighting inside turned up high. Michael crossed the threshold, his eyelids slammed shut in protest against the blinding glare.

Why was the light on?

Jack Tar surely couldn't reach the switch.

Who was in his office?

Forcing his eyelids open, he took a look around. Michael just stared when he saw the answer.

Jordy sat at the desk writing in his homework book, while Jack Tar, puffing on his pipe, stood beside the notebook, pointing at something on the page. They both looked up, boy and toy, as the door slammed against the wall. In a case of equal and opposite reaction, the abused door swung back and clicked shut with the leftover momentum. It barely missed Michael as it did so.

"Hey, Dad, did you know Jack was a navigator?" Jordy asked oblivious to the looming disaster in Michael's expression.

"No, boy. Yer great-great-great granddad, he was the one. But he taught me what he knew."

"Jordy? Aren't you supposed to be in bed? Why isn't your homework done? Why are you . . . ? Hell. Don't you think this is really odd? You're talking to a doll! You're letting a toy help you with your homework."

" 'S okay. Well, yeah, at first it was weird. But he's cool. It's like this. I just came in to check him out the other day—I wanted another look at him. And than it got dark and he stretched. He talked to me first, right, Jack? But it's like those Chucky movies, cool, huh? Anyway, he's not like Chucky. He isn't evil. Right, Jack? He told me all about everything. I looked it up. He's this uh, homocudas and similacron or something."

"Homunculus and simulacra. I know, son. I just didn't think you did."

"Well, I do. It's so, well, way better than any video game or anime. I mean like I wouldn't tell anyone, honest. It's so wicked!"

"Jordy. It's after midnight and a school night. Bed. Now. We'll talk all about this tomorrow."

Jordy looked to Jack Tar. Pipe clenched firmly between his teeth, Jack Tar cocked his head toward the doorway. Jordy slid off the chair, gathering his notebook. "I decided Jack'll be my math tutor. He's really good, man."

"Not a word of this to anyone. Not even your mother."

"Yeah, yeah. I get it. But it's so cool. . . ."

Jack Tar waited until Jordy was out of earshot. "The nipper's a might sickly, ain't he?"

The old toy's astute question hit home and took the wind out of Michael's fury. "Yes. He is. We're not sure what's wrong. The last round of tests were negative. They all come back that way. My wife and I have been worried sick. Doctors can't pinpoint what's wrong, but you can tell something is off by looking at the kid."

"They won't. Put the blame square where it lies. Lad. Your dad."

"What?" Of all the things he'd expected to hear, that was the unlikeliest.

Jack withdrew a match from his pocket and relit his pipe. " 'Tis obvious you never heard what you needed to hear."

"Yeah. My dad never talked much." Michael sat down, rubbing his forehead to ease his pounding head. "I suspect you'd agree."

"Yer great-great-granddad George, now he was a fine man. He had a gift for the stars and sailing. He went around the world more times than can be counted on two hands, and lived to tell the tale. But he was also a man of the heart and missed his family fierce. And he was able to put his longings into action. How else do ye think this can be? Me chatting with you all like nothing's amiss? He made me with his own hands and love he did. Right there on his travels, made me from bits and such to be company for yer great-granddad while he was at sea. But he knew that weren't enough. He needed someone he could trust to look after those he couldn't."

Jack pulled open his tobacco pouch, adding more leaf into the bowl of his pipe. " 'Twas in New Zealand. He saved the life of a young native being used as sport by a handful of ruffians. As a reward the bloke had all George's future generations and me blessed. But there were conditions. All the men of George's line had to be told and be straight up with the tale. Each son before thirteen had to know me and each dad had to add to me special gifts."

"Your gifts? Do I have to teach you how to drive or something?" asked Michael.

"Yer thinking down the wrong route. George gave me his wisdom tooth stitched under me cap for thinking and such. Charlie, yer granddad, chose a piece of moonstone here, here in me chest what helps in any journey's aid. Do ye see what I'm meaning?"

"No. This sounds like some kind of joke."

"Bloody hell, Michael. 'Tis no joke, whatever yer meaning there. George be a sailor true. He believed heartily in the four corners of the compass as special." Jack sighed with frustration at Michael's blank expression.

"George held to four creeds for life well lived. Wisdom, protection, health, and soul. But he were a man of things ye could see and hold."

"But I knew you," Michael protested.

"But not enough. The link first was weakened by Ralph when he chose to disbelieve, now worsened with you losing track o' me, but it be taking deadly toll on Jordy. He be coming onto thirteen and nothings been done to finish the four creeds and keep the line strong."

"This sounds preposterous," Michael stated.

"A doll what lives sundown to sunup and speaks don't sound a mite odd? A doll what watches over a family don't sound like a fishy sailor's tale?" retorted Jack Tar. "But here I stand. No mermaid tale here."

"You're talking to me in riddles!" yelled Michael. "If you're suppose to be here to watch over us just tell me what I need to do."

"If only I could, lad. I can sail ye on the route with an aye or nay to whatever yer thoughts be, but that be the only map clues I can give."

"Thanks, George." Michael sighed. "Great job."

"It weren't him that done it this way." Jack Tar seemed to have some sympathy for his pain. " 'Twas the blessing, to make each lifeline stronger than the next. Ye best think hard on it, Michael. Jordy's coming of age. Health and soul. Yer all sons of a sailor. Think hard, lad. Think hard."

Michael cancelled his future appointments until further notice, virtually closing himself to all things but family and research. He knew he couldn't share his burden with anyone. Health and soul, sons of a sailor, talking dolls, a sick son, a blessing that's a curse. It was up to him to find the answer.

He had a constant headache.

He felt this was the one thing in his life he could not share with Victoria. Not now, at least. She'd think he'd finally gone off the deep end. Once he solved the dilemma perhaps, or perhaps never. He was a CPA for crying out loud. He thought in nice logical linear patterns. He feared this kind of problem was beyond his scope.

Michael pushed the stack of library books away and stretched his aching back. Raising his arms over his head, he leaned backward. His eyes were blurry, his head spinning. He glanced over to the neat racks of books to his right. A colorful magazine page taped to a corner of the book stack caught his eye. For a break Michael idly read through the snippet from the gardening section.

"Jack! Jack, I found it." Michael dumped a wade of photocopied pages on the desk blotter. "The rowan. The bark, the berries, the leaves, the whole damn thing. Protection and health. And jam, the berries aren't poison. Jordy loves peanut butter and jam. What do you think?

"Rowan tree. Hmmm . . . health and protection. Should do the trick. A bit of bark, a berry put anywhere inside me. Yer close. Now what about soul? That's the lifeblood."

"You're right. Blood. Blood, where the essence of the soul survives. Damn, Jack, my blood. Just a drop of blood buried inside you somewhere near your heart. This is right. I know it is. This will work."

"Remember, lad, yer no sawbones. This here procedure before sunset if you please."

"Sure, sure. I'll get to eBay tonight and buy this rowan stuff. Good thing we don't need the whole tree."

"Ebay? What state's that city in?"

Some things were easier to demonstrate than to explain.

Michael elbowed his way out of the fabric store, seeking refuge in his car. He was way, way out of his comfort zone. That was the third attempt he'd made to purchase the needed supplies. "I deal in millions of dollars but I can't decide on the right sewing needle and thread. Sick. I'm sick," he pounded on the defenseless steering wheel. Resting his head against the seat, Michael closed his eyes, fighting his tears.

He and Jack Tar had decided to stitch the items they'd gathered into the toy's arms and leg. Since four seemed to be significant to George, after his vest was opened Michael would pour four drops of his own blood onto Jack Tar's bare chest and sew him back up.

Sounded simple enough. But the long crammed rows of sewing supplies against the shop wall were daunting, silently mocking Michael's certain knowledge that he knew nothing about sewing. He was scared. Scared he'd do it wrong. Scared he'd somehow hurt Jack Tar and in doing so hurt Jordy, too. Hurt his son more than he'd already been hurt so needlessly.

And he felt dirty. He hated keeping these monumental events from Victoria. He loved her, loved her deeply. Seeing the worry and pain in her eyes when she looked at Jordy made him feel ever guiltier. Knowing he held a possible hope for his son's well-being, no matter how absurd it might sound, Michael knew the time had come to come clean, then ask Victoria to help.

But he wasn't looking forward to it. How to tell her the circumstances? Now that was an exercise in itself. He was afraid she'd have him committed over it.

But the only way to do something was to just do it.

Jack Tar heard the raised voices through the closed door. Then he heard the sound of something fragile breaking.

"Ah, the gale's a' brewing," Jack Tar said to the images in the photograph. "Please don't hit the reef." All he could do now was wait.

Jack Tar checked the office wall clock when silence finally settled in the house. To his reckoning it had been a good two-hour brawl.

Victoria stormed into the office that evening. Jack Tar straightened to his full height and stood at attention. When she stood in front of the liquor cart Jack Tar snatched the cap off his head and bowed low. "A deep pleasure to properly be meeting the lady of the house."

She glared down at him, her mouth opening and closing, but no sound escaped. Jack Tar could only imagine the questions and thoughts racing through Victoria's mind at that moment.

With no inkling what would happen next, he stood and waited.

Michael stepped protectively behind his wife, ready to catch Victoria if her legs buckled from the shock. But his wife was even tougher than he'd imagined. Clearing her throat, Victoria gave a terse greeting to the figure apprehensively standing before her. "Michael informs me you can cure my son."

"Seems likely, ma'am."

"Good!" Victoria said. "Celebratory drinks anyone?" she asked in her finest hostess voice. "Mr. Tar, what's your pleasure?"

Michael beamed with pride.

*   *   *

Shrieks of laughter filled the kitchen. "Clara's going to quit when she see this mess we've made," warned Michael.

"We? I warned you about the blender top," Victoria countered, her cheeks glowing, her voice brimming with mirth.

"I thought you said jam making were easy," Jack Tar inquired from his seat on the toaster oven.

"It is, but Michael rushed and didn't check the lid of the blender was secured." Victoria looked down at her stained clothing and across at Michael. He was covered head to toe in squashed berries. "The kitchen isn't a problem but the clothes are definitely ruined."

"Ahh, guys," Jordy interjected. "How about just painting the ceiling red? Might be easier on everyone."

They all glanced up. Blotches of red berries dotted the length of the formerly white ceiling like psychedelic polka dots. A thick blob of juice and berries plopped down onto the tip of Jack Tar's nose. He wiped it off with a snort of disgust as Michael and Victoria doubled up in peals of laughter.

"Kid, you might have a point," Michael said.

By the time the last winter snows melted, Michael was more than ready for an outing with Jordy. They drove to the park, Jordy chattering the entire way. He stopped when Michael parked and turned off the ignition.

Jordy pushed the car door open with his foot. Holding the shoe box steady in both hands, he slammed the door closed with his hip. He bounced on balls of his feet waiting for Michael to get the large package out of the back.

"Hurry, dad."

"Relax. You don't want me to drop it, do you?"

"Heck, no!" His patience exhausted, Jordy began

to walk backward down the slope. "We'll meet you down there."

Michael watched Jordy race down the path, carefully holding the box outstretched for balance. *What a difference a few bits of tree and drops of blood can make in a life,* he thought. *A little magic is a wonderful thing.* Though still dressed head to foot in Goth black, his son's complexion glowed with health.

He met Jordy at the lake and together they unwrapped the radio-controlled sailing ship. They knelt at the water's edge, Michael holding the ship steady. Jody meticulously tied the sails onto the three masts and carefully pulled the Styrofoam packing material off the ship's rudder. Lovingly, Jordy opened the shoe box and placed Jack Tar behind the ship's wheel.

Nudging the ship a few inches farther onto the water, Michael handed Jordy the transmitter. Jordy turned the handle and watched the ship sail across the lake.

"You think Jack will like this, Dad?"

"We'll find out tonight."

Jack Tar did.

He liked it very much.

DANNY'S VERY LONG TRIP

Mike Moscoe

"Are we there yet?" Danny asked in the gentlest voice his four years allowed him.

"We just started," Mommy said from the front seat, interrupting her reading aloud to Dad, who was driving.

"When will we get there?" Danny asked, choosing his wheedling voice this time. That might help.

"We aren't even to Fry's," Dad said. "We've got to drive through all of Oregon and half of California to get to San Francisco."

Dad went to Fry's a lot to buy computer stuff and that was a long drive. Danny eyed his new best friend, Robot. He'd first met Robot at Fry's. Danny had told everyone that he wanted Robot for a friend, and had been taken to the car for being too noisy. Neither Danny nor Robot knew how much larger a drive it was from Fry's to San Francisco. Danny turned to Nikki.

Nikki was his big sister and six and went to school. She knew a lot more than Danny did. She said, "It's lots and lots and lots of far away."

Danny sighed. That was a *long* way!

Mommy went back to reading as Danny hugged Robot. Robot was his friend. Grandmama had promised Danny a robot if he'd start using the potty. Danny liked diapers; he didn't have to take time away from playing or anything. But then his fourth birthday had come and Mommy started using cloth diapers that felt really yucky and Danny decided that maybe using the potty like his big sister wasn't so bad.

And Grandmama had given him Robot just before Mommy and Dad came to get Danny for the trip. As soon as Danny saw Robot, he knew he was his very best friend.

Danny ran his hand over the smooth, silver robot and looked out the window. Trees and houses went by. There were just more and more of them. "Can we listen to songs?" Danny asked.

In the front seat, Mommy stopped reading. "No, Danny, I can't read to your father if the music is going. Why don't you listen to me?"

So Danny did . . . for a while. Mommy's story was about a boy, a big boy who went to school and was learning all about magic and playing with strange creatures. Danny looked out the window and didn't see anything new or strange . . . or fun for that matter.

He decided Robot wanted to go for a walk. The seat between him and Nikki was down, making a kind of table between them. So Danny helped Robot walk up the table.

"Ew," Nikki said, putting her hands over her ears. "Your toy is noisy."

"You look funny," Danny said, and big sister did look funny. She had her hands over her ears, but she was still holding a colored pencil in one, the paper she was drawing on in the other. She looked like an elephant with just one ear. Danny laughed.

"You kids pipe down," Dad said, and Nikki had to whisper "I am not funny," back at Danny.

Danny considered shouting "Oh, yes, you are," but Dad wanted quiet so Danny just hugged Robot. If he made the big people mad, they might take Robot away from him.

So he listened to Mommy talk about the magical boy and watched the houses and trees go by or watched sister Nikki draw. When she finished her first picture, she put it down on the table between them and Danny got his first good look.

You could never tell about sister Nikki's pictures. The sun was always round and yellow, but other things might be really different from what Danny usually saw. But Nikki was learning to draw at school and maybe all the trees and flowers there were blue or green or yellow. At least she could draw them. When Danny tried, his pictures were just a mess of lines.

Danny stared at Nikki's picture and the longer he stared at it, the more it looked like the castle at home where they played knights. Knights and dragons and gargoyles and dinosaurs and tanks and airplanes. The castle was good for a lot of things.

Danny walked Robot toward the picture. Then Robot turned at the waist, like Danny had never been able to make him. Robot reached out with his arm, clamped the three things like fingers onto Danny's shirtsleeve, and took two steps right into the picture.

And Danny went with him!

"I hope you aren't chilly. Castles are rather dank," Robot said.

"I am cold," Danny said, then clamped his hands over his mouth. Robot had never talked before. Slowly Danny took his hands off his mouth. "You can talk?"

"I can in here," Robot said.

Here, Danny saw, was in front of the gray plastic castle he shared with Nikki . . . usually. Only now the green plastic was real grass and the castle was made out of stones as rough as those at the hospital where Dad worked. Danny wished he could sit down in a thinking chair, like he did when he played Blues Clues and Think, Think, Think. He was only four, but he knew he needed to think about what was going on here.

"Where are we, Robot?"

"We are inside the picture Nikki drew with her magic pencils. Just like when they go into the pictures in *Blues Clues*," Robot said. The red light that kind of looked like a smile and that made him look so much like a friend flashed as Robot talked.

"I thought that was just TV pretend," Danny said, screwing up his face and trying to think even without a thinking chair.

"And this is my magic. You don't have to be a boy and go to school for a best friend robot to do magic here."

Danny thought about magic, and the book Mommy had been reading. He'd thought it was a pretend story. Maybe it wasn't.

"Are you still my friend here?" Danny asked, needing to have at least one thing safe to hang on to.

"Your Grandmama gave me to you. I will always be your friend. Are you my friend?"

"I want to be your friend," Danny said. From the castle came strange noises. He reached over for Robot. Here he was taller than Danny, almost a big person, but not quite. Danny held onto Robot's elbow. It always felt good to rub Grampa or Grandmama's elbow when strange things came on the TV. He hoped it worked now.

Atop the castle wall, a monster stood up. He was green and had a pointed nose and pointy ears. And wings. Danny recognized him for one of the monsters Grampa had given him last year to play with in the castle.

"Hi, Danny," the monster said.

"Hello," Danny said, and sidled around to put Robot between him and the monster when he got a look at the battle ax in his green hand. "Are you my friend?"

"I always have been," Green Monster said, then hopped and used his wings to glide down to stand beside Robot.

"Good to see you here," he said friendly like to Robot.

"Glad for the company," Robot said.

"Can I fly with your wings?" Danny asked Green Monster.

"I'm sorry, Danny. My wings don't come off here."

Danny was distracted from his disappointment by the sight of a horse clopping into view. No, not a horse. A pure white unicorn!

"Oh no, not that one," Green Monster said. "She's so prissy."

"What's so prissy about wanting clean hoofs and a sparkling horn?" Unicorn said, sounding very much like big sister Nikki. Grampa sometimes said big sister was "prissy," but Danny was never sure what it meant. It must have something to do with being like a unicorn.

"Hello," Danny said. "Are you my friend?"

"I'd like to be with Nikki," Unicorn said. "But I can be both your friends."

Somewhere off to the right . . . or left . . . Danny wasn't sure which was which . . . there was a loud bellow. Unicorn and Green Monster gave a worried glance in that direction. Even Robot turned that way. Danny immediately slipped behind Robot.

"What was that?" Danny asked.

"Either the T. Rex, or a dragon," Green Monster said, hefting his ax. "Whichever one it is, I don't think it's in a happy mood."

"Not at all," Unicorn agreed.

Then there was an even louder sliding noise and Danny grabbed Robot.

"Wake up, you've slept all the way to Grant's Pass," Dad said as he picked Danny up.

"Are we there yet?" Danny muttered as he wrapped his arms around Dad and Robot.

"Not yet," Dad said. "Why don't you leave your toy in the car? You might lose it."

Danny held on tight to Robot while he was carried into the hotel and as he watched a good-night movie. Nikki picked the movie. It was about a girl fighting monsters and working with a two-headed dragon to find a sword and return it to the king. Danny had seen it before and fell asleep before it got to the good part with the dragon. Mommy and Dad, even Grandmama and Grampa had said it was all pretend.

Now Danny wasn't so sure.

Next morning they were back in the van, with Mommy driving, driving, driving. Dad said that the mountains up ahead had snow and they should drive to the coast and around them.

Nikki and Danny both shouted gleefully that they'd love to play in the snow, but Mommy said they had to make San Francisco tonight and there was no time to play.

At least the drive was more fun. Mommy drove a smaller road that wound through fields with horses and cows and sheep. Danny saw houses that Nikki said were farms though they didn't look any different from houses. There were hills and then mountains away from the road with trees on them. And then the trees got very big and very tall and very close.

"Those are redwoods," Dad said, interrupting his reading about the boy and his magical adventures. Danny tried to tell Mommy about his magical adventure with Robot but the words didn't come our right. He told Nikki about seeing her friend Unicorn, but Nikki told him that she'd left Unicorn at home and Danny couldn't quite find the right words to tell her that Unicorn was in her picture. He got more and more frustrated, and maybe he did shout, because the big people both told him to quiet down.

So he did. He hugged Robot, but Robot said nothing.

Now Nikki was drawing a new picture. She was using the orange pencil, so the picture didn't look at all like what Danny was looking at out the window, but she had the trees with big trunks and lots of bushy stuff on top, not leaves. And all orange. Was Nikki learning that in school?

When Nikki finished her picture, she showed it to Dad who said it looked lovely. Nikki put it down on the table between them where the castle picture had been yesterday. It wasn't there now or Danny would have walked Robot into it already.

Now he started to walk Robot into this picture, but he stopped. Yesterday Unicorn said she wanted to play with Nikki. "Want to see Unicorn?" Danny asked.

Big sister just said "Humph," and reached for another sheet of paper and the green pencil. Danny reached for her hand, caught it for a second, and walked Robot into the new picture.

And Danny was in the forest.

The trees were brown and green. There were ferns all over the ground, as well as white and purple flowers. The wind was cool and soft and smelled of dirt and maybe mud puddles. And a butterfly flew by with all sorts of colors on its wings. Danny took off chasing it.

"Where is this?" Nikki demanded in her big sister voice.

Danny stopped, watched for a moment while the flutterby disappeared, then turned back to Nikki and Robot.

"We are in your picture. This is *some* picture."

Nikki eyed Robot, like Mommy did stray cats. "You're taller than me and Danny."

"Yes, I am here," Robot said.

"Where are Mom and Daddy?" Nikki demanded. "Where is the van?"

"Someplace else," Robot said. "Your magic pencils made this picture and this place, and my magic has brought you here."

"Magic," Nikki said, frowning at Robot like Grandmama frowned when she was really thinking.

"The magic of words and pictures to make things true," Robot went on. "Like the story your daddy is reading just now. The writer put the words on paper and now they are real to your mom and daddy. Nikki, can you write words yet?"

"Some of them," Nikki said, putting her hands behind her back and scuffing the ground with her shoe.

"Nikki can write lots of alphabets," Danny put in.

"It is important to write words," Robot said.

"But not with a pencil," Nikki said. "Grampa always writes with his computer."

Before Robot could answer that, Danny squealed with glee and waved. Green Monster was standing on a low hanging tree branch.

"Oh, hi, Danny, I'm glad to see you back." And Green Monster leaped into the air and glided on his wings down to land a few feet away from Danny. This time Danny didn't run to hide behind Robot, even when he saw Green Monster's axe.

Nikki, however, took two steps back. Then she caught sight of the axe and said, "Danny, you come here," in her most demanding voice.

Before Danny could say "No," which was his usual answer to that demanding voice, whether it was from Nikki or Mommy, there was a happy sound behind Nikki.

"Oh, I'm so glad that you could come this time," Unicorn said.

Nikki whirled at the words, shouted "Unicorn!" and ran to her. She ran her hands through Unicorn's white mane and rested her head against Unicorn's neck. "You can talk to me! This is wonderful!"

"Isn't this the bestest place ever?" Danny said, walking up to Robot and fingering his elbow. This was the bestest place ever, but it was still strange and it was nice to have a friend to stand beside and even hug.

And that was enough . . . for a while. Nikki walked along with Unicorn, talking about school things and how much fun recess was unless the bigger boys were hogging the tetherball games. But Unicorn reminded Nikki that she was just as big as most of those boys and that she had taken the game away from them several times. They laughed at that.

Danny and Robot found another butterfly to chase, and then found a grasshopper and hopped along with it for a while. There were also slugs that Nikki said were yucky but Danny thought were so cool. It was so much better to walk through the woods than be strapped into a car seat driving through the woods.

Then there was that bellow again. It made every tree shiver. Danny found himself hugging Robot and patting his elbow faster than he'd ever done Grampa's no matter what was on TV. Nikki held on tight to Unicorn. "What was that?" she said in a trembling voice like she had when they went to the doctor for shots.

"Either the dragon or the T. Rex," Green Monster said. "And it does sound like whichever one it is got up on the wrong side of the bed."

"There's a dragon here?" Nikki asked. "Why is there a dragon here?"

"Don't you have a dragon at home?" Robot said.

"Well, yes." Nikki agreed. "Grampa gave us all really cool dragons last Christmas. Dan and me and our cousins. So?"

"So if you have a really loved friend in your toybox, you have one here."

"We don't really have a toybox," Danny put in. "Our toys are kind of spread all over the place," he said like Mommy.

"You got a dragon there, you got one here," Green Monster said.

"But Grampa has a dragon next to his computer. All the big people have dragons," Nikki put in.

Green Monster hefted his ax and took a ready stance. "Me thinks he's figured out how to control his dragon. Dragons more likely. Most big people have learned how. Or made friends with theirs."

"How do I make a new friend of a dragon?" both Danny and Nikki said at the same time.

"Here's your chance," Robot said.

Through the trees was a clearing. In it sat the most wonderful creature Danny had ever seen. Even Robot paled beside this. It was huge, like a house. And it was beautiful. Its skin shone in every color of the rainbow. Its wings waved gently in the wind. No, they were what was making the wind. The wings were even more beautiful, glistening in soft pinks and golds. Even if Danny got as good at drawing as Nikki, he'd never be able to draw a picture as beautiful as this.

"That's a dragon," Nikki said softly.

"That it be," Green Monster answered.

"It's so lovely," Danny said.

"Yes," agreed Unicorn. "Lovely as truth. And just as dangerous. It looks beautiful now, untainted by lies and cunning and deceit. But look carefully at its underbelly. See those dark spots. Have you ever told a lie?"

"No," Nikki and Danny said.

The Unicorn's laughter was crystal pure in the forest air. In the meadow, the dragon's underbelly added another dark scale and the huge creature shivered and whimpered. "With every lie, the dragon turns darker, changes humor. For the dragon's sake, never tell a lie."

"I won't," Nikki and Danny said together. They really, really meant it, and the dragon's shine showed it by not getting another bit darker.

"Now you need to go make a new friend," Robot said.

Nikki squared her shoulders and took a step toward the meadow. Then she reached back for Danny's hand. He sniffed a little bit, and hunted around in his tiny soul for all the courage he had found to use the big people's potty and not worry about being flushed down with his poopy. Then he took his big sister's hand and stepped up beside her.

"Thank you," Nikki said.

"You're welcome," Danny answered, because the big people said it was good to be polite. Looking at the dragon, Danny figured he needed all the good on his side that he could get.

Hand in hand, the little brother, who was the taller, and the big sister, who was outweighed by twenty pounds, walked out into the clearing.

The dragon's head had been waving in the air, like the squirrels did when they came to rob the bird feeder. Then it caught sight of the two of them and brought its head down, resting its chin on the ground. Even then, its eyes were still level with the two of them. Danny gazed into huge liquid eyes that were kind of funny like cats' eyes. But they were also sad in a way that Danny did not understand. Maybe Nikki had learned about that at school.

Nikki was still walking toward the dragon, so Danny had to keep walking, too. He held on so tight to her hand; there was no way he'd let go of it. No way.

They were so close they could feel the dragon's warm breath when Nikki finally stopped. The dragon must have been eating peppermint candy cause its breath smelled of it. Or maybe that was just what dragons smelled like. Danny was discovering that having a toy dragon and meeting a real one were not the same thing at all.

"Hello," the dragon said in a voice and with a breath that almost shook Danny into little pieces.

"Hello," Danny stammered out a bit behind Nikki.

"Why have you come here?" the dragon asked.

Nikki didn't seem to know the answer to the question. She just looked and looked at the dragon, her mouth open a little bit, but no words coming out.

Danny said his usual greetings. "Will you be my new friend?"

Dragon's huge eyes blinked, long eyelashes fluttered, and she seemed to think on that for a moment. Then she raised her eyebrows like Grampa did in question and gazed hard at Nikki. "Like you did with those two boys?"

Danny liked to eat chicken stars at the place with the play place. He remembered the two boys who'd swaggered into the play area like they intended to boss everyone around. Nikki had squared her shoulders, swaggered right back up to them, and faced them off with her hands on her hips. After that, they became good friends.

"I would like very much to be your friend," Nikki said, then swallowed hard before going on. "And I would do my best to be a good friend to you, if we were friends."

The dragon nodded, batting her beautiful eyelashes again, and seemed to think about that long and hard. Like Grandmama did when Nikki and Danny pleaded to go to the ice cream place and Mommy said they hadn't been good enough and Grandmama was making up her own mind if they'd been good enough for ice cream.

Then the dragon turned to Danny. "You want to be my new friend?"

Danny nodded, finding words hard to come by.

"Just like you did those two little kids at the play place?"

"Which two?" Danny asked. He'd made a lot of new friends there. Hopefully, the dragon wasn't thinking of *those* two.

"The two you pushed down."

Oh, yes, those two. And their mommy. And Grampa said that Danny needed to be careful because he was so big for a four-year-old. And he had been. At least he tried to be.

"He tries very hard," Nikki put in.

The dragon eyed Danny for a long moment, then nodded gravely. "We big people have to be extra specially careful not to hurt people who are smaller than we are."

"You remember that," Nikki said in her bossy voice.

Almost, Danny shoved his sister. Just in time he remembered that the dragon was looking and she might not think that a shove was his way of telling big sister that he loved her.

"I will try real hard to remember that," Danny said.

"Then we can be friends."

"Oh boy," Nikki cried. "Can you take us for rides on your back like the kids do in Dragon Land? Can you? Can you?"

"I am sorry, Nikki, but as your Grampa told you, dragons are very big and our wings are just big enough to carry us up. I'm sorry. I can't carry you."

"Green Monster said he couldn't lend me his wings, either," Danny pointed out.

Nikki looked around. "Aren't there any airplanes here? Or space ships? We have plenty of them at home. Why aren't there any of them here?"

Robot had joined them. "Are any of them your very bestest friends?" he asked Danny.

Danny looked at Nikki, and they both shook there heads. "We like them a lot, but you can't really make friends with a rocket ship," Nikki explained.

"There is one way that I could fly you on my back," Dragon said.

"How? How? How?" Danny asked.

"Nikki could write a story that changed what Grampa said," Dragon told her.

"Write a long story?" Nikki said, sounding worried like she did when she had a lot of homework, three or four sheets, to do.

"It could be a short story," Dragon said. "A story just one sentence long. A story like 'My dragon has big wings.' Could you write that, Nikki?"

"I don't have any paper, or a pencil."

"You could write it in the dirt with a stick," Robot said.

"I could," Nikki said, sounding like she had just decided something very important, like whether to be a unicorn or princess for Halloween.

Danny found a stick, and Nikki knelt down beside some good clean dirt.

"Dad wrote 'I love you,' in the sand at the beach," Danny remembered.

"That is very special magic," Dragon said.

Nikki started by writing *my*, then paused. "How do you spell 'dragon'?"

"Sound it out," Dragon said and started. "Drrr."

Nikki wrote *dr*.

And there was a bellow so loud and so long that it made the ground shake.

Nikki dropped her stick. "What was that?" she got out. Danny would have said the same thing, but he was so scared he'd made a fist and stuffed it in him mouth to keep from screaming.

"That would have to be T. Rex," Green Monster said. "And he really sounds unhappy."

"Why is he unhappy?" Nikki asked.

"If he'd tell me, I'd be the first to do something about it, but T. Rex, he's not one for talking. He just bellows and bites and knocks things around."

"What can we do?" Danny asked.

"Nikki, could you write something and change this story?" Unicorn asked.

"What could I write?"

"Write 'bunny,'" Robot said. "That could turn T. Rex into a nice fluffy bunny."

Nikki grabbed for her stick just as T. Rex stomped into the far end of the meadow and bellowed again. His breath smelled sour like he'd been eating bad-tasting medicine.

"Nikki, rewrite the story," Robot said, moving forward. "We'll keep T. Rex busy."

"How do you spell 'bunny'?" Nikki yelled.

"Sound it out," Dragon said as she flew up into the air. Even with T. Rex bellowing and smelling up the meadow, Nikki and Danny had to take a moment to look at how beautiful Dragon was in flight.

"Hurry up," Unicorn called as she galloped out to meet T. Rex, Green Monster trotting along behind her.

Danny pushed Nikki. "Hurry up and write 'bunny.'"

"You do it if you're so smart," Nikki shoved back.

"Hurry up," Robot called over his shoulder as T. Rex stooped down to bite his head off. Robot dodged out of the way.

"Ba," Danny said. "What letter is ba?"

Nikki stooped and wrote *b*. Then said, "And there is the 'na' sound."

"N," Danny guessed.

"But there's the 'uh' sound first," Nikki insisted and wrote a *u* before writing an *n*.

"There's two ns" Dragon shouted as she finished a dive at T. Rex that had him dodging away.

Nikki quickly added a second *n*.

"Bunny," Danny said. "It ends with an 'e' sound. Write an e."

"No, no," Nikki said. "This is a hard one. It sounds just like e, but it isn't. What is it? I can't remember," she shouted.

"It's a y." Unicorn said, sounding like Grandmama did when she helped Nikki with a really hard bit of homework.

"Yes," Nikki shouted. "Yes, a y," and she finished the whole word with a flourish.

There it was, *bunny*, complete in the dirt.

In the meadow, T. Rex, mouth gapping wide, was about to swallow Unicorn. Then suddenly there wasn't a T. Rex in the meadow, but a huge, fluffy bunny with floppy ears, just as white as Unicorn was.

"Do you think he will want to be our friend?" Danny asked.

Then there was a huge scraping sound and Danny wanted to hug Robot close but Robot was out in the meadow.

"You kids slept all the way to San Francisco," Dad was saying as he picked up Nikki.

"Where's Robot?" Danny shouted, half awake, as Mommy picked him up.

"It's in the car somewhere," Dad said. "I'll come back and get it after I get you in the motel room."

But Danny wanted Robot now! And he told everyone in San Francisco that he did. So he got left in the room while Dad went to hunt. Nikki asked Daddy to bring in her picture, so Dad said he would.

Mommy tried to make it better by hugging Danny, but he couldn't stop crying, so she put him to bed. He cried more when Dad came back with no Robot. "He must have left it at the last motel."

Nikki got her pictures back, but only for a second because Mommy was so proud of them she wanted to show them to the friends they were visiting. Nikki got upset and was also sent to bed. There she hugged Danny and patted him on the back.

"We'll get Robot back," she told him. "We'll see Unicorn and Dragon again."

Danny tried to believe her, because she was six and the big sister, but the big people had the pictures and Robot was not there to walk them into the picture. Danny cried himself to sleep.

The next day Nikki told Danny to not feel so sad. She would think of a way out of this. But Danny did stay sad through the rest of the trip. Dad stopped on the way home at the first motel, but they didn't have Robot. Danny could have told Dad that they wouldn't, but Nikki shushed him.

They got home. Dad went back to work and Nikki

went back to school and Danny went back to pre-school. He tried to tell his friends there about Robot. And teacher too. But he couldn't find the right words. Teacher did tell him to bring Robot to show and tell. Mommy told teacher that Robot was lost.

By the end of the week, Danny was giving up hope that he'd ever see Robot again. But Mommy and Dad had to go to a meeting and that meant Danny would go to Grampa's house. Nikki said that she had an idea for something at Grandmama's house and asked Mommy if she could show Grandmama the pictures she drew on the trip.

Mommy left the pictures with Grandmama and rushed off to her meeting. After Danny got apple juice, Nikki asked Grandmama to see the pictures.

"Will you tell me about the pictures?" Grandmama said.

So Nikki did, and Danny tried too also, but the words just didn't come out right. Grandmama listened to them and told them it was a very wonderful story, but she made it sound like the kind of story you saw on TV. Pretend.

Danny really tried to tell Grandmama that this was real. He and Nikki had been there. But the big people just could not seem to understand him.

Nikki gave him a hug and told him not to worry. She had a plan.

Actually it was Grandmama who had a plan. "Nikki, where should we put your pictures?" she asked.

Nikki got very nice, like only a six-year-old big sister could and asked if it would be all right to put the pictures on the refrigerator.

Grandmama said yes, and used the magic stuff, magnets, that stuck things to the refrigerator. Then she asked Nikki what movie she'd like to see and Nikki picked one, but Danny just stood in front of the refrigerator and stared and stared at the pictures.

Look as hard as he could, Danny didn't see Green

Monster or Unicorn or Dragon looking back at him. Saddest of all, he did not see Robot.

After a long while, Nikki came in. She looked at the picture for a while. Then she reached up and tried to push her hand into the picture. It didn't go anywhere.

Finally Nikki folded her hands, shook her head, and scowled. "We need some magic of our own."

"Your magic pencil made the drawing," Danny said.

"But your robot walked us into the picture," Nikki said.

"You wrote 'bunny' and the T. Rex was a bunny," Danny said.

"I can't write a whole story that says Nikki and Danny can walk into the picture. That's too long." Nikki stomped her foot at that.

"Could you just write 'robot'?" Danny wheedled.

"Can you *spell* robot?" Nikki demanded.

"Grampa can," Danny was sure Grampa could spell anything.

The two of them ran into Grampa's office. He was working at the computer, writing words, not playing a game or something.

"Hi, crew," he said with a smile, even if he didn't look up from the words he was making appear on the computer.

"Hi, Grampa," both of them said.

Nikki ran over to the pile where Grampa put paper he'd already run through his printer and that he let Nikki and Danny draw on or cut up. Nikki picked out one that was full of words on Grampa's side and turned it over to its empty side.

"Grampa, can I borrow a pen?" Nikki asked.

Right, if any grown-up pen or pencil had magic in it, it would be Grampa's. Nikki was so smart.

Grampa finished typing and spun in his chair to face the two of them. He bent over so he could look right into their eyes . . . and they into his. "You aren't going to write on yourself, are you? Nikki, you know how sad that makes your mommy."

Grampa's voice sounded almost like a dragon. His eyes looked almost as sad as Dragon's. If any big person knew a dragon, Grampa would be the one.

Nikki stood very straight and looked right back at Grampa like she had Dragon. "I won't write on myself."

"Good," Grampa said and smiled as he pulled a blue pen out from his drawer. "Have fun and be careful."

Nikki went over to her place in Grampa's office, a low table in front of his couch. She stared at the pen, and she stared at the paper.

"How do you spell 'robot'?" Danny said softly.

"Grampa, how do you spell 'robot,'" Nikki said in a louder voice.

"Sound it out." And now Grampa sounded just like Dragon.

"Rrrr," Danny said.

"R," Nikki said and wrote an *r*.

"Roooo," Danny said.

"O," Nikki said, and wrote that letter.

"Bot," Grampa said.

"B," said Nikki and added that to her word.

"'Ot' is a hard one," Grampa said. "I'll give you the second o."

Nikki made a second *o* appear in her word.

"Bot," Danny said, making the last letter dance on his tongue.

"T," Nikki shouted and finished the word. Robot stood there on the page in front of them.

"Thank you, Grampa," Nikki said, and scrambled out of the office.

"Thank you," Danny remembered to say after Nikki. Then he raced after Nikki. There were a lot of reasons it was no fun being little brother, even if he was bigger than sister Nikki. She remembered to say "please" and "thank you" before he did and she was always headed places before he remembered he wanted to go there too.

Danny ran into the kitchen. Nikki was trying to hold the paper with *robot* on it up to the refrigerator while she tried to write it real small on her orange picture.

Danny ran up to the refrigerator and held the paper in place. Now Nikki could work hard on the word she was writing.

Nikki's tongue moved right and left—or was it left and right—as she made each letter. As she put the cross on the *t*, she reached over and grabbed Danny's arm.

And Nikki and Danny were walking through the forest.

Ahead of them there was a clearing. "Let's run," Nikki said but she didn't let go of Danny's hand. Together they ran through the trees right out into the meadow.

And there, across from them, were Robot and Green Monster, Unicorn and Dragon, and a large white Bunny having a tea party.

"Hello, Danny," Green Monster called when he saw them.

Unicorn turned around and called, "Hello, Nikki."

And then Dragon called hello and Danny really felt like he'd been helloed. But the nicest part of all was when Robot turned around and hugged Danny, and Danny patted his elbow and Robot said. "It's so nice to see you again, Danny."

And it was.

After tea and chocolate chip cookies they walked in the forest and chased a butterfly and studied an anthill and did lots of fun things. But all through it, Danny kept a hand on Robot and never let it go.

And when he heard the loud noise of a door opening, Danny hugged Robot closer.

"Shush," Grandmama said as Mommy and Dad came through her front door. "The little ones are asleep."

And Danny raised his head sleepily. He was under

a blanket on Grandmama's living-room floor. And Robot was in his arm.

"Where'd that come from?" Mommy said as she picked up Danny.

"I thought he lost that at Grant's Pass," Dad said as he picked up Nikki.

Danny hugged Robot and smiled at Nikki. Big sister winked back. Let the big people figure out this magic.

QUOTH THE SCREAMING CHICKEN

David Bischoff

The long, silly joke about the professor, his son, Frog, and the magic screaming rubber chicken started with this punch line:

A hideous, gulping shriek rose up from the dusk.

It should have been a joke, anyway. The noise sounded like some unlucky Christmas caroler waylaid with Scrooge's bough of holly through their heart.

"Daddy, Daddy!" cried the boy, clinging to Doctor Evan Marshall's hand. "Was that Santa getting hit by a Mack truck?"

Dusk had long since settled into the valley, dipping all in mist and gloom. The streetlights glowed like ghosts of fireflies. The smell of hot cheese, tomato sauce, oregano, and fresh baked bread wafted from the nearby pizza parlor. Cheerful yuletide Muzak and chatter spilled out from the Oregon University bookstore: warm inviting embers in a welcoming hearth fire.

"No, Teddy," said Professor Marshall, fatherly hand on his son's shoulder, guiding. "Santa's okay. Don't worry. Now come along, let's get to the party before—"

A jolly voice emerged from the thick fog, stopping

them in their tracks. "Hi there, friends. Have you seen the funniest joke book ever written?"

Teddy jumped. He was an excitable ball of energy, Teddy was, skinny and hyperactive with big gray eyes starting from his head as though they were too large for his skull. The professor's dearest wish was that Teddy would love books—any books, even comic books—as much as he. But the longest Teddy could sit still was to play a short video game.

"Daddy, Daddy," cried the little boy excitedly. "It's Santa! It's Santa!"

Doctor Evan Marshall's eyes rolled heavenward. Egad! Caught despite his very best efforts.

He sighed, exasperation leaking from him into the chill December air on 13th Street, Skinner, Oregon—Deadhead Central, the place where hippies went to die. Once a tall man, Marshall's shoulders were now humped a bit, as though from the weight of years of strain. His gray eyes, once bright and intelligent, were now bleary and dull with disappointment.

"No, Teddy," said the professor. "It's just Frog."

At first there was just the smile.

It rose out of the mist like the Cheshire Cat's in *Alice in Wonderland.*

Then the eyes: tufts of blue from a friendly sky, surrounded by a Brillo pad of hair, beaming above a big nose. The happy body rolled out along the sidewalk, a handful of colorful ragged pamphlets in mittened hands. If Santa Claus was some elf or pixie or some other enchanted being, then this cheerful fellow must be some cousin, albeit amphibious: for indeed, the knit wool cap that adorned his head was green with red eyes, with legs sprawling out behind suitable for a French king's supper.

For, despite his name, this Frog was just as human as Professor Marshall or Teddy. He was one of the more wonderful leftovers of the twentieth century counterculture clan who'd come years ago to see the Grateful Dead play at the Skinner Country Fair—a kind of mecca for hippies—and had liked Oregon so much, he stayed. Always an encyclopedia of jokes— many of which he made up himself—he'd learned that by typing a bunch of jokes down on two sides of letter-size paper, then stapling them together he could create very economically viable "books." A colored cover with an illustration by himself, along with a funny title and a couple of Kinko's staples in the middle, completed the product. They were a hit at the Skinner Country Fair and the local Sunday Market, these joke books, and when Frog discovered that university students would buy them, too, he started making a modest living from his vulgar art.

"Hello, Frog," said the professor morosely.

"Hello, professor," said Frog without a trace of resentment, despite their past encounters.

Teddy, unaware of any history between his father and this Dickensian apparition, seemed far more interested in Frog than in the Christmas party beyond. "Jokes!" he cried. "I like jokes! Tell me a joke!"

"Sure," said Frog, wiping a bit of sneeze drip from a silver nose ring. "Why do elephants paint their nails red, green, yellow, orange, and black?"

"Why?"

"So they can hide in jelly bean jars."

Teddy laughed with delight. His father cringed. Such horrible jokes!

"There's more jokes in my new book *The Frog Jokebook For Kids Picks A Scab*. Only two dollars!" said Frog, eyes shiny as newly minted pennies.

"Oh, Dad! I want that joke book. Please buy it for me."

Wanting to just get this over with, the professor pulled two dollars from his pocket and offered it to the street vendor.

"Oh, no, professor. As you may remember, you've got to put the money in the slot there and take out a joke book from the box."

"Fine," said the professor uneasily. "Very well."

When Teddy had his joke book, Frog beamed merrily. "Thank you. Now, young man. What's your name?"

"Teddy."

"Teddy, you get to squeeze the magic rubber chicken, direct from my good pal Santa's magic toybox."

The Professor rolled his eyes. The damned chicken.

From the side of a bag, Frog produced a yellow rubber featherless chicken, the kind you get from gag stores. From a distance, it looked lifelike and life-size: only up close could you see that its paint was chipping, and one of its toes had come off, revealing a patch of gray plastic.

"Squeeze it, Teddy!" said Frog.

Enchanted, Teddy stepped forward, gripped the chicken by its gnarly abdomen, and squeezed.

The horrible gulping squawk that had first attracted Teddy's attention rose up louder.

Teddy giggled with sheer delight.

"Why, Teddy, the chicken likes you! You'll have a wonderful Christmas!"

"Come on, Ted," said the professor, urging his son along. "Let's get to the party before it's over."

Teddy obeyed, but as they walked toward the sounds of Christmas, he kept looking back at Frog and this magic screaming rubber chicken, disappearing into the fog.

That should have been it.

It should have been over and done with.

That should have been the last time that Teddy saw that wretched street creature for a long time. The professor had, in fact, nearly dismissed the whole matter from his mind.

However, at breakfast the very next morning, Teddy produced an addendum to his Christmas want list.

"You want what?" said the professor.

"Frog's magic screaming chicken!" said Teddy. "It's

just the most wonderful toy I've ever seen! I want it! I really want it!"

Teddy's mom laughed merrily. "You liked that joke book, Teddy?"

"I sure did!" said Teddy

"But the magic screaming chicken belongs to Frog," said Mrs. Marshall. She was a sweet, understanding woman with mouse-brown hair and twinkling green eyes. She taught piano lessons part-time, mostly to beginners, and as a consequence had the patience of a saint.

"Maybe he'll sell it," said Teddy.

"I don't think so. You could ask, though."

The professor shot an angry look at his wife, but she narrowed her eyes at him. Their history concerning Frog was still a tough issue between them. Although she was sweet, Beatrice Marshall could be tough as saltwater taffy or old boots when she felt it was necessary.

The previous year, the professor, along with several other colleagues, had organized a petition to prevent the street vendor from hawking his wares at his favorite corner, where a steady traffic of students brought him steady trade. This Anti-Frog brigade discovered that it was actually illegal to sell books on 13th Street. However, a clever lawyer, bringing the case all the way to the State Supreme Court, won the day for the joke bookseller. Money could change hands—but it had to be placed in a box, and a joke book selected. Frog had crowed with triumph from the street ever since. From that day forward, the professor tried to avoid Frog's corner as much as possible.

"Nonsense," he said.

"Daddy. Is that like humbug?"

"Well, Ebenezer Scrooge?" said his wife.

The professor grumbled something incomprehensible in reply.

"I see," she said. She looked at her son. "Tell you what, I want to go down today, exchange some stuff at the bookstore, maybe buy some other things. You two can come along and we'll have lunch. We can ask Frog if maybe his rubber chicken is for sale."

"Absolutely not!" said the professor, but his wife kicked him under the table and gave him the Look. Later, when they were alone again, she explained to him that of course Frog wouldn't sell his screaming rubber chicken. He'd say no to Teddy, they could buy Teddy another joke book for two dollars, and the matter would be settled.

Alas for the professor, things did not work out quite that way.

"What? Buy my magic screaming chicken?" said Frog. "Oh goodness, I wish that were possible, Teddy."

"You see, Ted. Now let's go," said the professor.

"But!" continued Frog, breaking into an even wider grin. "But he can come visit you. He especially enjoys a nice hot dinner accompanied by some bottles of holiday brew. In fact, he can bring along his best friend, the magical mooing cow, who likes beer, too!"

"Oh, Mom, that would be awesome. That would be a real Christmas treat," said Teddy.

"Absurd!" said the professor.

"One quick dinner and the rubber chicken's gone," said his wife. "It's better than having a screaming rubber chicken around for years."

"Well, I won't be there," said the professor, screwing up his eyes, hardening up his heart.

"Professor, that's too bad," said Frog eagerly. "Can I sit in your professorial chair at the dinner table?"

"No!" said the professor. "You stay out of my chair, Frog."

"I'll be there too, because sometime I can't control the chicken. He'd cross a road to sit in a professor's chair!"

"Well, it's settled then, Frog. We'll pick you up here for a jolly Christmas dinner."

"One thing," said the professor sourly. "Frog, just how is this chicken supposed to be magical?"

"Oh, you don't know?" said Frog.

"Frog, I wouldn't be asking if I knew."

Frog grinned. "You'll find out, professor. I'll tell you all about it at dinnertime, after I drink a beer."

"Oh, very well," said the professor. "Come along, Teddy. Let's have lunch."

"Oh, professor. Did you know that I'm magical, too?" called Frog.

"Sure, Frog," said the professor in his best Alan Rickman tones of contempt. "Absolutely no question about it."

Teddy asked if they'd be having flies for dinner with Frog, and thought that was the funniest idea he'd ever heard of. He'd been reading Frog's joke book and could not stop telling bad jokes with silly puns and such.

He's just about the right age, his mother said, to be telling stupid jokes. Everyone told stupid jokes when they were kids. It was a rite of passage.

Dinner was going to be a Teddy favorite, fried chicken and mashed potatoes with pickled beets. Mrs. Marshall bought a case of seasonal microbrew, the sort of beer that came dark and thick and full of weird spices.

"Nobody can drink too much of this stuff," she assured the professor.

"I can't drink *any* of that stuff!" huffed the professor.

"Maybe it would be best if you stuck to nonalcoholic beverages this particular dinner."

"And dull knives," muttered the professor.

But, then, mused the professor, the world was a dull place anyway. Brown and gray, bound by duty and boredom from day to day. He seemed to ride some quotidian meridian in this sorry world, doomed to the mediocre.

It had not always been so.

Once when he was a student, in love with literature all the way from Arthur to Zelazny, he had dreamed he might someday pen great novels and stories. Oh he didn't have to be a Chaucer or a Dante, forging the basis for a Renaissance of language, human thought, and discourse —Just write what was in his heart and mind, show the insights he felt about life and the human heart. Out of college, taking on part-time jobs, he had written his stories and submitted them. He had even written his great American novel and found a New York agent who thought it good. Waiting for results, he changed pace and wrote an academic that which he submitted to an obscure publication that only paid in copies. The stories bounced. The novel was rejected soundly by many, many publishers, each rejection a wound. However, the obscure publication happily accepted his article, promising him two (2) copies for his trouble.

It seemed there was no other recourse. He reentered academia, working on a doctorate in literature. His thesis was accepted by the University of Kansas Press, and he sought a job. It happened to be a bad time to be looking for a job in his field. Only the academically moribund Skinner University was at all interested in him. He took the job. He taught Chaucer and Dante—and far too much boneheaded English. He met a graduate student and got married. Ten years later, he had a surprise son. The gray and dull world had closed in on him, and a cup of his heart would have killed a thousand Socrates.

Above all else, he despised jokes—especially silly, bad jokes—and so he had tried to rid his world of the creature known as Frog.

And now Frog was coming to dinner!

But being widely read in literature, the professor was well aware of irony as a device in fiction. He simply wished his life hadn't become a bad, boring Russian novel.

So it was that on that pre-Christmas day, the professor, his wife, and their son welcomed Frog to their home in the South Hills of Eugene. Frog came on bicycle, towing his weird plastic trailer of joke books. He was wrapped in a Doctor Who scarf and a Jethro Tull jacket, both long and ratty and down to his scuffed boots. But the green on his head was sharper than holly and the smile on his face was brighter than Rudolph the reindeer's nose. Little Teddy, watching from the front window, cried for joy as Frog opened his weird trailer and pulled out his magic rubber chicken. He held it up and squeezed.

The scream curdled in the professor's cold blood.

He hastened to his den where he knocked back a dram of whiskey from a flask, breathing deeply, trying to gain composure. When he struggled out to dinner at his wife's call, he was relieved to find Frog not sitting in his chair at the dining-room table, but several seats away, at a safe distance.

Frog was telling a joke, working on his second seasonal beer. "Why do ostriches have such long necks?" he asked Teddy.

"Why?" asked Teddy.

"Because it's such a long way to their heads!" answered Frog happily.

Teddy guffawed.

The professor rolled his eyes, resisting the temptation to dash back to his den and knock back another snort. Instead, he sat down.

"Arrrrrrrrrrrrwwwwwk!" quoth the screaming chicken.

The professor shot back out of his seat. He stared down in horror. There below him, filling back up with air, eyes bulging, beak open and red with defiance was the rubber chicken.

"Damn it! What's this thing doing in my chair!"

Teddy said, "But I just had it. Right here!"

"I told you it was magic!" said Frog in his piping, merry voice. The brew was already in his eyes and flecks of it were on his mustache and beard.

Teddy laughed. "It teleported! The screaming chicken teleported!"

"Frog, if I get bird flu, I'll sue!" said the professor. "I swear I'll sue!"

"Oh great!" said Frog. "Use my lawyer! He's always looking for more money!"

The mention of Frog's lawyer shut the professor up. He'd far rather suffer the pain of Frog's jokes than feel again the lash of Frog's lawyer.

"Get this thing out of my chair," demanded the professor.

Giggling, Teddy scurried over and removed the avian offender.

Folding his rumpled dignity around himself like feathers, the professor sat down to his dinner.

"This thing really is magic!" said Teddy.

"Absolutely. And if you'll give me another beer, Mrs. Professor, I'll have the chicken do another trick."

The professor's wife got another beer and set the frosty thing in front of her guest. Frog added much of its contents to his stomach, mustache, and beard.

"Okay, chicken," said Frog. "Show them."

"Thanks, Frog," said the chicken in a squeaking, kooky voice. "What's the difference between an onion and an accordion?"

"What?" said Teddy.

"You don't cry when you chop up an accordion!"

Teddy laughed in glee.

"Buy a joke book from me," continued the chicken. "And you get to squeeze the screaming rubber Frog."

"Very cute, Charlie McCarthy," said the professor. "But I think I saw Frog's lips move."

"You think so, huh?" said Frog. He picked up his beer and started to drink.

"A one-hump camel marries a two-hump camel and they have a no-hump camel baby," said the chicken. "What do they call it!"

"What?" said Teddy.

"Humphrey," said the chicken.

The professor sighed. "Okay, okay. A nice ventriloquist trick. Ventriloquism I can live with."

"You don't have to believe in magic, professor," said Frog. "But magic believes in you."

"Spare me!" said the Professor. "Dear? May I have a seasonal beer. I believe I'm ready for one."

And so dinner was eaten, drinks were drunk. Both the chicken and Frog told a few more jokes, and the professor learned to appreciate the soporific dark, hoppy, nasty seasonal beer. Finally, the fruit cake and whipped cream from a can gobbled, the coffee drunk, the magic chicken squeezed once more, Teddy allowed that this indeed had been a splendid Christmas gift.

"I shouldn't just want the screaming chicken all to myself," he said. "I should allow Frog to share it with the world."

They all saw Frog to the door. Smiling, Frog turned around to wave to them from the steps. He slipped on a patch of ice and went tumbling to the sidewalk far below, landing on the rubber chicken.

The rubber chicken screamed.

Fortunately both Frog and the rubber chicken survived.

Frog had a bump on his head and a badly sprained ankle.

"That's okay," he said, drinking yet another seasonal beer. "I'll be fine. I'll just call my lawyer. He'll pick me up and take me home."

"Nooooo!" said the Professor, aghast. Visions of lawsuits danced in his head, wearing hobnail boots. "No . . . please. I insist you stay here tonight. Yes, we have a spare room, Frog. And lots more beer. Yes, lots more. I'll go get more if we run out. Then tomorrow I'll call my personal doctor and make sure you get looked at!"

"Gee, Dad, that's so cool," said Teddy.

Frog slept late. The doctor came, pronounced his head just fine, and bandaged his foot.

"Stay off the foot for a full week and you'll be okay," said the doctor.

"But I need to go out and sell Frog joke books!" said Frog.

"No, no," said the professor exuberantly. "I totally insist. You stay here, rest. I'll buy your joke books for the family here."

"Gee, professor. I thought you hated my jokes!" said Frog.

"I'm just very concerned about my guests, I suppose," said the professor. "Now how do you like to relax, Frog? Do you need a nice comfy lilly pad or something?"

"Gosh, I like to watch TV Land and Nickeleodeon on cable TV," said Frog.

"Me, too," chirped Teddy.

"And football," continued Frog. "Gee, professor. I just love football on TV. With popcorn and beer."

"I see," said the professor through gritted teeth, for the professor hated football on TV, football anywhere. The professor also actively opposed the university sports program, which he felt drained away funds from truly academic college pursuits. However, far better Frog in front of his TV, stretched out with popcorn and football, than Frog in touch with a lawyer—especially as the professor had accidentally allowed his home insurance to lapse.

Fortunately Frog's steady new diet of TV and hand-and-foot service, to say nothing of seasonal beer, of which he had gotten uncommonly fond, shut both him and his rubber chicken up. Teddy watched *Gilligan's Island* with him, but after a couple of days, Teddy went on to other Christmas-type activities.

For the professor's part, he found his nerves frazzled to the point of fraying. Teddy had taken up telling bad jokes. His wife told bad jokes. Life itself seemed to be a silly bad joke, what with the constant drone of TV, popcorn munching and beer slurping, and *Gilligan's Island* in the background he found himself shutting himself in his den with his whiskey between bouts of nervously serving Frog and seeing to his needs.

Three nights after Frog's fall, the professor awoke with a start. There was something on his chest, something gangly and soft.

He opened his eyes.

There, staring down at him, was the rubber chicken, looking like the nightmare bird in *Reefer Madness.*

"This ham-and-cheese sandwich goes into a bar and orders a beer. 'Can't you read the sign?' says the bartender. 'We don't serve food.' "

The professor screamed.

When his wife turned on the light, however, the rubber chicken was no longer there.

"A nightmare," she assured him. "It was just a nightmare, dear."

But the real nightmare arrived the next evening.

The professor had just started settling down. Frog had not only started hobbling around, he'd helped put up the Christmas tree, the tinsel, and the decorations, a duty that the professor loathed.

Moreover, his continual good cheer suffused the entire household.

The wife had become a domestic goddess, baking cookies and pies, losing entirely her penchant for worry and holiday depression. The whole house was filled with the mouth-watering scents of vanilla, chocolate, nuts, and toasted buttery flour. And Teddy, who had been a present hound, didn't seem interested in what he was getting for Christmas. He'd not only read all of Frog's joke books, he seemed to have caught the reading bug and was now reading his other books, with much improved comprehension and pleasure.

Just as the family was about to settle down for dinner, however, the doorbell rang. At the door was Fredrick Hathaway, Frog's lawyer.

"Is Frog here?"

"No!" cried the Professor. "Actually, what I meant was . . . er . . . well, we were sitting down for dinner. Can you come back next week?"

"Counselor!" cried Frog. "Come in, come in! Have some of this delicious spiced seasonal beer!"

"Why, I think I will!" said Mr. Hathaway. "Just wondered what happened to you, Frog. Wanted to make sure you were okay—I mean, you've been here for days in the house of your enemy! A fellow who wanted to kick you off 13th Street! And—Frog, what happened to your leg?"

"I slipped on the ice on the steps outside!" said Frog. "Boy, I came down hard. *Bam!*"

The lawyers' eyes glittered with greed.

"Why don't we go out and have some dinner, Frog, and talk about this?" said Hathaway the lawyer.

"Sure. Can my friends come, too?" asked Frog innocently.

"Ah . . . No . . . I don't think so, Frog. Look you've been here long enough. Eugene needs you. You're going to have lots of new customers, with you on a set of crutches!"

"Will I?" said Frog happily.

"We were just sitting down to dinner," said Mrs. Marshall.

"Anyway," said the professor. "We're buying all of Frog's joke books."

"He can print more," said the lawyer.

"We'll buy those, too!" replied the professor.

"Oh!" said Frog. "That's great! It's kind of cold out there these days."

"Damn it, Frog," snapped Hathaway. "Don't you see? We can sue this guy!"

"Sue the professor?" said Frog, scratching his fuzzy head. "But he's my friend. And he's going to watch a football game with me tonight, aren't you professor?"

"Absolutely," replied the professor. "Rah rah rah, sis boom bah!"

"Oh, the heck with you, Frog," said the lawyer. "I'll see you after Christmas."

"Sure," said Frog. "Thanks for dropping by!"

"Hmmmmph!" replied the rebuffed lawyer

The lawyer stepped out the front door, started walking down the steps, and promptly slipped on a patch of black ice.

The lawyer screamed. The professor screamed.

The screaming chicken screamed.

The lawyer tumbled down to the bottom the steps, landing in a heap.

"Damn it, I'll sue!" said Hathaway. "I'll sue!"

He hopped up to his feet, shaking his fist upward.

"You can't sue the professor," said Frog. "That's my fault. My chicken. I left it on the steps."

Sure enough, there on the steps, exactly where the lawyer had tripped, lay the rubber chicken.

"But I just saw it back there on the couch—" said Teddy.

"Shut up!" said the professor.

The lawyer picked up the chicken and threw it at Frog. "Damn you, you crazy amphibian!" he shouted and then stomped off into the night.

"My lawyer and I have a hoppy relationship," explained Frog. "Very up and down."

"What's black and white and red all over?" asked Teddy. "A contract and a lawyer in a blender!"

"I told you it was a magic screaming rubber chicken," said Frog.

The professor laughed. He embraced Frog.

"No, professor! No—" said Frog.

The professor kissed Frog.

"Oh uh," said Frog. "Now you've done it!"

And Frog shrank, changing into an actual frog.

"Ribit," said Frog. "Ribit."

The rubber chicken got up from the steps and bounced up to the doorway. "Well, well," said the magic screaming rubber chicken. "It's finally happened. Frog got kissed by a Professor of Love."

"Ribit," said Frog. "Ribit."

"Is that good?" said Teddy.

"You bet it's good. Now we get to go back home to the Joke Dimension!" The chicken reached up with a claw and seemed to scratch the air. A rent opened, a rift into Somewhere Else. Canned laughter wafted out. "Come on, Frog. We're going home."

"Ribit," said Frog and hopped through the hole.

"Wait a minute!" said the professor. "People—especially his Lawyer—will think I killed him and buried him in the cellar or something."

"Don't worry. Frog will call people from time to time and tell them he's in his home country, Greenland. Trust me."

"Trust you? Why?"

"Because I'm a magic screaming rubber chicken!" said the screaming rubber chicken. "Ho ho ho! And a merry Christmas to all, and to all a good night."

And the chicken put a finger to his nose, and up through the rift in dimensions he rose.

It was, in short, the best Christmas the professor had ever had. His heart was so full of good cheer that he had a big party the day after to let his friends finish off the massive quantities of seasonal beer that were left and tell bad jokes. Everyone went home with a Frog joke book.

By New Year's Day, however, after a fantastic and romantic night away with Mrs. Marshall, the professor found himself watching football games on television, sighing, and making up jokes to himself.

The next day, going to the local university coffee shop, he was shocked to find Frog in his usual spot.

"Frog! Frog, you're back!" he said, resisting the temptation to hug his newly returned friend.

"Hi, professor," said Frog. "Yeah. The Joke Dimension got old, fast. My screaming rubber chicken stayed, though. He's the life of the party there."

"But how did you get back?" asked the professor.

"I got kicked out."

"Kicked out?"

"Yep!" said Frog. "Me and my new pal, the screaming brown scratch-and-sniff whoopee cushion! Buy my new book —*Frog Returns From Joke Hell*—and you get to sit on it!"

"Sure, Frog," said the professor. He'd buy the new joke book and make a windy ass of himself quite cheerfully.

LOSING DOLLY

Kristine Kathryn Rusch

Three days after Daddy died, Dolly disappeared. Annabeth thought she could live without Daddy or Dolly, but not both. Daddy hadn't been home a lot—he had his own flock to attend to, Momma said—but when he was there, the whole house centered on him.

Dolly, though, Dolly belonged to Annabeth and nobody else.

And Dolly was gone too.

Annabeth wasn't sure how to look for Dolly. She wasn't supposed to call attention to herself. She was supposed to be a good little girl and stay quiet, be polite to the guests, and never ever cry. They laid Daddy out in the parlor—his body, anyway, her brother Kyle had said—and he didn't look much like Daddy anymore. More like Daddy if they'd made Daddy into a china doll like Dolly. His skin was all white and gray, and his mustache drooped. Daddy's mustache never drooped, not before he died. Daddy's mustache twitched and wiggled and hid his smile. His eyes twinkled and his mouth curved up, making the mustache curve too.

Daddy would say, "Annabeth, you are my joy," and he'd scoop her in his arms, and hold her too tight,

then set her down and make her giggle. When she
giggled, he twitched his mustache, and she loved it.

Only now, his mustache didn't twitch. His eyes were
closed and his hands folded across his best sermon
suit. Momma wouldn't put his pocket watch on, like
Daddy used to do. When Annabeth's older sister,
Joan, suggested it, Momma told her different.

"That watch is worth money, Joan Marie," Momma
said. "We're not putting it in the ground for the
worms."

Only the worms wouldn't get Daddy. Daddy said
so. He said ashes to ashes, dust to dust, and then
the righteous would rise up and sit at the left hand
of God.

Annabeth told that to Kyle, who wouldn't go in the
parlor at all, and he told her she'd mixed up her
quotes and didn't know what she was talking about.
But Daddy said man shouldn't fear death, not if he
believed in God.

Daddy believed in God. Daddy was a man of God.
Everybody who crowded into the parlor to see him
would say to Momma, "He must've been a pure man
for God to take him so soon." Or "Only the beloved
of God die young."

Annabeth told Mean Old Mr. Nurberts that Daddy
wasn't young, and that God knew Daddy belonged
right here with his family and his flock. Mr. Nurberts
patted her on the head and said that God knew best,
little lady, then Momma came and grabbed Annabeth
by the hand and dragged her away and told her she
couldn't go in the parlor or outside unless Momma or
her oldest brother Peter or her sister Joan was nearby.
Even then, Annabeth wasn't supposed to talk to
anybody.

She just sat by the parlor fire and watched people
bow their heads over Daddy and look pious. Sometimes they closed their eyes and pretended to pray.
Sometimes they just stared. The Catholic priest, who
had a "friendly rivalry" with Daddy, put some oint-

ment on Daddy's forehead—"like Jesus," Annabeth later whispered to Kyle, but Kyle said that Jesus didn't anoint anybody, everybody anointed him.

She got so mad at him that afternoon. She pulled his hair and kicked him with her new shoes—the first new shoes she had ever got. They were black and shiny and made of something called patent leather and they pinched really, really hard.

When Annabeth told Aunt Marie that her shoes hurt, Aunt Marie said, "Then the tears in your eyes'll be genuine," as if Annabeth wouldn't've cried real tears for her daddy. Annabeth loved her daddy and missed him, but if it weren't for the body laid out in the parlor, she could pretend he was at church and it was Holy Week, and he was too busy to come home. She never liked Holy Week because Daddy even ate in his office. Joan got to bring him a boxed supper, and last April, on Maundy Thursday, Annabeth asked if she could do it, and Joan got all mad, said Annabeth was trying to steal Joan's time with Daddy.

Time with Daddy had always been important. When there was eight kids in the family, Momma used to say, each one barely got a piece of each parent.

And now there was only one parent. It was Momma and her face was gray just like Daddy's, only Aunt Marie said it was because of her new burden, not because she was sick. Aunt Marie was gonna move in for a few weeks, while the church looked for a new pastor, and help Momma through the holidays, and the packing, and the figuring out what was going to happen next.

What was going to happen next was the hardest part. Annabeth learned they didn't even own the house. She'd been born in the big bed upstairs—all eight of them had—and they'd lived there their whole lives, and now the church wanted the house for the next pastor and his family.

Momma and Aunt Marie sat at the kitchen table late last night and Momma cried and cried because they didn't have any real money. The church paid in kind—the house, the bills, food from the parishioners' gardens, and pin money for fabric and shoes and other necessities (some of which, Momma said, they got from the poor box in the back because the pin money never went far enough).

Now there'd be nothing. No Daddy, no house, no food.

And no Dolly.

Maybe Dolly ran away. Maybe she heard that there'd be no place to live and nothing to eat and no thread to fix her dress when it accidentally ripped or to stitch up her knee when Annabeth got careless.

Maybe Dolly decided to go to a new house, with people who had food and nice things and a daddy too.

Annabeth would do that if she could. She'd leave the parlor and the pinchy shoes and her crying brother, and she'd go someplace where Daddy's mustache still twitched and Momma laughed when Daddy came home early and the house always smelled of pie.

"They can't be good Christians if they leave the minister's wife and family destitute," Aunt Marie had said last night. "Especially now, with Godfried so newly dead and the blessed holiday season upon us. If they try to evict you, I'll fight them off. I'll tell them what I think, so help me I will."

Annabeth never heard Momma's reply because Joan found her and whisked her away, taking her to her bed in the smallest room in the house, under the eaves, with a blanket wall between her and Kyle. Only Dolly wasn't on the bed that night, leaning up against the pillow like she always used to be. Dolly wasn't there, and she wasn't under the bed, and she wasn't in the back parlor or the kitchen or the forbidden dining room or even in the privy (where Annabeth had left her one night by accident).

She'd been looking for Dolly when she heard Mean Old Mr. Nurberts say they'd have to get the family out soon so they could electrify the place and put in

real plumbing for the new family. No one would want
to live in this run-down place, especially not someone
from the city, not in the year 1925 when people'd
come to expect modern conveniences, even in a tiny
parish in a small town one hundred miles from the
biggest cities.

That was when she'd told Mr. Nurberts he was
wrong. She'd stay in that house, and she'd live without
electrification, and she'd wait for Daddy to come back
and make his mustache twitch, and Mean Old Mr.
Nurberts said God had taken Daddy, and she'd asked
what Mr. Nurberts knew of God (because Daddy said
that once—he'd said George Nurberts would never
know God, no matter how much money he gave to
the church), and Momma had come outside in time
to see Annabeth scream at Mr. Nurberts that Daddy
wasn't young and God didn't need him, that his family
and his flock needed him more, and God would send
him back. God would send him back and everybody
would see. And then Mr. Nurberts patted her head,
and said God knows best, little lady, and she kicked
him with those pinchy patent leather shoes and
Momma had hauled her away, telling her to apologize,
which Annabeth said she couldn't do because if she
apologized, she'd have to lie.

Mean Old Mr. Nurberts had given Momma a mean
smile and said death was hard on everybody, and
Momma apologized for Annabeth and sent her to her
room, and wouldn't listen about Dolly going missing
because she didn't seem to care. Momma didn't seem
to care about anything anymore, and the only one
running anything was Aunt Marie, who was older than
Momma and tougher and had never really liked
Daddy anyway.

What kind of man can't provide for his family?
She'd said to Uncle Otto when she thought nobody
was hearing. *He should've known better than to take
this post. For fifteen years he has it, and he has nothing
to show for it, except eight destitute children and a wife*

who can't see how to get to the next meal let alone the next week.

When Annabeth told Aunt Marie that Dolly was missing, Aunt Marie nodded. She said Dolly had to go away. She was real sick. And Annabeth's stomach ached because it was her fault Dolly got sick. She was supposed to be careful with Dolly—not drag her around, watch her hands and her head because they were made of china. Real expensive china. But she'd dropped Dolly two months ago, and Dolly got a hole in her chin and she lost a finger. Dolly told her it was all right, but nobody else said that. Everybody else told her she had to take better care of her things.

Dolly wasn't a thing. She was Annabeth's best friend, and she was gone. Gone, gone, gone.

And unlike Daddy, Dolly didn't even leave her body here. She disappeared completely, and Annabeth didn't know what to do.

Daddy had to stay in the parlor one more day until the big funeral. Annabeth didn't know how there could be a big funeral because Daddy always was in charge. He planned everything. He made sure there was crepe over the pulpit and the mirrors were covered in the church hallways and the pews were draped in black ribbon. He would stay up late at night, looking for good things to say about the "deceased" and he would thumb through his Bible to find "reassuring passages" for those left behind.

Now Annabeth was left behind, and so was the flock, and so were her brothers and sisters and her poor mother who looked paler and paler every day. Aunt Marie made sure there was food and Uncle Otto talked to the church elders all the time, talking and talking about Christian charity.

Kyle didn't know how come anybody wanted to talk about Christian charity at a time like this, and Annabeth tried not to listen, but she was looking and looking and looking through the house for Dolly. She looked under the fainting couch and the big chairs in the forbidden dining room, and even in the big cast-iron stove when the fire had been tamped down. She remembered to use a rag to open it because otherwise she'd burn her fingers, but she had to see if Dolly melted into a little puddle or had her tummy burned out.

But no Dolly. And Reverend Samuels, from three towns over, came to talk at the funeral because Reverend Samuels had gone to school with Daddy. Reverend Samuels was a tall man with a belly that stuck out like Aunt Lucinda's did when she had her baby and he had lots of whiskers on the side of his cheeks but no mustache. He had nice eyes, but they weren't Daddy's eyes, and that night, when he shared their dinner, Annabeth asked to talk to him.

He led her into the back parlor, all private, and lit the fire, even though Momma would say that was wasteful. They sat on the horsehair couch that Momma loved but Annabeth hated because it was scratchy, and Reverend Samuels said, "How are you, child?"

Annabeth didn't expect him to ask about her. She just wanted to tell him about the crepe and the bows and the mirrors, and she said that, and he put a fat finger against her mouth, shushing her. His finger smelled of tobacco and it made her stomach hurt, because Daddy used to smell of tobacco too. Now he smelled kinda funny, and even though she loved him, she wanted him out of the parlor. She could hardly look at him anymore.

"I'll take care of the funeral the way your father would want," Reverend Samuels said, "but how are you?"

Annabeth blinked. No grown-up had ever asked about her before, not even Daddy. She said, "My tummy hurts."

And Reverend Samuels nodded without running for

the camphor like Momma would've done. He took her little hand in his big one and didn't say anything.

So she said, "I get all mad."

He nodded again.

"People are dumb."

He said something about being insensitive.

She said, "Dolly's gone."

He said, "No, honey, Daddy's with God."

She said, "Not Daddy. Dolly. My dolly. She's gone too."

And he looked at her with such sadness that she wanted to tell him it was going to be all right.

"Momma says we have to leave. Mean Old Mr. Nurberts says he has to electrify the house and he can't because we're here. He says we have to go now so everything can get done before the new family comes."

Reverend Samuels frowned. "But they haven't even hired a new— "

He stopped like he said something bad. He looked away for a minute and his eyes got all wet, like a lot of people's had in the parlor, and then he blinked once.

"I'll talk to Mr. Nurberts."

He didn't yell at Annabeth for calling Mr. Nurberts names. He didn't say Annabeth didn't understand. He said he'd talk to him, which in grown-up speak meant he might do something.

"And put up the crepe?" Annabeth asked.

"And the bows," Reverend Samuels said. "Will you help me?"

"I can't tie a bow," she said.

"You can supervise." He smiled at her.

"I have to look for Dolly."

His smile went away. He sighed. "I'll see if we can find Dolly."

He squeezed her hand and stood up. As he started to leave the parlor, she said, "We got to bank the fire. Momma'll yell about the waste."

He looked back. He said, "You enjoy it, honey."

But she couldn't. All she could think about was a fire just for her alone, and how the day after tomorrow was the first Sunday in Advent and how Daddy used to bring home a tree and put it in the front parlor all by himself. He'd set up the candles and the bucket of water, and he'd let the baby hang the first ornament. And that was her. That was always her.

She couldn't ask Reverend Samuels for a tree. Daddy was in the front parlor, and they'd have to clean it, and no one would think about Christmas anyway. No one would know how to light the candles and keep them off the dry branches and no one would fuss with the water pails behind the tree like Daddy did, and no one would read Luke on Christmas morning in that deep Daddy voice: *There were shepherds watching their flocks by night. . . .*

She laid down on the horsehair, even though it was scratchy and closed her eyes. It was hot in the back parlor. Momma would yell at her for being alone with the fire, but Momma would yell more if she banked it all by herself. And since she couldn't bank it, and she couldn't leave it go to waste, she watched it, wishing it would tell her where Dolly was, and why Dolly had gone right now, when she needed Dolly so much.

Aunt Marie came to get her. Aunt Marie didn't yell about the fire or Annabeth's feet on the horsehair couch. Aunt Marie scooped her arms around Annabeth and said, "We've been ignoring you, haven't we, honey?"

Annabeth didn't say because she didn't know ignoring. Daddy used a lot of big words but never that one.

"Reverend Samuels said I have to tell you about Dolly."

Annabeth sat up. She rubbed her eyes. They were sore, like they got dry because of the heat. It was hot in here, heat she saved all for herself, selfish little girl that she was.

"Do you remember," Aunt Marie said, "how Dolly goes away before Christmas every year?"

Annabeth frowned. She thought she lost Dolly a lot.

"Then Dolly comes back all new and pretty. Remember?"

Her hurts fixed. Annabeth always thought she just healed. People get hurts and they get fixed. She thought dollies did too.

"How she'd be under the tree Christmas morning in her new dress, her face all shiny and her hands like new?"

Dolly was always here on Christmas, always. And Annabeth was happy somebody (Santa?) found her and brought her back. But Kyle said Daddy was Santa and no one would find her now. Because Daddy was gone too.

"Do you remember, Annabeth?"

Annabeth nodded. She didn't remember it quite like Aunt Marie said, but enough. Enough to nod and not get in trouble for lying before God.

"You didn't lose Dolly, honey," Aunt Marie said. "I took her to be fixed, just like your momma usually does. They give her a new face and new hands and she comes back better—"

"I don't want new!" Annabeth said.

"Honey, every year—"

"I want Dolly!" Annabeth said. "Give me Dolly!"

"I can't, honey. She's being fixed."

"I don't care that she's broke. I just want her back. Please bring her back."

"She'll be back, with a new face and—"

"With a new face, she's not Dolly. Please find her, Aunt Marie. Please."

"I'm sorry, baby," Aunt Marie said. "I thought I was being responsible. If we didn't send her now, she wouldn't get fixed in time for Christmas, and I wanted you to have a nice Christmas. I wanted—"

"How can there be Christmas," Annabeth said, "without Daddy?"

"Oh, honey." Aunt Marie folded her in her arms. She smelled of rosewater and fresh bread.

Annabeth let Aunt Marie hold her, but not too long. Too long, and she would fall asleep in the heat, on the horsehair couch, and Momma would be mad. Too long and Aunt Marie would forget to help Annabeth get Dolly back—Dolly with the hurt chin and the lost finger.

Dolly, the one that Annabeth loved.

The grown-ups talked about it after she went to bed. Mrs. Samuels offered to go to town to the waylay the package with the head and hands, but Aunt Marie thought it might be too late. Reverend Samuels said maybe a replacement might do, and Momma said Annabeth loved that doll to distraction. There was no replacing her.

Then they started talking about the church and church politics and Mean Old Mr. Nurberts and electrifying things and Momma started to cry and everything stopped or maybe, just maybe, Annabeth fell asleep.

Only it didn't seem like she fell asleep. One minute she was listening through that hole in the wall, the next she was in a place with a thousand heads. They looked like Dolly, but not like Dolly at the same time. There was batting and fabric and a really nice sewing machine that folded into a cabinet, like the kind Momma said she wanted but couldn't afford, and there were dresses and shoes and pretty things near the door.

In the back, broken dolls lay against the wall. Headless bodies and empty sleeves made Annabeth want to cry.

Annabeth . . .

She heard the voice, almost a whisper, and turned around. There was Dolly in a box that Momma had saved from last summer. Brown wrapping had been opened along it, and a note in Aunt Marie's pretty cursive was tucked against the straw someone used for packing.

Dolly sat up. It looked like sitting up hurt her.

Annabeth went to her side. "Dolly. I'm so sorry. I thought I lost you."

It's all right, Annabeth, Dolly said. *This is natural.*

Annabeth shook her head.

Everyone slows down. Everyone gets older. Everyone dies, Annabeth.

Only Dolly wasn't saying that now. Daddy was. He was on the big bed in his nightshirt, and he didn't look like Daddy. His eyes were all sunken and his mustache wet. His skin was red and dotted with sweat. Momma said he had a bad fever.

You have to trust God, Annabeth, he said.

She nodded.

When I go live with Him, Daddy said, *you have to trust God.*

Dolly was looking at her. Annabeth didn't know how she got back to this scary place when a minute ago, she'd been with Daddy. Just like that very last day.

Do you trust God, Annabeth? Only this time it was Dolly asking her. Dolly, her best friend.

"God stole my daddy," Annabeth said.

Your father was ready to go.

Annabeth shook her head. "My daddy would never leave me."

Dolly patted Annabeth with the broken hand. The hole where the finger had been scratched.

Your daddy is with God, Dolly said, *and God is always with you. Do you know what that means?*

Annabeth shook her head.

It means your Daddy is always with you.

He had said that too, his voice wheezing out of him like an accordion that got broken. He was leaning on the pillows and holding Annabeth's hand in his and his hands were so cold. She wanted to tell Momma, but she didn't know how. She forgot what he said because she was so worried. He was so cold.

"I want you here," she said to him. "With me."

I will be, he said.

"Like now," she said.

He shook his head. *Sometimes,* he said, *people break, and can't be fixed. So God takes them and makes them happy.*

"Are you broke?" she asked.

He nodded, then closed his eyes. And he never talked to her again.

Kyle found her, curled up and cold against the outside wall. He bundled her in the quilt Momma had made before she was born, and helped her back to bed.

"I'm worried about you, Annabeth," he said. "You don't cry."

She opened her eyes. "Dolly's broke," she said.

His lips got all thin. He looked away. "I know," he said.

"She's gonna be with God," Annabeth said.

He looked at her, that same look he gave her when he said Santa was Daddy. Then he put a hand on her cheek like she was a baby and he was all grown-up.

"I know that too," he said.

"I'm not sure I like God," Annabeth said.

He bit his lower lip, like he was thinking. After a long pause, he said, "I'm not sure I like Him either. But we have to be nice to Him. Daddy's with Him."

"And Dolly," Annabeth said.

"And Dolly, too," Kyle said. He wrapped the quilt around his body and snuggled against her. He didn't say any more. She didn't either.

And for the first time since the elders put Daddy in the parlor, Annabeth had a good night's sleep.

In the morning, Aunt Marie brought her a new

dress that was black like her shoes. Reverend Samuels took her to church early. They walked through the sanctuary, and he asked her where the bows went, where the winter flowers went, where the crepe went. And even though Reverend Samuels was in Daddy's place, she felt Daddy here like he had never left. She thought maybe once he'd appear behind the pulpit and his mustache would twitch when he saw her.

When she was helping with the candles, an elder— not Mean Old Mr. Nurberts—came for Reverend Samuels.

"You're right," the elder said. "We can't just evict them. I have a house I can donate to the church. We've voted to let her have it until she has her own money or until she goes. But we have no money to continue the stipend."

"A house is the first step," Reverend Samuels asked. "Is there room for a garden?"

"A large one," the elder said. "And there's a root cellar already full and a cistern from last summer's rains. We can take food collection, maybe ask for donations through the winter."

"It's a start," Reverend Samuels said. He looked over his shoulder. Annabeth looked over hers too, so he knew she was listening. Lying in church—even by omission, Daddy said—was a grievous sin.

The elders came in with the box that Daddy had been in. Only the lid was closed. They set it up front, near the pulpit, where he normally stood.

Reverend Samuels watched her. She stood near the family pew, near the black bow, and didn't say a word.

On top of the box, Dolly sat. *We'll always love you, Annabeth,* she whispered, then patted the top with her broken hand. *Your Daddy and me. We love you.*

She sat in the pew. Her feet hurt. The shoes pinched. The pinch went all the way to her heart.

Don't go, she wanted to say, but she couldn't. The words wouldn't come out of her throat. Her heart had pinched it closed.

So she watched as Dolly faded away, and people threaded into the church and slid into the pews, and Momma came, and Aunt Marie, and Uncle Otto, and all her brothers and sisters, and even the aunts from faraway, and other reverends from the seminary and Reverend Samuels disappeared for half a heartbeat to put on his robes.

When he finally went to the pulpit, he didn't look like Daddy. He was too big, too tall, too wide, his robes too dark, his eyes too sad. Daddy was never sad when somebody went to see God.

That's what Dolly was trying to tell her. Not to be sad. They were with God.

Like Daddy said that last day when he could hardly talk. *I worry for you, Annabeth,* he said. *You feel things so strongly. I worry that you'll lose your joy. Remember always that you are my heart.*

She touched hers through the starch of the new dress. "You're mine too, Daddy," she whispered. "You're mine too."

THE AFFAIR OF THE
WOODEN BOY

Mel Odom

1

Dark things are drawn to my husband. I know this to be true and I no longer question why. I love him, and I think it would be harder for me to imagine someone *not* feeling the way I do than in why it is so.

His physician, Dr. Theophilus Hyde-Whyte, thinks it was because my husband was born dead. His heart was not beating when he was taken from his mother's womb. Thankfully Dr. Hyde-Whyte had a hedgewitch on hand that knew about such things. She placed a palm over my beloved's chest and shocked his heart back to beating.

My husband believes the hedgewitch saved his life. I choose to believe he is so strong that his first breath could not be denied to him, and that his life will have to be torn from him because he will never willingly give it up.

His mother insists that he was born with a caul over his face and therefore sees the dark things in a different light than most. When he was a child of twelve, a fortune-teller predicted that my beloved's life will always be connected to the darkness.

I do hope so, for his interaction with the dark things

that come calling bring him joy and challenge. But I fear for him as well because everyone knows the darkness is unmerciful when it finds a weakness.

The gargoyles that perch on buildings and listen to secrets in the streets and in the structures they watch over come to life at night and whisper what they know to my husband. He has an arrangement with them, you see, based on favors he has done them in the past. Travelers searching for arcane objects and rumors of those objects consult with him and the vast library we keep in our large home. Hansom cab drivers across the city know to refer these people to my husband.

These visits from strangers seeking the mystical often prove diverting and titillating, making for long discussions in front of the roaring fire in my husband's study, which I am fortunate enough to be invited to partake in. My beloved trusts my instincts and judgments in such matters because I have proven quick-witted and insightful. He has always known me to be so, but I fear that wasn't the case before I met him. My continued association with him, my love for him and his love for me, have all contributed to changing my views of the world and of dark things.

Occasionally the Drummond Police Department detectives come calling. Usually Inspector Charles Kirklyn is sent round our way. Despite his hardened demeanor and quick temper—one the result of growing up in the Gutbucket, that section of Drummond where the poor and lawless live, and the other a mark of his heritage as Khellenan, though he didn't grow up as his forebears did on the Isle of Khell where kelpies sometimes still lure ships to their deaths—Kirklyn is a good man. I would like him even if he didn't treasure my husband's friendship; but he does and so I welcome him into our home without reservation.

The police send Kirklyn round only when they have exhausted all other avenues involving a particularly offensive and strange crime or murder they wish to solve. With any other inspector, though, I fear those meetings are more the result of suspicion about my husband than an attempt to gain his assistance.

My husband, a very intelligent man, always sees through their subterfuge and chooses not to feel threatened or slighted. I fear I am not so generous as he. But, should the puzzle prove challenging, he accepts the niggardly stipend they offer (though we are wealthy and do not need it) and applies his knowledge, wits, and—sometimes—sword and pistol to the solution of that mystery. He does love intrigues so.

I would prefer to live out the life we have together in our house in the city or—more my choice—at the manor house and lands that are ours in the countryside. But mysteries don't often find their way to our doorstep out there. So I abide, loving him and enjoying what I wish of Drummond's busy nightlife.

My beloved's name is James Stark, but he holds title in the Court of Lords as Lord Gallatin. Others know him as a consulting investigator, the only one in Drummond who specializes in the occult. He has cards printed that find their way into the hands of those who need his services, and those worthy of my husband's time and his precious blood are guided to our door by direction or by fate.

That night, when the case began—which I have taken the liberty of calling *The Affair of the Wooden Boy* for reasons which you'll quickly come to understand—we were home just after returning from a Siahnea play. Both of us had looked forward to the play, for it was the first of its culture to ever be imported to Drummond.

I had rather fancied the costumes, which were gay and festive and not ever to be worn by the ladies in Drummond, this according to Queen Isina's royal decree (I still don't think a monarch should decide what her subjects should and should not wear, or how they should behave in the privacy of their own homes!), and James had found favor with the swordplay, a whirling, two-bladed discipline that had filled the theater with the clangor of ringing steel during the choreographed fighting sequences.

"I have sent a message to Master Nilasta," my husband said. He took out the poker and turned the logs in the study fireplace. Whirling embers shot up the flue.

"Who is he?" I asked as I poured wine into glasses and brought it over to serve him.

As always, he looked incredibly handsome in his evening wear. In his early thirties, James is a tall man, two inches over six feet, with dark hair, eyes the color of cut jade, dimples in his cheeks, and a strong face. I am much fairer than he, and my long blond hair and gray eyes mark us as immediate contrasts. I am tall for a woman, though, five feet eight inches, which draws the attention of many men, but not so tall as my beloved, though I have been told we look very seemly together.

"Master Nilasta is the bladesmaster who taught the actors," he said. He relinquished the poker, at last satisfied with the cheery blaze that warmed the room.

"Why would you wish to talk to him?" I sat myself on the love seat we often shared during our nights there. The fire warmed me and made me feel wonderful. Or, perhaps, it was only being there with my beloved. I have found, over our years together, that I have often felt exactly that way while with him even in the harshest of circumstances with flesh-eating beasts possibly awaiting us round every turn.

"I would like to learn the bladework." My beloved smiled at me, and he reminded me once again of a boy whose interest flirts and flits through life like a honeybee. James has never truly been happy doing the same things again and again in his life. He seeks out that which is new and different.

When I first fell in love with him, I dreaded that aspect of him. Fearful of his charms and my own unwanted and unmatched weakness to swoon whenever

I was around him, I thought that he could love me one day and leave me the next.

So far, in eight years, I have never had reason to doubt him. He tells me I am his constant constellation, his one true star that helps him navigate his tempestuous life. I choose to believe him. Doubt about love only leads to madness and murder, and I have seen that in many of the cases my beloved has investigated.

"You already know the art of the sword," I replied, and sipped my wine.

"I would learn more, Mina," he told me.

In those words, I was reminded again how so many of our adventures together had begun because of that need within him. I suppose I could not help my reaction.

"You're laughing at me," he said, but he took no offense.

"No more so than usual, beloved," I told him. "Your infatuations are sometimes easy to predict."

He touched the marble chess set I had given him as a gift (all the pieces are night creatures and monsters from the works of the Brothers Taloch, whose frightful tales were once banned throughout all of the Empire—because many of them rattled uneasy skeletons in the closets of important personages throughout the Empire), then walked over to the vast collection of books we have accumulated. Many nights we spent hours playing chess, reading from books, exchanging ideas, and talking. Our life together is complete. Still my husband loves his diversions. And truthfully, upon occasion, I enjoy a good chase as much as he does.

"I don't mean to be inattentive, my love," he told me, "but I fear I'm descending into one of my despairing moods." He sighed. "I'm ready for something, *anything,* to come calling in need of my expertise."

As if the fates had joined together, there came a tentative knock at our door. Although we didn't know it at the time, my husband's claim to being ready for anything was about to be challenged.

He excused himself from my presence and went to answer the door. He had given Thom, our houseman, the evening off. Curious myself at who would come calling this late at night, knowing that it had to be connected to my husband's predilection for mysteries, murder, and mayhem, I stood and walked to the hallway to watch him answer the knock. Every now and again, I've been able to prevent harm that might otherwise befall him. He has his strengths and I have mine. We complement each other.

James reached into his pocket for the pistol he habitually carries. He had learned even before meeting me that his fascinations often proved dangerous. His body is scarred from swords, knives, and bullets.

When he opened the door, he didn't immediately invite in whoever stood there. Dark things, as you may know, often require an invitation to step into a person's home.

"Fascinating," he whispered.

Drawn by his surprise, I joined him at the door. Outside, thick white snowflakes tumbled through the air and drifted into masses that promised at least another foot on top of the winter's leavings thus far into the season. Cabs and coaches pulled by sure-footed horses, and sometimes exotic creatures less seen in the day, crossed the street in a rumble of wheels, heading in both directions. Gaslight streetlamps carved holes in the night. Golden glows played against a few other windows, for most of Drummond is early to bed and early to rise because it is a city of merchants and warehouses.

When I saw our prospective visitor, even I—who had seen nearly everything my husband had seen—was almost bowled over. For there on our doorstep, illuminated by the stoop lamp, stood a little wooden boy.

2

The wooden boy stood less than two feet tall. Soot covered him from head to toe. His glass eyes, set firmly into his wooden head, looked almost human. Blue and sad, they regarded first my beloved, then me. His hair, powdered by the falling snow, was sheep's wool dyed blue-black. A thin blade of a nose had been whacked into an appropriate space between and under his eyes and above his hinged mouth.

He wore only frayed brown twill knee pants that were held up by red suspenders, a white short-sleeved shirt displaying a garish collection of stains and a couple rips that needed mending, a missing button and a broken one, and a faded red and yellow kerchief around his spindly neck.

His feet and hands were made plain, only hinting at toes and fingers, all of them the same length. The arms and legs, hands and feet, were articulated and had holes bored in them. A child's puppet, I realized, and wondered immediately how he had come to our door. He surprised my beloved and me even more when he spoke.

"Good evening," the wooden boy said. His hinged jaw clacked and snapped open and shut. Of course there was no breath in him to fog the cold night air.

"Good evening," my husband replied.

"Is this 463 Candlestick Road?" the wooden boy asked.

"It is," James told him. He glanced to the side of the door and brushed snow from the brass plate that listed the house's address. The modest script also noted The Honorable James Stark, Lord Gallatin, Private Enquiry Agent.

"You are Lord Gallatin?" the wooden boy asked.

"I am. And who might you be?"

"I'm Simon," the wooden boy replied, and his voice trailed off into an anguished cry. "I n-need your h-help." With that, he clapped his wooden hands to his wooden head with solid thunks and began to cry in earnest. His hinged jaw trembled in a way that broke my heart.

My beloved looked at me. I could see that he was lost as to what to do. The wooden boy, after all, was a toy. But the anguish in our strange visitor's thin voice (even though it was somewhat jarring because his wooden jaws scraped against each other) moved me to action.

I reached out to the wooden boy and stroked the soaked sheep's wool hair, which was wet and thick. "You have come to the right place," I told Simon (for in that moment I chose to regard him as an individual with a name and not a toy) with all the brave confidence I could muster. "Lord Gallatin is very good with problems that many learned men might find otherwise daunting."

"Thank you, my lady," Simon said.

I noticed that he had very good manners for a wooden boy, although I wasn't certain what kind of manners to expect from a boy who had once been a woodchopper's log. Feeling much relieved, though James was still somewhat uncertain about how things would go, I reached down and took the wooden boy's hand. His rough wooden fingers curled slightly around mine.

"Come inside where it's warm," I told him.

He did so, clutching my hand as best he could with his stiff fingers.

Mindful that he might be cold from being so under-dressed in the dead of winter (even though he was a wooden boy), I led him straightaway to my beloved's study.

James checked outside again, then closed the door and followed us.

"Are you cold?" I asked a short time later when I had our unexpected guest in one of the chairs in the study.

Simon shook his head, but the effort looked somewhat ridiculous on him. "I don't . . . *feel* anything." He held one of his wooden hands out in front of him. "I can move, but this body . . . just *isn't* me." Seated on the chair with his feet hanging only halfway to the floor, he looked a pitiful sight.

"Well, Simon," James said, "what seems to be the problem?"

"I'm not myself today," Simon said.

"What do you mean?"

"I am not a wooden boy most days."

"Then what are you?"

"A flesh and blood boy."

"Who were you," I asked, "before you were a puppet?"

"Simon Delhalm," he answered. "My father is—"

"Courtland Delhalm," James said. He makes it a habit to read the papers every day and spend some time at his scrying bowl. Also, as I have mentioned, the gargoyles in the city often whisper their gossip to him.

A surprised look lifted the wooden boy's painted eyebrows. Obviously whatever magic had been used to animate him was strong.

"You know my father?" he asked hopefully.

"I know *of* your father," James said. "Our paths have never crossed."

"Oh." A forlorn look conveyed Simon's dashed hopes.

"Not to worry," my beloved told him. "If need be, I can meet your father. Does he know that you're a—" James, although he is quick of mind, sometimes falters at how to express himself properly.

"What my husband means to ask is whether your father knows of your condition?" I asked. I work at my beloved's side, and often I am better at dealing with people than he. That is especially true of children and women.

"No," Simon answered.

"When did this change occur?" James asked.

"Early this morning."

"If you can, tell us about it."

Nodding sadly, Simon began his tale. "I was at school. I attend Thornwood Academy. It's a private school for boys."

"The school is very well protected," James said. His brow furrowed and I knew he was intrigued by what was unfolding in the study. "Something like . . . *this* shouldn't have happened there."

"But it did. At lunch, I went to the loo. On the way back, Edgar Chalmers, one of the school custodians, put a knife to my neck and told me he'd slit my throat if I cried out for help."

Unconsciously, Simon touched his spindly wooden neck and I knew that was a memory that would never leave him no matter what my beloved was able to do for him. I resolved to kill the man or men behind the evil deed. No child should have to live with even the memory of such a threat. I fear that I am most times more vengeful than my beloved.

"Edgar Chalmers took me down into the basement," Simon continued in a tremulous voice. "I feared the worst, that I would be taken advantage of in some way. I also feared that he would kill me later, so that I couldn't tell on him." He shook his head and his neck squeaked in its socket. "In the basement, he placed me within a circle drawn in chalk when the other man commanded him to."

"What other man?" James asked instantly.

"I don't know. I had never seen him before."

"What did he look like?"

Simon contemplated for a moment. "He was a handsome man, taller than you, and more powerfully built. He had long red hair and a goatee."

"Did Edgar Chalmers ever call him by name?"

Squeaking once again, Simon shook his head. "I lay in the circle with Edgar Chalmers's knife at my throat." His voice broke and his hinged chin quivered.

"I didn't want to die, so I begged for my life. The man just laughed at me. He said I would live. That I had to."

My beloved nodded in understanding. "If he meant to use your body, he needed to keep your spirit alive. Otherwise the body would die as well."

"I didn't know that," Simon said. "Edgar Chalmers opened a bag and laid a child's stuffed gingerbread man in the circle with me."

That seemed to surprise my beloved. "Not this puppet?"

"No. A gingerbread man. Then the other man, the one I didn't know, began chanting." Simon's eyes grew round. "I knew he was a wizard then. As he talked, fire sprang up from the chalk lines of the circle. I felt myself being pushed into the gingerbread man."

"As you should have been," James said.

I wondered if it would have been any more surprising to find a stuffed gingerbread man on our doorstep.

"Where did the puppet come from?" James asked.

Simon held out his stick arms with the ill-made hands. "This is Mr. Jinx. He was my favorite toy for a long time. I kept him because I didn't want to throw him away." He paused. "During the wizard's spell, when I was about to sink into the gingerbread man, Mr. Jinx reached out for me and pulled me to him."

"How?"

Simon shook his head. "I don't know."

"Had Mr. Jinx ever before exhibited a magical nature?"

"When I was little, I used to think that he was alive. My friends sometimes made fun of me because I told them he would talk to me and play with me. Without me pulling his strings."

"Did he?"

"I don't remember now, but I think that he did. I was very small then."

"Simon," I asked, "how old are you?"

"Eleven," he said.

I could not remember being eleven. I could not ever imagine how afraid he must have felt. I smiled at him. "You're very brave," I said.

He smiled a little. "Thank you, Lady Gallatin."

"So you found yourself in Mr. Jinx's body instead of the gingerbread man?" James asked.

"Yes."

"Where was Mr. Jinx at the time?"

"In my house. I closed my eyes in the school basement, then opened them in my bedroom."

"Do you know what happened to—" Curbing his impatience to know the parameters of the intrigue confronting him, my beloved thought about what he was about to ask.

"My body?" Simon asked.

"Yes."

"It came home." Those blue eyes looked so sad again. "Someone else is wearing it. I had waited in my room, not knowing what to do. My father was at his offices and I didn't know how to find him on foot. As I am," he gestured to his wooden body, "I couldn't ask a hack to take me there."

"No," James replied, "I suppose you couldn't. Even in Drummond, which is known far and wide for its magical marvels, you couldn't very well be running through the city unescorted. Wasn't there anyone else at home you could have asked for help?"

"I was afraid. My father doesn't like anything to do with magic. My stepmother was home, but since her marriage to my father two years ago, we've never gotten on."

"So what happened when your body returned home?" James asked.

"He caught me and threw me onto the fireplace. Before I could get back out, he locked the grate." Simon touched his soot-covered cheeks. "At first I thought I would burn. Then I managed to climb up the chimney and escape the house."

"Did your opponent know you escaped?"

"He heard me running across the roof. I slipped and fell into the yard. By that time, he was at the window. He yelled the most frightful things at me, and promised that he would hack me to pieces with an axe."

"But wouldn't that have killed you?" I asked before I thought how callous that question was.

"No," my beloved said. "With the spell still in operation, Simon would have been trapped in the body of the gingerbread man."

He seemed predisposed now and I knew he'd turned his mind to the auguries of the puzzle set before him. Without thinking, he strode to the fireplace and turned the logs, never noticing as I did how Simon drew back from the fire.

"Only your relationship with your toy—with Mr. Jinx—saved you, you know," my beloved said after a moment. "Doubtless your kidnappers would have trapped you in the gingerbread man, bagged you, and stored you somewhere till you were driven insane by your captivity. They needed you alive, but they hadn't counted on your puppet." He smiled a little then. "I believe it had some magic in it. Perhaps you were right, Simon, when you believed Mr. Jinx talked to you and played with you when you were younger. Some fairy magic is delicate like that, connected only to the belief of a child. I think he protected you now."

"I was told by a talking horse that you could help me," Simon said. "He saw me in the street and called out to me."

I smiled. "I see Cobblepot is still spreading your name about, Beloved."

James grinned at that. The horse, Cobblepot, is a favorite of ours.

"I didn't believe him," Simon said, "even though I had heard of you and read about you in the papers. But it was the gargoyles that convinced me."

"The gargoyles in this city," James declared, with a mixture of resignation, irritation, and fondness, "have forever been busybodies. Worse than magpies."

"They directed me to your door."

"And now here we are," my husband said. "We need to figure out our next steps. I suppose you've tried to return home after your escape?"

"Yes. The man wearing my body waits there for me. I knocked on the door several times after my father got home, but the servants now have orders to destroy me on sight."

"Well that presents a problem, doesn't it?"

Simon was quiet for a moment. "I only want to return home, Lord Gallatin. I love my father very much."

"Well then," said my beloved with a conviction and passion that made me love him all the more, "we'll have to make that happen, won't we?"

3

We went visiting at eleven o'clock that night, after my husband called round to Mr. Courtland Delhalm's home through the scrying bowl. That Mr. Delhalm should welcome us into his home at such a late hour only testified to how highly my beloved was regarded.

Dressed in heavy outerwear against the winter's chill, even a coat for Simon, we took a hired cab to the Delhalm home. Simon was distraught the whole way, I could tell though he tried to hide it and the wooden face was difficult to read.

Outside the cab the snow swirled. The cab wheels shushed through the drifts. A haze clung around the full moons and all three of them appeared fragile and watchful. Clouds muted most of the stars, but there was enough light to watch the gargoyles and dragonets playing tag like children across the building roofs and in the sky.

For a moment, when we passed a small coach drawn

sive artillery piece and stood once more rigidly at attention. Snowflakes that settled on his metal hide hissed into oblivion.

Mr. Delhalm waved to us, ushering us to the house. James and I went along the shoveled walk. At the porch, we paused to stomp our feet and rid ourselves of the excess snow that didn't fall off on its own.

By that time a young woman had appeared in the doorway. No older than her early twenties, she had red-gold hair that trailed down her shoulders in rampant curls. A corset, obviously cinched very tightly given the effect it made, divided her body into its voluptuous hourglass shape. The milky white tops of her breasts lay exposed in the moonlight. Evidently she didn't follow the queen's rules for proper attire. A necklace gleamed in her throat. Bracelets shone at her wrists. Rings caught and reflected the moonlight.

"Lord Gallatin," the young woman said without awaiting a proper introduction, "please do come in. You'll catch your death out there in this cold."

"My wife," Mr. Delhalm said, gesturing to the young woman. "Mrs. Delhalm."

"Do call me Vivian," she said, offering her hand to my husband.

James, sometimes forgetful while he was on the hunt, started forward.

"Beloved," I said, "perhaps I should wait in the coach."

Recovering quickly, understanding what I needed, James took my elbow, shook his head as if chiding himself, and said, "Forgive me, my dear. I would forget my head were it not attached." Turning, he presented me to the Delhalms. "Mr. Delhalm, Mrs. Delhalm, may I present my beautiful wife, Lady Gallatin."

"Lady Gallatin," Vivian said, "please come inside. You're surely chilled standing out there. We can talk while the men do whatever it is they feel they must do."

On my husband's arm then, I stepped into the house where Simon no longer lived, and wondered when I might see their enchanted progeny.

After the maid took our coats in the foyer, James and Mr. Delhalm retired to the latter's study to discuss whatever business my beloved had concocted as a cover for his preliminary investigation into the household. I was left in the big parlor off the foyer with Mrs. Delhalm.

"Please," said my hostess, waving toward one of the overstuffed chairs in front of the fireplace, "do sit."

I sat and looked around. The room was overly large, ostentatious almost, and appointed with expensive things. I recognized several of the pieces as Siahnean in origin, which were austere in their strange craftsmanship rather than elegant. Most of the pieces had faces of animals and demons carved on them. Those images, I knew from my own interests and readings, came from the Siahnean mythology, filled with battles and beings with fierce powers.

Above the mantel on the fireplace hung a portrait of Mr. Delhalm and his pretty young wife. He occupied a large chair that sat even his considerable bulk comfortably. Vivian Delhalm stood behind him, one arm across her husband's chair and a smile on her beautiful face.

"That's a lovely portrait," I said, wishing to break into conversation as soon as was possible. I was somewhat uncomfortable around Vivian Delhalm, as I am around all highborn ladies. Despite the fact that I am now and will forever be Lady Gallatin, I was not born to a title.

"It is, isn't it?" She sat in a chair across from me, leaning back casually, well relaxed and at ease. Then she smiled and clapped her hands twice.

Immediately the picture above the fireplace changed and showed only Vivian Delhalm standing in a beautiful spring garden in full bloom. Three claps produced yet another portrait image in the frame, this one of Vivian Delhalm standing in a summer dress with a parasol near a brook. Listening closely, I heard the brook babbling in the background.

"It's enchanted, of course," said she, stating what was plainly obvious only to take pride in it. "Quite expensive, but my husband is a dear and indulges my whims."

At once I felt on more even footing with Vivian Delhalm. She might play the part of a highborn lady but I knew that she wasn't. No highborn would so casually flaunt wealth, nor remark upon it. No, I thought at the time, Vivian Delhalm's roots had not been among the elite, and I found that interesting.

We made small talk again for a while. She was much better at it than I. She knew the affairs of the Courts of Lords and their ladies and mistresses, and took great delight in recounting them. My subject matter for conversation tended more toward books, music, and art, though I was *not* going to comment any further on her gaudy portrait.

I listened with feigned interest, and I must have been quite convincing at the charade for she would not quiet herself and droned on. During one of those few times she had to stop to think of something she had not told me, I asked her, "I'd heard you had a son."

That stopped her in her tracks for a moment. Then she nodded. "We do. His name is Simon. Actually he is my husband's son from his previous marriage. The former Mrs. Courtland Delhalm died."

"Oh?"

"Yes. She was crossing Markham Bridge when her team bolted and dumped the coach into Traveler River." Vivian Delhalm put on a sad face but I knew straightaway it was only for show.

Markham Bridge was one of eleven bridges that crossed the river. In the early days of Drummond, in the infancy of the empire, explorers had come up

Traveler River and laid claim to all the lands. After that the river had become the main artery that allowed so much commerce to take place in the city. It was deep and held secrets of its own that sometimes spilled over into the Ghost Marshes and small cave systems right outside the city.

"I only met Courtland three years ago," Vivian Delhalm said. "He'd been grieving for his lost wife for six months. I was quite attracted to him. Men of power draw me to them like a lodestone, but there was something special about Courtland."

I thought to myself, perhaps a bit unkindly I'm afraid, that the attraction was rooted in her husband's great wealth.

"After a few weeks, I convinced him that grieving for the poor dear was over," she went on. "I mean, a few people talked about our quick nuptials, but when true love bites you, you can't just walk away."

I couldn't argue that. James and I had found each other quickly, and in our eight years together, our love has never wavered. "I know," I told her.

She smiled, looking deep into my eyes, which few people have been able to do. "You do know," she said. "You love your James the same way I love Courtland."

She would never understand how deeply I loved James. No one would. But I stilled my tongue despite its desperate attempts to free itself and tell her exactly that. But a small voice distracted me.

"Mother."

I turned and saw a young boy standing in the parlor doorway. He was young and intent, with a headful of blond curls and cerulean blue eyes. He was long and lanky, and his build promised strength and grace to come. He wore a dark suit cut to fit him.

"Simon," she said. "Whatever are you doing up at this late hour?"

"I heard voices," he replied.

Vivian Delhalm held her arms out to the imposter

posing as her stepson. He approached her and sat on her lap, though he was clearly too big to do so. "Did you have a bad dream?"

"I can't remember," he said. His gaze rested on me, though his stepmother's hands caressed his blond locks.

I got the strangest feeling that he knew me from somewhere, though I had no clue as to where that might have been. Many people in Drummond know of my husband, and—through him—of me.

I stared at him, wondering who would be cruel-hearted enough to steal a boy's body. The sad thing wasn't that I could think of those who would—the aged and infirm—but that I could think of so *many*.

Then I noticed the dark fleck on his lower lip. Closer inspection revealed it to be tobacco. Only then did my keen sense of smell detect the sweet odor of pipe tobacco on him.

Vivian Delhalm tenderly kissed her stepson's brow. "You've no fever." Then her eyes widened as she stared over my shoulder. "Wretched thing!" She pushed her stepson from her lap and stood up, grabbing the poker from the fireplace.

Looking over my shoulder, I saw the wooden face plainly in the window. The blue eyes looked forlorn. I shuddered to think what Simon must have been going through, seeing himself in a house he could not now enter.

"Wretched, wretched thing!" Vivian Delhalm screamed again, starting toward the window with the poker clutched in her fist.

The face disappeared from the window, but I didn't know if Simon would be able to effect a proper escape.

4

Vivian Delhalm's voice drew her husband's attention. He rushed from the study and James was behind him.

"There!" she shouted to her husband, pointing at the window where the wooden face had been but a moment ago. "It's back, Courtland!"

Her husband cursed and raced for the door, pausing only long enough to pick up a shotgun from the locked closet. "Why haven't the guards dealt with it?"

James threw open the door and bounded outside. I knew he was trying to save poor Simon, though our host and hostess didn't.

I followed, easily outrunning Vivian Delhalm who obviously didn't want to encounter the wooden boy. In seconds, we all stood out in the snow-covered yard. James and Mr. Delhalm's breath stained the night air as they searched for the wooden boy.

Trying not to be noticed, I crossed over to our rented coach. I looked up at Edmond, who was a coach driver my husband frequently employed while on his investigations. He is a slender man of indeterminate years, with ragged black hair and stubbled cheeks at all hours. Bundled into his winter clothes, he looked at me and gave an imperceptible nod.

I walked to the coach and peered in. Simon was a tight ball of odd angles and slats under one of the seats. He peered up at me fearfully, his knees and elbows clacking against the coach's bottom.

"I couldn't help it," he pleaded. "I just wanted to see. You were gone for ever so long."

"It's all right," I told him. "Just stay put this time."

"Yes, ma'am."

I returned to the coach beside Edmond.

"I didn't see 'im climb out, mum," he whispered. "First I knowed of 'im not bein' in 'is proper place was when the missus set up such a fuss inside."

"It's all right, Edmond," I told him. "He'll stay put now." I watched while James and Mr. Delhalm searched the yards and the dead gardens. Mr. Delhalm called the mechanical men to aid them, cursing them the whole time for not having seen the intruder.

Later, after they'd given up the search and I'd signaled to my beloved that all was well and that Simon was once more where he should have been, we stood once more in the foyer.

"Well, that's a nasty bit of business," Mr. Delhalm said. "I came home only this evening to hear my wife's story about that possessed puppet trying to break into the house. That's why I had the mechanical men patrolling the grounds."

"But you mustn't hurt Mr. Jinx, Papa!" the fake Simon cried.

I, of course, knew that whoever possessed Simon's body was only trying to play the son to the hilt for Mr. Delhalm.

"There, there, my boy," Mr. Delhalm said as he knelt in front of the boy and took his shoulders in hand. "We have to be quite careful at the moment. Someone has put a hex or a curse on Mr. Jinx, obviously turned him against us. I will put things aright. I give you my word."

"Come, Simon," Vivian Delhalm said, taking the boy by the hand. "You've had a frightful scare from that horrid thing. Let me tuck you in."

For a moment, Mr. Delhalm watched his wife and young son reenter the home. His love for both shone in his eyes.

"I didn't see what we were pursuing," James said. "You say it was a puppet?"

"Yes." Mr. Delhalm sighed. "Evidently someone— an enemy, perhaps, or a business rival—has magicked Simon's puppet, Mr. Jinx, and given it instructions to do us harm. Mrs. Delhalm told me about it when I arrived home earlier this evening. She found it awaiting her here. It attacked without warning, and she said she was very lucky to have escaped with her life."

"That's horrible," I said because I was a woman and was expected to say something like that under the circumstances.

Mr. Delhalm regarded me and nodded. "I'm quite certain, Lady Gallatin, that you've seen much worse, what with accompanying your husband in his endeavors, but Mrs. Delhalm is very sensitive."

"Have you notified the police?" James asked. "They have wizards and spellcasters in their employ."

"Not yet," Mr. Delhalm said. "But I shall. First thing in the morning."

Good, I thought to myself, knowing that James and I would have the rest of the night to search without tripping over the police. But that time would pass swiftly.

Mr. Delhalm shook his massive head. "After losing my first wife in such a tragic mishap, I try to be very careful with my second. And with Simon."

After a few more minutes, we took our leave. I was in a hurry to discuss my thoughts with James.

"I'm sorry," Simon said from under the coach seat once we were underway. "I worried that something had happened to you."

My husband extracted the wooden boy and sat him on the seat across from us. He patted Simon on the head.

"It's all right, lad," my beloved told Simon. "We're going to get to the bottom of this." He touched his heart. "Upon my honor as a gentleman, I pledge this to you."

James is not free with his pledges, and I knew that even though the boy didn't.

"Thank you," Simon whispered.

"Just give us a little more time," James said.

"We've only just begun this investigation." He smiled confidently. "Lady Gallatin and I are quite skilled in these matters, you see."

Simon nodded and his wooden head squeaked as it bobbed.

James turned to me then. "What did you think?"

"The imposter smokes," I said. "He had a fleck of tobacco on his lip and I smelled smoke on him."

"Obviously he can't give up his vices," James said. Then he grinned and looked at Simon. "Unless you're the one who smokes."

The puppet's painted eyebrows climbed almost to his woolen hairline in consternation. "No, sir!" Simon exclaimed. "I would never!"

"There's a good lad," James said. "Tell me, though, do you tie your own ties?"

"I do, but I'm not very good at it."

My husband nodded and I wondered at what he had seen. Even though he hadn't spent much time with the imposter, I knew my beloved had noticed something.

"Did your father teach you to tie your tie?" James asked.

"Yes, sir. He and the valet."

"Were either of them in the military?"

Simon thought for a moment. Unconsciously, his little wooden hand came up to scratch at his knobby wooden chin. "No sir. Not that I can remember."

I looked at my beloved: "Why do you ask about the military?"

"Because," he answered, "the boy's tie tonight was knotted in a military four-in-hand that's taught at the Veritas Military Academy. Not many people know how to tie them."

Over the years, James has made a study of esoterica. Inside our big house, he keeps rooms full of paraphernalia that he believes might come in handy some day. Soil samples, fabric swatches from the textile

mills, bottles of preserved lizards and snakes, stuffed
and mounted birds and animals, all add to the bizarre
collection he has managed.

I don't think anything about his excesses, but I'm
afraid many of our acquaintances would not be so
inclined. Once the Drummond Police inspectors even
took umbrage over a mummified body my beloved
had shipped in from far-off Safrik where ebony-hued
warriors are rumored to be cannibals who devour their
enemies. Of course, those inspectors were much more
lenient when that body solved a missing-person report
they had been stymied on. Especially when James had
also tracked down the murderer.

"But you do." I smiled.

He took my hand and kissed it, then grinned mis-
chievously. "But of course I do." He continued holding my hand and I felt the warmth and strength of
him. "So we know a little about the imposter from
Simon's description of him. He's tall and powerfully
built, with red hair and a goatee. He has passing ac-
quaintance with magic and the military, as evidenced
by the spell he used on Simon and the tie he wore
tonight. To that list, we can add the tobacco."

"The tobacco?" I asked.

My beloved nodded. "I smelled it on him. It's an
exotic blend. Not something you can just buy off the
shelves at even a well-stocked tobacconist's shop. The
blend is from the Confederacy of Ishplen, taken there
during the Dragon Campaigns, when mankind finally
succeeded in enforcing a peace with dragonkind."

That peace was a tenuous thing. If the dragons'
numbers hadn't been so severely cut during those vicious battles, the proud creatures would never have
agreed to peaceable surrender. Still these days dragons
walked among mankind—as many monsters do—
looking quite human.

"The blend has a mild narcotic in it," James went
on. "An herb called dreamweed. Something less
strong than the opium that the Siahnean have brought

to our shores, but still not something most smokers would use. As a result, few tobacconists keep the blend in stock. I happen to know of only two places in Drummond that carry it."

I smiled at him. "If it is a unique blend, especially one that contains contraband, we can find out who he is," I said.

"I believe so." James leaned back in the seat. "There is also the matter of the custodian, Mr. Edgar Chalmers. I should think I'd like to talk to him as well. To find out how deeply this conspiracy runs, and what the ultimate goal is."

Before he could say anything further, the horses bolted sideways in the street and Edmond's harsh voice rang out as he tried to control them. James threw his arm out to steady me, but I already had myself in hand and was holding on to poor Simon.

The coach came to a halt. James opened the door and peered out. The coach light lit him squarely and I saw him reach into his pocket for his pistol.

Naturally, I could not let him face alone whatever danger lay ahead. I opened the coach's other door even as he bade me stay inside.

Ahead of us, only a few feet from the rearing coach horses, the sewer cover suddenly shot away and a monstrosity heaved itself from the ill-smelling depths.

5

Covered in muck and slime, the Shambler stood ten feet tall, the height made even more impressive because of its slim build. Shamblers come in all sizes and shapes, each according to its maker's wish and ability, but the core materials for such an undertaking come from the unburied remains of a murder victim. Sometimes men who died on battlefields can be raised.

Vengeance burns in the remains of those victims, and the wizard or necromancer who brings a Shambler to life employs those leftover feelings to fill the creature with rage. Unfortunately such a resurrection generally drives the afflicted party totally mad, and little control remains. This one had been sent for us, for it charged at once. (They have a keen sense of smell, like that of a bloodhound, but after traveling through the sewer, I wonder as I set these events to page now how that thing could smell anything!)

James lifted his pistol and fired. His bullets struck the Shambler, erupting in small explosions of blue sparks and tearing away melon-size pieces of the creature. My beloved has his bullets blessed and charmed so they are proof against most creatures, normal flesh and blood as well as supernatural. Given time and sufficient ammunition, I was certain the pistol would bring our opponent down.

But the Shambler was determined we wouldn't be given that time. It went at James with flailing fists the size of nail kegs, missing him because my beloved is quick on his feet, and knocking potholes in the cobbled street.

Shoving his empty pistol back into his coat pocket, James drew forth the Ikari fighting knives he carried sheathed at his back. Both knives were fifteen inches long with razor-sharp double edges, also blessed and charmed. He is a master of the blade.

He went at the Shambler, ducking and weaving, raking the cruel knives along the beast and carving out hunks of it. The Shambler growled in pain, its huge round face—like that of a puffer fish, only dark green—ballooning up as it did so.

James likes to fight, but I feared for him and could not remain still. I seized the nearest lantern from the coach, then vaulted on top of the horses, running across them, then dropping to the street. I attacked the Shambler from behind, for I do not have the same honorable compulsions as my beloved and don't feel the need to face my enemy when I strike.

I swung the lantern as hard as I could, which was

considerable, and caught the back of the creature's head. Hammered by the blow, the Shambler stumbled and fell to its knees. Oil from the broken lantern cascaded down it. James struck again and again.

"Beloved," I called out to him. "Back away, please." When he was far enough away, by which time the Shambler pressed its knuckled fists against the street and once more heaved itself to its feet, I spoke a Word and threw out my hand. The heat of the spell (one of the few that I know because magic doesn't come easily to me—or to most for that matter) coursed along my arm, then poured from my palm. Green flames leaped for the Shambler, igniting the oil and covering the creature at once in a hungry blaze.

The Shambler screamed then, for I believe the creature knew even in its animalistic mind that its second life was now at an end, and those screams ululated in the urban canyon of multi-storied buildings. It whirled and flailed to escape the flames, but those efforts were to no avail. Based in magic, though steeped in whale oil, the fire did not relinquish its grip even after the Shambler collapsed and its smoldering remains hissed in the snow-covered street.

"The Shambler was set after us," James stated quietly as he put the Ikari fighting knives away and reloaded his pistol.

"I know."

His face hardened, as I knew it must, for I knew in my heart what he would do. "You were endangered, Mina. I cannot allow that." He peered harshly at the smoldering mass in the street. "I *will* not."

And I knew we were in it then, and my beloved would not rest till he had punished those responsible.

Only minutes later, we were at the first tobacconist's shop that James knew sold the specialized tobacco blend he had smelled on the imposter. The man lived in a small flat above his business. The neighborhood was at the fringe of the Gutbucket, that part of Drummond that was equally home to the hopeless and to the lawless.

A dressmaker's shop and a cobbler sat on either side of the tobacconist. As it turned out, the tobacconist was next door visiting with the dressmaker, and I could tell that we had interrupted them at their trysting by his nervous mannerisms and her protective gaze on him from her window.

Not wanting to conduct business out in the cold street, he let us into his shop and lit a lantern on the counter. The shop was small and filled with smoking accessories—carved pipes, papers, and ashtrays as well as personal humidors—and reeked of tobacco in many different scents.

"I apologize for having disturbed you at this late hour," James said, "but the matter that brought us here is of some import. I will pay you for your time." He handed the man five gold Stellars, which was more profit than the tobacconist would make in two months.

"Thankee, yer lordship," the tobacconist, whose name was Mr. Byars, gasped. He made the Stellars disappear with the trained skill of a cutpurse. "But nothing I could do could earn this, even at this late 'our."

I knew that he suspected he was going to be asked to do something illegal. Given that five Stellars were involved, he probably believed it would be something that would find him dangling from a noose.

"I'm searching for a man with a particular taste in tobacco," James said. "It's from the Confederacy of Ishplen. It's called Nocturne Rhapsody."

Mr. Byars looked unhappy, but he was five Stellars to the good, so that feeling couldn't long prevail against any loyalty he felt toward a patron. "That's an expensive blend, yer lordship."

"And an exotic one," James said, "because this one was laced with dreamweed."

Mr. Byars hesitated at that and scratched the back

of his neck. "Well now, yer lordship, dreamweed happens to be illegal 'ere in Drummond."

"Dreamweed is frowned upon in Drummond," James countered, "but the local constabulary don't often rouse themselves to jail someone for possession of it. In addition, Mr. Byars, I am not an officer of the court."

"I 'ave a few what pleasures themselves with such a dalliance," Mr. Byars admitted. "I fills their orders—in an effort to keep a roof over me 'ead."

"Understood." James gave a brief description of the red-haired man as we had put it together.

At that Mr. Byars relaxed. He had no compunction about selling out this particular customer.

"Ye're talkin' about Mr. Martin Landro," the tobacconist whispered.

"Who is Mr. Landro?"

" 'E's a bad 'un, yer lordship," Mr. Byars said. "One of them men ye'd truly be better of stayin' away from."

"I'm afraid I can't do that," James replied. "Where can I find Mr. Martin Landro?"

"In the Gutbucket," Mr. Byars said. "Usually he makes the rounds of the illegal sportin' events an' such. 'E's not a man for the light of day, that 'un. Even 'eard 'e might not be a man."

"You have my attention, Mr. Byars. I await elucidation."

The tobacconist shrugged. "Just them what says 'e's the cold-hearted devil 'imself. 'E's a killer near a dozen times over, an' women—" Here he looked at me, ashamed for having forgotten I was there, "forgive me coarseness, milady."

I told him that I did, that what he had to tell us was most important, and to please continue.

"An' women, them good 'uns what lives in the Gutbucket because they was born there an' can't get out, as well as them women what works there in the rough trade." Mr. Byars turned a little red with embarrassment at this point, "they stays away from Mr. Martin Landro. 'E's 'ard on 'em, 'e is."

James thanked Mr. Byars for the information and we took our leave. On our way back to the coach, James took my hand and showed me a grim smile. "You know what it means if the women of the Gutbucket avoid Landro."

"I do," I said, for sometimes I was as quick as my beloved. "It means that in order to avoid Mr. Martin Landro that they must first know where he is."

"Yes. You've got a good mind."

"I've got a good teacher," I replied.

Grinning but still somewhat deflected by his anger, he pulled me close and kissed me. Although few people were about, it was still not something he did easily because he is more bound by societal restraints than am I.

Hand in hand, then, we returned to the coach and headed into the Gutbucket.

The Gutbucket gets its name from the slaughterhouses that line the Merchant's Ward, which is behind the Dockyards along the Traveler River. The stink of blood and offal hang over the area so thick that people swore they can actually see it in the air on clear days.

Cows and sheep and chickens are killed and processed in the meatpacking plants. Part of the rendered meat is sold fresh to butchers, who further cut it up and sell it to people who can afford it in the Merchant's Ward, the Artisan's Ward, and on High Hill where most of the nobles and the truly wealthy lived.

But the tripes are hauled down to the Gutbucket where the poor pick over the remains, get as much as they can for a price they can afford, then make soups and coarse sausages from them. The stink never goes away, and the blood along the cobblestones from the dripping wagons carrying the leavings draws rats and other predators—not all of them truly animal—down into the ward. There is an unspoken caveat about the Gutbucket that no one goes there alone at night.

The houses are clapboard. Pieces torn from other wrecks and even shipyards where vessels are salvaged contribute to the building materials. Oiled parchment, not glass, filled most of the windows, and the light came from tallow candles. Low-grade coal that didn't burn cleanly heated homes and staved most of the winter's chill. Having food hauled in was too expensive. Three and four families slept tight and uncomfortable in two-room homes.

Whenever I go there, I always feel guilty. I know that my beloved experiences similar pangs.

Edmond halted the coach in front of the Boar's Tusk, a tavern where my husband and I are always welcome. Despite the lateness of the hour, Natty—the owner—was still tending bar for the longshoremen and visitors who didn't want to pay the price for a room for the night before sailing on the morrow.

Natty was an old gray fox of a man. Short and slight and balding, though he pulled his long gray hair back in a queue. He habitually wears sailor's breeches and dark sweaters and shaves once a week.

The Boar's Tusk was a quiet, desperate place for men who wished to drink their worries off their minds for as long as their money and time held out. Most of the furniture was brought in to trade for ale and liquor by sailors who came from all around the world.

Natty was tending bar that night when we went in. A dozen sailors and longshoremen and a few men only passing through held down chairs, swapped lies, and stared into the fire.

When he saw us, Natty came over at once. "Milord, milady," he greeted, pleased as always to see us.

"Hello, Natty," my beloved replied, taking the older man's hand.

"Come for a bite or a draft?" Natty asked. The Boar's Tusk offered a good but simple bill of fare.

"No," James told him. "I'm afraid we're working."

"In the Gutbucket?" Natty didn't like it when we did. Even though he knew from personal experience that we could take care of ourselves, he feared for us when we ventured into his home turf.

"We're looking for a man named Martin Landro," James said.

Natty shook his head. "A truly evil one, that man."

"So we've heard," I told him. "May I use the back room?"

"Of course, milady." He stood like a proper gallant and waved me to the back room.

I left James talking to Natty and went to the back room. I kept a change of clothes there, pants and a shirt that were more suitable for whatever action I might see in the Gutbucket. A quick change and I no longer looked like a lady from High Hill. My beloved, though, insists that I am beautiful no matter what I wear. I don't think so, but I'm glad that he does.

I added a pistol to my outfit, extra rounds in a pocket, then covered everything with an old cloak that would never draw attention from a cutpurse or any foolish or brave-hearted policemen who ventured down into the Gutbucket.

I added the weapon with reluctance. I don't prefer them as a general rule because I think they tend to dull a user's senses. I prefer quick wits to a quick trigger finger, but my beloved believes in them. So I carry one whenever he wants me to. After the attack by the Shambler, I knew I would be remiss in my beloved's eyes if I didn't arm myself.

Ready once more for the predators that run amok among the desperate denizens of the Gutbucket, I went to join my beloved to once more take up the hunt for the malefactor who had seized poor Simon Delhalm's body.

"Simon," I said, gazing into the blue eyes plunked into the wooden puppet's head, "I want you to stay here with Natty."

Not at all wanting to separate from us, Simon sat on one of the stools in front of the counter. Only a few of the tavern patrons gazed in our direction. Many strange things were seen in the Gutbucket. They didn't bother to hide there as much as they did in the other wards of Drummond.

"You will be safer here," I insisted.

In a truly childlike manner, Simon clasped his wooden hands together and ducked his head sadly. His neck squeaked with the effort.

"Simon," I said with a touch of sternness.

He looked up at me then and his eyes were pools of woe. "Do I have to?"

"Yes," I said, maintaining the firmness. "Where Lord Gallatin and I must go tonight is not safe." I gripped his shoulder. "I don't want to worry about you while I need to worry about my husband and myself. Do you understand?"

I had not thought it possible that a wooden puppet—a child's toy—like Mr. Jinx could look so lost and abandoned, but he did. My heart went out to the small boy trapped within the puppet but I made myself be strong.

"I understand," he told me. "But I'm just so scared." He turned to me then and held me around my neck, clinging tightly.

I held him back, knowing that even if he couldn't feel my arms around him, Simon at least knew I was there for him. "Soon," I whispered to him, "soon this will be over, Simon. Until that time, I ask you to be brave."

He nodded and withdrew.

"You'll be safe here with Natty," my beloved said. So caught up was I in the boy's pain that I hadn't heard James come up behind me. I resolved to pay more attention to my surroundings before my lack got James killed.

Together we went out into the night.

We found Edgar Chalmers at a ratting event in the Underground, the vast Labyrinth that runs beneath the Gutbucket, the Dockyards, and even underneath the Traveler River. Over the years as the metropolitan area developed, a number of businesses—mostly those involving smugglers—had created a network of tunnels that connected warehouses and dwellings to ferry in goods that avoided the queen's taxman.

When the poor and the desperate had needed places to live and to get away from the Drummond police, they ran through those tunnels and hid out till they thought they were safe. They weren't, of course, but they thought they were. There are Underground graveyards too, and rumors of people who have never left those earthen tunnels and cinderblock walls. Should the Traveler River ever find holes into the tunnel that runs under it, drowning victims will flush out into the Dockyards on both sides.

Natty had known Mr. Chalmers, and informed James that the man was a wastrel by any account, and not a brave man. Natty had said that Mr. Landro and Mr. Chalmers were often in each other's company of late, and were sometimes accompanied by a red-haired woman.

I immediately remembered that Mrs. Courtland Delhalm, Simon's stepmother, also had red hair, and I wondered at the coincidence. Mainly, I supposed, because my beloved didn't believe in coincidences.

Mr. Chalmers was at a gambling den, crowded around a cage where a tiny dragonet warred against two dozen rats as long as my arm. The dragonet was smaller, but it had wings and could fly inside the cage, had razor-sharp claws, and breathed flames.

Sometimes men catch the dragonets, which is

against Empire laws, and subject them to all manner of tortures. This is probably a result of the Dragon Campaigns. Dragonets are not true dragons, of course, for they only have the intelligence of mynah birds. They can be housebroken and taught a few words, but that is about the extent of their abilities. Still they are skilled combatants when fighting for their lives.

As we closed on Mr. Edgar Chalmers, who was skinny as a rake, marked by smallpox scarring, and jaundiced yellow from habitual drinking, the dragonet dropped from the side of the cage where it had hung and breathed fire on the crimson-toothed rat climbing up after it. The hungry rats had started feeding on their vanquished fellows, though they still preferred to savage their living foe.

The burning rat shrilled as it dropped from the cage's side, eliciting cheering from many of the men and curses from a few others. Money changed hands, most of it copper pels and every now and again a silver Lunar or a small gold Solar.

Not enthralled with his luck, Mr. Edgar Chalmers kicked the restraining wall. James and I slipped up on him in the crowd as he cursed the dragonet, which flew down and struck again, killing another rat with its breath.

I took Mr. Chalmers's arm on one side while James did the same on the other.

" 'Ere now!" he protested, trying to jerk away. James held him in a clever hold, one of those he no doubt learned from the open-handed boxers he trained with, while I closed my hand and surprised our captive with my strength. "Ye can't just—"

He stopped protesting then, and I knew that James had prodded him with the pistol or one of the Ikari knives.

"You'll come with us, Mr. Chalmers," James said in a low voice. His beautiful lips curved into a smile, but the effort never touched his hard eyes. "Or I'll kill you where you stand."

We led our prisoner through the crowd then, out the door, and up into the alley behind the warehouse where the ratter's pit was. Mr. Chalmers pleaded again and again to be set free, and he told us over and over that we obviously had the wrong man because he couldn't possibly be the man we were searching for.

Outside James put his hand in the center of the man's chest and pushed him up against the alley wall. He pressed his pistol against the man's nose, gaining his immediate and complete attention.

High above a Drummond police dirigible floated sedately by, projecting a beam of light across the city streets. Even if someone had seen us confronting Mr. Chalmers, the chances of someone—even the police—helping someone else in the Gutbucket were infinitesimal.

"I'm tellin' ye," Mr. Chalmers said again, "I'm not the man ye're lookin' for."

James stared into the man's eyes. "I am James Stark," my beloved said so fierce that excitement fluttered through me. "Called Lord Gallatin. Perhaps you've heard of me."

Mr. Chalmers blinked like a halfwit for a moment, then started trembling. "Aye," said he. "I've 'eard of ye."

"I want to know about young Simon Delhalm," James said. "About what you and Mr. Martin Landro have done to him."

"I can't," Mr. Chalmers said, shaking his head. "I can't tell ye anythin'. 'E'll kill me, 'e will."

"I'll kill you if you don't," James said. "You have my word on that. And I always keep my word. By my lights, you should swing from the gallows in Justice Square for what you've done to that poor boy."

Mr. Chalmers's fear of Mr. Landro was a strong thing, though, for he still did not talk.

James turned his face up to the top of the alley. I followed his gaze, as did Mr. Chalmers. As we watched, gargoyles circled and landed on the edges of the buildings. They sat, some of them looking moderately human and others resembling the vilest grotesqueries, and watched the action unfolding below.

"Come down," James said.

As one, at least forty gargoyles spread their bat-shaped wings and dropped to the alley floor with muffled thumps. The smallest was no taller than my knee and the biggest no taller than my waist. They ringed James and Mr. Chalmers.

Even I, who had been married to James for eight years, who had seen so many of the mysteries he'd unraveled, didn't know why the gargoyles loved him so.

"At a word from me," James told Mr. Chalmers, "they will rend you limb from limb and devour your flesh even before you are completely dead."

Anyone who had seen gargoyles feed on a victim knew that was true. They didn't often do such a thing because spells were in place to prevent it, but not everyone is protected by those spells.

Mr. Chalmers held out only for a few seconds. "All right. Don't let 'em eat me. Please. I'm beggin' ye."

"Tell me where I can find Mr. Martin Landro," James ordered.

"In Goodhaven Cemetery," Mr. Chalmers said. "In one of the mausoleums."

As hiding places went, I had to admit it was a most ingenious one. I would not have searched for him there. But what better place for a man nearly dead?

"Take us there," James commanded, and we were once more underway.

Goodhaven Cemetery was at the heart of the Gutbucket. The last funeral had probably been held there over a hundred years ago because all the graves and mausoleums were filled. Unadorned and plain, surrounded by tall iron fences sagging from the march of years as well as the weight of trees, brush, and dead vines, the cemetery sat silent and still without a light.

We went through the creaking gates and followed the winding trail that led within. I guessed that drunks and trespassers simply walked through the cemetery rather than around it to save time, for there were rotgut bottles and wine bottles everywhere.

Mr. Chalmers led us to one of the back mausoleums, then entered. Inside the Randall Family vault, the man told us that Mr. Martin Landro's comatose body had been laid to rest, all without benefit of removing the previous occupant. I lit a few of the candles sitting around the room while James and Mr. Chalmers lifted the heavy stone lid from the coffin.

Peering inside, James and I discovered that Mr. Martin Landro had been laid amid the bones of the coffin's rightful owner. He was a tall and powerfully built man, as Simon had described him. His burnished red hair caught the light from the candles. He was not an unhandsome man, but there laid upon him a veneer of cruelty that could be seen even in repose. I had known men like him all my life.

James looked up at Mr. Chalmers, who was in fear for his very life. "Why did Mr. Landro steal Simon Delhalm's body?"

"Because they were tired of waitin' for Mr. Courtland Delhalm to die," Mr. Chalmers said in a strained whisper.

" 'They'?" I repeated.

Mr. Chalmers nodded, trading on his words to continue his life. "Mr. Landro an' 'er. Mrs. Delhalm."

"Mrs. Delhalm plotted to kill her own husband?"

Intent though I was on Mr. Chalmers's reply, my mind already spinning with the complexity of what had truly been going on, I heard the scrape of shoe leather across the ground behind me. It was almost in time.

But then Mrs. Courtland Delhalm stepped into the room with a large pistol clutched in her hand. She looked different, grungier in hand-me-down shirt and pants, but she looked at home as well.

"Get your hands up," she admonished.

Since she was pointing the pistol directly at James, we did as she bade.

7

"Mrs. Delhalm." My husband greeted her as casually as though he'd been expecting her.

"Don't call me by that name," she snapped, stepping into the mausoleum room with the pistol leveled. "I hate that name. You can call me Vivian."

Three more men, all of them armed as well, followed her. All of them looked like they were on frequent terms with violence and death.

"I didn't just plan to steal my stepson's body and kill my husband," the woman said. "I also planned and killed my husband's former wife. The incident on Markham Bridge that resulted in her death was a carefully organized event. Just so you know I'm not someone to trifle with."

Somehow I was not surprised, for I had seen how she had acted around the imposter. And again she proved how vain she was by calling attention to her work.

Moving slowly Vivian Delhalm walked to the body lying in the coffin. "Martin," she called.

A moment later, Mr. Martin Landro roused from his slumber and stared up at us with naked hate showing in his brown eyes. Stiffly he clambered from the coffin and took his place beside Vivian Delhalm. He leaned down and kissed her.

"I've wanted to do that all day," he told her.

She laughed. "We'll have to let you grow up a bit first," she said. "Though I look forward to seeing you as a young man again."

Then it hit me what they'd planned to do. I was certain James had already figured it out, probably from the time we started looking for Mr. Chalmers.

"You *are* planning to kill your husband," I said.

She turned to me and smiled. "Of course I'm planning on killing him." She touched Mr. Landro. "This is my true husband. I've put up with Delhalm's pathetic attentions far too long. He should have died before I had to spend two years with him."

"The longer he lived, the older Simon got," James said.

"Yes," Vivian agreed. "Here in the Empire, everything is governed by the Law of Primogeniture. The eldest male child inherits everything." She smiled. "As I'm certain you know firsthand, Lord Gallatin. Even though I was a wife to Courtland Delhalm, his wealth was not mine to inherit. Still if he'd done me the favor of dying early enough, I could have diverted some of those funds before Simon grew old enough to know what I was doing."

"But you were running out of time," James told her. "The boy is eleven, after all."

"Yes." Vivian frowned. "And quite clever. I still don't know how he managed his escape from the spell."

He had Mr. Jinx thank for that, I thought. A child's love for a toy was a most amazing thing.

"So you sought to exchange bodies with Simon," James said. "Keep the boy trapped somewhere until you no longer needed him."

"Yes, then you decided to start meddling." Vivian frowned. "Why *did* you start meddling?"

"Your stepson came to me and asked for help."

Some of the confusion left her face then. "Ah, Mr. Jinx. I knew there was something going on when that cursed thing suddenly came to life. Where is he now?"

"Safe," I replied, taking a step toward my husband. I could not bear her pointing the weapon at him a moment longer.

"You know," Vivian said, "you could save Lady Gallatin a lot of torture if you simply told me where I could find that puppet."

I smiled at her to show her I had no fear of her.

"I think not," James said. "You made a mistake tonight when you sent the Shambler after us. You endangered Mina. That I will not tolerate."

"Then you can die," she said, taking more deliberate aim with the pistol, "and I'll find the damned puppet on my own." Her finger was already tightening on the trigger when I stepped into the path of the bullet.

"No!" James yelled, and I could tell from the sound of his voice that he'd already moved, possibly even gotten out of the way of the bullet. I'd known that he might be able to, but I just couldn't bring myself to take the chance.

The pistol shot rang out very loud inside the mausoleum. I felt a sledge slam into my heart. Stumbling, I fell onto my back, one hand clasped over the wound.

The other three men, Mr. Chalmers, and Mr. Landro drew their weapons.

Vivian looked at me, a smile spreading across her face as she thought about what she'd done.

Then I pushed myself back to my feet and saw her smile falter. "Surprise," I said.

Didn't I tell you in the beginning that dark things are drawn to my husband? I know I did. I looked and it's there. Dark things *are* drawn to my husband. I happen to be one of them. That was why the cold doesn't affect me, why I had to have my own invitation at the Delhalm home, why I am stronger than anyone human, why I can't bear children for my husband.

And why I can't be killed by a bullet through the heart.

James knows what I am, and he loves me for myself anyway. He knew I never set out to become what I am.

Vivian had to have suspected what I was at that point. So I opened my mouth and revealed my fangs to her.

"Vampiress!" she shouted. She brought up the pistol and fired again and again, the shots rolling like thunder in the enclosed space.

Two of the wild shots struck Mr. Chalmers and knocked him to the ground. From the corner of my eye, I saw that one of the shots went through Mr. Chalmers' eye. I smelled fresh death in the air.

Another shot struck me, again in the chest, but I knew from experience the wounds from the pistol would be healed before James and I returned home that night. With no trace of mercy in my heart (I was thinking only of Simon and how this woman had taken his mother and very nearly his own life from him!), I leaped at her and was on her like a striking lioness.

I grabbed the back of her hair and pulled her head back to bare her throat. James had his pistol in hand and shot with unerring marksmanship. By the time I had ripped Vivian's throat out and drunk her blood (I told you I am not so forgiving as my beloved), James had killed two of the men with his pistol and another with a thrown Ikari knife.

Mr. Martin Landro launched himself at me, pummeling me with his fists as he sought to tear me from his wife's body. I swept out a hand and knocked him back against the mausoleum wall. By that time, the beast part of me was ready to kill again.

I leaped at him, letting him think for just a moment that he might escape, then I picked him up by an arm and a leg as if he were a child, and I broke him in half. He died staring up at me, and all the while the beast in me cried out to drink his blood as well.

When I turned, I saw that James had stayed within the mausoleum. I stepped toward him and he raised his pistol and pointed it at me. I didn't doubt that he had reloaded, and I knew that his blessed and charmed bullets would probably kill me.

Still the beast in me cried out for his blood as well, and it took all my willpower to fight it off. I knew I must look horrible to him. I had seen vampires before that had their feeding faces on.

"Mina," he called to me softly. His pistol never wavered. He would die for me if ever there were the need, but he will not die at the hands of the beast inside me. He has told me that upon occasion. I knew that he would tell me again that night or in the morning.

You see, we each have something to fear in the other. I fear that James will someday turn his attentions to someone new and different who can offer him the child I can never give him, and he fears that one day—or night in our bedchamber—that I will no longer be able to control the hunger that pushes me.

"Mina," he called again.

Slowly I regained control of myself. When I was certain I had once more locked away that bestial side of myself, I went to him and held him in my arms.

"I'm sorry," I told him in a ragged whisper. "I thought she was going to kill you."

Handing me a kerchief so that I might clean my face, he held me and told me that everything would be fine, that we would be fine. After all we had lived through this. For a long time, there was only the sound of his breathing and his heart beating in the crypt, and I listened to them both and made them my own.

Later after I had cleaned up and we had once more returned to our normal clothing at the Boar's Tusk, James and I loaded Simon into the coach and headed home. Despite his anxiety, I knew that Simon was tired beyond measure. He had been through a lot.

"Are you sure my body is there?" he asked me again as we rode to his father's house.

"It is," I told him. James and I had decided to keep the particulars from him. It was going to be hard enough on him when he discovered that he had lost yet another mother, though this one—he already knew—didn't love him. But his father would feel the loss, and—in turn—so would Simon.

Instead James told Simon a clever tale of how we had tracked down the wizard who had enchanted him, stolen the wizard's cat, and threatened to never return it to him if he didn't free Simon's body.

"But you didn't hurt the cat, did you?" Simon asked, more concerned about the imaginary feline than he was in why the wizard would do something like that to him.

"It was a foul and vicious beast," James insisted. "One-eared and mangy. There surely wasn't one good and decent bone in its entire body." He paused, grinning. "Unless it had just eaten, of course."

Simon saw the humor in that and laughed. "When I get my body back," he said a little later, "you should come visit me."

I was stricken. I couldn't find my voice.

"We will," James said.

Turning his little wooden head to me, Simon said, "I think I'm cold now."

I held out my arms to him, then lifted him onto my lap. In his puppet body, he was nowhere near as big as an eleven-year-old boy. He curled up inside my arm, against my breast, and—after only a few moments—went to sleep.

Only a short time after that, I was no longer holding an enchanted boy. I held only a child's toy, a bundle of sticks covered in paint and glue. Regretfully I picked the puppet up and placed it in the opposite seat.

Then I cried and James held me, offering what comfort he could, but this was a pain so deep and raw that he could never hope to touch it.

The next day James and I went by the Delhalm home. After all he and Mr. Courtland Delhalm were now business associates so we had a ready excuse.

The house was in chaos, of course. Vivian Delhalm

had been found murdered in Goodhaven Cemetery in the Gutbucket and no answers for who might have done it or what she was doing there appeared to be forthcoming. Mr. Courtland Delhalm hadn't even known his wife was gone from the house until a Drummond police inspector told him that morning.

I saw Simon, but he kept his distance from James and me. His father said that the boy had had a bad dream he couldn't quite remember, but with everything that had happened to him, Simon was coping.

The fact that I might never get to talk to him again hurt. But I took as my solace that Simon would never rightly remember everything that had happened to him and it would fade in his memories as all nightmares did.

Mr. Courtland Delhalm buried the pieces of his second wife in Eternal Hope Cemetery the day after she was found. The newspapers and public scrying bowls stayed full of the news.

The night after that, I waited till sunset and went out to Eternal Hope Cemetery with a wooden stake, found Vivian's grave in the darkness, and sat down to wait. I'd known when I bit her that I'd turned her and she would rise again.

I've only turned two others in my long life, one by accident and the other because I thought he loved me and I hadn't wanted to lose him. He'd discovered I was a vampiress and promised to love me forever. He hadn't, and I soon found out he'd only lied to me to get me to turn him. I gave the first a final death, and looked forward to doing the same for the other should the chance ever present itself.

As I sat there at the foot of Vivian Delhalm's fresh grave running the two-foot-long stake through my hands, I thought about my relationship with my husband. Sometimes, like tonight, I wondered if he would love me were I not a vampire.

I didn't know.

I thought that he would, and I chose to believe that.

But I know that dark things are drawn to my husband, and he is drawn to them in return. It might be that he wouldn't.

Then the ground trembled in front of me and I saw Vivian thrust her hand through the fresh-turned soil. I smiled in anticipation and took a new hold on the stake.

When she sat up from her grave, doubtless aware of what had happened to her and of the relentless hunger that now filled her, she found me waiting.

"Hello, Vivian," I said. Then I shoved the stake through her dead heart and watched her turn to ash. I rather enjoyed the surprised look of anguish on her dirt-smeared features. Killing her the second time was as equally gratifying as killing her the first time.

I rose and dusted myself off. On the way back, I had Edmond stop for a fresh bottle of fruit wine, which was not meant to age, but to be drunk while it was new. I felt like celebrating finally for the first time in days. The darkness that was in my life and my husband's would draw us back in soon, I had no doubts about that, but I knew we could take a moment just to be ourselves, just to be in love.

LADY ROXANNE LA BELLE

Laura Resnick

If her problem had been a mere nuclear holocaust, she might have adjusted with grace.

If a plane crash had stranded her in a frozen tundra with nothing on the menu but the flesh of her fellow passengers. . . . If a tragic hairdressing accident had left her permanently bald. . . . If she and Donald Trump were the only two survivors of a sudden, devastating plague, so that she faced a choice between procreating with The Donald or else condemning civilization to certain oblivion. . . . She'd cope somehow. She'd manage. She was a hardy, resilient person. A survivor. She liked to think she had moxie. She'd always believed she possessed true grit.

So, yes, if something merely catastrophic happened, she'd deal with it and try not to complain too much.

But *this*?

No, this was too much. *This* was beyond the pale. It was beyond anything she had ever imagined having to survive. Beyond what she believed any woman *could* survive with her sanity intact.

It was the ultimate disaster: Due to circumstances beyond her control, she had recently moved back in with her parents.

Roxanne Bell awoke that morning in the bedroom

where she had slept every night as a child, and she stared morosely at the lavender ceiling.

She hated lavender. She had always hated lavender. But her mother hadn't believed her when she expressed this sentiment at the age of five. In Mom's worldview, girls loved lavender and boys loved green; so she had painted the rooms of her two children in those colors thirty years ago. Roxanne's brother Michael had, in fact, loved green, and he was perfectly content in his room for the rest of his youth, thus proving Mrs. Bell's point (as she said often, smugly, and to this very day). Roxanne continued to loathe lavender and confidently expected to loathe it for the rest of her life; but her mother remained convinced this was just a rebellious phase and she would one day confess that a lavender bedroom had been her heart's secret desire from birth. This was perhaps why, when redecorating the house a decade ago, Mrs. Bell had repainted these two bedrooms the exact same childhood colors they'd been painted for years.

Of course, this time around, the paint job was for her grandchildren. Michael's old bedroom was now reserved for Jeff, Roxanne's ten-year-old son. And Roxanne's lavender bedroom was intended for the granddaughter that Mrs. Bell remained convinced would soon be born.

Since Michael was gay, single, and fiercely childless, and since Roxanne's husband had just left her, there was little realistic chance of another grandchild. This, however, did not seem to alter Mrs. Bell's certainty that, any moment now, one of her two offspring would provide the lavender bedroom with a girlchild.

Roxanne stared at the ceiling and sighed.

Instead of contributing a granddaughter to the nauseating pale-purple room, she had moved back in here as an impoverished, abandoned mother in her mid-thirties.

If she ever saw Thack again, she would kill him.

Why did I even marry a man called "Thack" in the first place? What was I thinking?

Roxanne's husband hadn't returned from the golf course one Saturday afternoon last month. As dinner grew cold, she worried that his SUV had broken down because she hadn't gotten around to taking it in for its tune-up, and she wondered why Thack didn't answer his cell phone. It soon turned out, however, that Thack hadn't missed dinner that night due to car trouble, but rather because he was busy fleeing the country with a twenty-year-old manicurist whose breast implants he had charged to a credit card that was in Roxanne's name.

Soon thereafter Roxanne discovered that the house she and her husband owned was mortgaged to the hilt (foreclosure occurred about two weeks after Thack disappeared), they owed the IRS more than seventy thousand dollars, and their credit card debt exceeded the annual defense budget of some industrialized nations.

Evicted from her house and unable to rent an apartment while her bank account was empty and her credit rating was in the toilet, a shell-shocked Roxanne had seen no alternative to accepting her parents' invitation to move back "home." And even here, she was being hounded by terse collection agencies and ravening IRS employees.

Roxanne rolled onto her side, feeling depression weigh her down as her legs tangled in the lavender bedsheets. Her apathetic gaze drifted around the bedroom, which was drenched in cheery morning sunlight.

Her mother had gone overboard in her determined preparations for a granddaughter. Fussy lace curtains framed the window, and a ruffled skirt concealed the legs of a French provincial vanity table. On the wall, a likeness of the Lady of Shalott gazed sadly into the distance; she, too, had fallen for the wrong guy and paid a heavy price for it. And in the corner, taking up a good quarter of the room, a fairy-tale toy castle sat on a turntable.

The castle was a new addition to the room. Previously, there'd been a rocking chair in that corner. Mrs. Bell had recently bought the castle from a self-described "sorcerer" (how corny could you get?) at the local Renaissance Fair, thinking it would be the perfect thing for the granddaughter she was bound to have before long. The so-called sorcerer had recognized Mrs. Bell as a fanciful woman, and he had shrewdly jacked up the price of his merchandise with a good spiel about how it was an *enchanted* fairy-tale castle. It would, he claimed, one day reveal its secrets to a young lady whose heart was rich with longing, and he felt in his bones that Mrs. Bell was meant to take it home with her. Roxanne had endured her mother repeating this nonsense several times now, practicing the story she dreamed of one day telling her granddaughter. Each time she talked about the castle, Roxanne's father scowled and commented that the thing had cost a small fortune.

Despite the ruthlessly romantic sales pitch and steep price, Roxanne admitted to herself, as she gazed at in bleak depression, that it was a beautifully crafted toy castle.

It had four turrets, a drawbridge that really worked, a moat that gleamed as if it held real water (it was some ingenious plastic substance with incredibly tiny make-believe fish embedded in it), and a courtyard with hundreds of teensy-weensy hand-painted cobblestones. Small, sturdy wooden doors that actually opened and closed led to several halls and chambers of the castle, each of them furnished in exquisite detail. In the great hall, a tiny king sat on his throne while a white-bearded wizard, wearing a black robe with shiny silver dots on it, stood nearby, perhaps offering counsel. In one of the upstairs rooms, a princess in a dark blue gown stood at the window of a richly furnished chamber. She was gazing down into the courtyard, one graceful hand raised in farewell (it seemed) to a departing knight. He was dressed for battle and seemed to be on the verge of exiting via the drawbridge. Was he on his way to a joust? A war? A night out with the boys?

As Roxanne lay in bed, staring intently at the gorgeously detailed toy castle her mother had bought in her willful desire for a granddaughter, she heard the telephone ringing downstairs. It snatched her out of the fanciful world of fairy-tale princesses and knights in shining armor, bringing her back with a cold snap to her own appalling reality. She pulled a pillow over her head, supposing the telephone's ring heralded the first threatening phone call of the day from one of the many fiscal agencies determined to destroy her life now that her heavily indebted spouse had disappeared and left her holding the bag.

Sure enough, a moment later her mother's piercing voice floated up the stairs. "Roxannnnnne! Telephonnnnnnne!"

Roxanne kept her head hidden beneath the pillow and wished the problem away. Not surprisingly, that didn't work.

"Roxannne! Are you awaaaaaaaaaake yet?"

She lifted her head and shouted, "No!"

"Do you want to take this calllllllll?" her mother shouted up the stairs.

Roxanne got out of bed, went to the bedroom door, opened it a crack, and shouted, "Who is it?"

"The IRS!"

"Didn't I tell you that if the IRS, the bank, or any collection agencies call, you're to say that I'm not home and you don't know when I'll be back?"

"So you don't want to take it?" her mother called.

"No!"

"Are you sure?"

"Yes. I'm sure!"

"All right."

Roxanne leaned her head against the wall and

counted to ten. She and her mom had been having this conversation half a dozen times per day, every day, since she and her son had moved in. And as soon as even more collection agencies figured out where Roxanne was living now, she'd probably be having this conversation *twenty* times every day. No matter how many times she repeated that she did not want to take any phone calls from people trying to collect money that she didn't have, her mother persisted in believing that whoever called the house next to demand money might well be the exception to the rule.

Exhausted by this thought, Roxanne went back to bed.

A few minutes later the telephone rang.

Within moments, her mother called up the stairs, "Roxannnnnnne? It's for you!"

The caller was a credit card company to whom she owed more than ten thousand dollars for her husband's girlfriend's plastic surgery.

If there was one thing in this whole mess that Roxanne could be grateful for, it was her young son's emotional resilience. Though Jeff was upset by the sudden loss of his father and his home, he was fond of his doting grandparents and adjusting with reasonable equanimity to living in their house while his harassed mother tried to find a way out of the financial quicksand she was in. The boy spent a lot of time doing woodworking, fishing, leaf-raking, and other manly activities with his grandfather. Roxanne's dad was a gruff, quiet fellow who said little to his daughter beyond his daily reminder that he'd always disliked her husband and had warned her the marriage was destined to end badly. (In fact, her dad had been openly delighted when Roxanne married Thack, an ambitious advertising executive, and his first reaction to the announcement that Thack had left her was to ask what Roxanne had done to alienate her husband. In addition to woodworking, Roxanne's father practiced selective memory.)

Roxanne, who had a B.A. in English, had worked as a secretary for a few years after college, and then had become a stay-at-home mom soon after her marriage. For the past couple of years, in order to keep herself occupied now that Jeff was in school all day and she and Thack had decided not to have another baby, Roxanne had been doing a little part-time substitute teaching.

Now every single night at dinner, she again explained at length to her mother why her financial problems could not be solved with what she earned from substitute teaching, nor even with what she would earn if she could get a full-time job as a secretary again. Meanwhile her initial job search had revealed that she was, in any case, no longer qualified to be a secretary. Computers had changed so much during the decade since she'd last had a job that she could no longer operate one competently enough to get past the first stage of the application process at any company she contacted.

"So chances are," she said to her mother, "that I'm going to wind up waiting tables."

"Well, that'll be nice, dear," her mother said.

"*No,* Mom, being a thirty-five-year-old waitress won't really be that nice."

"But at least it'll solve your financial problems," her mother said.

Roxanne felt too drained to explain to her mother why waiting tables would not enable her to pay off the massive six-figure debt (with rapidly accruing penalties, fines, and exorbitant interest rates) that her snake of a husband had inflicted on her. Having vowed not to cry in front of her son, Roxanne fled to the safety of her hideous lavender bedroom, closed the door, and sank down into the carpet, too exhausted even to make it all the way to the bed before she gave in to silent sobs.

*   *   *

For the sake of her son, Roxanne tried to maintain
a positive demeanor during the next few days. But the
number of daily calls from creditors, collection agencies, and IRS agents continued increasing, as she'd
anticipated. A lawyer had advised her that bankruptcy
alone wouldn't eliminate all her debts, since they included back taxes and (she now learned) her husband's
student loans for his expensive MBA education. Her
employment prospects remained very discouraging,
and it was beginning to look as if *death* was the only
way she'd ever escape the towering financial disaster
Thack had left her with. In any case, the prospects
were very grim for moving out of her parents' house
ever (never mind the very next day, which was what
her frazzled nerves really needed).

So it wasn't long before she woke up one day and
felt too depressed to get out of bed. Ever again. She
lay there all morning, vaguely brushing off her mother's attempts to coax her into opening the door, and
just stared at the elaborate toy castle, feeling too
weary and defeated even to shed more tears.

She didn't want Thack back. (The very thought was
revolting.) She was so tired, she didn't even want justice or revenge anymore. Perhaps she would again,
someday. But right now, *all* she wanted was for the
problems he'd left her with to disappear magically. In
a puff of smoke. To evaporate. To go away.

She stared at the castle and felt her mother's roman-
ticism infecting her. It was a lovely thing—the towers,
the ramparts, the delicately painted walls, the maiden
in her rich blue gown waving at the handsome
knight. . . . It must have been lovely to have lived in
such a time and place. Roxanne was well read enough
to know that, in reality, life in medieval castles had
included appalling sanitary conditions, bitter cold in
winter, a complete lack of privacy, and societal values
that were distinctly unfriendly to feminist principles.
But the miniature castle in her bedroom made it look

like such a simple, elegant, appealing lifestyle, such a *safe* existence, compared to the hell she was living.

Drifting off to sleep in her exhausted depression, she thought longingly of how much she wished she were the begowned maiden who was looking out of her arched window and waving farewell to a departing knight on horseback.

"Where is La Belle? La Belle shall be told!"

Roxanne heard the distant shouting and pulled the pillow over her head, trying to stay lost in the oblivion of sleep.

Much closer to her, a different voice said, "Lady Roxanne! Sir Roderick is dead!"

Roxanne removed the pillow and made a frustrated sound.

Her parents needed to turn down the volume on the television set. The *booming* decibels at which they kept the TV on for several hours every evening was immensely irritating, and she figured if they weren't already deaf from the noise, they soon would be. But they usually only watched TV at night. She could tell by the sunshine pouring across her face that it was still daytime. So why was the TV on now? While two characters talked a blue streak?

"Does she weep for Sir Roderick?" The first voice sounded doubtful.

"Nay, I believe she sleeps," said a second voice. "She was not attached to Sir Roderick, you know."

"I believe she said he had an unpleasant odor."

"Indeed."

"Shall we rouse her?"

"Yes. My lady!"

"Oh, for pity's sake, turn it *down*," Roxanne muttered. It sounded as if the TV were right there in her bedroom! How deaf could her parents *be*?

"She wakens."

"Hark! She speaks!"

"That does it!" If her mother really wanted her to

get out of bed, she'd found the motivation. Roxanne would go downstairs and take a sledgehammer to the goddamn TV! *"Be quiet!"* Roxanne shouted, sitting up and opening her eyes as she did so. "Can't I have a little peace and qui-qu-qu . . . " Her voice trailed off in confusion as she stared at the two total strangers who were standing at the foot of her bed.

"Please forgive me, Lady Roxanne. I have come to tell you of Sir Roderick's unhappy fate."

Roxanne stared at them: a fresh-faced young woman, perhaps eighteen years old, and a slim, pale boy who looked about twelve.

"I regret disturbing your slumber," the young woman continued. "My humble apologies, my lady."

"What?" Roxanne said in confusion.

"I thought the sad news about Sir Roderick should be told."

"Sir . . . what?" Roxanne said.

"Have you not heard?"

"Heard?" she said.

"My lady," the boy said gravely, "it is our sad duty to tell you that Sir Roderick lives no more."

They were wearing strange clothes. The girl was in a plain gown with a high neck and a kerchief covering her hair. The boy seemed to be wearing some sort of rough tunic and a cap. They looked like characters in a historical movie. Or employees at a Renaissance fair.

From beyond the bedroom, a man's voice floated through the air. "Sir Roderick is no more! And yet, so soon, still another noble warrior has come to claim the right to wed La Belle!"

That was when Roxanne noticed this wasn't her bedroom. It was a strange room with stone floors that were mostly covered by some sort of woven matting, and stone walls with tapestries hung on them. A bed, a chair, a table, and a trunk were the only furnishings. She had no idea where she was, yet as she looked around, something about the room seemed vaguely familiar. . . .

"Lady Roxanne, shall you greet the new champion?"

"Champion of what?" she asked absently, wondering where she was and what was going on.

The boy and the young woman exchanged a puzzled glance. Then the boy supplied, "The champion who comes to claim the right to wed you."

The room, the furnishings, the setting . . . "Renaissance fair . . . " she murmured.

"What fair, my lady?"

She looked down at her body and saw she was clad in a dark blue gown of some rich material. "Oh, my God!"

The two young people standing at the foot of her bed gasped in shock at this blasphemy.

Ignoring them, Roxanne slid off the bed (which was frankly not that comfortable) and ran to the arched window. Sure enough, she found herself gazing down at a familiar courtyard. Only now it was very large, instead of miniature. The cobblestones looked real now, too—right down to a pile of horse manure that someone was shoveling off them.

"Good God!" she said.

The two young people gasped again.

From her vantage point, she looked around at the castle surrounding the courtyard. Sure enough, she could see the familiar towers and ramparts, and the various doors were right where she expected them to be.

She turned around and stared at the two people in the bedchamber. "But you're new."

They looked at each other, then looked at her. The young woman ventured, "New, my lady?"

"You're not in the castle."

They looked at the ceiling over their heads, the walls around them, and the floor. But despite their obvious conclusion, they did not contradict her.

"I mean," Roxanne amended, "you're not in the little castle. The miniature one. The one I look at every day. You're an addition. You're new." Pondering this, she wondered, "How did you get here? How did *I* get here? Am I really here? Are *you* really here?"

"Would you like us to leave you, my lady?" the boy asked, edging toward the door. His eyes had widened with every word she'd just spoken.

"Stop," she said. It was a tone she'd learned as a mother, and it invariably worked. The boy stopped just short of the door.

"Remind me of your name," she said to him.

"My name?"

"I'm feeling a little light-headed and can't think of it just now," she explained.

"Of course, my lady. I am John."

"John." Roxanne nodded and turned her gaze to the girl.

"I am Constance." After a moment, the young woman added helpfully, "And you are Lady Roxanne."

"Right. Gotcha."

"Rouse La Belle!" a voice cried outside the window. "She is summoned to the Great Hall by His Majesty the King!"

Roxanne asked, "And who is this La Belle they keep shouting about?"

"Er, that is you, my lady. You are La Belle."

"I thought I was Lady Roxanne."

"You are Lady Roxanne La Belle. La Belle means 'the beauty.' You are the beauty of the kingdom."

That gave her pause. *"I'm* the beauty of the kingdom?"

The girl nodded.

"Me? Really?"

"Yes, my lady."

"Well. That's . . . unexpected."

"Unexpected, my lady?"

"I mean, you know, considering that I was just

abandoned by my husband in favor of a younger woman with acrylic nails and breast implants."

John and Constance looked bewildered and alarmed.

"Your . . . husband, my lady?" John said.

"Lady Roxanne!" cried Constance. "Have you married Sir William in secret?"

"Okay, I'm lost, who's Sir William?"

Constance blinked. "Why . . . he is your true love, my lady."

"I have a true love?" When Constance nodded, Roxanne said, "I lead a busy life, don't I? So who was Sir Roderick? You know, the guy who's dead?"

"One of your suitors, my lady!"

"And now there's *another* suitor in the Great Hall? Hmm, so I get a lot of suitors, do I?" When they nodded in unison, she asked, "Why? Because I'm so, um, beautiful?"

"Well, that helps," Constance said.

"But it's not the whole story?"

"Well . . . you *are* wondrous rich, my lady," John said.

"You also play the harp quite well," Constance said, glaring at John.

"I'm rich?" Roxanne asked.

"Yes," said John.

"And the grace of your dancing is well known," said Constance, giving John a swift kick.

"Rich?" said Roxanne.

"Yes, my lady," said John.

"And you are much admired for your piety," said Constance.

"Me? *I* am rich?" said Roxanne.

"Yes, Lady Roxanne," said John.

"Very, *very* rich," Constance admitted.

"Who am I?" Roxanne wondered.

Looking patient, Constance replied, "You are Lady Roxanne La Belle, the beauty of the kingdom."

"No, I mean, how do I happen to be so rich?"

"Your father was very rich."

"Was? He's dead?"

"Yes." Evidently realizing more backstory was needed, Constance added, "You are now the king's ward."

"Ah." Roxanne nodded. "Okay, I think I get the picture."

"Picture?"

"Everyone wants to marry me because I'm very rich."

"Well, you also have a lively wit," said Constance.

"Uh-huh. I have a bridegroom in mind. This, uh, Sir William that you mentioned. But for some reason the king, who is my guardian, wants to marry me off elsewhere."

"His Majesty says that Sir William is too lowborn to deserve your hand."

"Why? He's got a title, hasn't he?"

"He is a mere knight."

"What about Sir Roderick? Wasn't he just a 'sir,' too?"

"He was a baron."

"That's a whole different thing?"

Constance and John nodded vigorously.

"And who is the new guy?" Roxanne asked.

"Lord Guy de Guise. The second son of a duke." Constance added, "Considered most suitable for a woman of your rank and fortune."

"So where is Sir William while these men are trying to court me?" Roxanne asked curiously.

"You mean . . . where is he *now*, my lady?"

"Uh-huh."

"*Right* now?"

"Yes."

John and Constance exchanged a guilty glance, then both studied the ceiling intently.

"Where *is* he?" When they still didn't respond, Roxanne clapped her hands and used her mom-tone. "Answer me!"

John flinched. "We may not tell."

"Why not?"

Constance said, "We swore we would not!"

"Who made you swear?"

"Sir William himself!"

"Why?"

"So you would not worry!"

"Why would I worry?"

"Because he has gone off to slay the dragon!" As soon as the words were out of her mouth, Constance's eyes bulged and she clapped her hands over her mouth.

John said accusingly to Constance, "You were not supposed to tell!"

"It was an accident!" Constance said defensively.

"There's a *dragon*?" said Roxanne.

John nodded. "The one that killed Sir Roderick."

"Whoa! It's, like, a *deadly* dragon?" Roxanne said.

"Is there any other kind?" Constance said.

"So Sir William is off trying to slay this dragon?" Roxanne asked, appalled. "The dragon that's already slain Sir Roderick?"

"As well as your other four suitors."

"Oh, my God!"

They gasped again at her language.

"Wait a minute! You're saying *that's* what a guy has to do to date me? He has to fight the dragon?"

"He has to *slay* the dragon," John corrected.

"Oh. Yes. That makes sense. I suppose dragon fights are a to-the-death sort of thing."

"Indeed," said Constance.

"So Sir William is off getting himself killed by this dragon because the king won't agree to our getting married?"

"He would have gone to face the dragon in combat sooner, but your tears have always forestalled him before."

"I would have thought that common sense would forestall him." A moment later, Roxanne muttered,

"But, as always, I see that's a vain hope when it comes to men."

"So he has gone without telling you, my lady. And he will either return dead, or with the dragon's treasure!"

"The dragon has a treasure?"

"Yes. Of course," said John.

"It's customary," said Constance.

"But if I'm rich, William doesn't need to. . . . Oh! I get it. He needs a fortune of his own to wed me?"

"Yes. Of course, proving his valor in battle against the dragon will also help raise his stature to yours in the eyes of the king."

"Wow. I really like the idea of a man who wants to bring his own fortune to the marriage. Who's not planning on just living off his rich wife. Or, for example, running up a huge debt and then abandoning her to deal with the consequences."

Looking puzzled again, Constance said amicably, "Sir William is a most noble man, my lady."

"I would have liked to have met him." Seeing their confused expressions, she added, "Er, again. Once more, I mean. You know, before the dragon kills him." Which seemed a likely fate, since five men were already dead.

"Take heart, my lady!" Constance impulsively embraced her. "Sir William is a most stalwart warrior."

"Well, that's good to know." Roxanne patted the girl's back, then extricated herself from the embrace. "Flattering though it may be, I would much rather men stopped dying for the privilege of marrying me."

"La Belle is summoned to the Great Hall!" a voice cried down in the courtyard. "Whence cometh La Belle? And *when*?"

"If I'm so wealthy and important," Roxanne said irritably, "shouldn't they summon me in a more polite manner?"

John and Constance looked at each other again.

Then John said, "That is how summoning is done, my lady."

"At the king's pleasure," Constance added.

"All right, I suppose I'd better go." Roxanne headed for the door, but then paused and asked, "The Great Hall is down the stairs and to the left?" She remembered this from looking so often at the toy castle.

They nodded.

She left the room. A moment later she stuck her head back in the doorway to ask, "Er, you're both servants?"

"Yes, my lady."

"Just checking."

As she made her way to the Great Hall, since it seemed best to cooperate with the locals until she could figure out what was going on, Roxanne wondered whether she was hallucinating, insane, or just having a very intense dream. She felt as if she were fully awake, but she knew from some previous dreams that this didn't necessarily mean she *was* awake. She didn't feel crazy or hallucinatory. But since she was wandering around a medieval castle, utterly convinced of its reality, and immersed in an adventure where she was the beauty of the kingdom and all her potential suitors had been slain by a dragon . . . she probably wasn't the best judge of her own sanity.

In any event, whatever the nature of this experience, she was enjoying it and half wished it were real. Until she got to the Great Hall, that was, and met her new suitor. Within minutes of being introduced to Lord Guy de Guise by the king, Roxanne decided he was a pompous ass who looked—to her utter disgust— a bit like Thack. The possibility that the king could marry her off to this man against her will was certainly a downside of her improbable fairy tale.

"Lady Roxanne plays the harp well and has quite a lively wit," the king was saying to Lord Guy when someone else entered the Great Hall. The king looked up and smiled. "Ah! Phineas! There you are!"

Roxanne turned to see the newcomer—and recognized the white-bearded sorcerer who inhabited the Great Hall of the toy castle in her lavender bedroom. He wore a flowing black robe covered with—she could now see clearly, for the first time—silver zodiac symbols.

The wizard bowed his head. "Your pardon, sire. I was deeply embroiled in a new experiment." His gaze met Roxanne's. "And I'm pleased to see it has worked. How nice to find you here, Lady Roxanne."

Her eyes widened and she gasped. He knew what was going on! She was certain of it! As soon as Lord Guy and the king were deep in discussion of Roxanne's fortune, she took the sorcerer aside and said, "I want answers."

"It is a wise person who is always in search of new knowledge," Phineas replied.

"I'm seeking knowledge from a particular source," Roxanne said.

"Oh?"

She nodded. "A so-called sorcerer at the Renaissance Fair who claimed he was selling my mother an 'enchanted' castle that would reveal its secrets to a woman with longing in her heart."

He smiled. "I believe I said *young* woman. And you, fair Roxanne, still qualify."

"How did I get here? How did *you* get here?"

"I got here through years of experimentation."

"Where are you really from?"

"Poughkeepsie, originally."

"So you're from . . . um, the other place? The real place?"

"What makes you think this place isn't equally real?"

"Well, for one thing, in *this* place, I'm the filthy rich beauty of the kingdom."

"Isn't that better than being an abandoned wife

ruthlessly hounded by creditors and the IRS since her husband ran off with Mindy the manicurist?"

Roxanne gasped. "How do you know all that?"

"I have a crystal ball."

"Oh! Of course. Is that how you knew what I longed for?"

"Yes. Plus all the tears you shed in that horrible lavender bedroom. *Who* came up with that décor?"

"So what's the deal? Am I trapped here? Can I go home?"

"You really want to go back?"

She sighed. "Look, I like it here. But I have a son back there."

"Also a mountain of debt. You should probably take some gold with you when you go."

She stared at him. "I can take some of Lady Roxanne's money with me?"

"It's *your* money. You are Lady Roxanne La Belle."

"How is that possible?"

"A little dimensional juggling." He added bashfully, "It's not really as hard as it sounds."

"So you . . . discovered this other dimension and left Poughkeepsie?"

"Wouldn't *you*?"

"Why were you selling a replica of this castle at a Renaissance fair?"

"Just using my skills to spread happiness and good fortune among the unhappy and deserving." He shrugged. "It's mitzvah. And I'm less noticeable at Renaissance fairs. Also you meet a different class of people there."

"Well, Phineas, I have enjoyed this more than I can say, but since I have pressing debts back home. . . ." She'd pay off the bank, the credit card companies, the government, and she'd buy a house for herself and Jeff. She'd also convince her mother to let her have the toy castle, in case she ever wanted to come back here!

"I'll have a treasure chest filled with a pile of your

gold and put in your chamber," Phineas said. "All you have to do is go back there and wish with a sincere heart to go home—to return to the other place."

"And I'll . . . land at home with a pile of gold?"

"Yes. But you're sure you don't want to stay for a while?"

"I'd love to, but I need to get home and take care of business."

"Well, you can always come back for another visit."

Suddenly someone cried, "The dragon is slain! The dragon is no more!"

"My goodness," Phineas breathed. "He did it!"

"He . . . Sir William?" Roxanne said.

"Your true love." Phineas added, "I figured you needed a love interest. When was the last time you got l—"

"None of your business," she snapped. "He's won? He's defeated the dragon?"

"I think this safely eliminates Guy de Guise from the competition for your hand."

"Well that's a relief. But since I didn't intend to stick around for my wedding anyhow. . . ."

There was some commotion at the entrance to the Great Hall, and then a page announced, "Enter Sir William Le Beau, who has slain the dragon!"

Everyone in the hall cheered. Even the king, which made Lord Guy scowl and sulk. Seeing that unhappy expression on a face that resembled Thack's was rather satisfying.

"The fierce dragon that has menaced my kingdom for so long is finally conquered!" cried the king. "And the brave and noble knight who slew the beast has won the right to wed my ward, Lady Roxanne!"

While everyone cheered again, Phineas said to Roxanne, "That dragon was hoarding treasure conservatively estimated to be worth a cool million. William has turned into quite a catch."

"I'm happy for him," Roxanne said, "but even so, I need to get go . . . go . . ." Her voice trailed off as a tall, muscular, blue-eyed, blond-haired man strode boldly into the hall. He was followed by a two dozen servants carrying six large chests, all of them filled with gold and precious gems—the dragon's treasure.

The man's eyes met Roxanne's, and she was seized by a wave of feeling, a hot mixture of awe and lust. He was gorgeous, golden, and powerful, his hard-won victory evident in the sweat, blood, and dragon soot that covered him, his sword and mace clanking at his side. His eyes shone triumphant when he entered the Great Hall, then turned tender and passionate as he looked at Roxanne.

When William passed her by, on his way to greet the king, he whispered, "Roxanne."

She stared, thunderstruck, as he knelt before the king to accept his liege lord's blessing.

Phineas said to her, "You were saying?"

"Hmmm?"

"Something about going?"

"Huh?"

"You felt a certain urgency to depart?"

Roxanne blinked and closed her gaping mouth. "Oh . . . that would be rude. I'm sure I can stay through dinner."

"Indeed?"

With the consent of the king, William rose to his feet, then turned and strode directly to Roxanne. He took her hands in his, kissed each palm once, and murmured, "Whatever I have done, I have done only to win you."

She said to Phineas, "Yeah, I'm definitely staying for dinner. And I'll be back for another visit. I'll be back very, very soon." She might even, she decided, eventually try to give her mother a new grandchild.

Author Notes

Jean Rabe is the author of eighteen fantasy novels and more than three dozen short stories. An avid, but truly lousy gardener, she tends lots of tomato plants so her dogs can graze in the late summer months. In her spare time (which she seems to have less of each week), she enjoys role-playing, board, and war games; visiting museums; and riding in the convertible with the top down and the stereo cranked up. Visit her web site at www.jeanrabe.com

Diane Duane is the author of more than forty novels, more than fifty screenplays, and a whole bunch of computer games, comics, and short stories. Over the twenty-five years of her career she has written for characters as disparate as Jean-Luc Picard, Siegfried the Volsung, Batman, and Scooby-Doo. She bears the peculiar distinction of having worked with Star Trek™ in more formats than anyone else alive, but she is probably now better known for the best-selling "Young Wizards" series of novels, presently counting down toward its ninth volume, *A Wizard of Mars*. Her most recently released work is the award-winning TV miniseries *Dark Kingdom: The Dragon King,* written in collaboration with her husband Peter Morwood.

Nebula Award winner Esther Friesner is the author of thirty-one novels and over one hundred short stories, in addition to being the editor of seven popular anthologies. Her works have been published in the United States, the United Kingdom, Japan, Germany, Russia, France, and Italy. Besides winning two Nebula Awards in succession for Best Short Story (1995 and 1996) she was a Nebula finalist three times and a Hugo finalist once. She received the Skylark Award from NESFA and the award for Most Promising New Fantasy Writer of 1986 from Romantic Times. Educated at Vassar College, she went on to receive her M.A. and Ph.D. from Yale University, where she taught Spanish for a number of years. She lives in Connecticut with her husband, two all-grown-up children, two rambunctious cats, and a fluctuating population of hamsters.

Dean Wesley Smith is the bestselling author of over eighty novels and one hundred short stories. He was the former publisher of Pulphouse Publishing. He has been writing full time now for over twelve years under varied names. Among his recent novels is *All Eve's Hallows.*

Karen Everson is an artist and writer and a mom. Her daughter is her biggest fan in all those pursuits. She lives in Michigan with her husband, her daughter and a cat, a rabbit, and assorted wildlife. She's currently working on the second novel in a series set in the same world as the one in "Incognito, Ergo Sum," her story in Esther Friesner's *The Chicks in the Mail.*

Jay Lake is the winner of the 2004 John W. Campbell Award for Best New Writer, as well as a nominee for the 2004 Hugo and World Fantasy Awards. His stories appear in half a dozen languages in markets around the world, as well as his collections *Greetings From Lake Wu, Dogs in the Moonlight* and *American Sorrows*. He lives in Portland, Oregon. Jay can be reached through his web site at http://www.jlake.com/

Peter Morwood is the author of the *Book of Years* series, their prequels the *Clan Wars*, the *Tales of Old Russia*, and a bunch of other novels, short stories and screenplays. His most recently released project, the movie/miniseries *Dark Kingdom: The Dragon King*, aired on The Sci-Fi Channel in 2006. He lives in rural Ireland with his wife and frequent collaborator Diane Duane, a collection of museum-quality replica swords, and eclectic library and a quartet of cats. He's currently working on the fifth *Book of Years*, the third *Clan Wars*, the fantasy-historical novel *Blood's Ruby*, and screenplays for a feature film and another miniseries.

Jody Lynn Nye lists her main career activity as "spoiling cats." She lives northwest of Chicago with two of the above and her husband, author and packager Bill Fawcett. She has published thirty books, including six contemporary fantasies, four SF novels, four novels in collaboration with Anne McCaffrey, including *The Ship Who Won*; edited a humorous anthology about mothers, *Don't Forget Your Spacesuit, Dear!;* and written more than eighty short stories. Her latest books are *The Lady and The Tiger,* third in her Taylor's Ark series, *Strong Arm Tactics* first in the Wolfe Pack series, and *Class Dis-Mythed,* co-written with Robert Asprin.

Gail Selinger is a writer, college lecturer, and teacher of pirate lore. Active in the Port Royal Privateer Re-Enactment Workshops, she has written *The Complete Idiots Guide to Pirates,* several pirate-themed romance novels, as well as serious articles for publications for pirate enthusiasts.

Mike Moscoe is the critically acclaimed author of many novels, including his Lost Millennium series, his Price of Peace books, and a book in the Mech Warrior series, as well as the Kris Longknife series, written under the name Mike Shepherd. He lives in the Pacific Northwest with his family.

David Bischoff was born in 1951 in Washington D.C. and attended the University of Maryland where he graduated in 1973. After years of a career at NBC Washington, he became a full-time writer and teacher of fiction and teleplay writing. He's written many novels, scripts, short stories and articles. You can read more about Dave (especially his teaching) at: www.davidbischoff.com. He now lives in Eugene, Oregon.

Kristine Kathryn Rusch is a best-selling, award-winning writer. Her work has won awards in a variety of languages. Most recently, her novella, "Diving into the Wreck" (*Asimov's* December 2005) won the prestigious UPC award given in Spain. Her latest novel is *Paloma: A Retrieval Artist Novel.*

Mel Odom is often trekking around in worlds of wonder when no one's looking, but he always reports back with the story. He's written dozens of novels over the past eleven years in several fields: fantasy, game related fiction, science fiction, movie novelizations, horror, young adult, juvenile, computer strategy guides, action-adventure, and comics. He lives in Moore, Oklahoma with his wife and five children, and welcomes comments and conversation at DenimByte@aol.com. When not facing down ferocious enemies with blade and spell-book, you can often find him cheering his children on at softball games, basketball games, wrestling matches, and baseball games.

Laura Resnick is the author of such fantasy novels as *Disappearing Nightly, In Legend Born, The Destroyer Goddess,* and *The White Dragon,* which made the "Year's Best" lists of *Publishers Weekly* and *Voya.* Winner of the 1993 Campbell Award for best new science fiction/fantasy writer, she has published more than fifty short stories, as well as dozens of columns and articles. Under the pseudonym Laura Leone, she is the award-winning author of more than a dozen romance novels, including *Fallen From Grace,* which was a finalist for the Romance Writers of America's Rita Award. You can find her on the Web at www.LauraResnick.com.

C.S. Friedman

The Coldfire Trilogy

"A feast for those who like their fantasies dark, and as emotionally heady as a rich red wine." —*Locus*

Centuries after being stranded on the planet Erna, humans have achieved an uneasy stalemate with the fae, a terrifying natural force with the power to prey upon people's minds. Damien Vryce, the warrior priest, and Gerald Tarrant, the undead sorcerer must join together in an uneasy alliance confront a power that threatens the very essence of the human spirit, in a battle which could cost them not only their lives, but the soul of all mankind.

BLACK SUN RISING	0-88677-527-2
WHEN TRUE NIGHT FALLS	0-88677-615-5
CROWN OF SHADOWS	0-88677-717-8

To Order Call: 1-800-788-6262

Tanya Huff

The Finest in Fantasy

To Order Call: 1-800-788-6262

Kristen Britain

GREEN RIDER

As Karigan G'ladheon, on the run from school, makes her way through the deep forest, a galloping horse plunges out of the brush, its rider impaled by two black arrows. With his dying breath, he tells her he is a Green Rider, one of the king's special messengers. Giving her his green coat with its symbolic brooch of office, he makes Karigan swear to deliver the message he was carrying. Pursued by unknown assassins, following a path only the horse seems to know, Karigan finds herself thrust into in a world of danger and complex magic....   0-88677-858-1

FIRST RIDER'S CALL

With evil forces once again at large in the kingdom and with the messenger service depleted and weakened, can Karigan reach through the walls of time to get help from the First Rider, a woman dead for a millennium?   0-7564-0209-3

To Order Call: 1-800-788-6262

Tad Williams

THE WAR OF THE FLOWERS

"A masterpiece of fairytale worldbuilding."
—*Locus*

"Williams's imagination is boundless."
—*Publishers Weekly*
(Starred Review)

"A great introduction to an accomplished
and ambitious fantasist."
—*San Francisco Chronicle*

"An addictive world ... masterfully plays
with the tropes and traditions of
generations of fantasy writers."
—*Salon*

"A very elaborate and fully realized setting
for adventure, intrigue, and more
than an occasional chill."
—*Science Fiction Chronicle*

0-7564-0181-X

To Order Call: 1-800-788-6262

DAW 45